WHY SIN AND DEATH exist . . . how men and women were created . . . divine miracles changing the course of history . . . why the Jewish race is unique among the nations—these and other subjects of great concern to the human family unfold in this worldwide best seller, an intriguing and rewarding book.

From Eternity Past

E. G. White

A condensation of
Patriarchs and Prophets

Pacific Press Publishing Association
Boise, Idaho
Montemorelos, Nuevo Leon, Mexico
Oshawa, Ontario, Canada

Cover design and cover illustration design by Tim Larson
Cover illustration by Eric Joyner
Inside illustrations by John Steel

This condensation is not a paraphrase. The author's own words are retained throughout, except when it has been necessary to substitute a proper noun for a pronoun to avoid confusion, to change a verb tense to maintain meaning and continuity, or to supply a word or phrase to make a sentence read more smoothly.

All biblical quotations are from the King James, Revised, or American Revised versions of the Bible.

Copyright © 1983, 1986 by
Pacific Press Publishing Association
Printed in United States of America
All Rights Reserved

ISBN 0-8163-0649-4

Why You Should Read This Book

Where did we come from? Why do international tensions threaten to wipe out civilization? Why is crime increasing? Why are moral standards sagging? Is God indifferent to all this? Is He doing anything to help us solve our problems?

This book—the first of a five-book series—answers these questions. It tells how our world began and how the human race originated. It describes the tragic rebellion that took place in heaven many thousands of years ago and makes plain how the great controversy between God and Satan affects every inhabitant of planet Earth.

With unusual skill the author describes the role of our world in the conflict between right and wrong, between truth and error. Best of all, the book reveals the wiles of Satan and points to the Power by which we may defeat him in our personal lives.

The author's straightforward style and plain, direct language help hold one's interest from beginning to end. However, besides these qualities, most readers find something else in this book. As they read, they become convinced that the author was divinely inspired.

We commend this volume to all who seek authoritative information about how our world began, all who are interested in sacred history, all who are perplexed by the strange mixture of good and evil in the natural world and in human hearts, all who desire a better understanding of the Holy Scriptures.

The Publishers

CONTENTS

1 / Why Was Sin Permitted?

"God is love." His nature, His law, is love. It ever
has been; it ever will be. Every manifestation of creative power is an expression of infinite love. The history of the great conflict between good and evil from
the time it first began in heaven is also a demonstration
of God's unchanging love.

The Sovereign of the universe was not alone in His
work of beneficence. He had an associate who could
appreciate His purpose and share His joy in giving happiness to created beings. See John 1:1, 2.

Christ the Word was one with the eternal Father,
one in nature, in character, in purpose. "His name
shall be called Wonderful, Counselor, The mighty
God, The everlasting Father, The Prince of Peace."
Isaiah 9:6. His "goings forth have been from of old,
from everlasting." Micah 5:2.

The Father wrought by His Son in the creation of all
heavenly beings. "By Him were all things created, . . .
whether they be thrones, or dominions, or principalities,
or powers." Colossians 1:16. Angels are God's ministers
speeding to execute His will. But the Son, the "express
image of His person," "the brightness of His glory,"
"upholding all things by the word of His power," holds
supremacy over them all. See Hebrews 1:3, 8.

God desires from all His creatures the service of
love—service that springs from an appreciation of His
character. He takes no pleasure in a forced obedience;
and to all He grants freedom of will, that they may render Him voluntary service.

So long as all created beings acknowledged the allegiance of love, there was perfect harmony throughout the universe of God. There was no note of discord to mar the celestial harmonies.

But a change came over this happy state. There was one who perverted the freedom that God had granted to His creatures. Sin originated with him, who, next to Christ, had been most honored of God and was highest among the inhabitants of heaven. Lucifer, "son of the morning" (Isaiah 14:12), was holy and undefiled. "Thus saith the Lord God: Thou sealest up the sum, full of wisdom, and perfect in beauty. . . . Thou art the anointed cherub that covereth; and I have set thee so. Thou wast upon the holy mountain of God; thou hast walked up and down in the midst of the stones of fire. Thou wast perfect in thy ways from the day that thou wast created, till iniquity was found in thee."

Little by little, Lucifer indulged the desire for self-exaltation. "Thine heart was lifted up because of thy beauty; thou hast corrupted thy wisdom by reason of thy brightness." Ezekiel 28:12-15, 17. "Thou hast said in thine heart, . . . I will exalt my throne above the stars of God; . . . I will be like the most High." Isaiah 14:13, 14. Though honored above the heavenly host, he ventured to covet homage due alone to the Creator. This prince of angels aspired to power that was the prerogative of Christ alone.

Now the perfect harmony of heaven was broken. In heavenly council the angels pleaded with Lucifer. The Son of God presented before him the goodness and justice of the Creator and the unchanging nature of His law. In departing from it, Lucifer would dishonor his Maker and bring ruin upon himself. But the warning given in infinite love and mercy only aroused resistance. Lucifer allowed his jealousy of Christ to prevail, and became the more determined.

The King of the universe summoned the heavenly hosts before Him, that in their presence He might set forth the true position of His Son and show the relation

He sustained to all created beings. The Son of God shared the Father's throne, and the glory of the eternal, self-existent One encircled both. About the throne gathered the holy angels, "ten thousand times ten thousand, and thousands of thousands." Revelation 5:11. Before the inhabitants of heaven, the King declared that none but Christ could fully enter into His purposes and execute the mighty counsels of His will. Christ was still to exercise divine power in the creation of the earth and its inhabitants.

The Battle in Lucifer's Heart

The angels joyfully acknowledged the supremacy of Christ and poured out their love and adoration. Lucifer bowed with them; but in his heart there was a strange, fierce conflict. Truth and loyalty were struggling against envy and jealousy. The influence of the holy angels seemed for a time to carry him with them. As songs of praise ascended, the spirit of evil seemed vanquished; unutterable love thrilled his entire being; his soul went out in harmony with the sinless worshipers in love to the Father and the Son. But again his desire for supremacy returned, and envy of Christ was once more indulged. The high honors conferred upon Lucifer called forth no gratitude to his Creator. He gloried in his brightness and aspired to be equal with God. Angels delighted to execute his commands, and he was clothed with glory above them all. Yet the Son of God was exalted above him. "Why," questioned this mighty angel, "should Christ have the supremacy?"

Lucifer went forth to diffuse the spirit of discontent among the angels. For a time he concealed his real purpose under an appearance of reverence for God. He insinuated doubts concerning the laws that governed heavenly beings, intimating that angels needed no such restraint, for their own wisdom was a sufficient guide. All their thoughts were holy; it was not more possible for them than for God Himself to err. The exaltation of the Son of God as equal with the Father was represented as an injustice to Lucifer. If this prince of angels could but attain to his true, exalted position, great good would accrue to the entire host of heaven, for it was his object to secure freedom for all. Subtle deceptions through the wiles of Lucifer were fast obtaining in the heavenly courts.

The true position of the Son of God had been the same from the beginning. Many of the angels were, however, blinded by Lucifer's deceptions. He so artfully instilled into their minds his own distrust and discontent that his agency was not discerned. Lucifer had presented the purposes of God in a false light to excite dissent and dissatisfaction. While claiming for himself perfect loyalty to God, he urged that changes were necessary for the stability of the divine government. While secretly fomenting discord and rebellion, he caused it to appear as his sole purpose to promote loyalty and to preserve harmony and peace.

While there was no open outbreak, division of feeling imperceptibly grew up among the angels. Some looked with favor upon Lucifer's insinuations. They were discontented and unhappy, dissatisfied with God's purpose in exalting Christ. But angels who were loyal maintained the wisdom and justice of the divine decree. Christ was the Son of God, one with Him before the angels were called into existence. He had ever stood at the right hand of the Father. Wherefore should there now be discord.

God bore long with Lucifer. The spirit of discontent was a new element, strange, unaccountable. Lucifer himself did not see whither he was drifting. But such efforts as infinite love and wisdom only could devise were made to convince him of his error. He was made to see what would be the result of persisting in revolt.

Lucifer was convinced that he was in the wrong. He saw that "the Lord is righteous in all His ways, and holy in all His works" (Psalm 145:17), that the divine statutes are just, and that he ought to acknowledge them as such before all heaven. Had he done this, he might have saved himself and many angels. Though he had left his position as covering cherub, yet had he been willing to fill the place appointed him in God's great plan, he would have been reinstated in his office. The time had come for a final decision; he must yield to the divine sovereignty or place himself in open rebellion. He nearly reached the decision to return, but pride forbade him. It was too great a sacrifice for one who had been so highly honored to confess that he had been in error!

Lucifer pointed to the long-suffering of God as an evidence of his own superiority, an indication that the King of the universe would yet accede to his terms. If the angels would stand firmly with him, he declared, they could yet gain all that they desired. He fully committed himself to the great controversy against his Maker. Thus it was that Lucifer, "the light bearer," became Satan, "the adversary" of God and holy beings.

Rejecting with disdain the entreaties of the loyal angels, he denounced them as deluded slaves. He would never again acknowledge the supremacy of Christ. He had determined to claim the honor which should have been given him. And he promised those who would enter his ranks a new and better government under which all would enjoy freedom. Great numbers of the angels signified their purpose to accept him as their leader. He hoped to win all the angels to his side, to become equal with God Himself, and to be obeyed by the entire host of heaven.

Still the loyal angels urged him and his sympathizers to submit to God; they set before them the inevitable result should they refuse. They warned all to close their ears against Lucifer's deceptive reasoning and urged him and his followers to seek the presence of God without delay and confess the error of questioning His wisdom and authority.

Many were disposed to repent of their disaffection and seek to be again received into favor with the Father and His Son. But Lucifer now declared that the angels who had united with him had gone too far to return; God would not forgive. For himself, he was determined never again to acknowledge the authority of Christ. The only course remaining was to assert their liberty and gain by force the rights which had not been accorded them.

Active Revolt in Heaven

God permitted Satan to carry forward his work until the spirit of disaffection ripened into active revolt. It was necessary for his plans to be fully developed, that their true nature might be seen by all. God's government included not only the inhabitants of heaven, but all the world that He had created; and Lucifer concluded that if he could carry the angels with him in rebellion, he could carry the worlds also. All his acts were so clothed with mystery that it was difficult to disclose the true nature of his work. Even the loyal angels could not fully discern his character or see to what his work was leading. Everything simple he shrouded in mystery, and by artful perversion cast doubt upon the plainest statements of God. And his high position gave greater force to his representations.

Why God Did Not Destroy Satan

God could employ only such means as were consistent with truth and righteousness. Satan could use what God could not—flattery and deceit. It was therefore necessary to demonstrate before the inhabitants of heaven and all the world that God's government is just, His law perfect. Satan had made it appear that he himself was seeking to promote the good of the universe. The true character of the usurper must be understood by all. He must have time to manifest himself by his wicked works.

All evil he declared to be the result of the divine administration. It was his own object to improve upon the statutes of God. Therefore God permitted him to demonstrate the nature of his claims, to show the working out of his proposed changes in the divine law. His own work must condemn him. The whole universe must see the deceiver unmasked.

Even when Satan was cast out of heaven, Infinite Wisdom did not destroy him. The allegiance of His creatures must rest upon a conviction of His justice and benevolence. The inhabitants of heaven and of the world could not then have seen the justice of God in the destruction of Satan. Had he been immediately blotted out of existence, some would have served God from fear rather than from love. The influence of the deceiver would not have been fully destroyed, nor would the spirit of rebellion have been utterly eradicated. For the good of the entire universe through ceaseless ages he must more fully develop his principles, that his charges against the divine government might be seen in their true light and that the justice of God and the immutability of His law might be forever placed beyond question.

Satan's rebellion was to be a lesson to the universe through all coming ages—a perpetual testimony to the nature of sin and its terrible results. Thus the history of this experiment of rebellion was to be a perpetual safeguard to all holy beings to prevent them from being deceived as to the nature of transgression.

"His work is perfect: for all His ways are judgment: a God of truth and without iniquity, just and right is He." Deuteronomy 32:4.

2 / Creation: God's Answer to Evolution

"By the word of the Lord were the heavens made; and all the host of them by the breath of His mouth. . . . For He spake, and it was done; he commanded, and it stood fast." Psalm 33:6-9.

As the earth came forth from the hand of its Maker, it was exceedingly beautiful. The fruitful soil everywhere produced a luxuriant growth of verdure. There were no loathsome swamps nor barren deserts. Graceful shrubs and delicate flowers greeted the eye at every turn. The air was clear and healthful. The entire landscape outvied in beauty the decorated grounds of the proudest palace.

After the earth with its teeming animal and vegetable life had been called into existence, man, the crowning work of the Creator, was brought upon the stage of action. "God said, Let Us make man in Our image, after Our likeness; and let them have dominion over . . . all the earth." "So God created man in His own image: . . . male and female created He them."

Here is clearly set forth the origin of the human race. God created man in His own image. There is no ground for the supposition that man evolved by slow degrees from lower forms of animal or vegetable life. Inspiration traces the origin of our race, not to a line of developing germs, mollusks, and quadrupeds, but to the great Creator. Though formed from the dust, Adam was "the son of God." Luke 3:38.

The lower orders of being cannot understand the sovereignty of God, yet they were made capable of lov-

This chapter is based on Genesis 1 and 2.

ing and serving man. "Thou madest him to have dominion over the works of Thy hands; Thou hast put all things under his feet, . . . the beasts of the field, the fowl of the air." Psalm 8:6-8.

Christ alone is "the express image" (Hebrews 1:3) of the Father, but man was formed in the likeness of God. His nature was in harmony with the will of God, his mind capable of comprehending divine things. His affections were pure; his appetites and passions were under the control of reason. He was holy and happy in bearing the image of God, and in perfect obedience to His will.

As man came forth from the hand of his Creator, his countenance glowed with the light of life and joy. Adam's height was much greater than that of men now living. Eve was somewhat less in stature, yet her form was noble and full of beauty. The sinless pair wore no artificial garments: they were clothed with a covering of glory such as the angels wear.

The First Marriage
After the creation of Adam, "God said, It is not good that the man should be alone; I will make him an help meet for him." God gave Adam a companion, "an help meet for him," one who was fitted to be his companion, and who would be one with him in love and sympathy. Eve was created from a rib taken from the side of Adam. She was not to control him as the head, nor to be trampled under his feet as an inferior, but to stand by his side as an equal, loved and protected by him. She was his second self, showing the close union that should exist in this relation. "For no man ever yet hated his own flesh, but nourisheth and cherisheth it." "Therefore shall a man leave his father and his mother, and shall cleave unto his wife; and they shall be one." Ephesians 5:29; Genesis 2:24.

"Marriage is honorable." Hebrews 13:4. It is one of the two institutions that, after the Fall, Adam brought with him beyond the gates of Paradise. When the divine principles are recognized and obeyed, marriage is a blessing; it guards the purity and happiness of the race and elevates the physical, the intellectual, and the moral nature.

"And the Lord God planted a garden eastward in Eden; and there He put the man whom He had formed." In this garden were trees of every variety, many of them laden with delicious fruit. There were lovely vines, growing upright, their branches drooping under their load of tempting fruit. It was the work of Adam and Eve to train the branches of the vine to form bowers, thus making for themselves a dwelling from living trees covered with foliage and fruit. In the midst of the garden stood the tree of life, surpassing in glory all other trees. Its fruit had the power to perpetuate life.

"The heavens and the earth were finished, and all the host of them." "And God saw everything He had made, and, behold, it was very good." No taint of sin or shadow of death marred the fair creation. "The morning stars sang together, and all the sons of God shouted for joy." Job 38:7.

The Blessing of the Sabbath

In six days the great work of creation had been accomplished. And God "rested on the seventh day from all His work which He had made. And God blessed the seventh day, and sanctified it; because that in it He had rested from all His work which God created and made." All was perfect, worthy of its divine Author; and He rested, not as one weary, but as well pleased with the fruits of His wisdom and goodness.

After resting on the seventh day, God set it apart as a day of rest. Following the example of the Creator, man was to rest upon this sacred day that he might reflect upon God's work of creation, that his heart might be filled with love and reverence for his Maker.

The Sabbath was committed to the whole human family, its observance to be a grateful acknowledgment that God was their creator and rightful sovereign. They were the work of His hands, the subjects of His authority.

God saw that a Sabbath was essential for man, even in Paradise. He needed to lay aside his own interests for one day of the seven. He needed a Sabbath to remind him of God and to awaken gratitude because all that he enjoyed came from the hand of the Creator.

God designs that the Sabbath shall direct the minds of men to His created works. The beauty that clothes the earth is a token of God's love. The everlasting hills, the lofty trees, the opening buds and delicate flowers all speak to us of God. The Sabbath, pointing to Him who made them all, bids men open the book of nature and trace therein the wisdom, power, and love of the Creator.

Our first parents, though created innocent and holy, were not placed beyond the possibility of wrongdoing. God made them free moral agents with liberty to yield or to withhold obedience. But before they could be eternally secure, their loyalty must be tested. At the beginning of man's existence a check was placed upon self-indulgence, the fatal passion that lay at the foundation of Satan's fall. The tree of knowledge was to be a test of the obedience, faith, and love of our first parents. They were forbidden to taste of this, on pain of death. They were to be exposed to the temptations of Satan; but if they endured the trial, they would be placed beyond his power, to enjoy perpetual favor with God.

The Beautiful Garden of Eden

God placed man under law, a subject of the divine government. God might have created man without the power to transgress; He might have withheld Adam from touching the forbidden fruit; but in that case man would have been a mere automaton. Without freedom of choice, his obedience would have been forced. Such a course would have been contrary to God's plan, unworthy of man as an intelligent being, and would have sustained Satan's charge of God's arbitrary rule.

God made man upright, with no bias toward evil. He presented before him the strongest possible inducements to be true. Obedience was the condition of eternal happiness and access to the tree of life.

The home of our first parents was to be a pattern for other homes as their children should go forth to occupy the earth. Men in their pride delight in magnificent and costly edifices and glory in the works of their own hands, but God placed Adam in a garden. This was a lesson for all time—true happiness is found not in the indulgence of pride and luxury, but in communion with God through His created works. Pride and ambition are never satisfied, but those who are truly wise will find pleasure in the enjoyment God has placed within the reach of all.

To the dwellers in Eden was committed the care of the garden, "to dress it and to keep it." God appointed labor as a blessing to man, to occupy his mind, to strengthen his body, and to develop his faculties. In mental and physical activity Adam found one of the highest pleasures of his holy existence. Those who regard work as a curse, attended though it be with weariness and pain, are cherishing an error. The rich often look down upon the working classes, but this is at variance with God's purpose in creating man. Adam was not to be idle. Our Creator, who understands what is for man's happiness, appointed Adam his work. The true joy of life is found only by working men and women. The Creator has prepared no place for stagnating indolence.

The holy pair were not only children under the fatherly care of God, but students receiving instruction from the all-wise Creator. They were visited by angels and were granted communion with their Maker with no obscuring veil between. They were full of vigor imparted by the tree of life, their intellectual power but little less than that of the angels. The laws of nature were opened to their minds by the infinite Framer and

Upholder of all. With every living creature, from the mighty leviathan among the waters to the insect mote that floats in the sunbeam, Adam was familiar. He had given to each its name, and he was acquainted with the nature and habits of all. On every leaf of the forest, in every shining star, in earth and air and sky, God's name was written. The order and harmony of creation spoke of infinite wisdom and power.

So long as they remained loyal to the divine law they would be constantly gaining new treasures of knowledge, discovering fresh springs of happiness, and obtaining clearer conceptions of the immeasurable, unfailing love of God.

3 / The Predicament of Our First Parents

No longer free to stir up rebellion in heaven, Satan found a new field in plotting the ruin of the human race. Moved by envy, he determined to bring upon them the guilt and penalty of sin. He would change their love to distrust and their songs of praise to reproaches against their Maker. Thus he would not only plunge these innocent beings into misery but cast dishonor upon God and cause grief in heaven.

Heavenly messengers opened to our first parents the history of Satan's fall and his plots for their destruction, unfolding the nature of the divine government which the prince of evil was trying to overthrow.

The law of God is a revelation of His will, a transcript of His character, the expression of divine love and wisdom. The harmony of creation depends upon perfect conformity to the law of the Creator. Everything is under fixed laws, which cannot be disregarded. But man alone, of all that inhabits the earth, is amenable to moral law. To man, God has given power to comprehend the justice and beneficence of His law, and of man unswerving obedience is required.

Like the angels, the dwellers in Eden had been placed upon probation. They could obey and live, or disobey and perish. He who spared not the angels that sinned, could not spare them; transgression would bring upon them misery and ruin.

The angels warned them to be on guard against the devices of Satan. If they steadfastly repelled his first insinuations, they would be secure. But should they

This chapter is based on Genesis 3.

once yield to temptation, their nature would become so depraved that in themselves they would have no power, and no disposition, to resist Satan.

The tree of knowledge had been made a test of their obedience and love to God. If they should disregard His will in this particular, they would incur guilt. Satan was not to follow them with continual temptations; he could have access to them only at the forbidden tree.

To accomplish his work unperceived, Satan employed a disguise. The serpent was one of the wisest and most beautiful creatures. It had dazzling brightness. Resting in the forbidden tree, regaling itself with the delicious fruit, it was an object to arrest attention and delight the eye. Thus in the garden of peace lurked the destroyer.

The angels had cautioned Eve to beware of separating from her husband. With him she would be in less danger than if alone. But she unconsciously wandered from his side. Unmindful of the angel's caution, she soon found herself gazing with mingled curiosity and admiration upon the forbidden tree. The fruit was beautiful, and she questioned why God had withheld it from them.

Now was the tempter's opportunity. "Yea, hath God said, Ye shall not eat of every tree of the garden?" Eve was startled to hear the echo of her thoughts. The serpent continued with subtle praise of her surpassing loveliness, and his words were not displeasing. Instead of fleeing from the spot, she lingered. She had no thought that the fascinating serpent could be the medium of the fallen foe.

She replied: "We may eat of the fruit of the trees of the garden; but of the fruit of the tree which is in the midst of the garden, God hath said, Ye shall not eat of it, neither shall ye touch it, lest ye die. And the serpent said unto the woman, Ye shall not surely die; for God doth know that in the day ye eat thereof, then your eyes shall be opened, and ye shall be as gods, knowing good and evil."

By partaking of this tree, he declared, they would attain a more exalted existence. He himself had eaten and had acquired the power of speech. He insinuated that the Lord had jealously withheld it from them, lest they be exalted to equality with Himself. It was because it imparted wisdom and power that He had prohibited them from tasting or touching it. The divine warning was merely to intimidate them. How could it be possible for them to die? Had they not eaten of the tree of life? God had been seeking to prevent them from reaching a nobler development and finding greater happiness.

Such has been Satan's work from the days of Adam to the present. He tempts men to distrust God's love and doubt His wisdom. In their efforts to search out what God has withheld, multitudes overlook truths which are essential to salvation. Satan tempts men to disobedience, to believe they are entering a wonderful field of knowledge. But this is all a deception. They are setting their feet in the path that leads to degradation and death.

The Subtlety of Satan's Appeal

Satan represented to the holy pair that they would gain by breaking the law of God. Today many talk of the narrowness of those who obey God's commandments, while they claim to enjoy greater liberty. What is this but an echo of the voice from Eden? "In the day ye eat thereof"—transgress the divine requirement—"ye shall be as gods." Satan did not let it appear that he had become an outcast from heaven. He concealed his own misery in order to draw others into the same position. So now the transgressor disguises his true character; but he is on the side of Satan, trampling upon the law of God and leading others to their eternal ruin.

Eve disbelieved the words of God, and this was what led to her fall. In the judgment, men will not be condemned because they conscientiously believed a lie, but because they did not believe the truth. We must set our hearts to know what is truth. Whatever contradicts God's Word proceeds from Satan.

The serpent plucked the fruit of the forbidden tree and placed it in the hands of the half-reluctant Eve. Then he reminded her of her own words, that God had forbidden them to touch it lest they die. Perceiving no evil results, Eve grew bolder. When she "saw that the tree was good for food, and that it was pleasant to the eyes, and a tree to be desired to make one wise, she took of the fruit thereof, and did eat." As she ate, she seemed to imagine herself entering upon a higher state of existence.

And now, having herself transgressed, she became the agent of Satan in working the ruin of her husband. In a state of strange, unnatural excitement, her hands filled with the forbidden fruit, she sought his presence.

Adam appeared astonished and alarmed. To the words of Eve he replied that this must be the foe against whom they had been warned. By the divine sentence she must die. In answer she urged him, "Eat," repeating the words of the serpent that they should not surely die. She felt no evidence of God's displeasure, but realized a delicious, exhilarating influence, thrilling every faculty with new life.

Adam understood that his companion had transgressed the command of God. There was a terrible struggle in his mind. He mourned that he had permitted Eve to wander from his side. But now the deed was done; he must be separated from her whose society had been his joy.

How could he have it thus? Adam had enjoyed the companionship of God and of holy angels. He understood the high destiny opened to the human race should they remain faithful to God. Yet all these blessings were lost sight of in the fear of losing that one gift which in his eyes outvalued every other. Love, gratitude, loyalty to the Creator—all were overborne by love to Eve. She was a part of himself, and he could not endure the thought of separation. If she must die, he would die with her. Might not the words of the wise serpent be true? No sign of death appeared in Eve, and he decided to brave the consequences. He seized the fruit and quickly ate.

After his transgression, Adam at first imagined himself entering upon a higher state of existence. But soon the thought of his sin filled him with terror. The love and peace which had been theirs was gone, and in its place they felt a sense of sin, a dread of the future, a nakedness of soul. The robe of light which had enshrouded them disappeared, and to supply its place they endeavored to fashion for themselves a covering. They could not, while unclothed, meet the eye of God and holy angels.

They now began to see the true character of sin. Adam reproached his companion for leaving his side and permitting herself to be deceived by the serpent. But they both flattered themselves that He who had given them so many evidences of His love would pardon this one transgression; they would not be subjected to so dire a punishment as they had feared.

Satan exulted. He had tempted the woman to distrust God's love, to doubt His wisdom, and to transgress His law; and through her he had caused the overthrow of Adam!

The Sad Change That Sin Produced

The great Lawgiver was about to make known to Adam and Eve the consequences of their transgression. In their innocence and holiness they had joyfully welcomed the approach of their Creator; now they fled in terror. But "the Lord God called unto Adam, and said unto him, Where art thou? And he said, I heard Thy voice in the garden, and I was afraid, because I was naked, and I hid myself. And He said, Who told thee that thou wast naked? Hast thou eaten of the tree, whereof I commanded thee that thou shouldest not eat?"

Adam cast the blame upon his wife, and thus upon God Himself: "The woman whom *Thou gavest* to be with me, she gave me of the tree, and I did eat." From love to Eve, he had deliberately chosen to forfeit the approval of God and an eternal life of joy; now he endeavored to make his companion, and even the Creator Himself, responsible for the transgression.

When the woman was asked, "What is this that thou hast done?" she answered, "The serpent beguiled me, and I did eat." "Why didst Thou create the serpent? Why didst Thou suffer him to enter Eden?"—these were the questions implied in her first excuse. Self-justification was indulged by our first parents as soon as they yielded to the influence of Satan and has been exhibited by all the sons and daughters of Adam.

The Lord then passed sentence upon the serpent: "Because thou hast done this, thou art cursed above all cattle, and above every beast of the field; upon thy belly shalt thou go, and dust shalt thou eat all the days of thy life." From the most beautiful of the creatures of the field it was to become the most groveling and detested of all, feared and hated by both man and beast. The words next addressed to the serpent applied to Satan himself, pointing to his ultimate defeat and destruction: "I will put enmity between thee and the woman, and between thy seed and her seed; it shall bruise thy head, and thou shalt bruise His heel."

Eve was told of the sorrow and pain that must be her portion. "Thy desire shall be to thy husband, and he shall rule over thee." God had made her the equal of Adam. But sin brought discord, and now their union could be maintained and harmony preserved only by submission on the part of one or the other. Eve had been the first in transgression. By her solicitation Adam sinned, and she was now placed in subjection to her husband. Man's abuse of the supremacy thus given him has too often rendered the lot of woman bitter and her life a burden.

Eve had been happy by her husband's side. But she

was flattered with the hope of entering a higher sphere than God had assigned her. In attempting to rise above her original position, she fell far below it. In their efforts to reach positions for which God has not fitted them, many leave vacant the place where they might be a blessing.

To Adam the Lord declared: "Because thou hast hearkened unto the voice of thy wife, and hast eaten of the tree, of which I commanded thee, saying, Thou shalt not eat of it; cursed is the ground for thy sake; in sorrow shalt thou eat of it all the days of thy life. Thorns also and thistles shall it bring forth to thee, and thou shalt eat the herb of the field. In the sweat of thy face shalt thou eat bread, till thou return unto the ground; for out of it wast thou taken; for dust thou art, and unto dust shalt thou return."

God had freely given them good and withheld evil. But they had eaten of the forbidden tree, and now they would have the knowledge of evil—all the days of their life. Instead of happy labor, anxiety and toil were to be their lot. They would be subject to disappointment, grief, and pain, and finally to death.

God made man ruler over the earth and all living creatures. But when he rebelled against the divine law, the inferior creatures were in rebellion against his rule. Thus the Lord in mercy would show men the sacredness of His law and lead them to see the danger of setting it aside, even in the slightest degree.

A Plan for Man's Recovery

The life of toil and care henceforth to be man's lot was appointed in love, a discipline rendered needful by his sin, to place a check upon the indulgence of appetite and passion, to develop habits of self-control. It was a part of God's great plan for man's recovery.

The warning given to our first parents—"In the day that thou eatest thereof thou shalt surely die"—did not imply they were to die on the very day they partook of the forbidden fruit. But on that day the irrevocable sentence would be pronounced. That very day they would be doomed to death.

In order to possess endless existence, man must continue to partake of the tree of life. Deprived of this, his vitality would gradually diminish until life should become extinct. It was Satan's plan that Adam and Eve would eat of the tree of life, and thus perpetuate an existence of sin and misery. But holy angels were commissioned to guard the tree of life. Around these angels flashed the appearance of a glittering sword. None of the family of Adam were permitted to pass that barrier; hence there is not an immortal sinner.

Is God Too Severe?

The tide of woe that flowed from the transgression of our first parents is regarded by man as too awful a consequence for so small a sin. But if they would look more deeply into this question, they might discern their error. In His great mercy God appointed Adam no severe test. The very lightness of the prohibition made the sin exceedingly great. Had some great test been appointed Adam, then those whose hearts incline to evil would have excused themselves saying, "This is a trivial matter, and God is not so particular about little things."

Many who teach that the law of God is not binding upon man urge that it is impossible to obey its precepts. But if this were true, why did Adam suffer the penalty of transgression? The sin of our first parents brought guilt and sorrow upon the world, and had it not been for the goodness and mercy of God, would have plunged the race into hopeless despair. Let none deceive themselves. "The wages of sin is death." Romans 6:23.

After their sin, Adam and Eve earnestly entreated that they might remain in the home of their innocence and joy. They pledged themselves for the future to yield strict obedience to God. But they were told that their nature had become depraved by sin. They had lessened their strength to resist evil. Now, in a state of conscious guilt, they would have less power to maintain their integrity.

In sadness they bade farewell to their beautiful home and went forth to dwell upon the earth, where rested the curse of sin. The atmosphere was now subject to marked changes, and the Lord mercifully provided them with a garment of skins as a protection from the cold.

As they witnessed in drooping flower and falling leaf the first signs of decay, Adam and his companion mourned more deeply than men now mourn over their dead. When the goodly trees cast off their leaves, the scene brought to mind the stern fact that death is the portion of every living thing.

The Garden of Eden remained upon the earth long after man had become an outcast from its pleasant paths. But when the wickedness of men determined their destruction by a flood of waters, the hand that had planted Eden withdrew it from the earth. In the final restitution, when there shall be "a new heaven and a new earth," it is to be restored more gloriously adorned than at the beginning. Revelation 21:1.

4 / The Plan of Redemption Is Unveiled

The fall of man filled all heaven with sorrow. There appeared no escape for those who had transgressed the law. Angels ceased their songs of praise.

The Son of God was touched with pity for the fallen race as the woes of the lost world rose up before Him. Divine love had conceived a plan whereby man might be redeemed. The broken law of God demanded the life of the sinner. Only one equal with God could make atonement for its transgression. None but Christ could redeem fallen man from the curse of the law and bring him again into harmony with Heaven. Christ would take upon Himself the guilt and shame of sin to rescue the ruined race.

The plan of salvation had been laid before the creation of the earth, for Christ is "the Lamb slain from the foundation of the world" (Revelation 13:8); yet it was a struggle with the King of the universe to yield up His Son to die for the guilty race. But "God so loved the world, that He gave His only begotten Son, that whosoever believeth in Him should not perish, but have everlasting life." John 3:16. Oh, the mystery of redemption! the love of God for a world that did not love Him!

God was to be manifest in Christ, "reconciling the world unto Himself." 2 Corinthians 5:19. Man had become so degraded by sin that it was impossible in himself to come into harmony with Him whose nature is purity and goodness. But Christ could impart divine power to unite with human effort. Thus by repentance toward God and faith in Christ, the fallen children of Adam might once more become "sons of God." 1 John 3:2.

The angels could not rejoice as Christ opened before them the plan of redemption. In grief and wonder they listened as He told them how He must come in contact with the degradation of earth, to endure sorrow, shame, and death. He would humble Himself as a man and become acquainted with the sorrows and temptations which man would have to endure in order that He might be able to succor them that should be tempted. See Hebrews 2:18. When His mission as a teacher should be ended, He must be subjected to every insult and torture that Satan could inspire. He must die the cruelest of deaths as a guilty sinner. He must endure anguish of soul, the hiding of His Father's face, while the sins of the whole world should be upon Him.

The angels offered to become a sacrifice for man. But only He who created man had power to redeem him. Christ was to be made "a little lower than the angels for the suffering of death." Hebrews 2:9. As He should take human nature upon Him, His strength would not be equal to theirs, and they were to strengthen Him under His sufferings. They were also to guard the subjects of grace from the power of evil angels.

When the angels should witness the agony and humiliation of their Lord, they would wish to deliver Him from His murderers, but they were not to interpose. It was a part of the plan that Christ should suffer the scorn and abuse of wicked men.

Christ assured the angels that by His death He would ransom many and recover the kingdom which man had lost by transgression. The redeemed were to inherit it with Him. Sin and sinners would be blotted out, nevermore to disturb the peace of heaven or earth.

Then inexpressible joy filled heaven. Through the celestial courts echoed the first strains of that song which was to ring out above the hills of Bethlehem,

Adam and Eve and their descendants were barred from entering the Garden of Eden.

"Glory to God in the highest, and on earth peace, good will toward men." Luke 2:14. "The morning stars sang together, and all the sons of God shouted for joy." Job 38:7.

God Promises a Saviour

In the sentence pronounced on Satan in the garden, the Lord declared, "I will put enmity between thee and the woman, and between thy seed and her seed; it shall bruise thy head, and thou shalt bruise His heel." Genesis 3:15. This was a promise that the power of the great adversary would finally be broken. Adam and Eve stood as criminals before the righteous Judge, but before they heard of the toil and sorrow which must be their portion or that they must return to dust, they listened to words that could not fail to give them hope. They could look forward to final victory.

Satan knew that his work of depraving human nature would be interrupted, that by some means man would be enabled to resist his power. Yet Satan rejoiced with his angels that, having caused man's fall, he could bring down the Son of God from His exalted position. When Christ should take upon Himself human nature, He also might be overcome.

Heavenly angels more fully opened to our first parents the plan for their salvation. Adam and his companion were not to be abandoned to Satan. Through repentance and faith in Christ, they might again become the children of God.

Adam and Eve saw as never before the guilt of sin and its results. They pleaded that the penalty might not fall upon Him whose love had been the source of all their joy; rather let it descend upon them and their posterity.

They were told that since the law of Jehovah is the foundation of His government, even the life of an angel could not be accepted as a sacrifice for transgression. But the Son of God, who had created man, could make an atonement for him. As Adam's transgression had brought wretchedness and death, so the sacrifice of Christ would bring life and immortality.

At his creation Adam was placed in dominion over the earth. But by yielding to temptation he became Satan's captive. The dominion passed to his conqueror. Thus Satan became "the god of this world." 2 Corinthians 4:4. But Christ by His sacrifice would not only redeem man, but recover the dominion he had forfeited. All that was lost by the first Adam will be restored by the second. See Micah 4:8.

God created the earth to be the abode of holy, happy beings. That purpose will be fulfilled when, renewed by the power of God and freed from sin and sorrow, it shall become the eternal abode of the redeemed.

The Terrible Fruits of Sin

Sin brought separation between God and man, and the atonement of Christ alone could span the abyss. God would communicate with man through Christ and angels.

Adam was shown that while the sacrifice of Christ would be sufficient to save the whole world, many would choose a life of sin rather than of repentance and obedience. Crime would increase through successive generations. The curse of sin would rest more and more heavily upon the human race and upon the earth. The days of man would be shortened by his own course of sin; he would deteriorate in physical, moral, and intellectual power until the world would be filled with misery. Through the indulgence of appetite and passion, men would become incapable of appreciating the great truths of the plan of redemption. Yet Christ would supply the needs of all who would come unto Him in faith. There would ever be a few who would preserve the knowledge of God and remain unsullied.

The sacrificial offerings were ordained to be a penitential acknowledgment of sin and a confession of faith in the promised Redeemer. To Adam the first sacrifice was painful. His hand must be raised to take life, which only God could give. It was the first time he had witnessed death. He knew that had he been obedient to God there would have been no death. He trembled at the thought that his sin must shed the blood of the spotless Lamb of God. This gave him a vivid sense of the greatness of his transgression, which nothing but the death of God's dear Son could expiate. A star of hope illumined the dark future.

The Wider Purpose of Redemption

But the plan of redemption had a yet broader and deeper purpose than the salvation of man. It was not merely that the inhabitants of this little world might regard the law of God as it should be regarded, but it was to vindicate the character of God before the universe. To this the Saviour looked forward when just before His crucifixion He said: "Now is the judgment of this world; now shall the prince of this world be cast out. And I, if I be lifted up from the earth, will draw all men unto Me." John 12:31, 32. Christ dying for the salvation of man would justify God and His Son in their dealing with the rebellion of Satan, establish the law of God, and reveal the nature and results of sin.

From the first, the great controversy had been upon the law of God. Satan had sought to prove that God was unjust, His law faulty, and that the good of the universe required it to be changed. In attacking the law he aimed to overthrow the authority of its Author.

When Satan overcame Adam and Eve, he thought he had gained possession of this world, "because," said he, "they have chosen me as their ruler." He claimed it was impossible that forgiveness be granted; the fallen race were his rightful subjects, and the world was his. But God gave His own Son to bear the penalty of transgression. Thus they might be restored to His favor and brought back to their Eden home. The great controversy begun in heaven was to be decided in the very world, on the same field, that Satan claimed as his.

It was the marvel of all the universe that Christ should humble Himself to save fallen man. When Christ came to our world in the form of humanity, all were intensely interested in following Him as He traversed the blood-stained path from the manger to Calvary. Heaven marked the insult and mockery that He received and knew that it was at Satan's instigation. They watched the battle between light and darkness as it waxed stronger. And as Christ upon the cross cried out, "It is finished!" a shout of triumph rang through every world and through heaven itself. The great contest was now decided, and Christ was conqueror. His death answered the question whether the Father and the Son had sufficient love for man to exercise self-denial and a spirit of sacrifice. Satan had revealed his true character as a liar and murderer. With one voice the loyal universe united in extolling the divine administration.

But if the law was abolished at the cross, as many claim, then the agony and death of God's dear Son were endured only to give to Satan just what he asked; then the prince of evil triumphed, and his charges against the divine government were sustained. The fact that Christ bore the penalty of man's transgression is a mighty argument that the law is changeless; that God is righteous, merciful, and self-denying; and that infinite justice and mercy unite in the administration of His government.

5/ The First Murderer and His Victim

Cain and Abel, the sons of Adam, differed widely in character. Abel saw justice and mercy in the Creator's dealings with the fallen race and gratefully accepted the hope of redemption. But Cain permitted his mind to run in the same channel that led to Satan's fall—questioning the divine justice and authority.

These brothers were tested to prove whether they would believe and obey the word of God. They understood the system of offerings which God had ordained. They knew they were to express faith in the Saviour, whom the offerings typified, and at the same time to acknowledge total dependence on Him for pardon. Without the shedding of blood, there could be no remission of sin. They were to show their faith in the blood of Christ as the promised atonement by offering the firstlings of the flock in sacrifice.

The two brothers erected their altars alike, and each brought an offering. Abel presented a sacrifice from the flock. "And the Lord had respect unto Abel and to his offering." Genesis 4:4. Fire flashed from heaven and consumed the sacrifice. But Cain, disregarding the Lord's direct command, presented only an offering of fruit. There was no token from heaven to show it was accepted. Abel pleaded with his brother to approach God in the divinely prescribed way, but his entreaties made Cain the more determined to follow his own will. As the eldest, he despised his brother's counsel.

Cain came before God with murmuring in his heart. His gift expressed no penitence, for it would be an ac-

This chapter is based on Genesis 4:1-15.

37

knowledgment of weakness to follow the exact plan marked out by God, of trusting his salvation wholly to the atonement of the promised Saviour. He would come in his own merits. He would not bring the lamb and mingle its blood with his offering, but would present his fruits, the products of his labor, as a favor done to God. Cain obeyed in building an altar, obeyed in bringing a sacrifice, but rendered only partial obedience. Recognition of the need of a Redeemer was left out.

These brothers were both sinners, and both acknowledged the claims of God to reverence and worship. To outward appearance their religion was the same up to a certain point, but beyond this the difference was great.

The Great Difference Between Cain and Abel

"By faith Abel offered unto God a more excellent sacrifice than Cain." Hebrews 11:4. Abel saw himself a sinner, and he saw sin and its penalty, death, standing between his soul and God. He brought the slain victim, thus acknowledging the claims of the law that had been transgressed. Through the shed blood he looked to Christ dying on the cross. Trusting in the atonement there to be made, he had the witness that he was righteous and his offering accepted.

Cain had the same opportunity of accepting these truths as had Abel. One brother was not elected to be accepted of God and the other rejected. Abel chose faith and obedience; Cain, unbelief and rebellion.

Cain and Abel represent two classes that will exist till the close of time. One avail themselves of the appointed sacrifice for sin; the other depend upon their own merits. Those who feel no need of the blood of Christ, who feel that they can by their own works secure the approval of God, are making the same mistake as did Cain.

Nearly every false religion has been based on the same principle—that man can depend upon his own efforts for salvation. It is claimed by some that the human race can refine, elevate, and regenerate itself. As Cain thought to secure divine favor by an offering that lacked the blood of a sacrifice, so do these expect to exalt humanity to the divine standard, independent of the atonement. The history of Cain shows that humanity does not tend upward toward the divine, but downward toward the satanic. Christ is our only hope. See Acts 4:12.

True faith will be manifested by obedience to all the requirements of God. From Adam's day to the present the great controversy has been concerning obedience to God's law. In all ages there have been those who claim a right to the favor of God while they disregard some of His commands. But by works is "faith made perfect," and without the works of obedience, faith "is dead." James 2:22, 17. He that professes to know God "and keepeth not His commandments, is a liar, and the truth is not in him." 1 John 2:4.

When Cain saw that his offering was rejected, he was angry that God did not accept man's substitute in place of the sacrifice divinely ordained and angry with his brother for choosing to obey God instead of joining in rebellion against Him.

God did not leave him to himself, but condescended to reason with the man who had shown himself so unreasonable. "Why art thou wroth? and why is thy countenance fallen? If thou doest well, shalt thou not be accepted? And if thou doest not well, sin lieth at the door." If he would trust to the merits of the promised Saviour and obey God's requirements, he would enjoy His favor. But should he persist in unbelief and transgression, he would have no ground for complaint because he was rejected by the Lord.

Instead of acknowledging his sin, Cain continued to complain of the injustice of God and to cherish jealousy and hatred of Abel. In meekness, yet firmly, Abel defended the justice and goodness of God. He pointed out Cain's error and tried to convince him the wrong was in himself. He pointed to the compassion of God in sparing the life of their parents when He might have punished them with instant death, and urged that God loved them or He would not have given His Son, innocent and holy, to suffer the penalty which they had incurred. All this caused Cain's anger to burn the hotter. Reason and conscience told him that Abel was in the right, but he was enraged that he could gain no sympathy in his rebellion. In fury he slew his brother.

So in all ages the wicked have hated those who were better than themselves. "Every one that doeth evil hateth the light, neither cometh to the light, lest his deeds should be reproved." John 3:20.

The murder of Abel was the first example of the enmity between the serpent and the seed of the woman, between Satan and his subjects and Christ and His followers. Whenever through faith in the Lamb of God a soul renounces the service of sin, Satan's wrath is kindled. The holy life of Abel testified against Satan's claim that it is impossible for man to keep God's law. When Cain saw that he could not control Abel, he was so enraged that he destroyed his life. And wherever any stand in vindication of the law of God, the same spirit will be manifested. But every martyr of Jesus has died a conqueror. See Revelation 12:9, 11.

Cain the murderer was soon called to answer for his crime. "The Lord said unto Cain, Where is Abel thy brother? And he said, I know not: am I my brother's keeper?" He resorted to falsehood to conceal his guilt.

The Punishment of Cain

Again the Lord said to Cain, "What hast thou done? The voice of thy brother's blood crieth unto me from the ground." Cain had had time to reflect. He knew the enormity of the deed he had done and the falsehood he had uttered to conceal it; but he was rebellious still, and sentence was no longer deferred. The divine voice pronounced the terrible words: "And now art thou cursed from the earth, which hath opened her mouth to receive thy brother's blood from thy hand. When thou tillest the ground, it shall not henceforth yield unto thee her strength. A fugitive and a vagabond shalt thou be in the earth.''

A merciful Creator still spared his life and granted him opportunity for repentance. But Cain lived only to harden his heart, to encourage rebellion against divine authority, and to be the head of a line of bold sinners. His influence exerted demoralizing power until the earth became so corrupt and filled with violence as to call for its destruction.

The dark history of Cain and his descendants was an illustration of what would have been the result of permitting the sinner to live on forever, to carry out his rebellion against God. The forbearance of God only rendered the wicked more bold and defiant. Fifteen centuries after the sentence pronounced upon Cain, crime and pollution flooded the earth. It was made manifest that the sentence of death on the fallen race was just and merciful. The longer men lived in sin, the more abandoned they became.

Satan is constantly at work to misrepresent the character and government of God and to hold the inhabitants of the world under his deception. God sees the end from the beginning. His plans were far-reaching and comprehensive, not merely to put down the rebellion, but to demonstrate to all the universe its nature, fully vindicating His wisdom and righteousness in His dealings with evil.

The inhabitants of other worlds were watching with the deepest interest the condition of the world before the Flood. They saw the results of the administration which Lucifer had endeavored to establish in heaven in casting aside the law of God. The thoughts of men's hearts were only evil continually (Genesis 4:25, 36), at war with the divine principles of purity, peace, and love. It was an example of awful depravity.

By the facts unfolded in the great controversy God carries with Him the sympathy of the whole universe as step by step His great plan advances to its fulfillment in the final eradication of rebellion. It will be seen that all who have forsaken the divine precepts have placed themselves on the side of Satan, in warfare against Christ. When the prince of this world shall be judged, and all who have united with him shall share his fate, the whole universe will declare, ''Just and true are Thy ways, Thou King of saints.'' Revelation 15:3.

6/ Seth: When Men Turned to God

To Adam was given another son to be the heir of the spiritual birthright. The name Seth, given to this son, signified "appointed," or "compensation"; "for," said the mother, "God hath appointed me another seed instead of Abel, whom Cain slew." Seth resembled Adam more closely than did his other sons, a worthy character following in the steps of Abel. Yet he inherited no more natural goodness than did Cain. Seth, like Cain, inherited the fallen nature of his parents. But he received also the knowledge of the Redeemer and instruction in righteousness. He labored, as Abel would have done, to turn the minds of sinful men to revere and obey their Creator.

"To Seth, to him also there was born a son; and he called his name Enos: then began men to call upon the name of Jehovah." The distinction between the two classes became more marked—an open profession of loyalty to God on the part of one, contempt and disobedience on the part of the other.

Before the Fall, our first parents had kept the Sabbath, which was instituted in Eden, and after their expulsion from Paradise they continued its observance. They had learned what everyone will sooner or later learn, that the divine precepts are sacred and immutable and that the penalty of transgression will surely be inflicted. The Sabbath was honored by all who remained loyal to God. But Cain and his descendants did not respect the day upon which God had rested.

Cain now founded a city, calling it after the name of

This chapter is based on Genesis 4:25 to 6:2.

43

his eldest son. He had gone out from the presence of the Lord to seek his possessions and enjoyment in the earth, standing at the head of that great class of men who worship the god of this world. In that which pertains to mere earthly and material progress his descendants became distinguished. But they were in opposition to the purposes of God for man. To the crime of murder, Lamech, the fifth in descent, added polygamy. Abel had led a pastoral life, and the descendants of Seth followed the same course, counting themselves "strangers and pilgrims on the earth," seeking "a better country, that is, an heavenly." Hebrews 11:13, 16.

For some time the two classes remained separate. The race of Cain, spreading from their first settlement, dispersed over the plains and valleys where the children of Seth had dwelt. The latter, in order to escape their contaminating influence, withdrew to the mountains and there maintained the worship of God in its purity. But in the lapse of time they ventured to mingle with the inhabitants of the valleys. "The sons of God saw the daughters of men that they were fair." The children of Seth displeased the Lord by intermarrying with them. Many of the worshipers of God were beguiled into sin by the allurements constantly before them, and they lost their holy character. Mingling with the depraved, they became like them. The restrictions of the seventh commandment were disregarded, "and they took them wives of all which they chose." The children of Seth went "in the way of Cain." Jude 11. They fixed their minds upon worldly prosperity and enjoyment and neglected the commandments of the Lord. Sin spread abroad in the earth.

Length of Adam's Life

For nearly a thousand years Adam sought to stem the tide of evil. He had been commanded to instruct his posterity in the way of the Lord, and he carefully treasured what God had revealed to him and repeated it to succeeding generations. To the ninth generation he described man's holy and happy estate in Paradise and repeated the history of his fall, telling them of the sufferings by which God had taught him the necessity of strict adherence to His law and explaining to them the merciful provisions for their salvation. Yet often he was met with bitter reproach for the sin that had brought such woe upon his posterity.

When he left Eden, the thought that he must die thrilled him with horror. Filled with remorse for his own sin and doubly bereaved in the death of Abel and the rejection of Cain, Adam was bowed down with anguish. Though the sentence of death had at first appeared terrible, yet after beholding for nearly a thousand years the results of sin, he felt that it was merciful for God to bring to an end a life of suffering and sorrow.

The antediluvian age was not, as has often been supposed, an era of ignorance and barbarism. The people possessed great physical and mental strength, and their advantages were unrivaled. Their mental powers were early developed, and those who cherished the fear of God continued to increase in knowledge and wisdom throughout their life. Illustrious scholars of our time would appear as greatly inferior in mental as in physical strength. As the years of man have decreased and his physical strength has diminished, so his mental capacities have lessened.

It is true that the people of modern times have the benefit of the attainments of their predecessors. Men of masterly minds have left their work for those who follow. But how much greater the advantages of the men of that time! They had among them for hundreds of years him who was formed in God's image. Adam had learned from the Creator the history of creation; he himself witnessed the events of nine centuries. The antediluvians had strong memories to retain that which was communicated to them and to transmit it unimpaired to their posterity. For hundreds of years there were seven generations living upon the earth contemporaneously, profiting by the knowledge and experience of all.

So far from being an era of religious darkness, that was an age of great light. All the world had opportunity to receive instruction from Adam, and those who feared the Lord had also Christ and angels for their teachers. And they had a silent witness to the truth in the garden of God, which for many centuries remained among men. Eden stood just in sight, its entrance barred by watching angels. The object of the garden, the history of its two trees, were undisputed facts. And the existence and supreme authority of God were truths which men were slow to question while Adam was among them.

Notwithstanding the prevailing iniquity, a line of holy men lived as in the companionship of heaven— men of massive intellect, of wonderful attainments. They had a great mission—to develop a character of righteousness, to teach a lesson of godliness, not only to men of their time, but for future generations. Only a few are mentioned in the Scriptures, but all through the ages God had faithful witnesses, true-hearted worshipers.

Enoch—the First Man Never to Die

Enoch lived sixty-five years and begat a son. After that he walked with God three hundred years. He was one of the preservers of the true faith, the progenitors of the promised seed. From the lips of Adam he had learned the story of the fall and of God's grace as seen in the promise, and he relied upon the Redeemer to come.

But after the birth of his first son, Enoch reached a higher experience. As he saw the child's love for its father, its simple trust in his protection, as he felt the deep tenderness of his own heart for that firstborn son, he learned a precious lesson of the wonderful love of God in the gift of His Son. The unfathomable love of God through Christ became the subject of his meditations day and night, and he sought to reveal that love to the people among whom he dwelt.

Enoch's walk with God was not in a trance or vision, but in all the duties of daily life. As a husband and father, a friend, a citizen, he was the unwavering servant of the Lord.

His heart was in harmony with God's will; for "can two walk together except they be agreed?" Amos 3:3. And this holy walk continued for three hundred years. Enoch's faith waxed stronger, his love more ardent, with the lapse of centuries.

Enoch was a man of extensive knowledge, honored with special revelations from God; yet he was one of the humblest of men. He waited before the Lord. To him prayer was as the breath of the soul; he lived in the very atmosphere of heaven.

Through holy angels God revealed to Enoch His purpose to destroy the world by a flood. He also opened more fully to him the plan of redemption and showed him the great events connected with the second coming of Christ and the end of the world.

Enoch had been troubled in regard to the dead. It had seemed to him that the righteous and the wicked would go to the dust together and that this would be their end. He could not see the life of the just beyond the grave. In prophetic vision he was instructed concerning the death of Christ and His coming in glory attended by all the holy angels to ransom His people from the grave. He also saw the corrupt state of the world when Christ should appear the second time— that there would be a boastful, self-willed generation trampling upon the law and despising the atonement. He saw the righteous crowned with glory and honor and the wicked destroyed by fire.

Enoch became a preacher of righteousness, making known God's messages to all who would hear. In the land where Cain had sought to flee from the divine presence, the prophet made known the wonderful scenes that had passed before his vision. "Behold," he declared, "the Lord cometh with ten thousands of His saints, to execute judgment upon all, and to convince all that are ungodly among them of all their ungodly deeds." Jude 14, 15.

While he preached the love of God in Christ, he rebuked the prevailing iniquity and warned that judgment would surely be visited upon the transgressor. It is not smooth things only that are spoken by holy men. God puts into the lips of His messengers truths that are keen and cutting as a two-edged sword.

Some gave heed to the warning, but the multitudes went on more boldly in their evil ways. So will the last generation make light of the warnings of the Lord's messengers.

In the midst of a life of active labor, Enoch steadfastly maintained his communion with God. After remaining for a time among the people, he would spend a season in solitude, hungering and thirsting for divine knowledge. Communing with God, Enoch came more and more to reflect the divine image. His face was radiant with the light that shines in the face of Jesus.

As year after year passed, deeper and deeper grew the tide of human guilt, darker and darker gathered the clouds of divine judgment. Yet Enoch held on his way, warning, pleading, striving to turn back the tide of guilt. Though his warnings were disregarded by a sinful, pleasure-loving people, he had the testimony that God approved. He continued to battle against evil until God removed him from a world of sin to the pure joys of heaven.

Enoch Is Translated to Heaven

The men of that generation had mocked him who sought not to build up possessions here. But Enoch's heart was upon eternal treasures. He had seen the King in His glory in the midst of Zion. His mind, his conversation, were in heaven. The greater the existing iniquity, the more earnest was his longing for the home of God.

For three hundred years Enoch had walked with God. Day by day he had longed for a closer union; nearer and nearer had grown the communion, until God took him to Himself. Now the walk with God, so long pursued on earth, continued, and he passed through the gates of the Holy City—the first from among men to enter there.

His loss was felt on earth. Some, both righteous and wicked, had witnessed his departure. Those who loved him made diligent search, but without avail. They reported that he "was not," for God had taken him.

By the translation of Enoch the Lord designed to teach an important lesson. There was danger that men would yield to discouragement because of the fearful results of Adam's sin. Many were ready to exclaim, "What profit is it that we have feared the Lord and have kept His ordinances, since a heavy curse is resting upon the race, and death is the portion of us all?" Satan was urging upon men the belief that there was no reward for the righteous or punishment of the wicked, and that it was impossible for men to obey the divine statutes. But in the case of Enoch, God shows what He will do for those who keep His commandments. Men were taught that it is possible to obey the law of God, that they were able by grace to resist temptation and become pure and holy. His translation was an evidence of the truth of his prophecy concerning the hereafter, with its award of immortal life to the obedient and of condemnation and death to the transgressor.

By faith Enoch "was translated that he should not see death, . . . for before his translation he had this testimony, that he pleased God." Hebrews 11:5. The godly character of this prophet represents the state of holiness which must be attained by those who shall be "redeemed from the earth" (Revelation 14:3) at Christ's second advent. Then, as before the Flood, iniquity will prevail. Men will rebel against the authority of Heaven. But like Enoch, God's people will seek for purity of heart and conformity to His will, until they shall reflect the likeness of Christ. Like Enoch they will warn the world of the Lord's second coming and by their holy example will condemn the sins of the ungodly. As Enoch was translated to heaven, so the living righteous will be translated from the earth before its destruction by fire. See 1 Corinthians 15:51, 52; 1 Thessalonians 4:16-18.

7/ When the World Was Destroyed by Water

In the days of Noah a double curse was resting upon the earth in consequence of Adam's transgression and the murder committed by Cain. Yet the earth was still beautiful. The hills were crowned with majestic trees; the plains were sweet with the fragrance of a thousand flowers. The fruits of the earth were almost without limit. The trees far surpassed in size and perfect proportion any now to be found. Their wood was of fine grain and hard substance, resembling stone and hardly less enduring. Gold, silver, and precious stones existed in abundance.

The human race yet retained much of its early vigor. There were many giants renowned for wisdom, skillful in devising the most cunning and wonderful works, but giving loose rein to iniquity.

God bestowed upon these antediluvians rich gifts, but they used His bounties to glorify themselves and turned them into a curse by fixing their affections on the gifts instead of the Giver. They endeavored to excel one another in beautifying their dwellings with skillful workmanship. They reveled in scenes of pleasure and wickedness. Not desiring to retain God in their knowledge, they soon came to deny His existence. They glorified human genius, worshiped the works of their own hands, and taught their children to bow down to graven images.

The psalmist describes the effect produced upon the worshiper by the adoration of idols: "They that make them are like unto them; so is every one that trusteth in

This chapter is based on Genesis 6 and 7.

them." Psalm 115:8. It is a law of the human mind that by beholding we become changed. If the mind is never exalted above the level of humanity, if it is not uplifted to contemplate infinite wisdom and love, man will be constantly sinking lower and lower. "God saw that the wickedness of man was great in the earth, and that every imagination of the thoughts of his heart was only evil continually. . . . The earth also was corrupt before God, and the earth was filled with violence." His law was transgressed, and every conceivable sin was the result. Justice was trampled in the dust, and the cries of the oppressed reached unto heaven.

Human Life Regarded With Indifference

Polygamy had been early introduced, contrary to the divine arrangement. The Lord gave to Adam one wife. But after the fall men chose to follow their own sinful desires. As the result, crime and wretchedness rapidly increased. Neither marriage nor the rights of property were respected. Men exulted in violence. They delighted in destroying animals, and the use of flesh for food rendered them still more cruel and bloodthirsty, until they came to regard human life with indifference.

The world was in its infancy, yet iniquity had become so deep and widespread that God said, "I will destroy man whom I have created, from the face of the earth." He declared that His Spirit should not always strive with the guilty race. If they did not cease their sins He would blot them from His creation; He would sweep away the beasts and the vegetation which furnished such an abundant supply of food and would transform the fair earth into one vast scene of ruin.

A Boat to Preserve Life

A hundred and twenty years before the Flood, the Lord declared to Noah His purpose and directed him to build an ark. He was to preach that God would bring a flood of water upon the earth. Those who would believe the message and would prepare by repentance and reformation should find pardon and be saved. Methuselah and his sons, who lived to hear the preaching of Noah, assisted in building the ark.

God gave Noah the exact dimensions of the ark and directions in regard to its construction. Human wisdom could not have devised a structure of so great strength and durability. God was the designer, and Noah the master builder. It was three stories high, with but one door in the side. Light was admitted at the top, and the different apartments were so arranged that all were lighted. The material was cypress or gopher wood, which would be untouched by decay for hundreds of years. Building this immense structure was a slow process. On account of the size of the trees and the nature of the wood, much more labor was required then than now to prepare timber. All that man could do was done to render the work perfect, yet the ark could not of itself have withstood the storm. God alone could preserve His servants upon the tempestuous waters.

"By faith Noah, being warned of God of things not seen as yet, moved with fear, prepared an ark to the saving of his house; by the which he condemned the world, and became heir of the righteousness which is by faith." Hebrews 11:7. While giving his warning message, his faith was perfected and made evident, an example of believing just what God says. All that he possessed he invested in the ark. As he began to construct that immense boat, multitudes came from every direction to see the strange sight and to hear the earnest words of the preacher.

Many at first appeared to receive the warning, yet they did not turn to God with true repentance. Overcome by the prevailing unbelief, they finally joined their former associates in rejecting the solemn message. Some were convicted and would have heeded the warning, but there were so many to ridicule, that they partook of the same spirit, resisted the invitations of mercy, and were soon among the most defiant scoffers. None go to such lengths in sin as do those who have once had light but have resisted the convicting Spirit of God.

The men of that generation were not all idolaters. Many professed to be worshipers of God. They claimed that their idols were representations of the Deity and that through them the people could obtain a clearer conception of the divine Being. This class were foremost in rejecting the preaching of Noah, and they finally declared that the divine law was no longer in force, that it was contrary to the character of God to punish transgression. Their minds had become so blinded by rejection of light that they really believed Noah's message to be a delusion.

The world was arrayed against God's justice and His laws, and Noah was regarded as a fanatic. Great men, worldly, honored, and wise, said, "The threatenings of God are for the purpose of intimidating and will never be verified. The destruction of the world by the God who made it and the punishment of the beings He has created will never take place. Fear not, Noah is a wild fanatic." They continued their disobedience and wickedness, as though God had not spoken through His servant.

But Noah stood like a rock amid the tempest. Connection with God made him strong in the strength of infinite power. For one hundred and twenty years his solemn voice fell upon the ears of that generation in regard to events which, so far as human wisdom could judge, were impossible.

Heretofore rain had never fallen; the earth had been watered by a mist or dew. The rivers had never yet passed their boundaries but had borne their waters safely to the sea. Fixed decrees had kept the waters from overflowing their banks. See Job 38:11.

But time passed on; men whose hearts had at times trembled with fear began to be reassured. They reasoned that nature is above the God of nature. If the message of Noah were correct, nature would be turned out of her course. They manifested their contempt for the warning of God by doing just as they had done before the warning was given. They continued their festivities and gluttonous feasts. They ate and drank, planted and builded, laying plans in reference to the future. They asserted that if there were any truth in what Noah had said, the men of renown—the wise, the prudent, the great men—would understand the matter.

The period of their probation was about to expire. The ark was finished in every part as the Lord had directed and was stored with food for man and beast. And now the servant of God made his last solemn appeal to the people. He entreated them to seek a refuge while it might be found. Again they rejected his words and raised their voices in scoffing.

Suddenly beasts of every description were seen coming from mountain and forest, quietly making their way toward the ark. Birds were flocking from all directions and in perfect order passed to the ark. Animals "went in, two and two, unto Noah into the ark," the clean beasts by sevens. Philosophers were called upon to account for the singular occurrence, but in vain. The doomed race banished their rising fears by merriment and seemed to invite upon themselves the awakened wrath of God.

God commanded Noah, "Come thou and all thy house into the ark; for thee have I seen righteous before Me in this generation." His influence and example resulted in blessings to his family. God saved all the members of his family with him.

An Angel Shuts the Door
The beasts of the field and the birds of the air had entered the place of refuge. Noah and his household were within the ark, "and the Lord shut him in." The massive door, impossible for those within to close, was slowly swung to its place by unseen hands. Noah was shut in and the rejecters of God's mercy were shut out. So when Christ shall cease His intercession for guilty men before His coming in the clouds of heaven, the

door of mercy will be shut. Then divine grace will no longer restrain the wicked, and Satan will have full control of those who have rejected mercy. They will endeavor to destroy God's people; but as Noah was shut into the ark, so the righteous will be shielded by divine power.

For seven days after Noah and his family entered the ark there appeared no sign of the coming storm. During this period their faith was tested. It was a time of triumph to the world without. They continued making a jest of the manifestations of God's power. They gathered in crowds about the ark, deriding its inmates with a daring violence never ventured upon before.

But upon the eighth day dark clouds overspread the heavens. There followed the muttering of thunder and the flash of lightning. Soon large drops of rain began to fall. The world had never witnessed anything like this, and the hearts of men were struck with fear. All were secretly inquiring, "Can it be that Noah was right and that the world is doomed?" The beasts were roaming about in the wildest terror. Then "the fountains of the great deep" were "broken up, and the windows of heaven were opened." Water appeared to come from the clouds in mighty cataracts. Rivers broke away from their boundaries and overflowed the valleys. Jets of water burst from the earth with indescribable force.

The people first beheld their splendid buildings and beautiful gardens and groves where they had placed their idols destroyed by lightning from heaven. Altars on which human sacrifices had been offered were torn down, and the worshipers were made to tremble at the power of the living God.

As the violence of the storm increased, the terror of man and beast was beyond description. Above the roar of the tempest was heard the wailing of a people that had despised the authority of God. Satan himself, compelled to remain in the midst of the warring elements, feared for his own existence. He now uttered imprecations against God. Many of the people, like Satan, blasphemed God. Others were frantic with fear, stretching their hands toward the ark, pleading for admittance. Conscience was at last aroused to know that there is a God who ruleth in the heavens.

They called upon Him earnestly, but His ear was not open to their cry. In that terrible hour they saw that transgression of God's law had caused their ruin. Yet they felt no true contrition, no abhorrence of evil. They would have returned to their defiance of Heaven had the judgment been removed.

Some clung to the ark until they were borne away by the surging waters or their hold was broken by collision with rocks and trees. The massive ark trembled in every fiber as it was beaten by the merciless winds. The cries of beasts within expressed their fear and pain. But it continued to ride safely. Angels were commissioned to preserve it.

Some of the people bound their children and themselves upon powerful animals, knowing that these would climb to the highest points to escape the rising waters. Some fastened themselves to lofty trees on the hills or mountains, but the trees were uprooted and hurled into the billows. As the waters rose higher the people fled for refuge to the loftiest mountains. Often man and beast would struggle together for a foothold until both were swept away.

From the highest peaks men looked abroad upon a shoreless ocean. The solemn warnings of God's servant no longer seemed a subject for ridicule. Those doomed sinners pleaded for one hour's probation, one more call from the lips of Noah! But love, no less than justice, demanded that God's judgments should put a check on sin. The despisers of God perished in the black depths.

Conditions Before the Flood

The sins that called for vengeance upon the antediluvian world exist today. The fear of God is banished from the hearts of men. His law is treated with indifference and contempt. "As in the days that were before the flood they were eating and drinking, marrying and giving in marriage, until the day that Noe entered into the ark, and knew not until the flood came, and took them all away; so shall also the coming of the Son of man be." Matthew 24:38, 39. God did not condemn the antediluvians for eating and drinking. He had given the fruits of the earth to supply their physical wants. Their sin consisted in taking these gifts without gratitude to the Giver, indulging appetite without restraint. It was lawful to marry. He gave special directions concerning this ordinance, clothing it with sanctity and beauty. But marriage was perverted and made to minister to passion.

Similar Conditions Today

A similar condition exists now. Appetite is indulged without restraint. Professed followers of Christ are eating and drinking with the drunken. Intemperance benumbs the moral and spiritual powers and prepares for indulgence of the lower passions. Multitudes become slaves of lust, living for the pleasures of sense. Extravagance pervades society. Integrity is sacrificed for luxury and display. Fraud, bribery, and theft stalk unrebuked. The issues of the press teem with records of crimes so cold-blooded that it seems as though every instinct of humanity were blotted out. And these atrocities have become so common that they hardly elicit surprise. The pent-up fires of lawlessness, having once escaped control, will fill the earth with woe and desolation. The antediluvian world represents the condition to which modern society is hastening.

God sent Noah to warn the world that the people might be led to repentance and escape the threatened destruction. As the time of Christ's second appearing draws near, the Lord sends His servants with a warning to prepare for that great event. Multitudes have been living in transgression of God's law, and now He in mercy calls them to obey its sacred precepts. All who will put away their sins by repentance and faith in Christ are offered pardon. But many reject His warnings and deny the authority of His law.

Of the vast population of the earth before the Flood, only eight souls believed and obeyed God's word through Noah. So before the Lawgiver shall come to punish the disobedient, transgressors are warned to repent; but with the majority these warnings will be in vain. "There shall come in the last days scoffers, walking after their own lusts, and saying, Where is the promise of His coming? for since the fathers fell asleep, all things continue as they were from the beginning." 2 Peter 3:3, 4.

Jesus asked the significant question, "When the Son of man cometh, shall He find faith on the earth?" Luke 18:8. "The Spirit speaketh expressly, that in the latter times some shall depart from the faith, giving heed to seducing spirits, and doctrines of devils." 1 Timothy 4:1. "In the last days perilous times shall come." 2 Timothy 3:1.

When Probation Closes

As the time of their probation was closing, the antediluvians gave themselves up to exciting amusements, engrossed with mirth and pleasure. In our day the world is absorbed in pleasure-seeking. A constant round of excitement prevents the people from being impressed by the truths which alone can save them from coming destruction.

In Noah's day philosophers declared it was impossible for the world to be destroyed by water. So now men of science endeavor to show that the world cannot be destroyed by fire. But when all regarded Noah's prophecy as a delusion, then it was that God's time had come. The Lawgiver is greater than the laws of nature. "As it was in the days of Noah," "even thus shall it be in the day when the Son of man is revealed." Luke 17:26, 30. "The day of the Lord will come as a thief in the night; in the which the heavens shall pass away with a great noise, and the earth also, and the works that are therein shall be burned up." 2 Peter 3:10.

When religious teachers are pointing forward to ages of peace and prosperity, and the world are absorbed in their planting and building, feasting and merrymaking, rejecting God's warnings and mocking His messengers—then it is that "sudden destruction cometh upon them, . . . and they shall not escape." 1 Thessalonians 5:3.

8 / After the Flood, a New Beginning

The waters rose above the highest mountains. It often seemed to the family within the ark that they must perish, as for five long months their boat was tossed about. It was a trying ordeal, but Noah's faith did not waver.

As the waters began to subside, the Lord caused the ark to drift into a spot protected by a group of mountains preserved by His power. These mountains were but a little distance apart, and the ark moved about in this quiet haven. This gave great relief to the weary, tempest-tossed voyagers.

Noah and his family longed to go forth again upon the earth. Forty days after the tops of the mountains became visible they sent out a raven to discover whether the earth had become dry. This bird, finding nothing but water, continued to fly to and from the ark. Seven days later a dove was sent forth, which finding no footing, returned to the ark. Noah waited seven days longer and again sent forth the dove. When she returned at evening with an olive leaf in her mouth, there was great rejoicing. Still Noah waited patiently for special directions to depart.

At last an angel opened the massive door and bade the patriarch and his household go forth upon the earth and take with them every living thing. Noah did not forget Him by whose gracious care they had been preserved. His first act was to build an altar and offer sacrifice, thus manifesting his gratitude to God for deliverance and his faith in Christ, the great sacrifice. This offering was pleasing to the Lord, and a blessing re-

This chapter is based on Genesis 7:20 to 9:7.

61

sulted not only to the patriarch and his family, but to all who should live upon the earth. "The Lord said in His heart, I will not again curse the ground any more for man's sake. . . . While the earth remaineth, seedtime and harvest, and cold and heat, and summer and winter, and day and night, shall not cease." Noah had come forth upon a desolate earth, but before preparing a house for himself, he built an altar to God. His stock of cattle was small, yet he cheerfully gave a part to the Lord as an acknowledgment that all was His. In like manner His mercy toward us should be acknowledged by devotion and gifts to His cause.

The Rainbow—Sign of God's Kindness

Lest men fear another flood the Lord encouraged the family of Noah by a promise: "I will establish My covenant with you; . . . neither shall there any more be a flood to destroy the earth. . . . I do set My bow in the cloud, and it shall be for a token of a covenant between me and the earth. . . . When I bring a cloud over the earth, . . . the bow shall be seen in the cloud; . . . and I will look upon it, that I may remember the everlasting covenant between God and every living creature."

How great the condescension of God and His compassion for His erring creatures!

This does not imply that He would ever forget, but He speaks to us in our own language. As the children should ask the meaning of the arch which spans the heavens, their parents should repeat the story of the Flood and tell them that the Most High had placed it in the clouds as an assurance that the waters should never again overflow the earth. It would testify of divine love to man and strengthen his confidence in God.

In heaven the semblance of the rainbow encircles the throne and overarches the head of Christ. See Ezekiel 1:28; Revelation 4:2, 3. When man by his great wickedness invites divine judgments, the Saviour, interceding with the Father, points to the bow in the clouds, to the rainbow around the throne, as a token of mercy toward the repentant sinner.

"As I have sworn that the waters of Noah should no more go over the earth; so have I sworn that I would not be wroth with thee, nor rebuke thee. . . . My kindness shall not depart from thee, neither shall the covenant of My peace be removed, saith the Lord that hath mercy on thee." Isaiah 54:9, 10.

As Noah looked upon the powerful beasts of prey that came forth from the ark, the Lord sent an angel with the assuring message: "The fear of you and the dread of you shall be upon every beast of the earth, and upon every fowl of the air, upon all that moveth upon the earth, and upon all the fishes of the sea; into your hand are they delivered. Every moving thing that liveth shall be meat for you; even as the green herb have I given you all things." Before this time God had given no permission to eat animal food, but now that every green thing had been destroyed, He allowed them to eat the flesh of the clean beasts that had been preserved in the ark.

The entire surface of the earth was changed at the Flood. Everywhere were strewn dead bodies. The Lord would not permit these to remain to decompose and pollute the air. A violent wind which was caused to dry up the waters moved them with great force, in some instances even carrying away the tops of mountains and heaping up trees, rocks, and earth above the bodies of the dead. By the same means the silver and gold, choice wood and precious stones, which had enriched the world before the Flood, were concealed, the violent action of the waters piling earth and rocks upon these treasures and even forming mountains above them. God saw that the more He enriched and prospered sinful men, the more they would corrupt their ways before Him.

The mountains, once beautiful, had become broken and irregular. Ledges and ragged rocks were now scattered upon the surface of the earth. Where once had been earth's richest treasures of gold, silver, and precious stones were seen the heaviest marks of the curse. And upon countries not inhabited and those where there had been the least crime, the curse rested more lightly.

More terrible manifestations than the world has yet beheld will be witnessed at the second advent of Christ. As lightnings from heaven unite with the fire in the earth, the mountains will burn like a furnace and pour forth terrific streams of lava, overwhelming gardens and fields, villages and cities. Everywhere there will be dreadful earthquakes and eruptions.

Thus God will destroy the wicked from off the earth. But the righteous will be preserved as Noah was preserved in the ark. Says the psalmist: "Because thou hast made the Lord, which is my refuge, even the most High, thy habitation, there shall no evil befall thee." Psalm 91:9, 10; see also verse 14 and Psalm 27:5.

The earth will burn like a furnace when it is finally cleansed of sin.

9/ The Beginning of the Literal Week

Like the Sabbath, the week originated at creation, and it has been preserved through Bible history. God Himself measured off the first week. It consisted of seven literal days. Six days were employed in the work of creation. Upon the seventh God rested, then set it apart as a day of rest for man. "For in six days the Lord made heaven and earth, the sea, and all that in them is, and rested the seventh day; wherefore the Lord blessed the Sabbath day, and hallowed it." Exodus 20:8-11.

This reason appears beautiful and forcible when we understand the days of creation to be literal. The first six days of each week are given to man for labor. On the seventh day man is to refrain from labor in commemoration of the Creator's rest.

But the assumption that the events of the first week required thousands upon thousands of years is infidelity in its most insidious and hence most dangerous form. Its real character is so disguised that it is held and taught by many who profess to believe the Bible. "By the word of the Lord were the heavens made; and all the host of them by the breath of His mouth." Psalm 33:6. The Bible recognizes no long ages in which the earth slowly evolved from chaos. Of each successive day of creation, the sacred record declares that it consisted of the evening and the morning, like all other days that have followed.

Geologists claim to find evidence from the earth that it is very much older than the Mosaic record teaches.

3-F.E.P.

Bones of men and animals much larger than any that now exist have been discovered, and from that it is inferred that the earth was populated long before the time brought to view in the record of creation. Such reasoning has led many professed Bible believers to adopt the position that the days of creation were vast, indefinite periods.

But apart from Bible history geology can prove nothing. Relics found in the earth do give evidence of conditions differing in many respects from the present, but the time when these conditions existed can be learned only from the Inspired Record. In the history of the Flood inspiration has explained that which geology alone could never fathom. In the days of Noah, men, animals, and trees many times larger than now exist were buried and thus preserved as an evidence to later generations that the antediluvians perished by a flood. God designed that the discovery of these things should establish faith in inspired history. But men, with their vain reasoning, fall into the same error as did the people before the Flood—the things which God gave them as a benefit they turn into a curse by making a wrong use of them.

There is a constant effort to explain creation as the result of natural causes, and human reasoning is accepted even by professed Christians in opposition to Scripture facts. Many oppose the investigation of the prophecies, especially Daniel and the Revelation, declaring that we cannot understand them. Yet these very persons eagerly receive the suppositions of geologists in contradiction of the Mosaic record. Just how God accomplished the work of creation He has never revealed to men; human science cannot search out the secrets of the Most High. See Deuteronomy 29:29.

Those who leave the Word of God to account for His created works on scientific principles are drifting without chart or compass upon an unknown ocean. The greatest minds, if not guided by the Word of God in their research, become bewildered in their attempts to trace the relations of science and revelation. Those who doubt the records of the Old and New Testaments will be led to go a step further and doubt the existence of God. Then, having lost their anchor, they are left to beat about upon the rocks of infidelity.

The Bible is not to be tested by men's ideas of science. Skeptics, through an imperfect comprehension of either science or revelation, claim to find contradictions between them: but rightly understood they are in perfect harmony. Moses wrote under the guidance of the Spirit of God, and a correct theory of geology will never claim discoveries that cannot be reconciled with his statements.

True Science and the Bible Agree

In the Word of God many queries are raised that scholars can never answer. There is much among the common things of everyday life that finite minds with all their boasted wisdom can never fully understand.

Yet men of science think they can comprehend the wisdom of God. The idea prevails that He is restricted by His own laws. Men either deny or ignore His existence or think to explain everything, even the operation of His Spirit upon the human heart; and they no longer reverence His name.

Many teach that the operations of nature are conducted in harmony with fixed laws with which God Himself cannot interfere. This is false science. Nature is the servant of her Creator. God does not annul His laws but is continually using them as His instruments. There is in nature the continual working of the Father and the Son. Christ says, "My Father worketh hitherto, and I work." John 5:17.

As regards this world, God's work of creation is completed. "The works were finished from the foundation of the world." Hebrews 4:3. But His energy is still exerted in upholding the objects of His creation. Every breath, every pulsation of the heart, is an evidence of the all-pervading care of Him in whom "we live, and move, and have our being." Acts 17:28. The hand of God guides the planets and keeps them in position. He "bringeth out their host by number; He calleth them all by names by the greatness of His might, for that He is strong in power, not one faileth." Isaiah 40:26. Through His power vegetation flourishes, the leaves appear, and the flowers bloom. He "maketh grass to grow upon the mountains" (Psalm 147:8), and by Him the valleys are made fruitful. "All the beasts of the forest . . . seek their meat from God" (Psalm 104:20, 21), and every living creature from the smallest insect to man is daily dependent upon His providential care.

All true science is in harmony with His works; all true education leads to obedience to His government. Science opens new wonders to our view; she soars high and explores new depths, but she brings nothing from her research that conflicts with divine revelation. The book of nature and the Written Word shed light upon each other.

Men may be ever searching, ever learning, and still there is an infinity beyond. The works of creation testify of God's power and greatness. See Psalm 19:1. Those who take the Written Word as their counselor will find in science an aid to understand God. "The invisible things of Him from the creation of the world are clearly seen, being understood by the things that are made, even His eternal power and Godhead." Romans 1:20.

10/ When Languages Were Changed

To repeople the desolate earth God had preserved but one family, the household of Noah. To him He declared, "Thee have I seen righteous before Me in this generation." Genesis 7:1. Yet in the three sons of Noah—Shem, Ham, and Japheth—were foreshadowed the character of their posterity.

Noah, speaking by divine inspiration, foretold the history of the three great races to spring from these fathers of mankind. Tracing the descendants of Ham through the son rather than the father, He declared, "Cursed be Canaan; a servant of servants shall he be unto his brethren." The unnatural crime of Ham revealed the vileness of his character. These evil characteristics were perpetuated in Canaan and his posterity.

On the other hand, the reverence manifested by Shem and Japheth for divine statutes promised a brighter future for their descendants. Concerning these sons it was declared, "Blessed be Jehovah, God of Shem; and Canaan shall be his servant. God shall enlarge Japheth, and he shall dwell in the tents of Shem; and Canaan shall be his servant." The line of Shem was to be that of the chosen people. From him would descend Abraham and the people of Israel, through whom Christ was to come. And Japheth "shall dwell in the tents of Shem." In the blessings of the gospel the descendants of Japheth were especially to share.

The posterity of Canaan descended to the most degrading forms of heathenism. Though the prophetic curse had doomed them to slavery, God bore with their

This chapter is based on Genesis 9:25-27; 11:1-9.

corruption until they passed the limits of divine forbearance. Then they became bondmen to the descendants of Shem and Japheth.

The prophecy of Noah did not fix the character and destiny of his sons. But it showed what would be the result of the course they had chosen and the character they had developed. As a rule, children inherit the dispositions and tendencies of their parents and imitate their example. Thus the vileness and irreverence of Ham were reproduced in his posterity, bringing a curse upon them for many generations.

On the other hand, how richly rewarded was Shem's respect for his father, and what an illustrious line of holy men appears in his posterity!

For a time, the descendants of Noah continued to dwell among the mountains where the ark had rested. As their numbers increased, apostasy led to division. Those who desired to forget their Creator and cast off the restraint of His law felt a constant annoyance from the teaching and example of their God-fearing associates. After a time they decided to separate. Accordingly they journeyed to Shinar on the banks of the Euphrates, attracted by the beauty of the situation and the fertility of the soil.

Here they decided to build a city and in it a tower of such height as should render it the wonder of the world. God had directed men to disperse throughout the earth, but these Babel builders determined to keep their community united and to found a monarchy that should embrace the whole earth. Thus their city would become the metropolis of a universal empire. Its glory would command the admiration and homage of the world. The magnificent tower, reaching to the heavens, was intended to stand as a monument of the power and wisdom of its builders.

The dwellers on the plain of Shinar disbelieved God's covenant that He would not again bring a flood upon the earth. One object in the erection of the tower was to secure their safety in case of another deluge.

And as they would be able to ascend to the region of the clouds, they hoped to ascertain the cause of the Flood. The whole undertaking was to exalt the pride of its projectors and to turn future generations away from God.

When the tower had been partially completed, suddenly the work that had been advancing so prosperously was checked. Angels were sent to bring to naught the purpose of the builders. The tower had reached a lofty height, and men were stationed at different points, each to receive and report to the one next below him the orders for needed material. As messages were passing from one to another, the language was confounded so that the directions delivered were often the reverse of those that had been given. All work came to a standstill. The builders were wholly unable to account for the strange misunderstandings among them and in their rage and disappointment reproached one another. Lightnings from heaven as an evidence of God's displeasure broke off the upper portion of the tower and cast it to the ground.

God's Purpose in Changing Their Language

Up to this time, all men had spoken the same language. Now those that could understand one another's speech united in companies. Some went one way and some another. "The Lord scattered them abroad from thence upon the face of all the earth." This dispersion was the means of peopling the earth; and thus the Lord's purpose was accomplished through the very means that men had employed to prevent its fulfillment.

But at what a loss! It was God's purpose that as men should go forth to different parts of the earth, they should carry with them the light of truth. Noah, the faithful preacher of righteousness, lived for three hundred and fifty years after the Flood, Shem for five hundred years; thus their descendants had opportunity to become acquainted with the requirements of God and the history of His dealings with their fathers. But they had no desire to retain God in their knowledge; and by the confusion of tongues they were in a great measure shut out from intercourse with those who might have given them light.

Satan was seeking to bring contempt upon the sacrificial offerings that prefigured the death of Christ. As the minds of the people were darkened by idolatry, he led them to counterfeit these offerings and sacrifice their own children upon the altars of their gods. As men turned away from God, the divine attributes—justice, purity, and love—were supplanted by oppression, violence, and brutality.

The men of Babel had determined to establish a government independent of God. Some among them, however, feared the Lord. For the sake of these faithful ones, the Lord delayed His judgments and gave the people time to reveal their true character. The sons of God labored to turn them from their purpose, but the people were fully united in their Heaven-daring undertaking. Had they gone on unchecked they would have demoralized the world in its infancy. Had this confederacy been permitted, a mighty power would have borne sway to banish righteousness—and with it peace, happiness, and security—from the earth.

Those that feared the Lord cried unto Him to interpose. "And the Lord came down to see the city and the tower, which the children of men builded." In mercy to the world He defeated the purpose of the tower-builders. In mercy He confounded their speech, putting a check on their rebellion. God bears long with the perversity of men, giving opportunity for repentance. From time to time the unseen hand is stretched out to restrain iniquity. Unmistakable evidence is given that the Creator of the universe is the Supreme Ruler of heaven and earth. None can with impunity defy His power!

The schemes of the Babel-builders ended in shame and defeat. The monument to their pride became the memorial of their folly. Yet men are continually pursuing the same course—depending upon self and rejecting God's law. It is the principle that Satan tried to carry out in heaven.

Today's Tower of Babel

There are tower builders in our time. Infidels presume to pass sentence upon God's moral government. They despise His law and boast of the sufficiency of human reason. Then, "because sentence against an evil work is not executed speedily, therefore the heart of the sons of men is fully set in them to do evil." Ecclesiastes 8:11.

Many turn from the plain teachings of the Bible and build up a creed from human speculations and pleasing fables. They point to their "tower" as a way to climb up to heaven. Lips of eloquence teach that the transgressor shall not die, that salvation may be secured without obedience to the law of God. If the professed followers of Christ would accept God's standard, it would bring them into unity, but so long as human wisdom is exalted above His holy Word there will be divisions and dissension. The existing confusion of conflicting creeds and sects is fitly represented by the term "Babylon," which prophecy applies to the world-loving churches of the last days. See Revelation 14:8; 18:2.

The time of God's investigation is at hand. His sovereign power will be revealed; the works of human pride will be laid low.

11/ Abraham, the Father of All Believers

After Babel, idolatry again became well-nigh universal, and the Lord finally left the hardened transgressors to follow their evil ways, while He chose Abraham of the line of Shem and made him the keeper of His law for future generations. God has ever preserved a remnant to preserve the precious revealings of His will. The son of Terah became the inheritor of this holy trust. Uncorrupted by the prevailing apostasy, he steadfastly adhered to the worship of God. The Lord communicated His will to Abraham and gave him a knowledge of His law and of salvation through Christ.

There was given to Abraham the promise, "I will make of thee a great nation, and I will bless thee, and make thy name great; and thou shalt be a blessing." To this was added the assurance that of his line the Redeemer of the world should come: "In thee shall all families of the earth be blessed." Yet, as the first condition of fulfillment, there was to be a test of faith; a sacrifice was demanded.

The message of God came to Abraham, "Get thee out of thy country, and from thy kindred, and from thy father's house, unto a land that I will show thee." Abraham must be separated from the influence of kindred and friends. His character must be peculiar, differing from all the world. He could not even explain his action so as to be understood by his friends. His motives were not comprehended by his idolatrous kindred.

Abraham's unquestioning obedience is one of the

This chapter is based on Genesis 12.

most striking evidences of faith in all the Bible. See Hebrews 11:8. Relying upon the divine promise, he abandoned home and kindred and native land and went forth to follow where God should lead. "By faith he became a sojourner in the land of promise as in a land not his own, dwelling in tents, with Isaac and Jacob." Hebrews 11:9.

There were strong ties to bind him to his country, his kindred, and his home. But he did not hesitate to obey the call. He had no question to ask concerning the land of promise—whether the soil was fertile, the climate healthful. The happiest place on earth was the place where God would have him to be.

Many are still tested as was Abraham. They do not hear the voice of God speaking directly from heaven, but He calls them by the teachings of His Word and the events of providence. They may be required to abandon a career that promises wealth and honor, and separate from kindred to enter upon what appears to be a path of self-denial and sacrifice. God has a work for them to do; the influence of friends and kindred would hinder it.

Who is ready at the call of Providence to renounce cherished plans, accept new duties, and enter untried fields? He who will do this has the faith of Abraham and will share with him that "far more exceeding and eternal weight of glory." 2 Corinthians 4:17; see also Romans 8:18.

The call from heaven first came to Abraham in "Ur of the Chaldees," and in obedience he moved to Haran. Thus far his father's family accompanied him. Here Abraham remained till the death of Terah.

Into the Unknown

But from his father's grave the divine voice bade him go forward. Besides Sarah, the wife of Abraham, only Lot chose to share the patriarch's pilgrim life. Abraham possessed extensive flocks and numerous servants. He was never to return, and he took with him all that he had, "their substance that they had gathered, and the souls that they had gotten in Haran." In Haran both Abraham and Sarah had led others to the worship of the true God. These accompanied him to the land of promise, "the land of Canaan."

The place where they first tarried was Shechem. In a wide, grassy valley, with its olive groves and gushing springs, Abraham made his encampment. It was a fair and goodly country, "a land of brooks of water, . . . of wheat, and barley, and vines, and fig trees, and pomegranates; a land of oil olive, and honey." Deuteronomy 8:7, 8. But a heavy shadow rested upon wooded hill and fruitful plain. In the groves were set up the altars of false gods, and human sacrifices were offered upon the neighboring heights.

Then "the Lord appeared unto Abram and said, Unto thy seed will I give this land." His faith was strengthened by this assurance. "And there builded he an altar unto the Lord, who appeared unto him." Still a wayfarer, he soon removed to a spot near Bethel and again erected an altar and called upon the name of the Lord.

Abraham set us a worthy example. His was a life of prayer. Wherever he pitched his tent, close beside was set up his altar, calling all within his encampment to the morning and evening sacrifice. When his tent was removed, the altar remained. Roving Canaanites received instruction from Abraham, and wherever one of these came to that altar, he there worshiped the living God.

Why God Permitted Abraham to Suffer Famine

Abraham continued to journey southward, and again his faith was tested. The heavens withheld their rain, and the flocks and herds found no pasture. Starvation threatened the whole encampment. All were eagerly watching to see what Abraham would do, as trouble after trouble came. So long as his confidence appeared unshaken, they felt that there was hope; they were assured that God was his friend and that He was still guiding him.

Abraham held fast the promise, "I will bless thee, and make thy name great; and thou shalt be a blessing." He would not allow circumstances to shake his faith in God's word. To escape the famine he went down to Egypt. He did not in his extremity turn back to the Chaldean land from which he came, but sought a temporary refuge as near as possible to the Land of Promise.

The Lord in His providence had brought this trial upon Abraham to teach him lessons for the benefit of all who should afterward be called to endure affliction. God does not forget or cast off those who put their trust in Him. The trials that task our faith most severely and make it seem that God has forsaken us are to lead us closer to Christ. We may lay all our burdens at His feet and experience the peace which He will give us in exchange.

It is in the heat of the furnace that the dross is separated from the true gold of Christian character. By close, testing trials God disciplines His servants. He sees that some have powers which may be used in the advancement of His work. In His providence He brings them into positions that test their character and reveal weaknesses hidden from their own knowledge. He gives them opportunity to correct these defects. He shows them their own weakness and teaches them to lean upon Him. Thus they are educated, trained, and disciplined, prepared to fulfill the grand purpose for which their powers were given them. Heavenly angels can unite with them in the work to be accomplished on earth.

Abraham's Sad Mistake

In Egypt, Abraham gave evidence that he was not free from human weakness. Sarah was "fair to look upon," and he doubted not that the Egyptians would covet the beautiful stranger and slay her husband. He reasoned that he was not guilty of falsehood in representing Sarah as his sister, for she was the daughter of his father, though not of his mother.

But this was deception. Through Abraham's lack of faith, Sarah was placed in great peril. The king of Egypt caused her to be taken to his palace, intending to make her his wife. But the Lord, in His great mercy, protected Sarah by sending judgment upon the royal household. By this means the monarch learned the deception practiced upon him. He reproved Abraham, saying, "What is this that thou hast done unto me? . . . Why saidst thou, She is my sister? so I might have taken her to me to wife: now therefore behold thy wife, take her, and go thy way."

Pharaoh's dismissal of Abraham was kind and generous, but he bade him leave Egypt. He had ignorantly been about to do Abraham a serious injury, but God had saved the monarch from committing so great a sin. Pharaoh saw in this stranger a man whom God honored. Should Abraham remain in Egypt, his increasing wealth and honor would likely excite the envy or covetousness of the Egyptians, and some injury might be done him which might again bring judgments upon the royal house.

The matter could not be kept secret, and it was seen that the God whom Abraham worshiped would protect His servant and that any injury done Him would be avenged. It is a dangerous thing to wrong one of the children of the King of heaven. The psalmist says that God "reproved kings for their sakes; saying, Touch not Mine anointed, and do My prophets no harm." Psalm 105:14, 15.

12/ Abraham, a Good Neighbor in Canaan

Abraham returned to Canaan "very rich in cattle, in silver and in gold." Lot was with him, and they came to Bethel and pitched their tents. In the midst of hardships and trials they had dwelt together in harmony, but in their prosperity there was danger of strife. The pasturage was not sufficient for the flocks and herds of both. It was evident that they must separate.

Abraham was the first to propose plans for preserving peace. Although the whole land had been given him by God Himself, he courteously waived this right. "Let there be no strife," he said, "between me and thee, and between my herdmen and thy herdmen; for we be brethren. Is not the whole land before thee? separate thyself, I pray thee, from me: if thou wilt take the left hand, then I will go to the right; or if thou depart to the right hand, then I will go to the left."

How many under similar circumstances would cling to their individual rights and preferences! How many households, how many churches have been divided, making the cause of truth a byword and a reproach among the wicked! The children of God the world over are one family, and the same spirit of love and conciliation should govern them. "Be kindly affectioned one to another with brotherly love; in honor preferring one another." Romans 12:10. A willingness to do to others as we would wish them to do to us would annihilate half the ills of life. The heart in which the love of Christ is cherished will possess that charity which "seeketh not her own." Philippians 2:4.

This chapter is based on Genesis 13 to 15; 17:1-16; 18.

Lot manifested no gratitude to his benefactor. Instead, he selfishly endeavored to grasp advantages. He "lifted up his eyes, and beheld all the plain of Jordan, that it was well watered everywhere, . . . even as the garden of the Lord, like the land of Egypt." The most fertile region in all Palestine was the Jordan Valley, reminding the beholders of the lost Paradise and equaling the beauty and productiveness of the Nile-enriched plains they had left. There were cities, wealthy and beautiful, inviting to profitable traffic. Dazzled with visions of worldly gain, Lot overlooked the moral evils encountered there. He "chose him all the plain of Jordan" and "pitched his tent toward Sodom." How little did he foresee the terrible results of that selfish choice.

Abraham soon after this moved to Hebron. In the free air of those upland plains with their olive groves and vineyards, their fields of grain, and the wide pasture of the encircling hills, he dwelt, content with his simple life, leaving to Lot the perilous luxury of Sodom.

Abraham did not shut away his influence from his neighbors. His life and character, in contrast to the worshipers of idols, exerted a telling influence in favor of the true faith. His allegiance to God was unswerving, while his affability and benevolence inspired confidence and friendship.

While Christ is dwelling in the heart, it is impossible to conceal the light of His presence. It will grow brighter as the mists of selfishness and sin that envelop the soul are dispelled by the Sun of Righteousness.

The people of God are lights in the moral darkness of this world. Scattered in towns, cities, and villages, they are God's channels through which He will communicate to an unbelieving world the knowledge and wonders of His grace. It is His plan that all who are partakers of salvation shall be lights that shine forth in the character, revealing the contrast with the darkness of the selfishness of the natural heart.

Abraham was wise in diplomacy and brave and skillful in war. Three royal brothers, rulers of the Amorite plains in which he dwelt, manifested friendship by inviting him to enter an alliance with them for greater security, for the country was filled with violence and oppression. An occasion soon arose for him to avail himself of this alliance.

Lot Rescued by Abraham

Chedorlaomer, king of Elam, had invaded Canaan years before and made it tributary to him. Several of the princes now revolted, and the Elamite king again marched into the country to reduce them to submission. Five kings of Canaan met the invaders, only to be completely overthrown. The victors plundered the cities of the plain and departed with rich spoil and many captives, among whom were Lot and his family.

Abraham learned from one of the fugitives the story of the calamity that had befallen his nephew. All his affection for him was awakened, and he determined that Lot should be rescued. Seeking divine counsel, Abraham prepared for war. From his own encampment he summoned three hundred eighteen trained servants, men trained in the fear of God, in the service of their master, and in the practice of arms. His confederates, Mamre, Eshcol, and Aner, joined him, and together they started in pursuit of the invaders. The Elamites had encamped at Dan, on the northern border of Canaan. Flushed with victory, they had given themselves up to reveling. The patriarch came upon the encampment by night. His attack, so vigorous and unexpected, resulted in speedy victory. The king of Elam was slain and his panic-stricken forces routed. Lot and his family, with all the prisoners and goods, were recovered, and a rich booty fell into the hands of the victors.

Abraham had not only rendered a great service to the country but had proved himself a man of valor. It was seen that Abraham's religion made him courageous in maintaining the right and defending the oppressed. On his return the king of Sodom came out to honor the conqueror, begging only that the prisoners be restored. The spoils belonged to the conquerors; but Abraham refused to take advantage of the unfortunate, only stipulating that his confederates receive the portion to which they were entitled.

Few, if subjected to such a test, would have resisted the temptation to secure so rich a booty. His example is a rebuke to self-seeking. "I have lifted up my hand," he said, "unto the Lord, the most high God, the possessor of heaven and earth, that I will not take from a thread even to a shoe latchet, and that I will not take anything that is thine, lest thou shouldest say, I have made Abram rich." God had promised to bless Abraham, and to Him the glory should be ascribed.

Another who came out to welcome the victorious patriarch was Melchizedek, king of Salem. As "priest of the most high God," he pronounced a blessing upon Abraham and gave thanks to the Lord, who had wrought deliverance by His servant. And Abraham "gave him tithes of all."

Abraham Is Afraid

Abraham had been a man of peace, so far as possible shunning strife. With horror he recalled the carnage he had witnessed. The nations whose forces he had defeated would doubtless renew the invasion and make him the special object of their vengeance. Furthermore, he had not entered upon the possession of Canaan, nor could he now hope for an heir, to whom the promise might be fulfilled.

In a vision of the night the divine voice was again heard. "Fear not, Abram: I am thy shield, and thy exceeding great reward." But how was the covenant promise to be realized while the gift of a son was withheld? "What wilt thou give me," he said, "seeing I go childless? . . . Lo, one born in my house is mine heir." He proposed to make his trusty servant Eliezer his son by adoption. But he was assured that a child of his own was to be his heir. Then he was told to look up to the unnumbered stars glittering in the heavens, and the words were spoken, "So shall thy seed be." "Abraham believed God, and it was counted unto him for righteousness." Romans 4:3.

The Lord condescended to enter into a covenant with His servant. And the voice of God was heard, bidding him not to expect immediate possession of the Promised Land, and pointing forward to the sufferings of his posterity before their establishment in Canaan. The plan of redemption was opened to him in the death of Christ, the great Sacrifice, and His coming in glory. Abraham saw also the earth restored to Eden beauty, given for an everlasting possession as the final and complete fulfillment of the promise.

When Abraham had been nearly twenty-five years in Canaan, the Lord appeared unto him and said, "Behold, My covenant is with thee, and thou shalt be a father of many nations." In token of the fulfillment of this covenant, his name Abram was changed to Abraham, "father of a great multitude." Sarai's name became Sarah—"princess," for "she shall be a mother of nations; kings of people shall be of her."

At this time circumcision was given to Abraham, to be observed by the patriarch and his descendants as a token that they were separated from idolaters and that God accepted them as His peculiar treasure. They were not to contract marriages with heathen, for by so doing they would be tempted to engage in the sinful practices of other nations and be seduced into idolatry.

Abraham Entertains Angels Unawares

God conferred great honor upon Abraham. Angels walked and talked with him. When judgments were about to be visited on Sodom, the fact was not hidden from him, and he became an intercessor with God for sinners.

In the hot summer noontide the patriarch was sitting

in his tent door when he saw in the distance three travelers. Before reaching his tent, the strangers halted. Without waiting for them to solicit favors, Abraham with the utmost courtesy urged them to honor him by tarrying for refreshment. With his own hands he brought water that they might wash the dust of travel from their feet. He selected food, and while they were at rest under the cooling shade, he stood respectfully beside them while they partook of his hospitality. Years later this act of courtesy was referred to by an inspired apostle: "Be not forgetful to entertain strangers; for thereby some have entertained angels unawares." Hebrews 13:2.

Abraham had seen in his guests only three tired wayfarers, little thinking that among them was One whom he might worship without sin. But the true character of the heavenly messengers was now revealed. They were on their way as ministers of wrath, yet to Abraham they spoke first of blessings. God takes no delight in vengeance.

Abraham had honored God and the Lord honored him, revealing to him His purposes. "Shall I hide from Abraham that thing which I do?" said the Lord. "The cry of Sodom and Gomorrah is great, and because their sin is very grievous, I will go down now, and see whether they have done altogether according to the cry of it, which is come unto me. And if not, I will know." God knew Sodom's guilt, but He expressed Himself after the manner of men, that His justice might be understood. He would go Himself to institute an examination of their course. If they had not passed the limits of divine mercy, He would grant them space for repentance.

Two of the heavenly messengers departed, leaving Abraham alone with Him whom he now knew to be the Son of God. And the man of faith pleaded for the inhabitants of Sodom. Once he had saved them by his sword; now he endeavored to save them by prayer. Lot and his household were still dwellers there, and

Abraham sought to save them from the storm of divine judgment.

With deep humility he urged his plea: "I have taken upon me to speak unto the Lord, which am but dust and ashes." He did not claim favor on the ground of his obedience or of the sacrifices he had made in doing God's will. Himself a sinner, he pleaded in the sinner's behalf. Yet Abraham manifested the confidence of a child pleading with a loved father. Though Lot had become a dweller in Sodom, he did not partake in the iniquity of its inhabitants. Abraham thought that in that populous city there must be other worshipers of the true God. He pleaded, "That be far from Thee . . . to slay the righteous with the wicked: . . . Shall not the Judge of all the earth do right?" As his requests were granted, he gained the assurance that if even ten righteous persons could be found in it, the city would be spared.

Abraham's prayer for Sodom shows that we should cherish hatred of sin, but pity and love for the sinner. All around us are souls going down to ruin. Every hour some are passing beyond the reach of mercy. Where are the voices of entreaty to bid the sinner flee from this fearful doom? Where are those who are pleading with God for him?

Who Prays for "Sodom" Today?

The spirit of Abraham was the spirit of Christ, Himself the great Intercessor in the sinner's behalf. Christ manifested toward the sinner a love which infinite goodness alone could conceive. In the agonies of the crucifixion, burdened with the awful weight of the sins of the whole world, He prayed for His murderers, "Father, forgive them; for they know not what they do." Luke 23:34.

The testimony of God is, "Abraham obeyed My voice, and kept My charge, My commandments, My statutes, and My laws." "I know him, that he will command his children and his household after him, and they shall keep the way of the Lord, to do justice and judgment; that the Lord may bring upon Abraham that which He hath spoken of him.'' It was a high honor to which Abraham was called, that of being father of the people who were the guardians of the truth of God for the world—through whom all nations should be blessed in the advent of the Messiah. Abraham would keep the law and deal justly and righteously. And he would not only fear the Lord himself but would instruct his family in righteousness.

Abraham's household comprised more than a thousand souls. Here, as in a school, they received such instruction as would prepare them to be representatives of the true faith. He was training heads of families, and his methods of government would be carried out in the households over which they should preside.

It was necessary to bind the members of the household together, to build up a barrier against the idolatry that had become widespread. Abraham sought to guard his encampment against mingling with the heathen and witnessing their idolatrous practices. Care was exercised to impress the mind with the majesty and glory of the living God as the true object of worship.

God Himself had separated Abraham from his idolatrous kindred that the patriarch might educate his family apart from the seductive influences in Mesopotamia, and that the true faith might be preserved in its purity by his descendants.

The Influence of Daily Living

Abraham's children and household were taught that they were under the rule of the God of heaven. There was to be no oppression on the part of parents and no disobedience on the part of children. The silent influence of his daily life was a constant lesson. There was a fragrance about the life, a nobility of character, which revealed to all that he was connected with Heaven. He did not neglect the humblest servant. In his household there was not one law for the master and another for the servant. All were treated with justice and compassion as inheritors with him of the grace of life.

How few in our day follow this example! On the part of too many parents there is a blind and selfish sentimentalism, miscalled love, manifested in leaving children to the control of their own will. This is cruelty to the youth and a great wrong to the world. Parental indulgence confirms in the young the desire to follow inclination instead of submitting to divine requirements. Thus they grow up to transmit their irreligious, insubordinate spirit to their children and children's children. Let obedience to parental authority be taught as the first step in obedience to the authority of God.

The teaching which has become widespread—that the divine statutes are no longer binding—is the same as idolatry in its effect on the morals of the people. Parents do not command their household to keep the way of the Lord. Children, as they make homes of their own, feel no obligation to teach their children what they themselves have never been taught. This is why there are so many godless families, why depravity is so widespread.

A reformation is needed, deep and broad. Parents, ministers, need to reform; they need God in their households. They must bring His Word into their families and teach their children kindly and untiringly how to live in order to please God. The children of such a household have a foundation that cannot be swept away by the incoming tide of skepticism.

In many households parents feel they cannot spare a few moments in thanksgiving to God for the sunshine and showers and for the guardianship of holy angels. They have no time to offer prayer. They go forth to labor as the ox or the horse, without one thought of God or heaven. The Son of God gave His life to ransom them, but they have little more appreciation of His goodness than beasts that perish.

If ever there was a time when every house should be

a house of prayer, it is now. Let the father as priest of the household lay upon the altar of God the morning and evening sacrifice, while the wife and children unite in prayer and praise. In such a household Jesus will love to tarry.

From every home love should flow out in thoughtful kindness, in gentle, unselfish courtesy. There are homes where God is worshiped and truest love reigns. His mercies and blessings descend upon the suppliants like morning dew.

A well-ordered household is a powerful argument in favor of the Christian religion. An influence at work in the family affects the children. The God of Abraham is with them. God speaks to every faithful parent: "I know him, that he will command his children and his household after him, and they shall keep the way of the Lord, to do justice and judgment."

13 / The Offering of Isaac: Test of Faith

Abraham had accepted the promise of a son but did not wait for God to fulfill His word in His own time and way. A delay was permitted to test his faith, but he failed to endure the trial.

In her old age, Sarah suggested, as a plan by which the divine purpose might be fulfilled, that one of her handmaidens be taken by Abraham as a secondary wife. Polygamy had ceased to be regarded as a sin but was a violation of the law of God and was fatal to the sacredness and peace of the family. Abraham's marriage with Hagar resulted in evil not only to his own household, but to future generations.

Flattered with her new position as Abraham's wife and hoping to be the mother of the great nation to descend from him, Hagar became proud. Mutual jealousies disturbed the peace of the once happy home. Forced to listen to the complaints of both, Abraham vainly endeavored to restore harmony. Though it was at Sarah's entreaty that he had married Hagar, she now reproached him as the one at fault. She desired to banish her rival. But Abraham refused to permit this, for Hagar was to be the mother of his child, as he fondly hoped, the son of promise. She was Sarah's servant, however, and he still left her to the control of her mistress. "When Sarai dealt hardly with her, she fled from her face."

She made her way to the desert and as she rested beside a fountain, lonely and friendless, an angel appeared. Addressing her as "Hagar, Sarai's maid," he

This chapter is based on Genesis 16; 17:18-20; 21:1-14; 22:1-19.

bade her, "Return to thy mistress, and submit thyself under her hands." Yet with the reproof were mingled words of comfort: "The Lord hath heard thy affliction." "I will multiply thy seed exceedingly, that it shall not be numbered for multitude." She was bidden to call her child Ishmael, "God shall hear."

When Abraham was nearly one hundred years old, the promise of a son was repeated: "Sarah thy wife shall bear thee a son indeed; and thou shalt call his name Isaac; and I will establish My covenant with him." "As for Ishmael," He said, "Behold, I have blessed him, . . . and I will make him a great nation."

Polygamy Brings Sorrow

The birth of Isaac filled the tents of Abraham and Sarah with gladness, but to Hagar this event was the overthrow of her fondly cherished ambitions. Ishmael had been regarded by all as the heir of Abraham's wealth and the inheritor of the blessings promised his descendants. Now he was suddenly set aside. Mother and son hated the child of Sarah.

The general rejoicing increased their jealousy, until Ishmael dared openly to mock the heir of God's promise. Sarah saw in Ishmael's turbulent disposition a perpetual source of discord, and she appealed to Abraham that Hagar and Ishmael be sent away.

The patriarch was thrown into great distress. How could he banish Ishmael his son, still dearly beloved? In his perplexity he pleaded for divine guidance. Through a holy angel the Lord directed him to grant Sarah's desire; only thus could he restore harmony and happiness to his family. The angel gave him the promise that Ishmael would not be forsaken by God and he would become the father of a great nation. Abraham obeyed, but not without keen suffering. The father's heart was heavy as he sent away Hagar and his son.

The sacredness of the marriage relation was to be a lesson for all ages. The rights and happiness of this relation are to be carefully guarded, even at great sacrifice. Sarah was the only true wife of Abraham. Her rights no other person was entitled to share. She was unwilling that Abraham's affections should be given to another, and the Lord did not reprove her for requiring the banishment of her rival.

An Example for All Generations

Abraham was to stand as an example of faith to succeeding generations. But his faith had not been perfect. He had shown distrust of God in his marriage with Hagar. That he might reach the highest standard, God subjected him to another test, the closest which man was ever asked to endure. In a vision of the night he was directed to offer his son as a burnt offering upon a mountain that should be shown him.

Abraham had reached the age of a hundred and twenty years. The ardor of youth had passed. One in the vigor of manhood may with courage meet difficulties and afflictions that would cause his heart to fail later in life. But God had reserved His most trying test for Abraham until the burden of years was heavy upon him and he longed for rest.

The patriarch was very rich and was honored as a mighty prince by the rulers of the land. Heaven seemed to have crowned with blessing a life of sacrifice and patient endurance.

Abraham Commanded to Offer Isaac

In the obedience of faith, Abraham had forsaken his native country and had wandered as a stranger in the land of his inheritance. He had waited long for the birth of the promised heir. At the command of God he had sent away Ishmael. And now, when the patriarch seemed able to discern the fruition of his hopes, a trial greater than all others was before him.

The command must have wrung with anguish that father's heart: "Take now thy son, thine only son Isaac, whom thou lovest, . . . and offer him there for a burnt offering." Isaac was the light of his home, the solace of his old age, the inheritor of the promised blessing; but he was commanded to shed the blood of that son with his own hand. It seemed a fearful impossibility.

Satan was at hand to suggest that he must be deceived, for the divine law commands, "Thou shalt not kill." God would not require what He had forbidden. Going outside his tent, Abraham recalled the promise that his seed should be as innumerable as the stars. If this promise was to be fulfilled through Isaac, how could he be put to death? Abraham bowed upon the earth and prayed as he had never prayed before for some confirmation of the command if he must perform this terrible duty. He remembered the angels sent to reveal God's purpose to destroy Sodom and who bore to him the promise of this same son Isaac. He went to the place where he had met the heavenly messengers, hoping to receive some further direction; but none came. The command of God was sounding in his ears, "Take now thy son, thine only son Isaac, whom thou lovest." That command must be obeyed. Day was approaching, and he must be on his journey.

Isaac lay sleeping the untroubled sleep of youth and innocence. For a moment the father looked upon the dear face of his son, then turned tremblingly away. He went to Sarah, who was also sleeping. Should he awaken her? He longed to unburden his heart to her and share with her this terrible responsibility; but he was restrained. Isaac was her joy and pride; the mother's love might refuse the sacrifice.

Three Sad Days

Abraham at last summoned his son, telling him of the command to offer sacrifice on a distant mountain. Isaac had often gone with his father to worship, and this excited no surprise. The wood was made ready and put upon the ass, and with two servants they set forth.

Father and son journeyed in silence, the patriarch pondering his heavy secret. His thoughts were of the proud, fond mother and the day when he should return to her alone. He knew that the knife would pierce her heart when it took the life of her son.

That day—the longest Abraham had ever experienced—dragged slowly to its close. He spent the night in prayer, still hoping that some heavenly messenger might say that the youth might return unharmed to his mother. But no relief came to his tortured soul.

Another long day. Another night of humiliation and prayer. The command that was to leave him childless was ringing in his ears. Satan was near to whisper doubts and unbelief, but Abraham resisted his suggestions.

As they were about to begin the journey of the third day, the patriarch saw the promised sign, a cloud of glory hovering over Mount Moriah. He knew that the voice which had spoken was from heaven.

Even now he did not murmur against God. This son had been unexpectedly given; had not He who bestowed the precious gift a right to recall His own? Then faith repeated the promise, "In Isaac shall thy seed be called"—a seed numberless as the grains of sand upon the shore. Isaac was the child of a miracle, and could not the power that gave him life restore it? Abraham grasped the divine word, "accounting that God was able to raise him up, even from the dead." Hebrews 11:19.

Yet none but God could understand how great was the father's sacrifice in yielding up his son to death. Abraham desired that none but God should witness the parting scene. He bade his servants remain behind, saying, "I and the lad will go yonder and worship, and come again to you."

The wood was laid upon Isaac, the father took a knife and the fire, and together they ascended toward the mountain summit. The young man at last spoke, "My father, . . . behold the fire and the wood; but where is the lamb for a burnt offering?"

What a test was this! How the endearing words, "my

father," pierced Abraham's heart! Not yet—he could not tell him now. "My son," he said, "God will provide Himself a lamb for a burnt offering."

At the appointed place they built the altar and laid the wood upon it. Then, with trembling voice, Abraham unfolded the divine message.

Trained to Obey

With terror and amazement Isaac learned his fate, but he offered no resistance. He could have escaped had he chosen. The old man, exhausted with the struggle of those three terrible days, could not have opposed the will of the vigorous youth. But Isaac had been trained from childhood to ready obedience, and as the purpose of God was opened before him, he yielded a willing submission. He was a sharer in Abraham's faith, and he felt honored in being called to give his life as an offering to God.

And now the last words of love were spoken, the last tears shed, the last embrace given. The father lifted the knife. Suddenly an angel of God called out of heaven, "Abraham, Abraham!" He quickly answered, "Here am I." Again the voice was heard, "Lay not thine hand upon the lad, neither do thou anything unto him: for now I know that thou fearest God, seeing thou hast not withheld thy son, thine only son from Me."

Then Abraham saw "a ram caught in a thicket," and quickly he offered it "in the stead of his son." In his joy and gratitude, Abraham gave a new name to the sacred spot—"Jehovah-jireh," "the Lord will provide."

The Promise to Abraham Repeated

On Mount Moriah God again confirmed with solemn oath the blessing to Abraham and to his seed: "Because thou hast done this thing, and hast not withheld thy son, thine only son: . . . in blessing I will bless thee, and in multiplying I will multiply thy seed as the stars of the heaven, and as the sand which is upon the seashore; and thy seed shall possess the gate of his enemies; and in thy seed shall all the nations of the earth be blessed; because thou hast obeyed My voice.''

Abraham's great act of faith stands like a pillar of light, illuminating the pathway of God's servants in all succeeding ages. During that three days' journey Abraham had sufficient time to reason and to doubt God. He might have reasoned that the slaying of his son would cause him to be looked upon as a murderer, a second Cain; it would cause his teaching to be rejected and despised, and thus destroy his power to do good to his fellowmen. He might have pleaded that age should excuse him from obedience. But the patriarch did not take refuge in excuses. Abraham was human; his passions and attachments were like ours; but he did not stay to reason with his aching heart. He knew that God is just and righteous in all His requirements.

"Abraham believed God, and it was imputed unto him for righteousness: and he was called the Friend of God." James 2:23. And Paul says, "They which are of faith, the same are the children of Abraham." Galatians 3:7. But Abraham's faith was made manifest by his works. "Was not Abraham our father justified by works, when he had offered Isaac his son upon the altar? Seest thou how faith wrought with his works, and by works was faith made perfect?" James 2:21, 22.

Many fail to understand the relation of faith and works. They say, "Only believe in Christ, and you are safe. You have nothing to do with keeping the law." But genuine faith will be manifest in obedience. Concerning the father of the faithful the Lord declares, "Abraham obeyed My voice, and kept My charge, My commandments, My statutes, and My laws." Genesis 26:5. Says the apostle James, "Faith, if it hath not works, is dead, being alone." James 2:17. And John, who dwells so fully upon love, tells us, "This is the love of God, that we keep His commandments." 1 John 5:3.

God "preached before the gospel unto Abraham." Galatians 3:8. And the patriarch's faith was fixed upon the Redeemer to come. Said Christ, "Your father

Abraham rejoiced that he should see My day; and he saw it, and was glad." John 8:56. The ram offered in place of Isaac represented the Son of God, who was to be sacrificed in our stead. The Father, looking upon His Son, said to the sinner, "Live: I have found a ransom."

The agony which Abraham endured during the dark days of that fearful trial was permitted that he might understand something of the greatness of the sacrifice made by God for man's redemption. No other test could have caused Abraham such torture of soul as did the offering of his son. God gave His Son to a death of agony and shame. The angels were not permitted to interpose, as in the case of Isaac. There was no voice to cry, "It is enough." To save the fallen race, the King of glory yielded up His life.

"He that spared not His own Son, but delivered Him up for us all, how shall He not with Him also freely give us all things?" Romans 8:32.

Lesson Book of the Universe

The sacrifice required of Abraham was not alone for his good nor for succeeding generations; it was also for the instruction of the sinless intelligences of heaven and other worlds. The field on which the plan of redemption is wrought out is the lesson book of the universe. Because Abraham had shown a lack of faith, Satan had accused him before angels and God. God desired to prove the loyalty of His servant before all heaven, to demonstrate that nothing less than perfect obedience can be accepted, and to open more fully before them the plan of salvation.

The trial brought upon Adam involved no suffering; but the command to Abraham demanded the most agonizing sacrifice. All heaven beheld with wonder and admiration Abraham's unfaltering obedience. All heaven applauded his fidelity. Satan's accusations were shown to be false. God's covenant testified that obedience will be rewarded.

As a result of the test he endured in offering up his son Isaac, Abraham understood as never before God's sacrifice of His Son Jesus.

When the command was given Abraham to offer his son, all heavenly beings with intense earnestness watched each step in the fulfillment of this command. Light was shed upon the mystery of redemption, and even the angels understood more clearly the wonderful provision that God had made for man's salvation. See 1 Peter 1:12.

14 / The Sin of Sodom and Gomorrah

Among the cities of the Jordan valley Sodom was "as the garden of the Lord" (Genesis 13:10) in its fertility and beauty. Rich harvests clothed the fields, and flocks and herds covered the encircling hills. Art and commerce enriched the proud city. The treasures of the East adorned her palaces, and caravans brought stores of precious things to her marts of trade. With little thought or labor, every want of life could be supplied.

Idleness and riches make the heart hard that has never been oppressed by want or burdened by sorrow. The people gave themselves up to sensual indulgence. "This was the iniquity of thy sister Sodom, pride, fullness of bread, and abundance of idleness was in her and in her daughters, neither did she strengthen the hand of the poor and needy. And they were haughty, and committed abomination before Me; therefore I took them away as I saw good." Ezekiel 16:49, 50. Satan is never more successful than when he comes to men in their idle hours.

In Sodom there was mirth, revelry, feasting, and drunkenness. The vilest passions were unrestrained. People openly defied God and His law and delighted in violence. Though they had before them the example of the antediluvian world and knew of their destruction, they followed the same course of wickedness.

At the time of Lot's removal to Sodom, corruption had not become universal, and God in mercy permitted rays of light to shine amid the moral darkness. Abra-

This chapter is based on Genesis 19.

ham was not a stranger to the people of Sodom, and his victory over greatly superior forces excited wonder and admiration. None could avoid the conviction that a divine power had made him conqueror. His noble and unselfish spirit, so foreign to the self-seeking inhabitants of Sodom, was another evidence of the superiority of the religion he had honored. God was speaking to that people by His providence, but the last ray of light was rejected as all before had been.

Now the last night of Sodom was approaching. But men perceived it not. While angels drew near on their mission of destruction, men were dreaming of prosperity and pleasure. The last day was like every other that had come and gone. A landscape of unrivaled beauty was bathed in the rays of the declining sun. Pleasure-seeking throngs were passing to and fro, intent upon the enjoyment of the hour.

In the twilight, two strangers drew near to the city gate. None could discern in those wayfarers the mighty heralds of divine judgment. The careless multitude little dreamed that in their treatment of these heavenly messengers that very night they would reach the climax of guilt which doomed their city.

Lot Entertains Angels Unawares

But one man manifested kindly attention toward the strangers and invited them to his home. Lot did not know their true character, but politeness and hospitality were habitual with him—lessons he had learned from Abraham. Had he not cultivated a spirit of courtesy, he might have been left to perish with Sodom. Many a household, in closing its doors against a stranger, has shut out God's messenger who would have brought blessing. The unpretending acts of daily self-denial, performed with a cheerful, willing heart, God smiles upon.

Seeing the abuse to which strangers were exposed in Sodom, Lot made it one of his duties to guard them by offering entertainment at his own house. He was sitting at the gate as the travelers approached and rose from his place to meet them, and bowing courteously, said, "Behold now, my lords, turn in, I pray you, into your servant's house, and tarry all night." They seemed to decline, saying, "Nay; but we will abide in the street." Their object in this answer was twofold—to test the sincerity of Lot and to appear ignorant of the character of the men of Sodom, as if they supposed it safe to remain in the street at night. Lot pressed his invitation until they yielded and accompanied him to his house.

Their hesitation and his persistent urging caused them to be observed, and before they retired for the night, a lawless crowd gathered about the house, an immense company, youth and aged men alike inflamed by the vilest passions. The strangers had been making inquiry in regard to the character of the city, when the hooting and jeers of the mob were heard, demanding that the men be brought out to them.

Lot went out to try persuasion on them. "I pray you, brethren," he said, "do not so wickedly," using the term "brethren" in the sense of neighbors and hoping to conciliate them. But their rage became like the roaring of a tempest. They mocked Lot and threatened to deal worse with him than they had purposed toward his guests. They would have torn him in pieces had he not been rescued by the angels of God. The heavenly messengers "put forth their hand, and pulled Lot into the house to them, and shut to the door." "They smote the men that were at the door of the house with blindness, both small and great; so that they wearied themselves to find the door." Had they not been visited with double blindness, being given up to hardness of heart, the stroke of God upon them would have caused them to desist from their evil work. That last night was marked by no greater sins than many others before it; but mercy, so long slighted, had at last ceased its pleading. The fires of God's vengeance were about to be kindled.

The angels revealed to Lot the object of their mission: "We will destroy this place, because the cry of them is waxen great before the face of the Lord; and the Lord hath sent us to destroy it." The strangers whom Lot had endeavored to protect, now promised to protect him and all his family who would flee with him from the wicked city. The mob had wearied themselves out and departed, and Lot went out to warn his children. "Up, get you out of this place; for the Lord will destroy this city." But they laughed at what they called his superstitious fears. His daughters were influenced by their husbands. They could see no evidence of danger. They had great possessions and could not believe it possible that beautiful Sodom would be destroyed.

Lot Loses Everything Except His Life

Lot returned sorrowfully to his home and told the story of his failure. Then the angels bade him take his wife and two daughters who were yet in the house and leave. But Lot delayed. He had no true conception of the debasing iniquity practiced in that vile city. He did not realize the terrible necessity for God's judgments to put a check on sin. Some of his children clung to Sodom, and the thought of leaving those whom he held dearest on earth seemed more than he could bear. It was hard to forsake his luxurious home and all the wealth of his whole life, to go forth a destitute wanderer. Stupefied with sorrow, he lingered. But for the angels, they would all have perished. The heavenly messengers took him and his wife and daughters by the hand and led them out of the city.

In all the cities of the plain, even ten righteous persons had not been found. (See page 85.) But in answer to the patriarch Abraham's prayer, the one man who feared God was snatched from destruction. The command was given with startling vehemence: "Escape for thy life; look not behind thee, neither stay thou in all the plain; escape to the mountain." To cast one lingering look upon the city, to tarry for one moment from regret to leave so beautiful a home, would cost their life. The storm of divine judgment was only waiting that these poor fugitives might escape.

But Lot, confused and terrified, pleaded that he could not do as he was required. Living in that wicked city, his faith had grown dim. The Prince of heaven was by his side, yet he pleaded for his own life as though God, who had manifested such love for him, would not still preserve him. He should have trusted himself wholly to the divine Messenger. "Behold now, this city is near to flee unto, and it is a little one: Oh, let me escape thither, (is it not a little one?) and my soul shall live." Zoar was but a few miles from Sodom, and, like it, was corrupt and doomed to destruction. But Lot asked that it might be spared, urging that this was but a small request. His desire was granted. The Lord assured him, "I have accepted thee concerning this thing also, that I will not overthrow this city, for the which thou hast spoken."

Again the command was given to hasten, for the fiery storm would be delayed but little longer. But one of the fugitives cast a look backward to the doomed city, and she became a monument of God's judgment. If Lot himself had earnestly fled toward the mountains without one word of remonstrance, his wife also would have made her escape. His example would have saved her from the sin that sealed her doom. But his hesitancy caused her to lightly regard the divine warning. While her body was on the plain, her heart clung to Sodom, and she perished with it. She rebelled against God because His judgments involved her possessions and children in the ruin. She felt severely dealt with because the wealth that had taken years to accumulate must be left to destruction. Instead of thankfully accepting deliverance, she presumptuously looked back to desire the life of those who rejected the divine warning.

There are Christians who say, "I do not care to be saved unless my companion and children are saved." They feel heaven would not be heaven without the presence of those who are so dear. But have those who cherish this feeling forgotten that they are bound by the strongest ties of love and loyalty to their Creator and Redeemer? Because our friends reject the Saviour's love, shall we also turn away? Christ has paid an infinite price for our salvation, and no one who appreciates its value will despise God's mercy because others choose to do so. The fact that others ignore His claims should arouse us to greater diligence, that we may honor God and lead all whom we can to accept His love.

Sodom Destroyed

"The sun was risen upon the earth when Lot entered into Zoar." The bright rays of morning seemed to speak only prosperity and peace to the cities of the plain. The stir of active life began in the streets; men were going their various ways, intent on the business or pleasure of the day. The sons-in-law of Lot were making merry at the fears and warnings of the weak-minded old man.

Suddenly and unexpectedly as thunder from an unclouded sky, the tempest broke. The Lord rained brimstone and fire upon the cities and the plain. Palaces and temples, costly dwellings, gardens, vineyards, and the pleasure-seeking throngs that only the night before had insulted the messengers of heaven— all were consumed. The smoke went up like a great furnace. The fair vale of Siddim became a place never to be built up or inhabited—a witness to all generations of the certainty of God's judgments upon transgression.

There are greater sins than that for which Sodom and Gomorrah were destroyed. Those who hear the gospel invitation calling to repentance, and heed not, are more guilty than the dwellers in the vale of Siddim. The fate of Sodom is a solemn admonition, not merely to those guilty of outbreaking sin, but to all who are trifling with Heaven-sent light and privileges.

The Saviour watches for a response to His offers of

love and forgiveness with more tender compassion
than that which moves the heart of an earthly parent to
forgive a wayward son. "Return unto Me, and I will
return unto you." Malachi 3:7. But if one persistently
refuses that tender love, he will at last be left in darkness. The heart that has long slighted God's mercy becomes hardened in sin, no longer susceptible to the influence of the grace of God. It will be more tolerable in
the day of judgment for the cities of the plain than for
those who have known the love of Christ and yet have
turned away to the pleasure of sin. In the books of
heaven there is a record kept of the impieties of nations, of families, of individuals. Calls to repentance,
offers of pardon may be given; yet a time will come
when the account will be full. The soul's decision has
been made. By his own choice, man's destiny has been
fixed. Then the signal will be given for judgment to be
executed.

Another Sodom

In the religious world today God's mercy has been
trifled with. Multitudes make void the law, "teaching
for doctrines the commandments of men." Matthew
15:9. Infidelity prevails in many churches, not infidelity in its broadest sense—an open denial of the Bible—
but an infidelity undermining faith in the Bible as a revelation from God. Vital piety has given place to hollow
formalism. As the result, apostasy and sensualism prevail. Christ declared, "As it was in the days of Lot . . .
even thus shall it be in the day when the Son of man is
revealed." Luke 17:28-30. The world is fast becoming
ripe for destruction.

Said our Saviour: "Take heed to yourselves, lest at
any time your hearts be overcharged with surfeiting,
and drunkenness, and cares of this life, and so that day
come upon you unawares. For as a snare shall it come
on all them that dwell on the face of the whole earth"—
all whose interests are centered in this world. "Watch
ye therefore, and pray always, that ye may be ac-

counted worthy to escape all these things that shall come to pass, and to stand before the Son of man." Luke 21:34-36.

Before the destruction of Sodom, God sent a message to Lot, "Escape for thy life." The same voice of warning was heard before the destruction of Jerusalem: "When ye shall see Jerusalem compassed with armies, then know that the desolation thereof is nigh. Then let them which are in Judea flee to the mountains." Luke 21:20, 21. They must not tarry but must escape.

There was a coming out, a decided separation from the wicked, an escape for life. So it was in the days of Noah; so with Lot; so with the disciples prior to the destruction of Jerusalem; and so it will be in the last days. Again the voice of God is heard, bidding His people separate from the prevailing iniquity.

The state of corruption and apostasy in the last days was presented to the prophet John in the vision of Babylon, "that great city, which reigneth over the kings of the earth." Revelation 17:18. Before its destruction the call is to be given from heaven, "Come out of her, My people, that ye be not partakers of her sins, and that ye receive not of her plagues." Revelation 18:4. As in the days of Noah and Lot, there must be no compromise between God and the world, no turning back to secure earthly treasures. See Matthew 6:24.

The people are dreaming of prosperity and peace. The multitudes cry, "Peace and safety," while Heaven declares that swift destruction is about to come upon the transgressor. On the night prior to their destruction, the cities of the plain rioted in pleasure and derided the warnings of the messenger of God. But that very night the door of mercy was forever closed to the careless inhabitants of Sodom. God will not always be mocked.

The great mass of the world will reject God's mercy and will be overwhelmed in swift and irretrievable ruin. But those who heed the warning shall dwell "in the secret place of the most High," and "abide under the shadow of the Almighty." Psalm 91:1.

Not long after, Zoar was consumed as God had purposed. Lot made his way to the mountains and abode in a cave.

But the curse of Sodom followed him even here. The sinful conduct of his daughters was the result of the evil associations of that vile place. Lot had chosen Sodom for its pleasure and profit, yet he had retained in his heart the fear of God. He was saved at last as "a brand plucked out of the fire," yet stripped of his possessions, bereaved of his wife and children, dwelling in caves, and covered with infamy in his old age. And he gave to the world, not a race of righteous men, but two idolatrous nations, at enmity with God and warring upon His people, until, their cup of iniquity being full, they were appointed to destruction. How terrible the results that followed one unwise step!

"Labor not to be rich; cease from thine own wisdom." "He that is greedy of gain troubleth his own house." "They that will be rich fall into temptation and a snare, and into many foolish and hurtful lusts, which drown men in destruction and perdition." Proverbs 23:4; 15:27; 1 Timothy 6:9.

When Lot entered Sodom, he fully intended to keep himself free from iniquity and command his household after him. But he failed. The result is before us.

Like Lot, many see their children ruined, and barely save their own souls. Their lifework is lost; their life is a sad failure. Had they exercised true wisdom, their children might have had less worldly prosperity, but they would have made sure of a title to the immortal inheritance.

The heritage that God has promised is not in this world. Abraham "sojourned in the land of promise, as in a strange country, dwelling in tabernacles with Isaac and Jacob, the heirs with him of the same promise: for he looked for a city which hath foundations, whose builder and maker is God." We must dwell as pilgrims and strangers here if we would gain "a better country, that is, an heavenly." Hebrews 11:9, 10, 16.

15 / Isaac's Marriage: The Happiest in the Bible

Abraham had become an old man; yet one act remained for him to do. Isaac was divinely appointed to succeed him as the keeper of the law of God and the father of the chosen people; but he was yet unmarried.

The inhabitants of Canaan were given to idolatry, and God had forbidden intermarriage between His people and them, knowing that such marriages would lead to apostasy. Isaac was gentle and yielding in disposition. If united with one who did not fear God, he would be in danger of sacrificing principle for the sake of harmony. In the mind of Abraham, the choice of a wife for his son was of grave importance; he was anxious to have him marry one who would not lead him from God.

In ancient times, marriage engagements were generally made by the parents, and this was the custom among those who worshiped God. None were required to marry those whom they could not love, but the youth were guided by the judgment of their God-fearing parents. It was a dishonor to parents, even a crime, to pursue a course contrary to this.

Isaac, trusting his father, was satisfied to commit the matter to him, believing also that God Himself would direct in the choice made. The patriarch's thoughts turned to his father's kindred in Mesopotamia. Though not free from idolatry, they cherished the knowledge of the true God. Isaac must not go to them, but it might be that among them could be found one who would leave her home and unite with him in maintaining the pure worship of the living God.

This chapter is based on Genesis 24.

Abraham committed the important matter to "his eldest servant," a man of experience and sound judgment who had rendered him long and faithful service. He required this servant to make a solemn oath that he would not take a wife for Isaac of the Canaanites, but would choose a maiden from the family of Nahor in Mesopotamia. If a damsel could not be found who would leave her kindred, then the messenger would be released from his oath. The patriarch encouraged him with the assurance that God would crown his mission with success. "The Lord God of heaven," he said, "which took me from my father's house, and from the land of my kindred, . . . He shall send His angel before thee."

The messenger set out without delay. Taking ten camels for his own company and the bridal party that might return with him and also gifts for the intended wife and friends, he made the long journey beyond Damascus to the plains that border on the great river of the East.

Arrived at Haran, "the city of Nahor," he halted outside the walls near the well to which the women came at evening for water. It was a time of anxious thought with him. Important results, not only to his master's household but to future generations, might follow from the choice he made. Remembering that God would send His angel with him, he prayed for positive guidance. In the family of his master he was accustomed to constant kindness and hospitality, and he now asked that an act of courtesy might indicate the maiden whom God had chosen.

Hardly was the prayer uttered before the answer was given. Among the women at the well, the courteous manners of one attracted his attention. As she came from the well, the stranger went to meet her, asking for some water from the pitcher upon her shoulder. The request received a kind answer with an offer to draw water for the camels also.

Thus the desired sign was given. The maiden "was

very fair to look upon," and her ready courtesy gave evidence of a kind heart and an active, energetic nature. Thus far the divine hand had been with him. The messenger asked her parentage, and on learning that she was the daughter of Bethuel, Abraham's nephew, "he bowed down his head, and worshiped the Lord."

The man revealed his connection with Abraham. Returning home, the maiden told what had happened, and Laban, her brother, at once hastened to bring the stranger to share their hospitality.

Eliezer would not partake of food until he had told his errand, his prayer at the well, with all the circumstances attending it. Then he said, "Now, if ye will deal kindly and truly with my master, tell me: and if not, tell me; that I may turn to the right hand, or to the left." The answer was, "The thing proceedeth from the Lord: we cannot speak unto thee bad or good. Behold, Rebekah is before thee, take her, and go, and let her be thy master's son's wife, as the Lord hath spoken."

Rebekah Believes God Has Spoken

Rebekah herself was consulted as to whether she would go to so great a distance from her father's house to marry the son of Abraham. She believed that God had selected her to be Isaac's wife, and said, "I will go."

The servant, anticipating his master's joy, was impatient to be gone, and with the morning they set out on the homeward journey. Abraham dwelt at Beersheba, and Isaac, who had been attending the flocks in the adjoining country, had returned to his father's tent to await the messenger from Haran. "And Isaac went out to meditate in the field at the eventide: and he lifted up his eyes, and saw, and, behold, the camels were coming. And Rebekah lifted up her eyes, and when she saw Isaac, she lighted off the camel. For she had said unto the servant, What man is this that walketh in the field to meet us? And the servant said, It is my master:

therefore she took a veil, and covered herself. And the servant told Isaac all things that he had done. And Isaac brought her into his mother Sarah's tent, and took Rebekah, and she became his wife; and he loved her: and Isaac was comforted after his mother's death.''

Abraham had marked the result of the intermarriage of those who feared God and those who feared Him not, from the days of Cain to his own time. His own marriage with Hagar and the marriage connections of Ishmael and Lot were before him. The father's influence upon his son Ishmael was counteracted by that of the mother's idolatrous kindred and by Ishmael's connection with heathen wives. The jealousy of Hagar and of the wives whom she chose for Ishmael surrounded his family with a barrier that Abraham endeavored in vain to overcome.

Abraham's early teachings had not been without effect upon Ishmael, but the influence of his wives resulted in the establishment of idolatry in his family. Separated from his father and embittered by the strife and contention of a home destitute of the love and fear of God, Ishmael was driven to choose the wild, marauding life of the desert chief, "his hand against every man, and every man's hand against him." Genesis 16:12. In his latter days he repented and returned to his father's God, but the stamp of character given to his posterity remained. The powerful nation descended from him were a turbulent, heathen people.

The wife of Lot was a selfish, irreligious woman, and her influence was exerted to separate her husband from Abraham. But for her, Lot would not have remained in Sodom. The influence of his wife and the associations of that wicked city would have led him to apostatize from God, had it not been for the faithful instruction he had early received from Abraham.

No one who fears God can without danger connect himself with one who fears Him not. "Can two walk together, except they be agreed?" Amos 3:3. The happiness and prosperity of marriage depends upon the unity of the parties; but between the believer and the unbeliever there is a radical difference of tastes, inclinations, and purposes. However pure and correct one's principles, the influence of an unbelieving companion will have a tendency to lead away from God.

He who has entered marriage while unconverted is by his conversion placed under stronger obligation to be faithful to his companion, however they may differ in religious faith. Yet the claims of God should be placed above every earthly relationship, even though trials and persecution result. The spirit of love and fidelity may win the unbelieving one. But marriage with the ungodly is forbidden in the Bible. "Be ye not unequally yoked together with unbelievers." 2 Corinthians 6:14.

Before One Marries

Isaac was inheritor of the promises through which the world was to be blessed; yet when forty years of age he submitted to his father to choose a wife for him. And the result of that marriage is a tender and beautiful picture of domestic happiness: "Isaac brought her into his mother Sarah's tent, and took Rebekah, and she became his wife; and he loved her: and Isaac was comforted after his mother's death."

Young people too often feel that the bestowal of their affections is a matter in which self alone should be consulted. They think themselves competent to make their own choice, without the aid of their parents. A few years of married life usually show them their error, but too late. The same lack of wisdom and self-control that dictated the hasty choice is permitted to aggravate the evil, until marriage becomes a galling yoke. Many thus wreck their happiness in this life and their hope of the life to come.

If ever the Bible was needed as a counselor, if ever divine guidance should be sought in prayer, it is before taking a step that binds persons together for life.

Parents should never lose sight of their responsibility for the future happiness of their children. While Abraham required his children to respect parental authority, his daily life testified that that authority was not selfish or arbitrary, but was founded in love and had their welfare and happiness in view.

Fathers and mothers should guide the affections of youth that they may be placed upon suitable companions. Mold the character of the children from their earliest years that they will be pure and noble, attracted to the good and true. Let love for truth, purity, and goodness be early implanted in the soul, and youth will seek the society of those who possess these characteristics.

Let parents seek to exemplify the love of the heavenly Father. Let home be full of sunshine. This will be worth more to your children than lands or money. Let the home love be kept alive in their hearts, that they may look back upon the home of their childhood as a place of peace and happiness next to heaven.

True love is a high and holy principle, altogether different from that love which, awakened by impulse, suddenly dies when severely tested. In the parental home youth are to prepare themselves for homes of their own. Let them here practice self-denial, kindness, courtesy, and Christian sympathy.

He who goes out from such a household to stand at the head of a family will know how to promote the happiness of her whom he has chosen as a companion for life. Marriage, instead of being the end of love, will be only its beginning.

16 / Jacob and Esau

Jacob and Esau, the twin sons of Isaac, present a striking contrast in character and in life. This unlikeness was foretold by the angel of God before their birth. In answer to Rebekah's troubled prayer, he declared that two sons would be given her. He opened to her their future history, that each would become the head of a mighty nation, but that one would be greater than the other, and the younger would have the pre-eminence.

Esau grew up loving self-gratification, centering all his interest in the present. Impatient of restraint, he delighted in the chase and the life of a hunter. Yet he was the father's favorite. This elder son fearlessly ranged over mountain and desert, returning home with game and exciting accounts of his adventurous life.

Jacob, thoughtful, diligent, ever thinking more of the future than the present, was content to dwell at home, occupied in the care of the flocks and tillage of the soil. His patient perseverance, thrift, and foresight were valued by the mother. His gentle attentions added more to her happiness than the boisterous, occasional kindnesses of Esau. To Rebekah, Jacob was the dearer son.

Esau and Jacob were taught to regard the birthright as a matter of great importance, for it included not only an inheritance of worldly wealth, but spiritual pre-eminence. He who received it was to be the priest of his family, and in the line of his posterity the Redeemer of the world would come.

This chapter is based on Genesis 25:19-34; 27.

On the other hand, there were obligations resting upon the possessor of the birthright. He who should inherit its blessings must devote his life to the service of God. In marriage, in his family relations, in public life, he must consult the will of God.

Isaac made known to his sons these privileges and conditions and plainly stated that Esau as the eldest was the one entitled to the birthright. But Esau had no love for devotion, no inclination to a religious life. The requirements that accompanied the spiritual birthright were an unwelcome and even hateful restraint. The law of God, the condition of the divine covenant with Abraham, was regarded by Esau as a yoke of bondage. Bent on self-indulgence, he desired nothing so much as liberty to do as he pleased. To him power and riches, feasting and reveling, were happiness. He gloried in the unrestrained freedom of his wild, roving life.

Rebekah remembered the words of the angel and read with clearer insight than her husband the character of their sons. Convinced that the heritage of divine promise was intended for Jacob, she repeated to Isaac the angel's words. But the father's affections were centered upon the elder son, and he was unshaken in his purpose.

Jacob had learned from his mother that the birthright should fall to him, and he was filled with desire for the privileges it would confer. It was not his father's wealth that he craved; the spiritual birthright was the object of his longing. To commune with God as Abraham, to offer the sacrifice of atonement, to be progenitor of the chosen people of the promised Messiah, to inherit the immortal possessions embraced in the covenant—here were the privileges and honor that kindled his ardent desires.

He listened to all that his father told concerning the spiritual birthright; he carefully treasured what he had learned from his mother. The subject became the absorbing interest of his life. But Jacob had not an experimental knowledge of the God whom he revered. His heart had not been renewed by divine grace. He constantly studied to devise some way whereby he might secure the blessing which his brother held so lightly, but which was so precious to himself.

Esau Sells His Treasure

Esau, coming home one day faint and weary from the chase, asked for the food that Jacob was preparing. The latter seized upon his advantage and offered to satisfy his brother's hunger at the price of the birthright. "Behold, I am at the point to die," cried the reckless, self-indulgent hunter, "and what profit shall this birthright do to me?" For a dish of red pottage he parted with his birthright and confirmed the transaction by an oath. To satisfy the desire of the moment he carelessly bartered the glorious heritage God Himself had promised his fathers. His whole interest was in the present. He was ready to sacrifice the heavenly to the earthly, to exchange a future good for a momentary indulgence.

"Thus Esau despised his birthright." In disposing of it he felt a sense of relief. Now he could do as he liked. For this wild pleasure, miscalled freedom, many are still selling their birthright to an inheritance eternal in the heavens!

Esau took two wives of the daughters of Heth. Worshipers of false gods, their idolatry was a bitter grief to Isaac and Rebekah. Esau had violated one of the conditions of the covenant, which forbade intermarriage between the chosen people and the heathen; yet Isaac was still determined to bestow upon him the birthright.

Years passed. Isaac, old and blind, soon to die, determined no longer to delay the bestowal of the blessing upon his elder son. But knowing the opposition of Rebekah and Jacob, he decided to perform the solemn ceremony in secret. The patriarch bade Esau, "Go out to the field, and take me some venison; and make me savory meat, . . . that my soul may bless thee before I die."

Rebekah told Jacob what had taken place, urging immediate action to prevent the bestowal of the blessing upon Esau. She assured her son that if he would follow her directions, he might obtain it as God had promised. Jacob did not readily consent. The thought of deceiving his father caused great distress. Such a sin would bring a curse rather than a blessing.

But his scruples were overborne, and he proceeded to carry out his mother's suggestions. It was not his intention to utter a direct falsehood, but once in the presence of his father he seemed to have gone too far to retreat, and he obtained by fraud the coveted blessing.

Consequences of Deception

Jacob and Rebekah succeeded in their purpose but gained only trouble and sorrow by deception. God had declared that Jacob receive the birthright, and His word would have been fulfilled had they waited in faith for Him to work. Rebekah bitterly repented the wrong counsel she had given her son. Jacob was weighed down with self-condemnation. He had sinned against his father, his brother, his own soul, and against God. In one short hour he had made work for a lifelong repentance. This scene was vivid before him in afteryears when the wicked course of his own sons oppressed his soul.

No sooner had Jacob left his father's tent than Esau entered. Though he had sold his birthright, he was now determined to secure its blessing. With the spiritual was connected the temporal birthright, which would give him the headship of the family and a double portion of his father's wealth. "Let my father arise," he said, "and eat of his son's venison, that thy soul may bless me."

Trembling with astonishment and distress, the blind old father learned the deception that had been practiced upon him. He keenly felt the disappointment that must come upon his elder son. Yet the conviction flashed upon him that it was God's providence which had brought about the very thing he had determined to prevent. He remembered the words of the angel to Rebekah, and he saw in Jacob the one best fitted to accomplish the purpose of God. While the words of blessing were upon his lips, he had felt the Spirit of Inspiration upon him; and now he ratified the benediction unwittingly pronounced upon Jacob: "I have blessed him; yea, and he shall be blessed."

Esau Could Not Repent

Esau had lightly valued the blessing while it seemed within his reach, but now that it was gone from him his grief and rage were terrible. "Bless me, even me also, O my father!" "Hast thou not reserved a blessing for me?" But the birthright which he had so carelessly bartered, he could not regain. "For one morsel of meat," for a momentary gratification of appetite that had never been restrained, Esau sold his inheritance.

But when he saw his folly, it was too late to recover the blessing. "He found no place of repentance, though he sought it carefully with tears." Hebrews 12: 17. Esau was not shut out from seeking God's favor by repentance, but he could find no means of recovering the birthright. His grief did not spring from conviction of sin; he did not desire to be reconciled to God. He sorrowed because of the results of his sin, but not for the sin itself.

Esau is called in Scripture "a profane person." Verse 16. He represents those who lightly value the redemption purchased for them by Christ and are ready to sacrifice their heirship to heaven for the perishable things of earth. Multitudes live with no thought or care for the future. Like Esau they cry, "Let us eat and drink; for tomorrow we die." 1 Corinthians 15:32. The claims of appetite prevail, and God and heaven are virtually despised. When the duty is presented of cleansing themselves from all filthiness of the flesh and spirit, perfecting holiness in the fear of God, they are offended.

Multitudes are selling their birthright for sensual indulgence. Health is sacrificed, the mental faculties are enfeebled, and heaven forfeited, all for a temporary pleasure, both weakening and debasing in its character. Esau awoke too late to recover his loss. So it will be in the day of God with those who have bartered their heirship to heaven for selfish gratifications.

17 / Jacob's Flight and Exile

Threatened with death by Esau, Jacob went out from his father's home a fugitive, but with the father's blessing. Isaac had renewed to him the covenant promise and had bidden him seek a wife of his mother's family in Mesopotamia.

Yet it was with a deeply troubled heart that Jacob set out on his lonely journey. With only his staff in his hand he must travel hundreds of miles through a country inhabited by wild, roving tribes. In his remorse and timidity he sought to avoid men, lest he should be traced by his angry brother. He feared that he had lost forever the blessing God had purposed to give him, and Satan was at hand to press temptations upon him.

The evening of the second day found him far away from his father's tents. He felt he was an outcast, and he knew that all his trouble had been brought upon him by his own wrong course. Despair pressed upon his soul, and he hardly dared to pray. But he was so lonely that he felt the need of protection from God as never before. With weeping he confessed his sin and entreated for some evidence that he was not utterly forsaken. He had lost all confidence in himself, and he feared that God had cast him off.

But God's mercy was still extended to His erring, distrustful servant. The Lord compassionately revealed just what Jacob needed—a Saviour. He had sinned, but he saw revealed a way by which he could be restored to the favor of God.

Wearied, the wanderer lay down on the ground, a

This chapter is based on Genesis 28 to 31.

stone for his pillow. As he slept, he beheld a ladder whose base rested on the earth while the top reached to heaven. Upon this ladder angels were ascending and descending. Above it was the Lord of glory and from the heavens His voice was heard: "I am the Lord God of Abraham thy father, and the God of Isaac." "In thee and in thy seed shall all the families of the earth be blessed." This promise had been given to Abraham and to Isaac, and now it was renewed to Jacob. Then the words of comfort and encouragement were spoken: "Behold, I am with thee, and will keep thee in all places whither thou goest, and will bring thee again into this land; for I will not leave thee, until I have done that which I have spoken to thee of."

The Lord in mercy opened up the future before the repentant fugitive, that he might be prepared to resist the temptations that would come to him when alone amid idolaters and scheming men. The knowledge that through him the purpose of God was reaching its accomplishment would constantly prompt him to faithfulness.

In this vision the plan of redemption was presented to Jacob in such parts as were essential to him at that time. The mystic ladder revealed in his dream was the same to which Christ referred in His conversation with Nathanael: "Ye shall see heaven open and the angels of God ascending and descending upon the Son of man." John 1:51. The sin of Adam and Eve separated earth from heaven, so that man could not have communion with his Maker. Yet the world was not left in hopelessness. The ladder represents Jesus, the appointed medium of communication. Christ connects man in his weakness and helplessness with the source of infinite power.

All this was revealed to Jacob in his dream. Although his mind at once grasped a part of the revelation, its great and mysterious truths were the study of his lifetime and unfolded to his understanding more and more.

Jacob awoke in the deep stillness of night. The vision had disappeared. Only the dim outline of lonely hills and the heavens bright with stars now met his gaze. But he had a solemn sense that God was with him. "Surely the Lord is in this place," he said, "and I knew it not. . . . This is none other but the house of God, and this is the gate of heaven."

"And Jacob rose up early in the morning, and took the stone that he had put for his pillows, and set it up for a pillar, and poured oil upon the top of it." He called the place Bethel, or "the house of God." And then he made the solemn vow, "If God will be with me, and will keep me in this way that I go, and will give me bread to eat, and raiment to put on, so that I come again to my father's house in peace; then shall the Lord be my God: and this stone, which I have set for a pillar, shall be God's house: and of all that Thou shalt give me I will surely give the tenth unto Thee."

Jacob was not seeking to make terms with God. The Lord had already promised him prosperity, and this vow was the outflow of a heart filled with gratitude for the assurance of God's mercy. Jacob felt that the special tokens of divine favor demanded a return.

The Christian should often recall with gratitude the precious deliverances that God has wrought for him, opening ways before him when all seemed dark and forbidding, refreshing him when ready to faint. In view of innumerable blessings he should often ask, "What shall I render unto the Lord for all His benefits toward me?" Psalm 116:12.

Why the Tithe Is Sacred

Whenever a special deliverance is wrought in our behalf, or new and unexpected favors are granted us, we should acknowledge God's goodness by gifts or offerings to His cause. As we are continually *receiving* the blessings of God, so we are to be continually *giving*.

"Of all that Thou shalt give me," said Jacob, "I will surely give the tenth unto Thee." Shall we who enjoy the full light of the gospel be content to give less to God than was given by those who lived in the former dispensation? Are not our obligations correspondingly increased? But how vain to measure with mathematical rules, time, money, and love, against a love so immeasurable and a gift of such inconceivable worth. Tithes for Christ! Oh, meager pittance, shameful recompense for that which cost so much! From the cross of Calvary, Christ calls for unreserved consecration of all that we have, all that we are.

With new faith and assured of the presence of heavenly angels, Jacob pursued his journey to "the land of the children of the East." But how differently his arrival from that of Abraham's messenger nearly a hundred years before! The servant had come with a train of attendants riding on camels, with rich gifts of gold and silver; the son was a lonely, foot-sore traveler, with no possession save his staff. Like Abraham's servant, Jacob tarried beside a well, and it was here that he met Rachel, Laban's younger daughter. On making known his kinship, he was welcomed to the home of Laban. A few weeks showed the worth of his diligence and skill, and he was urged to tarry. It was arranged that he should render Laban seven years' service for the hand of Rachel.

Jacob's Love for Rachel

In early times, custom required the bridegroom, before the marriage engagement, to pay a sum of money or its equivalent in other property, according to his circumstances, to the father of his wife. This was regarded as a safeguard to the marriage. Fathers did not think it safe to trust the happiness of their daughters to men who had not made provision for the support of a family. If they had not sufficient thrift and energy to manage business and acquire cattle or lands, it was feared that their life would prove worthless. But provision was made to test those who had nothing to pay for a wife. They were permitted to labor for the father whose daughter they loved, the length of time regulated by the value of the dowry required. When the suitor was faithful and proved worthy, he obtained the daughter as his wife.

Generally the dowry which the father had received was given her at her marriage. In the case of both Rachel and Leah, however, Laban selfishly retained the dowry that should have been given them. They referred to this when they said, just before the removal from Mesopotamia, "He hath sold us, and hath quite devoured also our money."

When the suitor was thus required to render service to secure his bride, a hasty marriage was prevented. There was opportunity to test the depth of his affections, as well as his ability to provide for a family. In our time it is often the case that persons before marriage have little opportunity to become acquainted with each other's habits and disposition. They are virtually strangers when they unite their interests at the altar. Many find, too late, that they are not adapted to each other, and lifelong wretchedness is the result. Often the wife and children suffer from the indolence or vicious habits of the husband and father. If the character of the suitor had been tested before marriage according to the ancient custom, great unhappiness might have been prevented.

Seven years of faithful service Jacob gave for Rachel, and the years that he served "seemed unto him but a few days, for the love he had to her." But selfish Laban practiced a cruel deception in substituting Leah for Rachel. The fact that Leah herself was a party to the cheat caused Jacob to feel he could not love her. His indignant rebuke to Laban was met with the offer of Rachel for another seven years' service. But the father insisted that Leah should not be discarded. Jacob was thus placed in a most painful and trying position: he finally decided to retain Leah and marry Rachel. Rachel was ever the one best loved, but his life was embittered by the rivalry between the sister-wives.

For twenty years Jacob remained in Mesopotamia in the service of Laban, who was bent upon securing to himself all the benefits of their connection. Fourteen years of toil he demanded for his two daughters, and during the remaining period Jacob's wages were ten times changed.

Yet Jacob's service was diligent and faithful. During some portions of the year it was necessary for him to be constantly with the flocks in person, to guard them in the dry season against perishing from thirst, and during the coldest months from becoming chilled with heavy night frosts. Jacob was the chief shepherd; the servants in his employ were the undershepherds. If any of the sheep were missing, the chief shepherd suffered the loss, and he called the servants to a strict account if the flock was not found in a flourishing condition.

We Have a Faithful Shepherd

The shepherd's life of care-taking and compassion for the helpless creatures illustrates some precious truths of the gospel. Christ is compared to a shepherd. He saw His sheep doomed to perish in the dark ways of sin. To save these wandering ones He left the honors and glories of His Father's house. He says, "I will seek that which was lost, and bring again that which was driven away, and will bind up that which was broken, and will strengthen that which was sick." I will "save My flock, and they shall no more be a prey." "Neither shall the beast of the land devour them." Ezekiel 34:16, 22, 28. His voice is heard calling them to His fold, "a shadow in the daytime from the heat, and for a place of refuge, and for a covert from storm and from rain." Isaiah 4:6. He strengthens the weak, relieves the suffering, gathers the lambs in His arms, and carries them in His bosom. His sheep love Him. "And a stranger will they not follow, but will flee from him; for they know not the voice of strangers." See John 10: 1-15.

The church of Christ has been purchased with His blood, and every shepherd imbued with the spirit of Christ will imitate His self-denying example, constantly laboring for the welfare of his charge, and the flock will prosper under his care. "When the chief Shepherd shall appear," says the apostle, "ye shall receive a crown of glory that fadeth not away." 1 Peter 5:4.

Jacob, growing weary of Laban's service, proposed to return to Canaan. He said to his father-in-law, "Send me away, that I may go unto mine own place, and to my country. Give me my wives and my children, for whom I have served thee, and let me go: for thou knowest my service which I have done thee." But Laban urged him to remain, declaring, "I have learned by experience that the Lord hath blessed me for thy sake."

Said Jacob, "It was little which thou hadst before I came, and it is now increased unto a multitude." But as time passed, Laban became envious of the greater prosperity of Jacob, who "increased exceedingly." Laban's sons shared their father's jealousy, and their malicious speeches came to Laban's ears. He "hath taken away all that was our father's; and of that which was our father's hath he gotten all this glory. And Jacob beheld the countenance of Laban, and, behold, it was not toward him as before."

Jacob would have left his crafty kinsman long before but for the fear of encountering Esau. Now he felt that he was in danger'from the sons of Laban, who, looking upon his wealth as their own, might endeavor to secure it by violence. He was in great perplexity and distress. But mindful of the gracious Bethel promise, he carried his case to God. In a dream his prayer was answered: "Return unto the land of thy fathers, and to thy kindred; and I will be with thee."

The flocks and herds were speedily gathered and sent forward, and with his wives, children, and servants, Jacob crossed the Euphrates, urging his way toward Gilead, on the borders of Canaan. After three days, Laban set forth in pursuit, overtaking the company on the seventh day of their journey. He was hot with anger and bent on forcing them to return. The fugitives were indeed in great peril.

God himself interposed for the protection of his servant. "It is in the power of my hand to do you hurt," said Laban, "but the God of your father spake unto me yesternight, saying, Take thou heed that thou speak not to Jacob either good or bad." That is, he should not force him to return, or urge him by flattering inducements.

Laban had withheld the marriage dowry of his daughters and treated Jacob with craft and harshness, but he now reproached him for his secret departure which had given the father no opportunity to make a feast or even bid farewell to his daughters and their children.

In reply, Jacob plainly set forth Laban's selfish and grasping policy and appealed to him as a witness to his own faithfulness and honesty. "Except the God of my father, the God of Abraham, and the fear of Isaac, had been with me," said Jacob, "surely thou hadst sent me away now empty. God hath seen mine affliction and the labor of my hands, and rebuked thee yesternight."

Laban could not deny the facts and now proposed a covenant of peace. Jacob consented, and a pile of stones was erected as a token of the compact. To this pillar Laban gave the name Mizpah, "Watchtower," saying, "The Lord watch between me and thee, when we are absent one from another. . . . The God of Abraham, and the God of Nahor, the God of their father, judge betwixt us. And Jacob sware by the fear of his father Isaac."

To confirm the treaty, the parties held a feast. The night was spent in friendly communing, and at dawn Laban and his company departed. With this separation ceased all connection between the children of Abraham and the dwellers in Mesopotamia.

18 / Jacob's Terrible Night of Wrestling

With many misgivings Jacob retraced the road he had trodden as a fugitive twenty years before. His sin in the deception of his father was ever before him. He knew that his long exile was the direct result of that sin. He pondered over these things day and night, an accusing conscience making his journey very sad. As the hills of his native land appeared before him in the distance, all the past rose vividly before him. With the memory of his sin came also the promises of divine help and guidance.

The thought of Esau brought troubled foreboding. Esau might be moved to violence not only by revenge, but to secure undisturbed possession of the wealth he had long looked upon as his own.

Again the Lord granted Jacob a token of divine care; two hosts of heavenly angels advanced with his company, as if for their protection. Jacob remembered the vision at Bethel so long before, and his burdened heart grew lighter. The divine messengers who brought him hope and courage at his flight from Canaan were to be the guardians of his return. And he said, "This is God's host."

Yet Jacob felt that he had something to do to secure his own safety. He therefore dispatched messengers with a conciliatory greeting to Esau. The servants were sent to "my lord Esau." They were to refer to their master as "thy servant Jacob." And to remove the fear that he was returning to claim the inheritance, Jacob was careful to state in his message, "I have oxen, and

This chapter is based on Genesis 32 and 33.

asses, flocks, and menservants, and womenservants."

But no response was sent to the friendly message. It appeared certain that Esau was coming to seek revenge. Terror pervaded the camp. "Jacob was greatly afraid and distressed." His company, unarmed and defenseless, were wholly unprepared for a hostile encounter. He sent from his vast flocks generous presents to Esau, with a friendly message. He did all in his power to atone for the wrong to his brother and to avert the threatened danger. Then he pleaded for divine protection: "I am not worthy of the least of all the mercies, and of all the truth, which Thou hast showed unto Thy servant. . . . Deliver me, I pray Thee, from the hand of my brother, from the hand of Esau: for I fear him, lest he will come and smite me, and the mother with the children."

Jacob decided to spend the night in prayer, alone with God. God could soften the heart of Esau. In Him was the patriarch's only hope.

An Angel Wrestles With Jacob

It was a lonely, mountainous region, the haunt of wild beasts, robbers, and murderers. Unprotected, Jacob bowed in deep distress upon the earth. It was midnight. All that made life dear to him were exposed to danger and death. Bitter was the thought that his own sin had brought this peril upon the innocent.

Suddenly a strong hand was laid upon him. He thought that an enemy was seeking his life. In the darkness the two struggled for the mastery. Not a word was spoken, but Jacob put forth all his strength and did not relax his efforts for a moment. While battling for his life, his guilt pressed upon his soul; his sins rose up to shut him out from God.

But in his terrible extremity he remembered God's promises. The struggle continued until near break of day, when the stranger placed his finger on Jacob's thigh, and he was crippled instantly. The patriarch now knew that he had been in conflict with a heavenly mes-

Jacob wrestled with the angel until the break of day, when at last he discovered that his opponent was none other than Christ Himself.

senger. This was why his almost superhuman effort had not gained the victory. It was Christ, "the Angel of the covenant." Jacob was now disabled and suffering the keenest pain, but he would not loosen his hold. Penitent and broken, he clung to the Angel; "he wept, and made supplication," pleading for a blessing. He must have the assurance that his sin was pardoned. The Angel urged, "Let Me go, for the day breaketh"; but Jacob answered, "I will not let Thee go, except Thou bless me." His was the assurance of one who confesses his unworthiness yet trusts the faithfulness of a covenant-keeping God.

Jacob "had power over the Angel, and prevailed." Hosea 12:4. This sinful, erring mortal prevailed with the Majesty of heaven. He had fastened his trembling grasp upon the promises of God, and the heart of Infinite Love could not turn away the sinner's plea.

Jacob's Name Becomes "Israel"

The error that had led to Jacob's sin in obtaining the birthright by fraud was now clearly set before him. He had not trusted God's promises but had sought by his own efforts to bring about that which God would have accomplished in His own time and way. As an evidence that he had been forgiven, his name was changed to one that commemorated his victory. "Thy name," said the Angel, "shall be called no more Jacob [supplanter], but Israel: for as a prince hast thou power with God and with men, and hast prevailed."

The crisis in his life was past. Doubt, perplexity, and remorse had embittered his existence, but now all was changed. Sweet was the peace of reconciliation with God. Jacob no longer feared to meet his brother. God could move the heart of Esau to accept his humiliation and repentance.

While Jacob was wrestling with the Angel, another heavenly messenger was sent to Esau. In a dream, Esau beheld his brother for twenty years an exile; he witnessed his grief at finding his mother dead; he saw him encompassed by the hosts of God. The God of his father was with him.

The two companies at last approached each other, the desert chief leading his men of war, and Jacob with his wives and children followed by long lines of flocks and herds. Leaning upon his staff, the patriarch went forward, pale and disabled from his recent conflict. He walked slowly and painfully, but his countenance was lighted up with joy and peace.

At sight of that crippled sufferer, "Esau ran to meet him, and embraced him, . . . and they wept." Even the hearts of Esau's rude soldiers were touched. They could not account for the change that had come over their captain.

In his night of anguish Jacob had been taught how vain is the help of man, how groundless is trust in human power. Helpless and unworthy, he pleaded God's promise of mercy to the repentant sinner. That promise was his assurance that God would pardon and accept him.

The Future "Time of Jacob's Trouble"

Jacob's experience during that night of wrestling and anguish represents the trial through which the people of God must pass just before Christ's second coming. "We have heard a voice of trembling, of fear, and not of peace. . . . Alas! for that day is great, so that none is like it: it is even the time of Jacob's trouble; but he shall be saved out of it." Jeremiah 30:5-7.

When Christ shall cease His work as mediator in man's behalf, this time of trouble will begin. Then the case of every soul will have been decided, and there will be no atoning blood to cleanse from sin. The solemn announcement is made, "He that is unjust, let him be unjust still: and he which is filthy, let him be filthy still: and he that is righteous, let him be righteous still: and he that is holy, let him be holy still." Revelation 22:11. As Jacob was threatened with death by his angry brother, so the people of God will be in peril from the wicked. The righteous will cry to God day and night for deliverance.

Satan had accused Jacob before the angels of God, claiming the right to destroy him because of his sin; he endeavored to force upon him a sense of his guilt in order to discourage him and break his hold on God. When Jacob made supplication with tears, the heavenly Messenger, in order to try his faith, also reminded him of his sin and endeavored to escape from him. But Jacob had learned that God is merciful. As he reviewed his life, he was driven almost to despair, but he held fast the Angel, and with earnest, agonizing cries urged his petition until he prevailed.

The Final Struggle

Such will be the experience of God's people in their final struggle with the powers of evil. God will test their faith, their perseverance, their confidence in His power. Satan will endeavor to terrify them with the thought that their sins have been too great to receive pardon. As they review their lives, their hopes will sink. But remembering God's mercy and their own sincere repentance, they will plead His promises. Their faith will not fail because their prayers are not immediately answered. The language of their souls will be, "I will not let Thee go, except Thou bless me."

Had not Jacob previously repented of his sin in obtaining the birthright by fraud, God could not have mercifully preserved his life. So in the time of trouble, if the people of God had unconfessed sins to appear before them while tortured with fear and anguish, despair would cut off their faith, and they could not have confidence to plead with God for deliverance. But they will have no concealed wrongs to reveal. Their sins will have been blotted out by the atoning blood of Christ, and they cannot bring them to remembrance.

All who endeavor to excuse or conceal their sins and permit them to remain upon the books of heaven, unconfessed and unforgiven, will be overcome by Satan. The more exalted their profession and the more honorable the position which they hold, the more certain is the triumph of the great adversary.

Jacob's history is an assurance that God will not cast off those who have been betrayed into sin, but have returned unto Him with true repentance. God taught His servant that divine grace alone could give him the blessing he craved. Thus it will be with those who live in the last days. In all our helpless unworthiness we must trust in the merits of the crucified and risen Saviour. None will ever perish while they do this.

Jacob's experience testifies to the power of importunate prayer. It is now that we are to learn this lesson of unyielding faith. The greatest victories are not those gained by talent, education, wealth, or the favor of men. They are gained in the audience chamber with God, when earnest, agonizing faith lays hold upon the mighty arm of power.

All who will lay hold of God's promises as did Jacob, and be as earnest and persevering as he, will succeed as he succeeded.

19 / Jacob Comes Home

Crossing the Jordan, "Jacob came in peace to the city of Shechem, which is in the land of Canaan." Here he "bought the parcel of ground, where he had spread his tent, at the hand of the children of Hamor, Shechem's father, for a hundred pieces of money. And he erected there an altar." It was here also that he dug the well to which, seventeen centuries later, came Jacob's Son and Saviour, and beside which, resting during the noontide heat, He told His wondering hearers of that "well of water springing up into everlasting life." John 4:14.

The tarry of Jacob and his sons at Shechem ended in bloodshed. One daughter of the household had been brought to shame and sorrow; two brothers were involved in the guilt of murder; a whole city had been given to ruin and slaughter in retaliation for the lawless deed of one rash youth. The beginning that led to results so terrible was the act of Jacob's daughter venturing to associate with the ungodly. He who seeks pleasure among those that fear not God is inviting temptations.

The treacherous cruelty of Simeon and Levi toward the Shechemites was a grievous sin. The tidings of their revenge filled Jacob with horror. Heartsick at the deceit and violence of his sons, he said, "Ye have troubled me to make me to stink among the inhabitants of the land, . . . I being few in number, they shall gather themselves together against me, and slay me; and I shall be destroyed, I and my house."

This chapter is based on Genesis 34; 35; 37.

Jacob felt that there was cause for deep humiliation. Cruelty and falsehood were in the character of his sons. False gods and idolatry had to some extent gained a foothold even in his household.

While Jacob was thus bowed down with trouble, the Lord directed him to journey southward to Bethel. The thought of this place reminded the patriarch not only of his vision of the angels and of God's promises of mercy, but of the vow he had made there that the Lord should be his God. Determined that before going to this sacred spot his household should be freed from the defilement of idolatry, he gave direction to all, "Put away the strange gods that are among you, and be clean, and change your garments. And let us arise, and go up to Bethel; and I will make there an altar unto God, who answered me in the day of my distress, and was with me in the way which I went."

Jacob Relates His Earlier Bethel Experience

With deep emotion, Jacob repeated the story of his first visit to Bethel and how the Lord had appeared to him in the night vision. His own heart was softened; his children also were touched by a subduing power. He had taken the most effectual way to prepare them to join in the worship of God when they should arrive at Bethel. "And they gave unto Jacob all the strange gods which were in their hand, and all their earrings which were in their ears; and Jacob hid them under the oak which was by Shechem."

God caused a fear to rest upon the inhabitants of the land, so that they made no attempt to avenge the slaughter of Shechem. The travelers reached Bethel unmolested. Here the Lord again appeared to Jacob and renewed to him the covenant promise.

From Bethel it was only two days' journey to Hebron, but it brought to Jacob a heavy grief in the death of Rachel. Twice seven years' service he had rendered for her sake, and his love had made the toil light. Deep and abiding that love had been.

Before her death, Rachel gave birth to a second son. With her parting breath she named the child Benoni, "son of my sorrow." But his father called him Benjamin, "son of my right hand," or "my strength."

At last Jacob came to his journey's end, "unto Isaac his father unto Mamre, . . . which is Hebron." Here he remained during the closing years of his father's life. To Isaac, infirm and blind, the kind attentions of this long-absent son were a comfort during years of loneliness and bereavement.

Jacob and Esau met at the deathbed of their father. The elder brother's feelings had greatly changed. Jacob, well content with the spiritual blessings of the birthright, resigned to the elder brother the inheritance of their father's wealth, the only inheritance Esau sought or valued. No longer estranged, they parted, Esau removing to Mount Seir. God, who is rich in blessing, had granted to Jacob worldly wealth, in addition to the higher good that he had sought. This separation was in accordance with the divine purpose concerning Jacob. Since the brothers differed so greatly in regard to religious faith, it was better for them to dwell apart.

Esau and Jacob both were free to walk in God's commandments and to receive His favor; but the two brothers had walked in different ways, and their paths would continue to diverge more and more widely.

There was no arbitrary choice on the part of God by which Esau was shut out from the blessings of salvation. There is no election but one's own by which any may perish. God has set forth in His Word the conditions upon which every soul will be elected to eternal life—obedience to His commandments through faith in Christ. God has elected a character in harmony with His law, and anyone who shall reach the standard of His requirement will have an entrance into the kingdom of glory. As regards man's final salvation, this is the only election brought to view in the Word of God.

Every soul is elected who will work out his own salvation with fear and trembling, who will put on the armor and fight the good fight of faith. He is elected who will watch unto prayer, search the Scriptures, flee from temptation, have faith continually, and be obedient to every word that proceedeth out of the mouth of God. The *provisions* of redemption are free to all; the *results* will be enjoyed by those who have complied with the conditions.

Esau had despised the blessings of the covenant. By his own deliberate choice he was separated from the people of God. Jacob had chosen the inheritance of faith. He had endeavored to obtain it by craft, treachery, and falsehood; but God had permitted his sin to work out its correction. Jacob never swerved from his purpose or renounced his choice. From that night of wrestling Jacob had come forth a different man. Self-confidence had been uprooted. Henceforth, in place of craft and deception, his life was marked by simplicity and truth. The baser elements of character were consumed in the furnace fire; the true gold was refined until the faith of Abraham and Isaac appeared undimmed in Jacob.

The sin of Jacob and the train of events to which it led revealed its bitter fruit in the character of his sons. These sons developed serious faults. The results of polygamy were manifest in the household. This terrible evil tends to dry up the springs of love, and its influence weakens the most sacred ties. The jealousy of the several mothers had embittered the family relation; the children had grown up contentious, impatient of control. The father's life was darkened with anxiety and grief.

There was one, however, of a widely different character—the elder son of Rachel, Joseph, whose rare personal beauty seemed to reflect an inward beauty of mind and heart. Pure, active, and joyous, the lad gave evidence of moral earnestness and firmness. He listened to his father's instructions and loved to obey God. The qualities that afterward distinguished him in

Egypt—gentleness, fidelity, and truthfulness—were already manifest. His mother being dead, his affections clung the more closely to the father. Jacob's heart was bound up in this child of his old age. He "loved Joseph more than all his children."

But this affection was to become a cause of trouble and sorrow. Jacob unwisely manifested preference for Joseph, and this excited the jealousy of his other sons. Joseph ventured gently to remonstrate with them but only aroused still further their hatred and resentment. He could not endure to see them sinning against God and laid the matter before his father.

With deep emotion Jacob implored them not to bring reproach upon his name and above all not to dishonor God by such disregard of His precepts. Ashamed that their wickedness was known, the young men seemed to be repentant but only concealed their real feelings, which were rendered more bitter by this exposure.

The father's gift to Joseph of a costly coat, usually worn by persons of distinction, excited a suspicion that he intended to pass by his elder children to bestow the birthright upon the son of Rachel.

The boy one day told them of a dream that he had had. "We were binding sheaves in the field, and, lo, my sheaf arose, and also stood upright; and, behold, your sheaves stood round about, and made obeisance to my sheaf."

"Shalt thou indeed reign over us? or shalt thou indeed have dominion over us?" exclaimed his brothers in envious anger.

Soon he had another dream which he also related: "Behold, the sun and the moon and the eleven stars made obeisance to me." The father, who was present, spoke reprovingly, "Shall I and thy mother and thy brethren indeed come to bow down ourselves to thee?" Notwithstanding the apparent severity of his words, Jacob believed that the Lord was revealing the future to Joseph.

As the lad stood before his brothers, his beautiful

countenance lighted up with the Spirit of Inspiration. They could not withhold their admiration, but hated the purity that reproved their sins.

The brothers were obliged to move from place to place to secure pasturage for their flocks. After the circumstances just related, they went to Shechem. Some time passed bringing no tidings, and the father began to fear for their safety on account of their former cruelty toward the Shechemites. He therefore sent Joseph to find them. Had Jacob known the real feeling of his sons toward Joseph, he would not have trusted him alone with them.

With a joyful heart, Joseph parted from his father, neither the aged man nor the youth dreaming of what would happen before they should meet again. When Joseph arrived at Shechem, his brothers and their flocks were not to be found. Upon inquiring for them, he was directed to Dothan. He hastened on, forgetting his weariness in the thought of relieving the anxiety of his father and meeting the brothers whom he still loved.

His brothers saw him approaching; but no thought of the long journey he had made to meet them, of his weariness and hunger, of his claims upon their hospitality and brotherly love softened the bitterness of their hatred. The sight of the coat, the token of their father's love, filled them with frenzy. "Behold, this dreamer cometh." Envy and revenge now controlled them. "Let us slay him," they said, "and cast him into some pit, and we will say, Some evil beast hath devoured him; and we shall see what will become of his dreams."

But Reuben shrank from the murder of his brother and proposed that Joseph be cast alive into a pit and left there to perish; secretly intending, however, to rescue him and return him to his father. Having persuaded all to consent to his plan, Reuben left, fearing that his real intentions would be discovered.

Joseph came on, unsuspicious of danger. But instead

of the expected greeting, he was terrified by the angry and revengeful glances which he met. He was seized and his coat stripped from him. Taunts and threats revealed a deadly purpose. His entreaties were unheeded. Those maddened men rudely dragged him to a deep pit, thrust him in, and left him there to perish.

Joseph Is Sold as a Slave

Soon a company of travelers was seen approaching. It was a caravan of Ishmaelites on their way to Egypt with merchandise. Judah now proposed to sell their brother instead of leaving him to die. While he would be effectually put out of their way, they would remain clear of his blood; "for," he urged, "he is our brother and our flesh." All agreed, and Joseph was quickly drawn out of the pit.

As he saw the merchants, the dreadful truth flashed upon him. To become a slave was more to be feared than death. In an agony of terror he appealed to one and another of his brothers, but in vain. Some were moved with pity, but all felt that they had now gone too far to retreat. Joseph would report them to the father. Steeling their hearts against his entreaties, they delivered him into the hands of the heathen traders. The caravan moved on and was soon lost to view.

Reuben returned to the pit, but Joseph was not there. Upon learning the fate of Joseph he was induced to unite in the attempt to conceal their guilt. Having killed a kid, they dipped Joseph's coat in its blood and took it to their father, telling him that they had found it in the fields. "Know now," they said, "whether it be thy son's coat or no." They were not prepared for the heart-rending anguish, the utter abandonment of grief, which they were compelled to witness. "It is my son's coat," said Jacob; "an evil beast hath devoured him. Joseph is without doubt rent in pieces." Vainly his sons and daughters attempted to comfort him. He "rent his clothes, and put sackcloth upon his loins, and mourned for his son many days." "I will go down into the grave unto my son mourning," was his despairing cry.

The young men, terrified at what they had done, yet dreading their father's reproaches, still hid in their own hearts the knowledge of their guilt, which even to themselves seemed very great.

20 / The Amazing Story of Joseph

Meanwhile, Joseph with his captors was on the way to Egypt. The boy could discern in the distance the hills among which lay his father's tents. Bitterly he wept at thought of that loving father in his loneliness and affection. The stinging, insulting words that had met his agonized entreaties at Dothan were ringing in his ears. With a trembling heart he looked forward to the future. Alone and friendless, what would be his lot in the strange land to which he was going? For a time, Joseph gave himself up to uncontrolled grief and terror.

But even this experience was to be a blessing to him. He had learned in a few hours that which years might not otherwise have taught him. His father had done him wrong by his partiality and indulgence. This had angered his brothers and provoked the cruel deed that had separated him from his home. In his character, faults had been encouraged. He was becoming self-sufficient and exacting. He felt that he was unprepared to cope with the difficulties before him in the bitter, uncared-for life of a slave.

Then his thoughts turned to his father's God. Often he had listened to the story of the vision that Jacob saw as he fled from his home an exile and a fugitive. He had been told of the Lord's promises to Jacob, and how, in the hour of need, angels had come to instruct, comfort, and protect him. He had learned of the love of God in providing a Redeemer. Now all these precious lessons came vividly before him. Joseph believed that the God

This chapter is based on Genesis 39 to 41.

141

of his fathers would be his God. He then and there gave himself fully to the Lord and prayed that the Keeper of Israel would be with him in his exile.

His soul thrilled with the high resolve to prove true to God, to act as a subject of the King of heaven. He would meet the trials of his lot with fortitude and perform every duty with fidelity. One day's terrible calamity had transformed him from a petted child to a man, thoughtful, courageous, and self-possessed.

Arriving in Egypt, Joseph was sold to Potiphar, captain of the king's guard. For ten years he was here exposed to temptations in the midst of idolatry, surrounded by all the pomp of royalty, the wealth and culture of the most highly civilized nation then in existence. Yet Joseph preserved his fidelity to God. The sights and sounds of vice were all about him, but he was as one who saw and heard not. His thoughts were not permitted to linger upon forbidden subjects. The desire to gain the favor of the Egyptians could not cause him to conceal his principles. He made no effort to hide the fact that he was a worshiper of Jehovah.

"And the Lord was with Joseph, and he was a prosperous man. . . . And his master saw that the Lord was with him, and that the Lord made all that he did to prosper in his hand." Potiphar's confidence in Joseph increased daily, and he finally promoted him to be his steward, with full control over all his possessions. "And he left all that he had in Joseph's hand; and he knew not aught he had, save the bread which he did eat."

Joseph's industry, care, and energy were crowned with the divine blessing; even his idolatrous master accepted this as the secret of his prosperity. God was glorified in the faithfulness of His servant. It was His purpose that the believer in God should appear in marked contrast to the worshipers of idols. Thus the light of heavenly grace might shine forth amid the darkness of heathenism.

The chief captain came to regard Joseph as a son

rather than a slave. The youth was brought in contact with men of rank and learning, and he acquired a knowledge of science, languages, and affairs—an education needful to the future prime minister of Egypt.

The Almost Overmastering Temptation

But Joseph's master's wife endeavored to entice the young man to transgress the law of God. He had remained untainted by the corruption teeming in that heathen land; but this temptation, so sudden, so strong, so seductive—how should it be met?

Joseph knew well the consequence of resistance. On the one hand were concealment, favor, and rewards; on the other, disgrace, imprisonment, perhaps death. His whole future life depended upon the decision of the moment. Would Joseph be true to God? With inexpressible anxiety, angels looked upon the scene.

Joseph's answer reveals the power of religious principle. He would not betray the confidence of his master on earth, and, whatever the consequences, he would be true to his Master in heaven. Joseph's first thought was of God. "How can I do this great wickedness, and sin against God?" he said.

Let the young ever remember that wherever they are and whatever they do, they are in the presence of God. No part of our conduct escapes observation. We cannot hide our ways from the Most High. To every deed there is an unseen witness. Every act, every word, every thought is as distinctly marked as though there were only one person in the whole world.

Joseph suffered for his integrity. His tempter revenged herself by causing him to be thrust into prison. Had Potiphar believed his wife's charge against Joseph, the young Hebrew would have lost his life; but the modesty and uprightness that had characterized his conduct were proof of his innocence. Yet to save the reputation of his master's house, he was abandoned to disgrace and bondage.

At first Joseph was treated with great severity by his

jailers. The psalmist says, "His feet they hurt with fetters; he was laid in chains of iron: until the time that his word came to pass; the word of the Lord tried him." Psalm 105:18, 19.

Joseph in Prison

But Joseph's real character shone even in the dungeon. His years of faithful service had been most cruelly repaid, yet this did not render him morose or distrustful. He had peace and trusted his case with God. He did not brood upon his own wrongs, but forgot his sorrow in trying to lighten the sorrows of others. He found a work to do, even in the prison. God was preparing him in the school of affliction for greater usefulness, and he did not refuse the needful discipline. He learned lessons of justice, sympathy, and mercy that prepared him to exercise power with wisdom and compassion.

Joseph gradually gained the confidence of the keeper of the prison and was finally entrusted with the charge of all the prisoners. The part he acted in the prison— the integrity of his daily life and his sympathy for those in trouble and distress—opened the way for his future prosperity and honor. Every kind word spoken to the sorrowful, every act to relieve the oppressed, and every gift to the needy, if prompted by a right motive, will result in blessings to the giver.

The chief baker and chief butler of the king had been cast into prison for some offense, and they came under Joseph's charge. One morning, observing that they appeared very sad, he kindly inquired the cause and was told that each had had a remarkable dream, of which they were anxious to learn the significance. "Do not interpretations belong to God?" said Joseph, "tell me them, I pray you."

As each related his dream, Joseph made known its import. In three days the butler was to be reinstated in his position and give the cup into Pharaoh's hand as before; but the chief baker would be put to death by the king's command. Both events occurred as foretold.

The king's cupbearer had professed deep gratitude to Joseph for the cheering interpretation of his dream and for many acts of kind attention. In return Joseph, referring to his own unjust captivity, entreated that his case be brought before the king. "Think on me," he said, "when it shall be well with thee, and show kindness, I pray thee, unto me, and make mention of me unto Pharaoh, and bring me out of this house: for indeed I was stolen away out of the land of the Hebrews; and here also have I done nothing that they should put me into the dungeon."

The chief butler saw the dream fulfilled in every particular; but when restored to royal favor, he thought no more of his benefactor. For two years longer, Joseph remained a prisoner. The hope that had been kindled in his heart gradually died out, and to all other trials was added the bitter sting of ingratitude.

But a divine hand was about to open the prison gates. The king of Egypt had in one night two dreams, apparently pointing to the same event and seeming to foreshadow some great calamity. The magicians and wise men could give no interpretation. The king's perplexity increased, and terror spread throughout his palace. The general agitation recalled to the chief butler his own dream; with it came the memory of Joseph and remorse for his forgetfulness and ingratitude. He at once informed the king how his own dream and that of the chief baker had been interpreted by a Hebrew captive and how the prediction had been fulfilled.

It was humiliating to Pharaoh to consult a slave, but he was ready if his troubled mind might find relief. Joseph was immediately sent for; he put off his prison attire and was conducted to the king.

"And Pharaoh said unto Joseph, I have dreamed a dream, and there is none that can interpret it; and I have heard say of thee, that thou canst understand a dream to interpret it. And Joseph answered Pharaoh, saying, It is not in me: God shall give Pharaoh an answer of peace.'' Joseph modestly disclaimed the honor of possessing in himself superior wisdom. God alone can explain these mysteries.

Pharaoh then proceeded to relate his dreams: ''Behold, there came up out of the river seven kine, fat-fleshed and well favored; and they fed in a meadow: and, behold, seven other kine came up after them, poor and very ill favored and leanfleshed, such as I never saw in all the land of Egypt for badness: and the lean and the ill favored kine did eat up the first seven fat kine: and when they had eaten them up, it could not be known that they had eaten them; but they were still ill favored, as at the beginning. So I awoke. And I saw in my dream, and, behold, seven ears came up in one stalk, full and good: and, behold, seven ears, withered, thin, and blasted with the east wind, sprung up after them: and the thin ears devoured the seven good ears: and I told this unto the magicians; but there was none that could declare it to me.''

The Interpretation of Pharaoh's Dream

Said Joseph, ''God hath showed Pharaoh what He is about to do.'' There were to be seven years of great plenty. Field and garden would yield more abundantly than ever before. And this period was to be followed by seven years of famine. ''And the plenty shall not be known in the land by reason of that famine following; for it shall be very grievous.'' ''Now therefore,'' he continued, ''let Pharaoh look out a man discreet and wise, and set him over the land of Egypt. Let Pharaoh do this, and let him appoint officers over the land, and take up the fifth part of the land of Egypt in the seven plenteous years. And let them gather all the food of those good years that come, and lay up corn under the hand of Pharaoh, and let them keep food in the cities. And that food shall be for store to the land against the seven years of famine.''

The interpretation was reasonable and consistent. The policy it recommended was sound and shrewd.

But who was to be entrusted with the execution of the plan? Upon the wisdom of this choice depended the nation's preservation.

For some time the matter of the appointment was under consideration. Through the chief butler the monarch had learned of the wisdom and prudence displayed by Joseph in the management of the prison. It was evident that he possessed administrative ability in a pre-eminent degree. In all the realm, Joseph was the only man gifted with wisdom to point out the danger that threatened the kingdom and the preparation necessary to meet it. There were none among the king's officers of state so well qualified to conduct the affairs of the nation at this crisis. "Can we find such a one as this, a man in whom the Spirit of God is?" said the king to his counselors.

From Prisoner to Prime Minister

To Joseph the astonishing announcement was made, "Forasmuch as God hath showed thee all this, there is none so discreet and wise as thou art: thou shalt be over my house, and according unto thy word shall all my people be ruled: only in the throne will I be greater than thou." "And Pharaoh took off his ring from his hand, and put it upon Joseph's hand, and arrayed him in vestures of fine linen, and put a gold chain about his neck; and he made him to ride in the second chariot which he had; and they cried before him, Bow the knee."

From the dungeon, Joseph was exalted to be ruler over all the land of Egypt, a position of high honor, yet beset with peril. One cannot stand upon a lofty height without danger. The tempest leaves unharmed the lowly flower of the valley, while it uproots the stately tree upon the mountaintop. So those who have maintained their integrity in humble life may be dragged down by the temptations that assail worldly success and honor. But Joseph's character bore the test alike of adversity and prosperity. He was a stranger in a heathen land, separated from his kindred, but he fully believed that the divine hand had directed his steps. In constant reliance upon God he faithfully discharged the duties of his position. The attention of the king and great men of Egypt was directed to the true God, and they learned to respect the principles revealed in the worshiper of Jehovah.

In his early years Joseph had consulted duty rather than inclination; and the integrity, the simple trust, the noble nature of the youth bore fruit in the deeds of the man.

The varied circumstances that we meet day by day are designed to test our faithfulness and qualify us for greater trusts. By adherence to principle the mind becomes accustomed to hold the claims of duty above pleasure and inclination. Minds thus disciplined are not wavering between right and wrong like the reed trembling in the wind. By faithfulness in that which is least, they acquire strength to be faithful in greater matters.

An upright character is of greater worth than the gold of Ophir. Without it none can rise to an honorable eminence. The formation of a noble character is the work of a lifetime. God gives opportunities; success depends upon the use made of them.

21 / Joseph and His Brothers

Under the direction of Joseph, immense storehouses were erected throughout the land of Egypt for preserving the surplus of the expected harvest. During the seven years of plenty the amount of grain laid in store was beyond computation.

And now the seven years of dearth began, according to Joseph's prediction. "And the dearth was in all lands; but in all the land of Egypt there was bread. And when all the land of Egypt was famished, the people cried to Pharaoh for bread: and Pharaoh said unto all the Egyptians, Go unto Joseph; what he saith to you, do. And the famine was over all the face of the earth: and Joseph opened all the storehouses, and sold unto the Egyptians."

The famine was severely felt in the country where Jacob dwelt. Hearing of the abundant provision made by the king of Egypt, ten of Jacob's sons journeyed thither to purchase grain. They were directed to the king's deputy and came to present themselves before the ruler of the land. And they "bowed down themselves before him with their faces to the earth." "Joseph knew his brethren, but they knew not him." His Hebrew name had been changed, and there was little resemblance between the prime minister of Egypt and the stripling they had sold to the Ishmaelites. As Joseph saw his brothers stooping and making obeisance, his dreams and the scenes of the past rose vividly before him. His keen eye discovered that Benjamin was not among them. Had he also fallen victim to treacher-

This chapter is based on Genesis 41:54-56; 42 to 50.

149

ous cruelty? He determined to learn the truth. "Ye are spies," he said sternly; "to see the nakedness of the land ye are come."

They answered, "Nay, my lord, but to buy food are thy servants come. . . . We are true men; thy servants are no spies." He wished to draw from them some information in regard to their home; yet he knew how deceptive their statements might be. He repeated the charge, and they replied, "Thy servants are twelve brethren, the sons of one man in the land of Canaan; and, behold, the youngest is this day with our father, and one is not."

Professing to doubt their story, the governor declared that he would require them to remain in Egypt till one of their number should go and bring their youngest brother. If they would not consent, they were to be treated as spies. But to such an arrangement the sons of Jacob could not agree, since the time required would cause their families to suffer for food; and who among them would undertake the journey alone, leaving his brothers in prison? It appeared probable that they were to be put to death or made slaves; and if Benjamin were brought, it might be only to share their fate. They decided to remain and suffer together rather than bring additional sorrow upon their father by the loss of his only remaining son. They were accordingly cast into prison.

Wicked Men Had Learned Repentance

These sons of Jacob had changed in character. Envious, turbulent, deceptive, cruel, and revengeful they had been; but now, tested by adversity, they were unselfish, true to one another, devoted to their father, and, themselves middle-aged men, subject to his authority.

Three days in the Egyptian prison were days of bitter sorrow as the brothers reflected upon their past sins. Unless Benjamin could be produced, their conviction as spies appeared certain.

On the third day, Joseph caused the brothers to be brought before him. He dared not detain them longer. Already his father and the families with him might be suffering for food. "This do, and live," he said; "for I fear God: if ye be true men, let one of your brethren be bound in the house of your prison: go ye, carry corn for the famine of your houses: but bring your youngest brother unto me; so shall your words be verified, and ye shall not die."

Joseph had communicated with them through an interpreter. Having no thought that the governor understood them, they conversed freely with one another in his presence. "We are verily guilty concerning our brother, in that we saw the anguish of his soul, when he besought us, and we would not hear; therefore is this distress come upon us." Reuben, who had formed the plan delivering Joseph at Dothan, added "Spake I not unto you, saying, Do not sin against the child; and ye would not hear? therefore, behold, also his blood is required."

Joseph, listening, could not control his emotions, and he went out and wept. On his return, he commanded that Simeon be bound before them and again committed to prison. In the cruel treatment of their brother, Simeon had been the instigator and chief actor.

Before permitting his brothers to depart, Joseph gave directions that they should be supplied with grain and that each man's money should be secretly placed in the mouth of his sack. On the way, one of the company, opening his sack, was surprised to find his bag of silver. The others were alarmed and said, "What is this that God hath done unto us?"

Jacob was anxiously awaiting the return of his sons, and on their arrival the whole encampment gathered eagerly around as they related to their father all that had occurred. Apprehension filled every heart. The conduct of the Egyptian governor seemed to imply some evil design, and their fears were confirmed when, as they opened their sacks, the owner's money was found in each. In his distress the aged father exclaimed, "Me have ye bereaved of my children: Joseph is not, and Simeon is not, and ye will take Benjamin away: all these things are against me." "My son shall not go down with you; for his brother is dead, and he is left alone: if mischief befall him by the way in the which ye go, then shall ye bring down my gray hairs with sorrow to the grave."

But the drought continued, and the supply of grain from Egypt was nearly exhausted. Deeper and deeper grew the shadow of approaching famine. In the anxious faces of all in the encampment, the old man read their need. At last he said, "Go again, buy us a little food."

Judah answered, "The man did solemnly protest unto us, saying, Ye shall not see my face, except your brother be with you. If thou wilt send our brother with us, we will go down and buy thee food; but if thou wilt not send him, we will not go down; for the man said unto us, Ye shall not see my face, except your brother be with you." Seeing that his father's resolution began to waver, he said, "Send the lad with me, and we will arise and go; that we may live, and not die, both we, and thou, and also our little ones." He offered to be surety for his brother and to bear the blame forever if he failed to restore Benjamin to his father.

Jacob could no longer withhold his consent. He bade his sons take to the ruler a present of such things as the famine-wasted country afforded—"a little balm, and a little honey, spices and myrrh, nuts and almonds," also a double quantity of money. "Take also your brother," he said, "and arise, go again unto the man." As his sons were about to depart on their doubtful journey, the aged father arose, and raising his hands to heaven, uttered the prayer, "God Almighty give you mercy before the man, that he may send away your other brother, and Benjamin."

Again they journeyed to Egypt and presented themselves before Joseph. As his eye fell upon Benjamin, his own mother's son, he was deeply moved. He concealed his emotion but ordered that they be taken to his house to dine with him. The brothers were greatly alarmed, fearing to be called to account for the money found in their sacks. They thought that it might have been placed there to furnish occasion for making them slaves. In proof of their innocence they informed the steward of the house that they had brought back the money found in their sacks, also other money to buy food; and they added, "We cannot tell who put our money in our sacks." The man replied, "Peace be to you, fear not: your God, and the God of your father, hath given you treasure in your sacks: I had your money." Their anxiety was relieved; and when Simeon, released from prison, joined them, they felt that God was indeed gracious to them.

Joseph's Dreams Again Fulfilled

When the governor again met them, they presented their gifts and humbly "bowed themselves to him to the earth." Again his dreams came to his mind, and he hastened to ask, "Is your father well, the old man of whom ye spake? Is he yet alive?" "Thy servant our father is in good health, he is yet alive," was the answer, as they again made obeisance. Then his eye rested upon Benjamin, and he said, "Is this your younger brother, of whom ye spake unto me?" "God be gracious unto thee, my son," but overpowered by feelings of tenderness, he could say no more. "He entered into his chamber, and wept there."

Having recovered his self-possession, he returned. By the laws of caste, the Egyptians were forbidden to eat with people of any other nation. The sons of Jacob had therefore a table by themselves, while the governor, on account of his high rank, ate by himself. The Egyptians also had separate tables. When all were seated, the brothers were surprised to see that they were arranged in exact order, according to their ages. Joseph "sent messes unto them from before him," but

Benjamin's was five times as much as any of theirs. He hoped to ascertain if the youngest brother was regarded with the envy and hatred that had been manifested toward himself. Still supposing that Joseph did not understand their language, the brothers freely conversed with one another; thus he had good opportunity to learn their real feelings. Still he desired to test them further. Before their departure he ordered that his own drinking cup of silver be concealed in the sack of the youngest.

Final Test of Their Repentance

Joyfully they set out on their return. Simeon and Benjamin were with them, their animals were laden with grain, and all felt that they had safely escaped the perils that had seemed to surround them. But they had only reached the outskirts of the city when they were overtaken by the governor's steward, who uttered the scathing inquiry, "Wherefore have ye rewarded evil for good? Is not this it in which my lord drinketh, and whereby indeed he divineth? Ye have done evil in so doing." This cup was supposed to possess the power of detecting any poisonous substance placed therein. Cups of this kind were highly valued as a safeguard against murder by poisoning.

To the steward's accusation the travelers answered, "Wherefore saith my lord these words? God forbid that thy servants should do according to this thing: behold, the money, which we found in our sacks' mouths, we brought again unto thee out of the land of Canaan: how then should we steal out of thy lord's house silver or gold? With whomsoever of thy servants it be found, both let him die, and we also will be my lord's bondmen."

"Let it be according to your words," said the steward; "he with whom it is found shall be my servant; and ye shall be blameless."

The search began immediately. "They speedily took down every man his sack to the ground," and the steward examined each, beginning with Reuben's, and taking them in order down to that of the youngest. In Benjamin's sack the cup was found.

The brothers rent their garments in utter wretchedness and slowly returned to the city. By their own promise, Benjamin was doomed to slavery. They followed the steward to the palace, and finding the governor yet there, prostrated themselves before him.

"What deed is this that ye have done?" he said. "Wot ye not that such a man as I can certainly divine?" Joseph designed to draw from them an acknowledgment of their sin.

Judah answered, "What shall we say unto my lord? what shall we speak? or how shall we clear ourselves? God hath found out the iniquity of thy servants: behold, we are my lord's servants, both we, and he also with whom the cup is found."

"God forbid that I should do so," was the reply, "but the man in whose hand the cup is found, he shall be my servant; and as for you, get you up in peace unto your father."

Judah's Plea

In his distress, Judah drew near the ruler. Eloquently he described his father's grief at the loss of Joseph and his reluctance to let Benjamin come with them to Egypt, as he was the only son left of his mother, Rachel, whom Jacob so dearly loved. "Now therefore," he said, "when I come to thy servant my father, and the lad be not with us; seeing that his life is bound up in the lad's life; it shall come to pass, when he seeth that the lad is not with us, that he will die: and thy servants shall bring down the gray hairs of thy servant our father with sorrow to the grave. For thy servant became surety for the lad unto my father, saying, If I bring him not unto thee, then I shall bear the blame to my father forever. Now therefore, I pray thee, let thy servant abide instead of the lad a bondman to my lord; and let the lad go up with his brethren. For how shall I go up to my father, and the lad be not with me? lest peradventure I see the evil that shall come on my father."

Joseph was satisfied. He had seen in his brothers the fruits of true repentance. He gave orders that all but these men should withdraw. Then, weeping aloud, he cried, "I am Joseph; doth my father yet live?"

Reconciliation!

His brothers stood motionless, dumb with fear and amazement. The ruler of Egypt their brother Joseph, whom they had envied and would have murdered, and finally sold as a slave! All their ill treatment of him passed before them. They remembered how long they had despised his dreams and had labored to prevent their fulfillment. Yet they had acted their part in fulfilling these dreams. Now that they were completely in his power, he would, no doubt, avenge the wrong that he had suffered.

Seeing their confusion, he said kindly, "Come near to me, I pray you"; and as they came near, he continued, "I am Joseph your brother, whom ye sold into Egypt. Now therefore be not grieved, nor angry with yourselves, that ye sold me hither: for God did send me before you to preserve life." Feeling that they had suffered enough for their cruelty toward him, he nobly sought to banish their fears and lessen the bitterness of their self-reproach.

"God sent me before you to preserve you a posterity in the earth, and to save your lives by a great deliverance. So now it was not you that sent me hither but God: and He hath made me a father to Pharaoh, and lord of all his house, and a ruler throughout all the land of Egypt. Haste ye, and go up to my father, and say unto him, Thus saith thy son Joseph, God hath made me lord of all Egypt: come down unto me, tarry not: and thou shalt dwell in the land of Goshen. . . ; for yet there are five years of famine; lest thou, and thy household, and all that thou hast, come to poverty." "And he fell upon his brother Benjamin's neck, and wept;

and Benjamin wept upon his neck. Moreover he kissed all his brethren, and wept upon them; and after that his brethren talked with him." They humbly confessed their sin and entreated his forgiveness.

The news of what had taken place was quickly carried to the king. He confirmed the governor's invitation to his family, saying, "The good of all the land of Egypt is yours." The brothers were sent away abundantly supplied with provision and everything necessary for the removal of all their families and attendants to Egypt.

The sons of Jacob returned to their father with the joyful tidings. "Joseph is yet alive, and he is governor over all the land of Egypt." At first the aged man was overwhelmed; he could not believe what he heard; but when he saw the long train of wagons and loaded animals, and when Benjamin was with him once more, he was convinced. In the fullness of his joy he exclaimed, "It is enough; Joseph my son is yet alive: I will go and see him before I die."

Another act of humiliation remained for the ten brothers. They now confessed to their father the deceit and cruelty that for so many years had embittered his life and theirs. Jacob had not suspected them of so base a sin, but he forgave and blessed his erring children.

The father and his sons, with their families, their flocks and herds, and numerous attendants, were soon on the way to Egypt. In a vision of the night the divine word came: "Fear not to go down into Egypt; for I will there make of thee a great nation: I will go down with thee into Egypt; and I will also surely bring thee up again."

The promise had been given to Abraham of a posterity numberless as the stars; but as yet the chosen people had increased but slowly. And the land of Canaan was in the possession of powerful heathen tribes that were not to be dispossessed until "the fourth generation." If the descendants of Israel were to become a numerous people, they must either drive out the inhabitants of the land or disperse themselves among them. Should they mingle with the Canaanites, they would be in danger of being seduced into idolatry. Egypt, however, offered the conditions necessary to the divine purpose. A section of country, well-watered and fertile, was open to them there, affording every advantage for their speedy increase. And they would remain a distinct and separate people, shut out from participation in the idolatry of Egypt.

Upon reaching Egypt, the company proceeded directly to the land of Goshen. Thither came Joseph in his chariot of state, attended by a princely retinue. One thought alone filled his mind, one longing thrilled his heart. As he beheld the travelers approaching, the love whose yearnings had for so many years been repressed would no longer be controlled. He sprang from his chariot and hastened to bid his father welcome. "And he fell on his neck, and wept on his neck a good while. And Israel said unto Joseph, Now let me die, since I have seen thy face, because thou art yet alive."

Joseph sought to save his brothers from the temptations to which they would be exposed at a heathen court; therefore he counseled them to tell the monarch frankly their occupation. The sons of Jacob followed this counsel, being careful also to state that they had come to sojourn in the land, not to become permanent dwellers, thus reserving the right to depart if they chose.

Jacob's Sunset Years

Not long after their arrival, Joseph brought his father to be presented to the king. The patriarch was a stranger in royal courts; but amid the sublime scenes of nature he had communed with a mightier Monarch. Now, in conscious superiority, he raised his hands and blessed Pharaoh.

In his first greeting to Joseph, Jacob had spoken as if, with this joyful ending to his long anxiety and sorrow, he was ready to die. But seventeen years were yet to be granted him in the peaceful retirement of Goshen. These years were in happy contrast to those that had preceded them. He saw in his sons evidence of true repentance; he saw his family surrounded by all the conditions needful for the development of a great nation; and his faith grasped the sure promise of their future establishment in Canaan. He himself was surrounded with every token of love and favor that the prime minister of Egypt could bestow.

As Jacob felt death approaching, he sent for Joseph and exacted a solemn oath to lay him beside his fathers in the cave of Machpelah.

Another important matter demanded attention—the sons of Joseph were to be instated among the children of Israel. Joseph, coming for a last interview with his father, brought with him Ephraim and Manasseh. These youths were connected through their mother with the highest order of the Egyptian priesthood; and the position of their father opened to them the avenues to wealth and distinction, should they choose to connect themselves with the Egyptians. It was Joseph's desire, however, that they should unite with their own people. He manifested his faith in the covenant promise, in behalf of his sons renouncing all the honors that the court of Egypt offered, for a place among the despised shepherd tribes, to whom had been entrusted the oracles of God.

Said Jacob, "Thy two sons, Ephraim and Manasseh, which were born unto thee in the land of Egypt, before I came unto thee into Egypt, are mine; as Reuben and Simeon, they shall be mine." They were to be adopted as his own and to become the heads of separate tribes.

As they came nearer, the patriarch embraced and kissed them, solemnly laying his hands upon their heads in benediction. Then he uttered the prayer, "God, before whom my fathers Abraham and Isaac did walk, the God which fed me all my life long unto this day, the Angel which redeemed me from all evil, bless the lads." There was no complaint of the evil days in as things against him. Memory recalled only God's mercy and loving-kindness who had been with the patriarch throughout his pilgrimage.

All the sons of Jacob were gathered about his dying bed. And Jacob called unto his sons, and said, "Gather yourselves together, . . . that I may tell you that which shall befall you in the last days."

Jacob Foretells the Future of His Sons

The Spirit of Inspiration rested upon him, and before him in prophetic vision the future of his descendants was unfolded. One after another the names of his sons were mentioned, the character of each was described, and the future history of the tribe was briefly foretold.

Reuben, thou art my firstborn,
My might, and the beginning of my strength,
The excellency of dignity and the excellency of
    power.

But Reuben's grievous sin at Edar had made him unworthy of the birthright blessing. Jacob continued,

Unstable as water.
Thou shalt not excel.

The priesthood was apportioned to Levi, the kingdom and the Messianic promise to Judah, and the double portion of the inheritance to Joseph. The tribe of Reuben never rose to any eminence in Israel; it was not so numerous as Judah, Joseph, or Dan, and was among the first that were carried into captivity.

Next were Simeon and Levi. They had been united in cruelty toward the Shechemites and had been the most guilty in the selling of Joseph.

I will divide them in Jacob,
And scatter them in Israel.

Moses, in his last blessing to Israel before entering Canaan, made no reference to Simeon. In the settlement of Canaan, this tribe had only a small portion of Judah's lot, and such families as afterward became powerful formed different colonies and settled in territory outside the borders of the Holy Land. Levi also

When the governor's cup was found in Benjamin's sack, Judah offered to be held in Egypt in his place.

received no inheritance except forty-eight cities. However their fidelity when the other tribes apostatized secured their appointment to the sacred service of the sanctuary; thus the curse was changed into a blessing.

The crowning blessings of the birthright were transferred to Judah:

> Judah, thou art he whom thy brethren shall
> praise;
> Thy hand shall be in the neck of thine enemies;
> Thy father's children shall bow down before
> thee. . . .
> The scepter shall not depart from Judah,
> Nor a lawgiver from between his feet,
> Until Shiloh come;
> And unto Him shall the gathering of the people be.

The lion, king of the forest, is a fitting symbol of this tribe, from which came David, and the Son of David, Shiloh, the true "Lion of the tribe of Judah," to whom all powers shall finally bow and all nations render homage.

For most of his children, Jacob foretold a prosperous future. At last the name of Joseph was reached, and the father's heart overflowed as he invoked blessings upon "the head of him that was separate from his brethren":

> Joseph is a fruitful bough,
> Even a fruitful bough by a well;
> Whose branches run over the wall.
> The archers have sorely grieved him,
> And shot at him, and hated him;
> But his bow abode in strength,
> And the arms of his hands were made strong
> By the hands of the mighty God of Jacob; . . .
> The blessings of thy father have prevailed
> Above the blessings of my progenitors
> Unto the utmost bound of the everlasting hills:
> They shall be on the head of Joseph,
> And on the crown of the head of him that was separate from his brethren.

Jacob was a man of deep affection; his love for his sons was strong and tender. He had forgiven them all, and he loved them to the last. His paternal tenderness would have found expression only in words of encouragement and hope; but the power of God rested upon him. Under the influence of Inspiration he was constrained to declare the truth, however painful.

Jacob's last years brought an evening of tranquillity and repose after a troubled and weary day. Clouds had gathered dark above his path, yet his sun set clear, and the radiance of heaven illumined his parting hours. Says the Scripture, "At evening time it shall be light." Zechariah 14:7. "Mark the perfect man, and behold the upright: for the end of that man is peace." Psalm 37:37.

Inspiration faithfully records the faults of good men who were distinguished by the favor of God. This has given the infidel occasion to scoff at the Bible. But it is one of the strongest evidences of the truth of Scripture that facts are not glossed over nor the sins of its chief characters suppressed. Had the Bible been written by uninspired persons, it would no doubt have presented the character of its honored men in a more flattering light.

Seeing where others struggled through discouragements like our own, where they fell under temptation as we have done and yet took heart again and conquered through the grace of God, we are encouraged in our striving after righteousness. As they, though sometimes beaten back, recovered their ground and were blessed of God, so we too may be overcomers in the strength of Jesus. On the other hand, the record of their lives may serve as a warning to us. God sees sin in His most favored ones, and He deals with it in them even more strictly than in those who have less light and responsibility.

After the burial of Jacob, fear again filled the hearts of Joseph's brothers. Conscious guilt made them distrustful and suspicious that Joseph would now visit upon them the long-deferred punishment for their crime. They dared not appear before him but sent a message: "Thy father did command before he died, saying, So shall ye say unto Joseph, Forgive, I pray thee now, the trespass of thy brethren, and their sin; for they did unto thee evil: and now, we pray thee, forgive the trespass of the servants of the God of thy father."

This message affected Joseph to tears, and, encouraged by this, his brothers came and fell down before him with the words, "Behold, we be thy servants." Joseph was pained that they could regard him as cherishing a spirit of revenge. "Fear not," he said; "for am I in the place of God? But as for you, ye thought evil against me: but God meant it unto good, to bring to pass, as it is this day, to save much people alive. Now therefore fear ye not: I will nourish you, and your little ones."

Seeing Christ in Joseph

The life of Joseph illustrates the life of Christ. It was envy that moved the brothers of Joseph to sell him as a slave; they hoped to prevent him from becoming greater than themselves. They flattered themselves that they were to be no more troubled with his dreams, that they had removed all possibility of their fulfillment. But their course was overruled by God to bring about the very event they designed to hinder. So the priests and elders were jealous of Christ. They put Him to death to prevent Him from becoming king, but they were thus bringing about this result.

Joseph, through his bondage in Egypt, became a savior to his father's family; yet this fact did not lessen the guilt of his brothers. So the crucifixion of Christ by His enemies made Him the Redeemer of mankind, the Saviour of the fallen race, and Ruler over the whole world; but the crime of His murderers was just as heinous as though God's providential hand had not controlled events.

Joseph was falsely accused and thrust into prison because of his virtue; so Christ was despised and rejected because His righteous, self-denying life was a rebuke to sin; and though guilty of no wrong, He was condemned upon the testimony of false witnesses. And Joseph's patience under injustice, his ready forgiveness and noble benevolence toward his unnatural brothers represent the Saviour's uncomplaining endurance of the malice and abuse of wicked men and His forgiveness of all who come to Him confessing their sins and seeking pardon.

Joseph witnessed the increase and prosperity of his people, and through all the years his faith in God's restoration of Israel to the Land of Promise was unshaken.

When he saw that his end was near, his last act was to signify that his lot was cast with Israel. His last words were, "God will surely visit you, and bring you out of this land unto the land which He sware to Abraham, to Isaac, and to Jacob." "So Joseph died, being an hundred and ten years old; and they embalmed him, and he was put in a coffin in Egypt."

Through the centuries of toil which followed, that coffin testified to Israel that they were only sojourners in Egypt and bade them keep their hopes fixed upon the Land of Promise, for the time of deliverance would surely come.

22 / Moses, the Leader of God's People

On account of the service that Joseph had rendered the Egyptian nation, the children of Jacob were not only granted a part of the country as a home but were exempted from taxation and liberally supplied with food during the famine. The king publicly acknowledged that it was through the God of Joseph that Egypt enjoyed plenty while other nations were perishing from famine. He saw, too, that Joseph's management had greatly enriched the kingdom, and his gratitude surrounded the family of Jacob with royal favor.

But as time rolled on, the great man to whom Egypt owed so much passed to the grave. And "there arose up a new king over Egypt, which knew not Joseph." Not that he was ignorant of Joseph's services to the nation, but he wished to make no recognition of them, and, so far as possible, to bury them in oblivion. "And he said unto his people, Behold, the people of the children of Israel are more and mightier than we: come on, let us deal wisely with them; lest they multiply, and it come to pass, that, when there falleth out any war, they join also unto our enemies, and fight against us, and so get them up out of the land."

The Israelites already "were fruitful, and increased abundantly, and multiplied, and waxed exceeding mighty; and the land was filled with them." But they had kept themselves a distinct race, having nothing in common with the Egyptians in customs or religion; and their increasing numbers now excited the fears of the king and his people.

This chapter is based on Exodus 1 to 4.

Many of them were able and understanding workmen, and they added greatly to the wealth of the nation. The king needed such laborers for the erection of his magnificent palaces and temples. Accordingly he ranked them with the Egyptians who had sold themselves with their possessions to the kingdom. Soon taskmasters were set over them, and their slavery became complete. "The Egyptians made the children of Israel to serve with rigor: and they made their lives bitter with hard bondage, in mortar, and in brick, and in all manner of service in the field." "But the more they afflicted them, the more they multiplied and grew."

The king and his counselors had hoped to subdue the Israelites with hard labor, decrease their numbers, and crush out their independent spirit. Orders were now issued to the women whose employment gave them opportunity to destroy the Hebrew male children at their birth. Satan knew that a deliverer was to be raised up among the Israelites, and by leading the king to destroy their children he hoped to defeat the divine purpose. But the women feared God and dared not execute the cruel mandate.

The king, angry at the failure of his design, made the command more urgent and extensive. "Pharaoh charged all his people, saying, Every son that is born ye shall cast into the river, and every daughter ye shall save alive."

Moses Born in the Worst of Times

While this decree was in full force, a son was born to Amram and Jochebed, Israelites of the tribe of Levi. The parents, believing that the time of Israel's release was drawing near and that God would raise up a deliverer for His people, determined that their little one should not be sacrificed. Faith in God strengthened their hearts, "and they were not afraid of the king's commandment." Hebrews 11:23.

The mother concealed the child for three months. Then, finding that she could no longer keep him safely, she prepared a little ark of rushes, making it watertight by means of slime and pitch; and, laying the babe therein, she placed it among the flags at the river's brink. His sister Miriam lingered near, anxiously watching to see what would become of her little brother.

And there were other watchers. The mother had committed her child to the care of God; and angels, unseen, hovered above his lowly resting place. Angels directed Pharaoh's daughter thither. Her curiosity was excited by the little basket, and as she looked upon the beautiful child within, the tears of the babe awakened her compassion; her sympathies went out to the unknown mother who had resorted to this means to preserve her precious little one. She determined that he should be saved; she would adopt him as her own.

Miriam, perceiving that the child was tenderly regarded, ventured nearer, and at last said, "Shall I go and call to thee a nurse of the Hebrew women, that she may nurse the child for thee?" Permission was given.

The sister hastened to her mother with the happy news and without delay returned with her to the presence of Pharaoh's daughter. "Take this child away, and nurse it for me, and I will give thee thy wages," said the princess.

Twelve Short Years

God had heard the mother's prayer. With deep gratitude she entered upon her now safe and happy task, to educate her child for God. She knew that he must soon be given up to his royal mother, to be surrounded with influences that would tend to lead him away from God. She endeavored to imbue his mind with the fear of God and the love of truth and justice. She showed him the folly and sin of idolatry and early taught him to bow down and pray to the living God, who alone could hear him and help him in every emergency.

She kept the boy as long as she could but was obliged to give him up when he was about twelve years old. From his humble cabin home he was taken to the royal palace, to the daughter of Pharaoh, "and he became her son." Yet even here the lessons learned at his mother's side could not be forgotten. They were a shield from the pride, the infidelity, and the vice that flourished amid the splendor of the court.

The whole future life of Moses, the great mission which he fulfilled as the leader of Israel, testifies to the importance of the work of the mother. There is no other work that can equal this. The mother is dealing with developing minds and characters, working not alone for time, but for eternity. She is sowing seed that will spring up and bear fruit, either for good or for evil. She has not to paint a form of beauty upon canvas or to chisel it from marble, but to impress upon a human soul the image of the divine. The impressions made upon developing minds will remain all through life. Children are placed in our care to be trained, not as heirs to the throne of an earthly empire, but as kings unto God, to reign through unending ages.

In the solemn day of accounts it will be found that many crimes have resulted from the ignorance and neglect of those whose duty it was to guide childish feet in the right way. Then it will be found that many who have blessed the world with the light of genius and truth and holiness owe their success to a praying mother.

At the court of Pharaoh, Moses received the highest civil and military training. The monarch determined to make his adopted grandson his successor on the throne, and the youth was educated for his high station. "And Moses was learned in all the wisdom of the Egyptians, and was mighty in words and in deeds." Acts 7:22. His ability as a military leader made him a favorite with the armies of Egypt, and he was generally regarded as a remarkable character. Satan had been defeated in his purpose. The very decree condemning the Hebrew children to death had been overruled by God for the training of the future leader of His people.

The elders of Israel were taught by angels that the time for their deliverance was near and that Moses was the man whom God would employ. Angels instructed Moses also that Jehovah had chosen him to break the bondage of His people. He, supposing they were to obtain their freedom by arms, expected to lead the Hebrew host against the armies of Egypt.

How Young Moses Was Tested

By the laws of Egypt, all who occupied the throne of the Pharaohs must become members of the priestly caste. Moses, as the heir apparent, was to be initiated into the mysteries of the national religion. But he could not be induced to participate in the worship of the gods. He was threatened with the loss of the crown and warned that he would be disowned by the princess should he persist in the Hebrew faith. But he was unshaken in his determination to render homage to none save the one God, the Maker of heaven and earth. He reasoned with priests and worshipers, showing the folly of their superstitious veneration of senseless objects. For the time his firmness was tolerated on account of his high position and the favor with which he was regarded by both the king and the people.

"By faith Moses, when he was come to years, refused to be called the son of Pharaoh's daughter; choosing rather to suffer affliction with the people of God, than to enjoy the pleasures of sin for a season; esteeming the reproach of Christ greater riches than the treasures in Egypt: for he had respect unto the recompense of the reward." Hebrews 11:24-26. Moses was fitted to take pre-eminence among the great of the earth, to shine in the courts of its most glorious kingdom, and to sway the scepter of its power. As historian, poet, philosopher, general of armies, and legislator, he stands without a peer. Yet with the world before him, he had the moral strength to refuse wealth, greatness, and fame, "choosing rather to suffer affliction with the people of God."

The magnificent palace of Pharaoh and the throne were held out as an inducement to Moses; but he knew that the sinful pleasures that make men forget God were in its lordly courts. He looked beyond the palace, beyond a monarch's crown, to the high honors that will be bestowed on the saints of the Most High in a kingdom untainted by sin. He saw by faith an imperishable crown that the King of heaven would place on the brow of the overcomer. This faith led him to join the humble, poor, despised nation that had chosen to obey God rather than to serve sin.

Moses remained at court until he was forty. He visited his brethren in their servitude and encouraged them with the assurance that God would work for their deliverance. One day, seeing an Egyptian smiting an Israelite, he sprang forward and slew the Egyptian. Except the Israelite, there had been no witness to the deed, and Moses immediately buried the body in the sand. He had now shown himself ready to maintain the cause of his people, and he hoped to see them rise to recover their liberty. "He supposed his brethren would have understood how that God by his hand would deliver them: but they understood not." Acts 7:25. They were not yet prepared for freedom.

On the following day Moses saw two Hebrews striving together, one of them evidently at fault. Moses reproved the offender, who at once retaliated upon the reprover, denying his right to interfere and basely accusing him of crime: "Who made thee a prince and a judge over us?" he said. "Intendest thou to kill me, as thou killedst the Egyptian?"

The whole matter soon reached the ears of Pharaoh. It was represented to the king that this act meant much, that Moses designed to lead his people against the Egyptians, to overthrow the government, and to seat himself upon the throne. It was at once determined by the monarch that he should die, but becoming aware of his danger, Moses fled toward Arabia.

The Lord directed his course, and he found a home

with Jethro, the priest and prince of Midian, who was a worshiper of God. After a time Moses married one of the daughters of Jethro; and here, as keeper of his flocks, he remained forty years.

It was not God's will to deliver His people by warfare, as Moses thought, but by His own mighty power, that the glory might be ascribed to Him alone. Moses was not prepared for his great work. He had yet to learn the same lesson of faith that Abraham and Jacob had been taught—not to rely upon human strength or wisdom but upon the power of God for the fulfillment of His promises. In the school of self-denial and hardship he was to learn patience, to temper his passions. His own heart must be fully in harmony with God before he could teach the knowledge of His will to Israel and exercise a fatherly care over all who needed his help.

Doing God's Work the Wrong Way

Moses had been learning much that he must unlearn. The influences that had surrounded him in Egypt had left deep impressions upon his developing mind and had molded to some extent his habits and character. Time could remove these impressions. It would require on the part of Moses himself a struggle as for life to renounce error and accept truth, but God would be his helper when the conflict should be too severe for human strength.

"If any of you lack wisdom, let him ask of God, that giveth to all men liberally, and upbraideth not; and it shall be given him." James 1:5. But God will not impart to men divine light while they are content to remain in darkness. In order to receive God's help, man must realize his weakness and deficiency; he must apply his own mind to the great change to be wrought in himself; he must be aroused to earnest and persevering prayer and effort.

Shut in by the bulwarks of the mountains, Moses was alone with God. In the solemn grandeur of the everlasting hills he beheld the majesty of the Most High, and in contrast realized how powerless were the gods of Egypt. Here his pride and self-sufficiency were swept away. The results of the luxury of Egypt disappeared. Moses became patient, reverent, and humble, "very meek, above all the men which were upon the face of the earth" (Numbers 12:3), yet strong in faith.

As the years rolled on, his prayers for Israel ascended by day and by night. Here, under the inspiration of the Holy Spirit, he wrote the book of Genesis. The long years spent amid the desert solitudes were rich in blessing to the world in all ages.

The Time for Freedom Comes!

"In process of time . . . the king of Egypt died: and the children of Israel sighed by reason of the bondage, and they cried, and their cry came up unto God. . . . And God looked upon the children of Israel, and God had respect unto them." The time for deliverance had come.

God's purpose was to be accomplished in a manner to pour contempt on human pride. The deliverer was to go forth as a humble shepherd, with only a rod in his hand, but God would make that rod the symbol of His power.

Leading his flocks one day near Horeb, "the mountain of God," Moses saw a bush in flames, yet not consumed. He drew near when a voice from out of the flame called him by name. With trembling lips he answered, "Here am I." He was warned not to approach irreverently: "Put off thy shoes from off thy feet, for the place whereon thou standest is holy ground. . . . I am the God of thy father, the God of Abraham, the God of Isaac, and the God of Jacob. And Moses hid his face; for he was afraid to look upon God."

As Moses waited in awe before God, the words continued: "I have surely seen the affliction of My people which are in Egypt, and have heard their cry by reason of their taskmasters; for I know their sorrows; and I am come down to deliver them out of the hand of the Egyptians, and to bring them up out of the land unto a good land and a large, unto a land flowing with milk and honey. . . . Come now therefore, and I will send thee unto Pharaoh, that thou mayest bring forth My people the children of Israel out of Egypt.''

Amazed and terrified, Moses drew back, saying, ''Who am I, that I should go unto Pharaoh, and that I should bring forth the children of Israel out of Egypt?''

Moses thought of the blindness, ignorance, and unbelief of his people. Many were almost destitute of a knowledge of God. ''Behold,'' he said, ''when I . . . shall say unto them, The God of your fathers hath sent me unto you; and they shall say to me, What is His name? what shall I say unto them?'' The answer was, ''I AM THAT I AM: . . . I AM hath sent me unto you.''

Moses was commanded first to assemble the elders of Israel, who had long grieved because of their bondage, and to declare to them a message from God. Then he was to go before the king, and say: ''The Lord God of the Hebrews hath met with us: and now let us go, we beseech thee, three days' journey into the wilderness, that we may sacrifice to the Lord our God.''

Moses was forewarned that Pharaoh would resist the appeal. Yet the courage of God's servant must not fail. The Lord would manifest His power. ''And I will stretch out My hand, and smite Egypt with all My wonders which I will do in the midst thereof: and after that he will let you go.''

The Lord declared, ''It shall come to pass, that, when ye go, ye shall not go empty: but every woman shall borrow of her neighbor, and of her that sojourneth in her house, jewels of silver, and jewels of gold, and raiment.'' The Egyptians had been enriched by the labor unjustly exacted from the Israelites, and it was right for the latter to claim the reward of their years of toil. God would give them favor in the sight of the Egyptians. The requests of the bondmen would be granted.

What proof could Moses give his people that God had indeed sent him? "Behold," he said, "they will not believe me, nor hearken unto my voice: for they will say, The Lord hath not appeared unto thee." He was told to cast his rod upon the ground. As he did so, "it became a serpent; and Moses fled from before it." He was commanded to seize it, and in his hand it became a rod. He was bidden to put his hand into his bosom. He obeyed, and "when he took it out, behold, his hand was leprous as snow." Being told to put it again into his bosom, he found on withdrawing it that it had become like the other. By these signs his own people, as well as Pharaoh, would be convinced that One mightier than the king of Egypt was manifest among them.

Moses Is Reluctant

But in his distress and fear the servant of God now pleaded as an excuse a lack of ready speech: "O my Lord, I am not eloquent. . . . I am slow of speech, and of a slow tongue." He had been so long away from the Egyptians that he had not so ready use of their language as when he was among them.

Moses entreated that a more competent person be selected. But after the Lord had promised to remove all difficulties and give him final success, any further complaining of his unfitness showed distrust of God. It implied a fear that God was unable to qualify him or that He had made a mistake in the selection of the man.

Aaron, his elder brother, having been in daily use of the language of the Egyptians, was able to speak it perfectly. He was told that Aaron was coming to meet him. The next words from the Lord were an unqualified command.

"Thou shalt speak unto him, and put words in his mouth. . . . And he shall be thy spokesman unto the people: and he shall be, even he shall be to thee instead of a mouth, and thou shalt be to him instead of God. And thou shalt take this rod in thine hand, wherewith thou shalt do signs.'' He could make no further resistance, for all ground for excuse was removed.

Having once accepted the work, Moses entered upon it with his whole heart, putting all his trust in the Lord. God blessed his ready obedience, and he became eloquent, hopeful, self-possessed, and well fitted for the greatest work ever given to man.

A man will gain power and efficiency as he accepts the responsibilities that God places upon him. However humble his position or limited his ability, that man will attain true greatness who seeks to perform his work with fidelity. The fact that a man feels his weakness is at least some evidence that he realizes the magnitude of the work appointed him; he will make God his counselor and his strength.

A secret dread of Pharaoh and the Egyptians, whose anger had been kindled against him forty years before, had rendered Moses reluctant to return to Egypt; but after he had set out to obey the divine command, the Lord revealed to him that his enemies were dead.

On the way from Midian, an angel appeared to Moses in a threatening manner, as if he would destroy him. No explanation was given; but Moses remembered that he had disregarded one of God's requirements. He had neglected to perform the rite of circumcision upon their youngest son. Such a neglect on the part of Israel's chosen leader could not but lessen the force of the divine precepts upon the people. Zipporah, fearing that her husband would be slain, performed the rite herself, and the angel then permitted Moses to pursue his journey. His life could be preserved only through the protection of holy angels. But while living in neglect of a known duty, he would not be secure; for he could not be shielded by the angels of God.

In the time of trouble just before the coming of Christ, the righteous will be preserved through the ministrations of angels, but there will be no security for the transgressor of God's law. Angels cannot protect those who are disregarding one of the divine precepts.

23 / The Ten Plagues of Egypt

Aaron, being instructed by angels, went forth to meet his brother amid the desert solitudes near Horeb. Here Moses told Aaron "all the words of the Lord who had sent him, and all the signs which He had commanded him." Exodus 4:28. Together they journeyed to Egypt, to assemble the elders of Israel. "The people believed: and when they heard that the Lord had visited the children of Israel, and that He had looked upon their affliction, then they bowed their heads and worshiped." Exodus 4:31.

With a message for the king, the two brothers entered the palace of the Pharaohs as ambassadors from the King of kings: "Thus saith Jehovah, God of Israel, Let My people go, that they may hold a feast unto Me in the wilderness."

"Who is the Lord, that I should obey His voice to let Israel go?" demanded the monarch; "I know not the Lord, neither will I let Israel go."

Their answer was, "The God of the Hebrews hath met with us: let us go, we pray thee, three days' journey into the desert, and sacrifice unto the Lord our God; lest He fall upon us with pestilence, or with the sword."

The king's anger was kindled. "Wherefore do ye, Moses and Aaron, let [hinder] the people from their works?" he said. "Get you unto your burdens." Already the kingdom had suffered loss by the interference of these strangers. At thought of this he added,

This chapter is based on Exodus 5 to 10.

176

"Behold, the people of the land now are many, and ye make them rest from their burdens."

In their bondage the Israelites had to some extent lost the knowledge of God's law, and the Sabbath had been generally disregarded. The exactions of their taskmasters made its observance apparently impossible. But Moses had shown his people that obedience to God was the condition of deliverance; and the efforts made to restore the observance of the Sabbath had come to the notice of their oppressors. (See Appendix, Note 1.)

The king, thoroughly roused, suspected the Israelites of a design to revolt from his service. He would see that no time was left them for dangerous scheming. And he at once adopted measures to tighten their bonds and crush their independent spirit. The most common building material was sun-dried brick; and the manufacture of brick employed great numbers of the bondmen. Cut straw being intermixed with the clay to hold it together, large quantities were required. The king now directed that no more straw be furnished; the laborers must find it for themselves, while the same amount of brick should be exacted.

The Egyptian taskmasters appointed Hebrew officers to oversee the work. When the requirement of the king was put in force, the people scattered to gather stubble instead of straw; but they found it impossible to accomplish the usual amount of labor. For this failure the Hebrew officers were cruelly beaten.

These officers went to the king with their grievances. Their remonstrance was met by Pharaoh with a taunt: "Ye are idle, ye are idle: therefore ye say, Let us go and do sacrifice to the Lord." They were ordered back to their work; their burdens were in no case to be lightened. Returning, they met Moses and Aaron, and cried out to them, "The Lord look upon you, and judge; because ye have made our savour to be abhorred in the eyes of Pharaoh, and in the eyes of his servants, to put a sword in their hand to slay us."

Moses was distressed. The sufferings of the people had been increased. All over the land a cry of despair went up from old and young. All united in charging upon him the disastrous change in their condition. In bitterness of soul he went before God. "Lord, wherefore hast Thou so evil entreated this people? Why is it that Thou hast sent me? For since I came to Pharaoh to speak in Thy name, he hath done evil to this people; neither hast Thou delivered Thy people at all."

The answer was, "Now shalt thou see what I will do to Pharaoh: for with a strong hand shall he let them go, and with a strong hand shall he drive them out of his land."

The elders of Israel endeavored to sustain the sinking faith of their brethren by repeating the promises made to their fathers and the prophetic words of Joseph foretelling their deliverance from Egypt. Some would listen and believe. Others refused to hope. The Egyptians, informed of what was reported among their bondmen, derided their expectations and scornfully denied the power of their God. They tauntingly said, "If your God is just and merciful and possesses power above that of the Egyptian gods, why does He not make you a free people?" They worshiped deities termed by the Israelites false gods, yet they were a rich and powerful nation. Their gods had blessed them with prosperity and had given them the Israelites as servants. Pharaoh himself boasted that the God of the Hebrews could not deliver them from his hand.

Words like these destroyed the hopes of many of the Israelites. True, they were slaves. Their children had been slain, and their own lives were a burden. Yet they were worshiping the God of heaven. Surely He would not thus leave them in bondage to idolaters. But those who were true to God understood that it was because of Israel's departure from Him, because of their disposition to marry with heathen nations, thus being led into idolatry, that the Lord had permitted them to become bondmen. They confidently assured their brethren that He would soon break the yoke of the oppressor.

But the Hebrews were not yet prepared for deliverance. They had little faith in God. Many were content to remain in bondage rather than meet the difficulties attending removal to a strange land; and the habits of some had become so much like those of the Egyptians that they preferred to dwell in Egypt. Therefore the Lord overruled events more fully to develop the tyrannical spirit of the Egyptian king and also to reveal Himself to His people. The task of Moses would have been much less difficult had not many of the Israelites become so corrupted that they were unwilling to leave Egypt. Says the Scripture, "They hearkened not . . . for anguish of spirit, and for cruel bondage."

Again the divine message came to Moses, "Go in, speak unto Pharaoh king of Egypt, that he let the children of Israel go out of his land." In discouragement he replied, "Behold, the children of Israel have not hearkened unto me; how then shall Pharaoh hear me?" He was told to take Aaron with him and go before Pharaoh and again demand "that he send the children of Israel out of his land."

Pharaoh Could Yet Save Egypt
He was informed that the monarch would not yield until God should visit judgments upon Egypt and bring out Israel by the signal manifestation of His power. Before the infliction of each plague, Moses was to describe its nature and effects, that the king might save himself from it if he chose. Every punishment rejected would be followed by one more severe, until his proud heart would be humbled, and he would acknowledge the Maker of heaven and earth as the true and living God. The Lord would punish the people of Egypt for their idolatry and silence their boasting, that other nations might tremble at His mighty acts, and that His people might be led to turn from idolatry and render Him pure worship.

Again Moses and Aaron entered the lordly halls of the king of Egypt. There, surrounded by lofty columns and glittering adornments, by the rich paintings and sculptured images of heathen gods, stood the two representatives of the enslaved race. The king demanded a miracle in evidence of their divine commission. Aaron now took the rod and cast it down before Pharaoh. It became a serpent. The monarch sent for his "wise men and the sorcerers," who "cast down every man his rod and they became serpents: but Aaron's rod swallowed up their rods." The king, more determined than before, declared his magicians equal in power with Moses and Aaron. He denounced the servants of the Lord as impostors, yet was restrained by divine power from doing them harm.

Satan's Counterfeits

The magicians did not really cause their rods to become serpents; but by magic, aided by the great deceiver, they were able to produce this appearance. The prince of evil, though possessing all the wisdom and might of an angel fallen, has not power to create or to give life; this is the prerogative of God alone. But he produced a counterfeit.

To human sight the rods were changed to serpents. Such they were believed to be by Pharaoh and his court. Though the Lord caused the real serpent to swallow up the spurious ones, this was regarded by Pharaoh not as a work of God's power, but as the result of a kind of superior magic.

Pharaoh was seeking some pretext for disregarding the miracles that God had wrought through Moses. Satan gave him just what he wanted. He made it appear that Moses and Aaron were only magicians and sorcerers and that the message they brought could not claim respect as coming from a superior being. Thus Satan's counterfeit caused Pharaoh to harden his heart against conviction. Satan hoped also to shake the faith of Moses and Aaron.

The prince of evil well knew that Moses prefigured Christ, who was to break the reign of sin over the human family. He knew that when Christ should appear, mighty miracles would be an evidence to the world that God had sent Him. By counterfeiting the work of God through Moses, Satan hoped not only to prevent the deliverance of Israel, but through future ages to destroy faith in the miracles of Christ by making them appear to be the result of human power.

The Plagues Strike Egypt

Moses and Aaron were directed to visit the riverside next morning. The overflowing of the Nile being the source of food and wealth for all Egypt, the river was worshiped as a god, and the monarch came thither daily to pay his devotions. The two brothers again repeated the message to him and then stretched out the rod and smote upon the water. The sacred stream ran blood, the fish died, and the river became offensive to the smell. The water in the houses, the supply in the cisterns was likewise changed to blood. But "the magicians of Egypt did so with their enchantments," and "Pharaoh turned and went into his house, neither did he set his heart to this also." For seven days the plague continued, but without effect.

Again the rod was stretched out, and frogs came up from the river. They overran the houses, took possession of the bedchambers, and even the ovens and kneading troughs. The frog was regarded as sacred by the Egyptians, and they would not destroy it; but the slimy pests now swarmed even in the palace of the Pharaohs, and the king was impatient to have them removed. The magicians had appeared to produce frogs, but they could not remove them.

Upon seeing this, Pharaoh was somewhat humbled. He sent for Moses and Aaron, and said, "Entreat the Lord, that He may take away the frogs from me, and from my people; and I will let the people go, that they may do sacrifice unto the Lord." They requested him to appoint a time when they should pray for the removal of the plague. He set the next day, secretly hoping the frogs might disappear of themselves and thus save him from the bitter humiliation of submitting to the God of Israel. The plague, however, continued till the time specified, when throughout all Egypt the frogs died. But their putrid bodies, which remained, polluted the atmosphere.

The Lord could have caused them to return to dust in a moment; but He did not do this, lest the king and his people should pronounce it the result of enchantment like the work of the magicians. The frogs died and were then gathered together in heaps, evidence that this work was not accomplished by magic but was a judgment from the God of heaven.

"When Pharaoh saw that there was respite, he hardened his heart." At the command of God, Aaron stretched out his hand, and the dust of the earth became lice throughout all the land of Egypt. Pharaoh called upon the magicians to do the same, but they could not. The magicians acknowledged, "This is the finger of God." But the king was still unmoved.

Another judgment was inflicted. Flies filled the houses, so that "the land was corrupted by reason of the swarms of flies." These flies were large and venomous, and their bite was extremely painful. As foretold, this visitation did not extend to the land of Goshen.

Pharaoh Hardens His Heart

Pharaoh now offered the Israelites permission to sacrifice in Egypt, but they refused. "It is not meet," said Moses; "lo, shall we sacrifice the abomination of the Egyptians before their eyes, and will they not stone us?" The animals which the Hebrews would be required to sacrifice were among those regarded as sacred by the Egyptians. To slay one even accidentally was a crime punishable with death.

Moses again proposed to go three days' journey into the wilderness. The monarch consented and begged the servants of God to entreat that the plague might be removed. They promised to do this but warned him against dealing deceitfully with them. The plague was stayed, but the king's heart had become hardened by persistent rebellion, and he still refused to yield.

A more terrible stroke followed—murrain upon all the Egyptian cattle. Both the sacred animals and the beasts of burden, kine and oxen and sheep, horses, and camels and asses, were destroyed. It had been distinctly stated that the Hebrews were to be exempt; and Pharaoh, on sending messengers to the home of the Israelites, proved the truth of this. "Of the cattle of the children of Israel died not one." Still the king was obstinate.

Moses was next directed to take ashes of the furnace and "sprinkle it toward heaven in the sight of Pharaoh." The fine particles spread over the land of Egypt, and wherever they settled, produced boils "breaking forth with blains upon man, and upon beast." The priests and magicians had encouraged Pharaoh in his stubbornness, but now a judgment had reached even them. Smitten with a loathsome and painful disease, they were no longer able to contend against the God of Israel. The magicians were not able to protect even their own persons.

Still the heart of Pharaoh grew harder. And now the Lord sent a message to him, "I will at this time send all My plagues upon thine heart, and upon thy servants, and upon thy people; that thou mayest know that there is none like Me in all the earth. . . . And in very deed for this cause have I raised thee up, for to show in thee My power." God's providence had overruled events to place him upon the throne at the very time appointed for Israel's deliverance.

Though this haughty tyrant had forfeited the mercy of God, his life had been preserved that through his stubbornness the Lord might manifest His wonders in Egypt. God's people were permitted to experience the grinding cruelty of the Egyptians, that they might not be deceived concerning the debasing influence of idolatry. In His dealing with Pharaoh, the Lord manifested His hatred of idolatry and His determination to punish cruelty and oppression.

God had declared concerning Pharaoh, "I will harden his heart, that he shall not let the people go." Exodus 4:21. There was no exercise of supernatural power to harden the heart of the king, but the seeds of rebellion that he sowed when he rejected the first miracle produced their harvest. As he continued to venture from one degree of stubbornness to another, his heart became more and more hardened, until he was called to look upon the cold, dead faces of the first-born.

How Stubbornness Develops

God speaks to men through His servants, rebuking sin. If one refuses to be corrected, divine power does not interpose to counteract the tendency of his own action. He is hardening the heart against the influence of the Holy Spirit.

He who has once yielded to temptation will yield more readily the second time. Every repetition lessens his power of resistance, blinds his eyes, and stifles conviction. God works no miracle to prevent the harvest. "Whatsoever a man soweth, that shall he also reap." Galatians 6:7. It is thus that multitudes come to listen with stoical indifference to the truths that once stirred their souls. They sowed neglect and resistance to the truth, and such is the harvest they reap.

Those who quiet a guilty conscience think that after casting their influence on the side of the great rebel, when danger compasses them about they will change leaders. But this is not easily done. A life of sinful indulgence has so molded the character that they cannot then receive the image of Jesus. Had no light shone upon their pathway, mercy might interpose; but after light has been long despised, it will be finally withdrawn.

A plague of hail was next threatened upon Pharaoh.

"Send therefore now, and gather thy cattle, . . . for upon every man and beast which shall be found in the field, . . . and shall not be brought home, the hail shall come down upon them, and they shall die." Such a storm as was foretold had never been witnessed. The report spread rapidly, and all who believed the word of the Lord gathered in their cattle, while those who despised the warning left them in the field. Thus in the midst of judgment the mercy of God was displayed, and it was shown how many had been led to fear God.

The storm came, thunder and hail and fire mingled with it, "very grievous, such as there was none like it in all the land of Egypt since it became a nation. And the hail smote throughout all the land of Egypt all that was in the field, both man and beast; and the hail smote every herb of the field, and brake every tree of the field." Ruin and desolation marked the path of the destroying angel. The land of Goshen alone was spared.

Pharaoh at Last Relents

All Egypt trembled before the divine judgment. Pharaoh hastily sent for the two brothers: "I have sinned this time: the Lord is righteous, and I and my people are wicked. Entreat the Lord (for it is enough) that there be no more mighty thunderings and hail; and I will let you go, and ye shall stay no longer."

Moses knew that the contest was not ended. Pharaoh's confessions and promises were not the effect of any radical change in his mind but were wrung from him by terror and anguish. Moses promised, however, to grant his request, for he would give him no occasion for further stubbornness. The prophet went forth, unheeding the fury of the tempest, and Pharaoh and all his host were witnesses to the power of Jehovah to preserve His messenger. Moses "spread abroad his hands unto the Lord: and the thunders and hail ceased, and the rain was not poured upon the earth." But no sooner had the king recovered from his fears than his heart returned to its perversity.

Then the Lord would give unmistakable evidence to the difference He placed between Israel and the Egyptians and would cause all nations to know that the Hebrews were under the protection of the God of heaven. Moses warned the monarch that a plague of locusts would be sent, which would cover the earth and eat up every green thing that remained; they would fill the houses, even the palace itself; such a scourge, he said, as "neither thy fathers, nor thy fathers' fathers have seen, since the day that they were upon the earth unto this day."

The counselors of Pharaoh stood aghast. The nation has sustained great loss in the death of the cattle. Many of the people had been killed by the hail. The forests were broken down and the crops destroyed. They were fast losing all that had been gained by the labor of the Hebrews. The whole land was threatened with starvation. Princes and courtiers pressed about the king and demanded, "How long shall this man be a snare unto us? let the men go, that they may serve the Lord their God: knowest thou not yet that Egypt is destroyed?"

Moses and Aaron were again summoned, and the monarch said to them, "Go, serve the Lord your God: but who are they that shall go?"

Pharaoh Again Hardens His Heart

The answer was, "We will go with our young and with our old, with our sons and with our daughters, with our flocks and with our herds will we go; for we must hold a feast unto the Lord."

The king was filled with rage. He cried, "Not so: go now ye that are men, and serve the Lord; for that ye did desire. And they were driven out from Pharaoh's presence." Pharaoh pretended to have deep interest in their welfare and a tender care for their little ones, but his real object was to keep the women and children as surety for the return of the men.

Moses now stretched forth his rod over the land, and an east wind brought locusts. "Very grievous were they; before them there were no such locusts as they, neither after them shall be such." They filled the sky till the land was darkened and devoured every green thing remaining.

Pharaoh sent for the prophet in haste, and said, "I have sinned against the Lord your God, and against you. . . . Entreat the Lord your God, that He may take away from me this death only." They did so, and a strong west wind carried away the locusts toward the Red Sea. Still the king persisted in his stubborn resolution.

The people of Egypt were ready to despair, and they were filled with fear for the future. The nation had worshiped Pharaoh as a representative of their god; but many were now convinced that he was opposing himself to One who made all the powers of nature the ministers of His will. The Hebrew slaves were becoming confident of deliverance. Throughout Egypt there was a secret fear that the enslaved race would rise and avenge their wrongs. Everywhere men were asking, What will come next?

Suddenly a darkness settled upon the land, so thick and black that it seemed a "darkness which may be felt." Breathing was difficult. "They saw not one another, neither rose any from his place for three days: but all the children of Israel had light in their dwellings." The sun and moon were objects of worship to the Egyptians. In this mysterious darkness the people and their gods alike were smitten. (See Appendix, Note 2.) Yet fearful as it was, this judgment is an evidence of God's compassion and unwillingness to destroy. He would give the people time for reflection and repentance before bringing upon them the last and most terrible of the plagues.

At the end of the third day of darkness Pharaoh summoned Moses and consented to the departure of the people, provided the flocks and herds were permitted to remain. "There shall not a hoof be left behind," replied the resolute Hebrew. The king's anger burst forth beyond control. "Get thee from me," he cried, "take heed to thyself, see my face no more; for in that day thou seest my face thou shalt die."

The answer was, "Thou hast spoken well; I will see thy face again no more."

"The man Moses was very great in the land of Egypt, in the sight of Pharaoh's servants, and in the sight of the people." The king dared not harm him, for the people looked upon him as alone possessing power to remove the plagues. They desired that the Israelites might be permitted to leave Egypt. It was the king and the priests that opposed to the last the demands of Moses.

24 / The First Passover

When the demand for Israel's release had been first presented to the king of Egypt, the warning of the most terrible of the plagues had been given. "Thus saith the Lord, Israel is My son, even My firstborn: And I say unto thee, Let My son go, that he may serve Me: and if thou refuse to let him go, behold, I will slay thy son, even thy firstborn." Exodus 4:22, 23.

God has a tender care for the beings formed in His image. If the loss of their harvests and their flocks and herds had brought Egypt to repentance, the children would not have been smitten; but the nation had stubbornly resisted the divine command. Now the final blow was about to fall.

Moses had been forbidden, on pain of death, to appear again in Pharaoh's presence; but again Moses came before him, with the terrible announcement: "Thus saith the Lord, About midnight will I go out into the midst of Egypt: and all the firstborn in the land of Egypt shall die, from the firstborn of Pharaoh that sitteth upon his throne, even unto the firstborn of the maidservant that is behind the mill; and all the firstborn of beasts. And there shall be a great cry throughout all the land of Egypt, such as there was none like it, nor shall be like it any more. But against any of the children of Israel shall not a dog move his tongue, against man or beast: that ye may know how that the Lord doth put a difference between the Egyptians and Israel."

Before the execution of this sentence the Lord

This chapter is based on Exodus 11; 12:1-32.

189

through Moses gave direction to the children of Israel concerning their departure from Egypt and their preservation from the coming judgment. Each family, alone or in connection with others, was to slay a lamb or a kid "without blemish," and with a bunch of hyssop sprinkle its blood on "the two sideposts and on the upper doorpost" of the house, that the destroying angel at midnight might not enter that dwelling. They were to eat the flesh roasted, with unleavened bread and bitter herbs, at night, as Moses said, "with your loins girded, your shoes on your feet, and your staff in your hand; and ye shall eat it in haste: it is the Lord's passover."

The Lord declared: "I will pass through the land of Egypt this night, and will smite all the firstborn in the land of Egypt, both man and beast; and against all the gods of Egypt I will execute judgment. . . . And the blood shall be to you for a token upon the houses where ye are: and when I see the blood, I will pass over you, and the plague shall not be upon you to destroy you."

In commemoration of this great deliverance, a feast was to be observed yearly by Israel in all future generations—"the sacrifice of the Lord's passover, who passed over the houses of the children of Israel in Egypt, when he smote the Egyptians, and delivered our houses."

The Passover Points to Christ

The Passover was to be both commemorative and typical, not only pointing back to the deliverance from Egypt, but forward to the greater deliverance which Christ was to accomplish in freeing His people from the bondage of sin. The sacrificial lamb represents "the Lamb of God," in whom is our only hope of salvation. Says the apostle, "Christ our passover is sacrificed for us." 1 Corinthians 5:7. It was not enough that the paschal lamb be slain; its blood must be sprinkled upon the doorposts; so the merits of Christ's blood must be applied to the soul. We must believe, not only that He died for the world, but that He died for us individually.

The hyssop was the symbol of purification. "Purge me with hyssop, and I shall be clean; wash me, and I shall be whiter than snow." Psalm 51:7.

The lamb was to be prepared whole, not a bone being broken; so not a bone was to be broken of the Lamb of God, who was to die for us. See John 19:36.

The flesh was to be eaten. It is not enough that we believe on Christ for the forgiveness of sin; we must by faith be constantly receiving spiritual nourishment from Him through His Word. Said Christ, "Except ye eat the flesh of the Son of man, and drink His blood, ye have no life in you. Whoso eateth My flesh, and drinketh My blood, hath eternal life." "The words that I speak unto you, they are spirit, and they are life." John 6:53, 54, 63. The followers of Christ must assimilate the Word of God so that it shall become the motive power of life and action. By the power of Christ they must be changed into His likeness and reflect the divine attributes.

The lamb was to be eaten with bitter herbs, as pointing back to the bitterness of the bondage in Egypt. So when we feed upon Christ, it should be with contrition of the heart, because of our sins. The use of unleavened bread also was significant. The leaven of sin must be put away from all who would receive life and nourishment from Christ. So Paul writes to the Corinthian church, "Purge out therefore the old leaven, that ye may be a new lump. . . . Let us keep the feast, not with old leaven, neither with the leaven of malice and wickedness; but with the unleavened bread of sincerity and truth." 1 Corinthians 5:7, 8.

Before obtaining freedom, the bondmen must show their faith in the great deliverance. The blood must be placed upon their houses, and they must separate themselves and their families from the Egyptians and gather within their own dwellings. All who failed to heed the Lord's directions would lose their firstborn by the hand of the destroyer.

How Faith Must Be Shown

By obedience the people were to give evidence of their faith. So all who hope to be saved by the blood of Christ should realize that they themselves have something to do in securing their salvation. We are to turn from sin to obedience. Man is to be saved by faith, not by works; yet his faith must be shown by his works. Man must appreciate and use the helps that God has provided; he must believe and obey all the divine requirements.

As Moses rehearsed to Israel the provisions of God for their deliverance, "the people bowed the head and worshiped." Many of the Egyptians had been led to acknowledge the God of the Hebrews as the only true God, and these now begged to find shelter in the homes of Israel when the destroying angel should pass through the land. Gladly welcomed, they pledged to serve God and go forth from Egypt with His people.

The Israelites obeyed the directions God had given. Their families were gathered, the paschal lamb slain, the flesh roasted with fire, the unleavened bread and bitter herbs prepared. The father and priest of the household sprinkled the blood upon the doorpost. In haste and silence the paschal lamb was eaten. Fathers and mothers clasped in their arms their loved firstborn, as they thought of the fearful stroke that was to fall that night. The sign of blood—the sign of a Saviour's protection—was on their doors, and the destroyer entered not.

At midnight "there was a great cry in Egypt; for there was not a house where there was not one dead." All the firstborn in the land, "from the firstborn of Pharaoh that sat on his throne unto the firstborn of the captive that was in the dungeon; and all the firstborn of cattle" had been smitten. The pride of every household had been laid low. Shrieks and wails filled the air.

At midnight, the firstborn of every Egyptian household died—even the firstborn of Pharaoh.

King and courtiers, trembling, stood aghast at the overmastering horror. His heaven-daring pride humbled in the dust, Pharaoh "called for Moses and Aaron by night, and said, Rise up, and get you forth from among my people, both ye and the children of Israel; and go, serve the Lord, as ye have said. . . . Be gone; and bless me also."

25/ The Israelites Leave Egypt

Before the morning broke, the people of Israel were on their way. During the plagues the Israelites had gradually assembled in Goshen. Some provision had already been made for the necessary organization and control of the moving multitudes, they being divided into companies under appointed leaders.

And they went out, "about six hundred thousand on foot that were men, besides children. And a mixed multitude went up also with them"—not only those actuated by faith in the God of Israel but also a far greater number who desired only to escape from the plagues. This class were ever a hindrance and a snare to Israel.

The people took with them "flocks and herds, even very much cattle." Before leaving Egypt, the people claimed a recompense for their unpaid labor; and the bondmen went forth laden with the spoil of their oppressors.

"And it came to pass . . . that the Lord did bring the children of Israel out of the land of Egypt by their armies." The Israelites bore with them the bones of Joseph, which, during the dark years of bondage, had been a reminder of Israel's promised deliverance.

Instead of pursuing the direct route to Canaan through the country of the Philistines, the Lord directed their course southward toward the shores of the Red Sea. "For God said, Lest peradventure the people repent when they see war, and they return to Egypt." The Philistines, regarding them as slaves escaping

This chapter is based on Exodus 12:34-51; 13 to 15.

194

from their masters, would not have hesitated to make war upon them. The Israelites had little knowledge of God and little faith in Him, and they would have become terrified and disheartened. They were unarmed and unaccustomed to war, their spirits were depressed by long bondage, and they were encumbered with women and children, flocks and herds. In leading them by the Red Sea, the Lord revealed Himself as a God of compassion.

The Pillar of Cloud

"And they took their journey from Succoth, and encamped in Etham, in the edge of the wilderness. And the Lord went before them by day in a pillar of cloud, to lead them the way; and by night in a pillar of fire, to give them light; to go by day and by night: He took not away the pillar of the cloud by day, nor the pillar of fire by night, from before the people." Says the psalmist, "He spread a cloud for a covering; and fire to give light in the night." Psalm 105:39. See also 1 Corinthians 10:1, 2. It served as a protection from the burning heat, and by its coolness and moisture afforded grateful refreshment in the parched, thirsty desert. By night it became a pillar of fire, illuminating their encampment and constantly assuring them of the divine presence.

Across a dreary, desertlike expanse they journeyed. Already they were becoming weary with the toilsome way, and some hearts began to fear pursuit by the Egyptians. But the cloud went forward, and they followed. Now the Lord directed Moses to turn aside into a rocky defile and encamp beside the sea. It was revealed to him that Pharaoh would pursue them but that God would be honored in their deliverance.

Pharaoh's counselors declared to the king that their bondmen had fled, never to return. Their great men, recovering from their fears, accounted for the plagues as the result of natural causes. "Why have we done this, that we have let Israel go from serving us?" was the bitter cry.

Pharaoh collected his forces, "six hundred chosen chariots, and all the chariots of Egypt," horsemen, captains, and foot soldiers. The king himself, attended by the great men of his realm, headed the attacking army. The Egyptians feared lest their forced submission to God should subject them to the derision of other nations. If they should now go forth with a great show of power and bring back the fugitives, they would redeem their glory, as well as recover the services of their bondmen.

The Hebrews were encamped beside the sea, a seemingly impassable barrier before them, while on the south a rugged mountain obstructed their further progress. Suddenly they beheld in the distance flashing armor and moving chariots. Terror filled the hearts of Israel. The greater part hastened to Moses with their complaints: "Because there were no graves in Egypt, hast thou taken us away to die in the wilderness? . . . It had been better for us to serve the Egyptians, than that we should die in the wilderness."

True, there was no possibility of deliverance unless God Himself should interpose for their release; but having been brought into this position in obedience to the divine direction, Moses felt no fear of the consequences. His calm and assuring reply to the people was, "Fear ye not, stand still, and see the salvation of the Lord, which He will show to you today: for the Egyptians whom ye have seen today, ye shall see them again no more forever. The Lord shall fight for you, and ye shall hold your peace."

The hosts of Israel, lacking discipline and self-control, became violent and unreasonable. Their wailings and lamentations were loud and deep. The wonderful pillar of cloud had been followed as the signal of God to go forward; but now had it not led them on the wrong side of the mountain, into an impassable way? The angel of God appeared to their deluded minds as the harbinger of disaster.

As the Egyptian host approached them, the cloudy

column rose majestically into the heavens, passed over the Israelites, and descended between them and the armies of Egypt. The Egyptians could no longer discern the camp of the Hebrews and were forced to halt. But as night deepened, the wall of cloud became a great light to the Hebrews.

Then hope returned to the hearts of Israel. "And the Lord said unto Moses, . . . speak unto the children of Israel, that they go forward: but lift thou up thy rod, and stretch out thine hand over the sea, and divide it: and the children of Israel shall go on dry ground through the midst of the sea."

As Moses stretched out his rod, the waters parted, and Israel went into the midst of the sea, upon dry ground, while the waters stood like a wall upon each side. The light from God's pillar of fire lighted the road cut like a furrow through the waters.

The End of Pharaoh's Army

"The Egyptians pursued, and went in after them to the midst of the sea, even all Pharaoh's horses, his chariots, and his horsemen. And it came to pass, that in the morning watch the Lord looked unto the host of the Egyptians through the pillar of fire and of the cloud, and troubled the host of the Egyptians."

Thunders pealed and lightning flashed. The Egyptians were seized with confusion. They endeavored to retrace their steps, but Moses stretched out his rod, and the piled-up waters rushed together and swallowed the Egyptian army in their black depths.

As morning broke, it revealed to Israel all that remained of their mighty foes—mail-clad bodies cast upon the shore. From the most terrible peril, Jehovah had brought complete deliverance, and to Him their hearts were turned in gratitude and faith. The Spirit of God rested upon Moses, and he led the people in a triumphant anthem of thanksgiving, the earliest and one of the most sublime known to man.

It was taken up by the women of Israel, Miriam, the

sister of Moses, leading the way, as they went forth with timbrel and dance. Far over desert and sea rang the joyous refrain, and the mountains re-echoed the words of their praise, "Sing ye to Jehovah, for He hath triumphed gloriously."

That song does not belong to the Jewish people alone. It points forward to the destruction of all the foes of righteousness and the final victory of the Israel of God. The prophet of Patmos beheld the white-robed multitude that "have gotten the victory," standing on the "sea of glass mingled with fire," having "the harps of God. And they sing the song of Moses, the servant of God, and the song of the Lamb." Revelation 15:2, 3.

In freeing our souls from the bondage of sin, God has wrought for us a deliverance greater than that of the Hebrews at the Red Sea. Like the Hebrew host, we should praise the Lord with heart and soul and voice for His "wonderful works to the children of men." What compassion, what matchless love, has God shown in connecting us with Himself, to be to Him a peculiar treasure! What a sacrifice has been made by our Redeemer, that we may be called children of God!

The Redeemed Will Sing

"Whoso offereth praise," says the Creator, "glorifieth Me." Psalm 50:23. All the inhabitants of heaven unite in praising God. Let us learn the song of the angels now, that we may sing it when we join their shining ranks.

God brought the Hebrews into the mountain fastnesses before the sea that He might manifest His power and signally humble the pride of their oppressors. He chose this method to test their faith and strengthen their trust in Him. If the people had held back when Moses bade them advance, God would never have opened the path for them. It was "by faith" that "they passed through the Red Sea as by dry land." Hebrews 11:29. In marching down to the very water, they showed that they believed the word of God spoken by Moses. Then the Mighty One of Israel divided the sea to make a path for their feet.

Often life is beset by dangers, and duty seems hard to perform. Imagination pictures impending ruin. Yet the voice of God speaks clearly, "Go forward." We should obey this command, even though our eyes cannot penetrate the darkness, and we feel the cold waves about our feet. Those who defer obedience till every uncertainty disappears and there remains no risk of failure or defeat will never obey at all; but faith courageously urges an advance. The path where God leads may lie through the desert or the sea, but it is a safe path.

26/ Israel Meets With Difficulties

From the Red Sea the hosts of Israel again set forth on their journey under the guidance of the pillar of cloud. They were full of joy in the consciousness of freedom, and every thought of discontent was hushed.

But for three days, as they journeyed, they could find no water. The supply which they had taken with them was exhausted. There was nothing to quench their burning thirst as they dragged wearily over the sun-burnt plains. Moses, who was familiar with this region, knew what the others did not—at Marah, where springs were found, the water was unfit for use. With a sinking heart he heard the glad shout, "Water! water!" echo along the line. Men, women, and children in joyous haste crowded to the fountain, when, lo, a cry of anguish burst forth—the water was bitter.

In their despair they reproached Moses, not remembering that the divine presence in that mysterious cloud had been leading him as well as themselves. Moses did what they had forgotten to do; he cried earnestly to God for help. "And the Lord showed him a tree, which when he had cast into the waters, the waters were made sweet." Here the promise was given to Israel: "If thou wilt diligently hearken to the voice of the Lord thy God, and wilt do that which is right in His sight, and wilt give ear to His commandments, and keep all His statutes, I will put none of these diseases upon thee, which I have brought upon the Egyptians: for I am the Lord that healeth thee."

From Marah the people journeyed to Elim, where

This chapter is based on Exodus 15:22-27; 16 to 18.

200

they found "twelve wells of water." Here they remained several days.

When they had been a month absent from Egypt, their store of provisions had begun to fail. How was food to be supplied for these vast multitudes? Even the rulers and elders of the people joined in complaining against the leaders of God's appointment: "Would to God we had died by the hand of the Lord in the land of Egypt, when we sat by the fleshpots, and when we did eat bread to the full; for ye have brought us forth into this wilderness, to kill this whole assembly with hunger."

They had not as yet suffered hunger; but they feared for the future. In imagination they saw their children famishing. The Lord permitted difficulties to surround them and their supply of food to be cut short, that their hearts might turn to Him who had been their Deliverer. If in their want they would call upon Him, He would still grant them tokens of His love and care. It was sinful unbelief on their part to anticipate that they or their children might die of hunger.

It was necessary for them to encounter difficulties and endure privations. God was bringing them from degradation to occupy an honorable place among the nations and to receive sacred trusts. Had they possessed faith in Him, in view of all that He had wrought for them, they would cheerfully have borne inconvenience, privation, and even real suffering. But they forgot the goodness and power of God displayed in their deliverance from bondage. They forgot how their children had been spared when the destroying angel slew all the firstborn of Egypt. They forgot the grand exhibition of divine power at the Red Sea. They forgot that their enemies, attempting to follow them, had been overwhelmed by the waters of the sea.

Instead of saying, "God has done great things for us; whereas we were slaves, He is making of us a great nation," they talked of the hardness of the way and wondered when their weary pilgrimage would end.

God would have His people in these days review the trials through which ancient Israel passed, that they may be instructed in their preparation for the heavenly Canaan. Many look back to the Israelites and marvel at their unbelief, feeling that they themselves would not have been so ungrateful; but when their faith is tested even by little trials, they manifest no more faith or patience than did ancient Israel. They murmur at the process by which God has chosen to purify them. Though their present needs are supplied, many are in constant anxiety lest poverty come upon them and their children be left to suffer. Obstacles, instead of leading them to seek help from God, separate them from Him because they awaken unrest and repining.

Why should we be ungrateful and distrustful? Jesus is our friend; all heaven is interested in our welfare. Anxiety and fear grieve the Holy Spirit of God. It is not the will of God that His people should be weighed down with care.

Our Lord does not tell us there are no dangers in our path, but He points us to a never-failing refuge. He invites the weary and care-laden, "Come unto Me, all ye that labor and are heavy laden, and I will give you rest." Lay off the yoke of anxiety and care that you have placed on your own neck, and "take My yoke upon you, and learn of Me; for I am meek and lowly in heart; and ye shall find rest unto your souls." Matthew 11:28, 29. Instead of murmuring and complaining, the language of our hearts should be, "Bless the Lord, O my soul, and forget not all His benefits." Psalm 103:2.

God was mindful of the wants of Israel. He said to their leader, "I will rain bread from heaven for you." Directions were given that the people gather a daily supply, with a double amount on the sixth day, that the sacred observance of the Sabbath might be maintained.

Moses assured the congregation that their wants were to be supplied. "The Lord shall give you in the evening flesh to eat, and in the morning bread to the full." And he added, "What are we? your murmurings are not against us, but against the Lord." They must be taught that the Most High, not merely Moses, was their leader.

At nightfall the camp was surrounded by vast flocks of quails, enough to supply the entire company. In the morning there lay upon the ground "a small round thing, . . . like a coriander seed, white." The people called it "manna." Moses said, "This is the bread which the Lord hath given you to eat." The people found that there was an abundant supply for all. They "ground it in mills, or beat it in a mortar, and baked it in pans, and made cakes of it." "And the taste of it was like wafers made with honey." Numbers 11:8; Exodus 16:31.

They were directed to gather daily an omer for every person and not to leave of it until the morning. The provision for the day must be gathered in the morning, for all that remained upon the ground was melted by the sun. "He that gathered much had nothing over, and he that gathered little had no lack."

How the Sabbath Was Honored

On the sixth day the people gathered two omers for every person. The rulers hastened to acquaint Moses with what had been done. His answer was, "This is that which the Lord hath said, Tomorrow is the rest of the holy Sabbath unto the Lord: bake that which ye will bake today, and seethe that ye will seethe; and that which remaineth over lay up for you to be kept until the morning." They did so, and found that it remained unchanged. And Moses said, "Eat that today; for today is a Sabbath unto the Lord: today ye shall not find it in the field. Six days ye shall gather it; but on the seventh day, which is the Sabbath, in it there shall be none."

God requires that His holy day be as sacredly observed now as in the time of Israel. The day before the

Sabbath should be made a day of preparation, that everything may be in readiness for its sacred hours. In no case should our own business be allowed to encroach upon holy time. God has directed that the sick be cared for; the labor required to make them comfortable is a work of mercy and no violation of the Sabbath; but all unnecessary work should be avoided. Work that is neglected until the beginning of the Sabbath should remain undone until it is past.

The Israelites witnessed a three-fold miracle to impress their minds with the sacredness of the Sabbath: a double quantity of manna fell on the sixth day, none on the seventh, and the portion needed for the Sabbath was preserved sweet and pure.

Sabbath Before Sinai

In the giving of the manna, we have conclusive evidence that the Sabbath was not instituted when the law was given at Sinai. Before the Israelites came to Sinai they understood the Sabbath to be obligatory upon them. In being obliged to gather every Friday a double portion of manna in preparation for the Sabbath, the sacred nature of the day of rest was continually impressed upon them. And when some of the people went out on the Sabbath to gather manna, the Lord asked, "How long *refuse ye* to keep My commandments and my laws?"

"The children of Israel did eat manna forty years, . . . until they came into the borders of the land of Canaan." For forty years they were daily reminded of God's unfailing care and tender love. God gave them "of the corn of heaven. Man did eat angels' food" (Psalm 78:24, 25)—that is, food provided for them by the angels. They were daily taught that they were as secure from want as if surrounded by fields of waving grain on the fertile plains of Canaan.

The manna was a type of Him who came from God to give life to the world. Said Jesus, "I am that bread of life. Your fathers did eat manna in the wilderness, and are dead. This is the bread which cometh down from heaven. . . . If any man eat of this bread, he shall live forever: and the bread that I will give is My flesh, which I will give for the life of the world." John 6:48-51.

After leaving the wilderness of Sin, the Israelites encamped in Rephidim. Here there was no water, and again they distrusted the providence of God. The people came to Moses with the demand, "Give us water that we may drink." They cried in anger, "Wherefore is this, that thou hast brought us up out of Egypt, to kill us and our children and our cattle with thirst?" When they had been so abundantly supplied with food, they remembered with shame their unbelief and promised to trust the Lord in the future; but they failed at the first trial of their faith. The pillar of cloud that was leading them seemed to veil a fearful mystery. And Moses—who was he? What could be his object in bringing them from Egypt? Suspicion and distrust filled their hearts, and in the tumult of rage they were about to stone him.

Water From a Rock

In distress Moses cried to the Lord, "What shall I do unto this people?" He was directed to take the elders of Israel and the rod wherewith he had wrought wonders in Egypt, and to go on before the people. And the Lord said unto him, "Behold, I will stand before thee there upon the rock in Horeb; and thou shalt smite the rock, and there shall come water out of it, that the people may drink." He obeyed, and the waters burst forth in a living stream that abundantly supplied the encampment. The Lord in His mercy made the rod His instrument to work their deliverance.

It was the Son of God who, veiled in the cloudy pillar, stood beside Moses and caused the life-giving water to flow. All the congregation beheld the glory of the Lord; but had the cloud been removed, they would have been slain by the terrible brightness of Him who abode therein.

The unbelief manifested was criminal, and Moses

feared that the judgment of God would rest upon them. He called the name of the place Massah, "temptation," and Meribah, "chiding," as a memorial of their sin.

War With Amalek

A new danger now threatened them. Because of their murmuring against Him, the Lord suffered them to be attacked by their enemies. The Amalekites came out against them and smote those who, faint and weary, had fallen into the rear. Moses directed Joshua to choose from the different tribes a body of soldiers and lead them against the enemy, while he himself would stand on an eminence nearby with the rod of God in his hand. Accordingly the next day Joshua and his company attacked the foe, while Moses, Aaron, and Hur were on a hill overlooking the battlefield. With arms outstreched toward heaven and holding the rod of God in his right hand, Moses prayed for the success of the armies of Israel. It was observed that so long as his hands were reaching upward, Israel prevailed; but when they were lowered, the enemy was victorious. As Moses became weary, Aaron and Hur stayed up his hands until the going down of the sun, when the enemy was put to flight.

The act of Moses was significant, showing that God held their destiny in His hands; while they made Him their trust, He would fight for them and subdue their enemies. But when they should let go their hold upon Him and trust in their own power, they would be weak and their foes would prevail against them.

Divine strength is to be combined with human effort. Moses did not believe that God would overcome their foes while Israel remained inactive. While the great leader was pleading with the Lord, Joshua and his brave followers were putting forth their utmost efforts to repulse the enemies of Israel and of God.

Just before his death Moses delivered to his people the solemn charge: "Remember what Amalek did unto thee by the way, when ye were come forth out of

Egypt; how he met thee by the way, and smote the hindmost of thee, even all that were feeble behind thee, when thou wast faint and weary; and he feared not God. . . . Thou shalt blot out the remembrance of Amalek from under heaven; thou shalt not forget it." Deuteronomy 25:17-19. Concerning this wicked people the Lord declared, "The hand of Amalek is against the throne of Jehovah." Exodus 17:16, margin.

The Amalekites were not ignorant of God's character or of His sovereignty, but they had set themselves to defy His power. The wonders wrought by Moses before the Egyptians were made a subject of mockery. They had taken oath by their gods that they would destroy the Hebrews and boasted that Israel's God would be powerless to resist them. They had not been threatened by the Israelites. Their assault was unprovoked. To manifest their defiance of God they sought to destroy His people. The Amalekites had long been high-handed sinners, yet God's mercy had still called them to repentance; but when the men of Amalek fell upon the wearied and defenseless ranks of Israel, they sealed their nation's doom. Over all who love and fear Him, God's hand extends as a shield; let men beware that they smite not that hand; for it wields the sword of justice.

Jethro, the father-in-law of Moses, now set out to visit the Hebrews and restore to Moses his wife and two sons. Moses, the great leader, went out with joy to meet them and conducted them to his tent.

Jethro's Wise Advice

As Jethro remained in the camp, he soon saw how heavy were the burdens that rested upon Moses. Not only the general interests and duties of the people, but the controversies that arose among them, were referred to him. He said, "I do make them know the statutes of God, and His laws." But Jethro remonstrated, saying, "This thing is too heavy for thee; thou art not able to perform it thyself alone." "Thou wilt surely wear away." He counseled Moses to appoint proper persons as rulers of thousands, others as rulers of hundreds, and others of tens. These were to judge in all matters of minor consequence, while the most difficult and important cases should still be brought before Moses. This counsel was accepted, and it not only brought relief to Moses, but more perfect order among the people.

The fact that he had been chosen to instruct others did not lead Moses to conclude that he himself needed no instruction. The chosen leader of Israel listened gladly to the suggestions of the godly priest of Midian and adopted his plan.

From Rephidim the people continued their journey, following the movement of the cloudy pillar. Their route had led across barren plains, over steep ascents, and through rocky defiles. Now before them in solemn majesty Mount Sinai lifted its massive front. The cloudy pillar rested upon its summit, and the people spread their tents upon the plain beneath. Here was to be their home for nearly a year. At night the pillar of fire assured them of divine protection, and while they were locked in slumber, the bread of heaven fell gently upon the encampment.

Here Israel was to receive the most wonderful revelation ever made by God to men. Here the Lord had gathered His people that He might impress upon them the sacredness of His requirements by declaring with His own voice His holy law. Radical changes were to be wrought in them; for the degrading influences of servitude and idolatry had left their mark upon habits and character. God was working to lift them to a higher moral level by giving them a knowledge of Himself.

27 / God Gives His Law on Mount Sinai

Soon after the encampment at Sinai, Moses was called up into the mountain to meet with God. Israel was now to be taken into a close and peculiar relation to the Most High—to be incorporated as a church and a nation under the government of God. "Ye have seen what I did unto the Egyptians, and how I bare you on eagles' wings, and brought you unto Myself. Now therefore, if ye will obey My voice indeed, and keep My covenant, then ye shall be a peculiar treasure unto Me above all people: for all the earth is Mine: and ye shall be unto Me a kingdom of priests, and an holy nation."

Moses returned to the camp, and to the elders of Israel he repeated the divine message. Their answer was, "All that the Lord hath spoken we will do." Thus they entered into a solemn covenant with God, pledging themselves to accept Him as their ruler, by which they became, in a special sense, the subjects of His authority.

God purposed to make the occasion of speaking His law a scene of awful grandeur. Everything connected with the service of God must be regarded with the greatest reverence. The Lord said to Moses, "Go unto the people, and sanctify them today and tomorrow, and let them wash their clothes, . . . for the third day the Lord will come down in the sight of all the people upon Mount Sinai." All were to occupy the time in solemn preparation to appear before God. Their person and their clothing must be freed from impurity. They

This chapter is based on Exodus 19 to 24.

were to devote themselves to humiliation, fasting, and prayer that their hearts might be cleansed from iniquity.

On the morning of the third day, Sinai's summit was covered with a thick cloud, black and dense, sweeping downward until the entire mountain was wrapped in darkness and mystery. Then a sound as of a trumpet was heard, summoning the people to meet with God. From the thick darkness flashed lightnings, while peals of thunder echoed among the surrounding heights. "And Mount Sinai was altogether on a smoke, because the Lord descended upon it in fire: . . . and the whole mount quaked greatly." The hosts of Israel shook with fear and fell upon their faces before the Lord. Even Moses exclaimed, "I exceedingly fear and quake." Hebrews 12:21.

Now the thunders ceased; the trumpet was no longer heard; the earth was still. There was a period of solemn silence; then the voice of God was heard. Speaking out of the thick darkness as He stood upon the mount, surrounded by angels, the Lord made known His law.

"I am the Lord thy God, which have brought thee out of the land of Egypt, out of the house of bondage." He who had brought them forth from Egypt, making a way for them through the sea, and overthrowing Pharaoh and his hosts—He it was who now spoke His law.

God honored the Hebrews by making them the guardians and keepers of His law, but it was to be held as a sacred trust for the whole world. The precepts of the Decalogue are adapted to all mankind, and they were given for the instruction and government of all. Ten precepts, brief, comprehensive, and authoritative, cover the duty of man to God and to his fellowman, and all based upon the great fundamental principle of love. "Thou shalt love the Lord thy God with all thy heart, and with all thy soul, and with all thy strength, and with all thy mind; and thy neighbor as thyself." Luke 10:27. In the Ten Commandments these principles are made applicable to man.

1. "Thou shalt have no other gods before Me." Whatever we cherish that tends to lessen our love for God or to interfere with the service due Him, of that do we make a god.

2. "Thou shalt not make unto thee any graven image, or any likeness of anything that is in heaven above, or that is in the earth beneath, or that is in the water under the earth: Thou shalt not bow down thyself to them, nor serve them."

Conceptions of God Affect Human Behavior

Many heathen nations claimed that their images were mere symbols by which the Deity was worshiped; but God has declared such worship to be sin. The attempt to represent the Eternal One by material objects would lower man's conception of God. The mind would be attracted to the creature rather than to the Creator. As his conceptions of God were lowered, so would man become degraded.

"I the Lord thy God am a jealous God." The close relation of God to His people is represented under the figure of marriage. Idolatry being spiritual adultery, the displeasure of God against it is fitly called jealousy.

"Visiting the iniquity of the fathers upon the children unto the third and fourth generation of them that hate Me." Children are not punished for parents' guilt, except as they participate in their sins. It is usually the case, however, that by inheritance and example the sons become partakers of the father's sin. Wrong tendencies, perverted appetites, and debased morals, as well as physical disease and degeneracy, are transmitted as a legacy from father to son, to the third and fourth generation.

"Showing mercy unto thousands of them that love Me, and keep My commandments." To those who are faithful in His service, mercy is promised, not merely to the third and fourth generation as is the wrath threatened against those who hate Him, but to thousands of generations.

3. "Thou shalt not take the name of the Lord thy God in vain; for the Lord will not hold him guiltless that taketh His name in vain."

This commandment forbids us to use the name of God in a light or careless manner. By the thoughtless mention of God in common conversation, and by frequent, thoughtless repetition of His name, we dishonor Him. "Holy and reverend is His name." Psalm 111:9. It should be uttered with reverence and solemnity.

4. "Remember the Sabbath day, to keep it holy. Six days shalt thou labor, and do all thy work: but the seventh day is the Sabbath of the Lord thy God: in it thou shalt not do any work, thou, nor thy son, nor thy daughter, thy manservant, nor thy maidservant, nor thy cattle, nor thy stranger that is within thy gates: for in six days the Lord made heaven and earth, the sea, and all that in them is, and rested the seventh day: wherefore the Lord blessed the Sabbath day, and hallowed it."

The Sabbath is not introduced as a new institution but as having been founded at creation. Pointing to God as the Maker of the heavens and the earth, it distinguishes the true God from false gods. Thus the Sabbath is the sign of man's allegiance to God. The fourth commandment is the only one of the ten in which are found both the name and the title of the Lawgiver, the only one that shows by whose authority the law is given. Thus it contains the seal of God.

God has given men six days wherein to labor, and He requires that their own work be done in the six working days. Acts of necessity and mercy are permitted on the Sabbath. The sick and suffering are at all times to be cared for; but unnecessary labor is to be strictly avoided. To keep the Sabbath holy, we should not even allow our minds to dwell upon things of a worldly character. And the commandment includes all within our "gates." The inmates of the house are to lay aside their worldly business during the sacred hours. All should unite to honor God by willing service upon His holy day.

5. "Honor thy father and thy mother that thy days may be long upon the land which the Lord thy God giveth thee."

Parents are entitled to a degree of love and respect due to no other person. He who rejects the rightful authority of his parents is rejecting the authority of God. The fifth commandment requires children not only to yield respect, submission, and obedience to their parents, but also to give them love and tenderness, to lighten their cares, to guard their reputation, and to succor and comfort them in old age. It also enjoins respect for ministers and rulers.

6. "Thou shalt not kill."

All acts of injustice that tend to shorten life; the spirit of hatred and revenge, or the indulgence of any passion that leads to injurious acts toward others (even to wish them harm, for "whoso hateth his brother is a murderer"); a selfish neglect of caring for the needy; self-indulgence or excessive labor that tends to injure health—all these are, to a greater or less degree, violations of the sixth commandment.

7. "Thou shalt not commit adultery."

Purity is demanded not only in the outward life but in the secret intents and emotions of the heart. Christ, who taught the far-reaching obligation of the law of God, declared the evil thought or look to be as truly sin as is the unlawful deed.

8. "Thou shalt not steal."

This prohibition condemns manstealing and slave dealing, wars of conquest, theft and robbery. It demands strict integrity in the minutest details of life. It forbids overreaching in trade and requires the payment of just debts or wages. Every attempt to advantage one's self by the ignorance, weakness, or misfortune of another is registered as fraud in the books of heaven.

9. "Thou shalt not bear false witness against thy neighbor."

An intention to deceive is what constitutes falsehood. By a glance of the eye, a motion of the hand, an expression of the countenance, a falsehood may be told as effectually as by words. Even the statement of facts in such a manner as to mislead is falsehood. Every effort to injure our neighbor's reputation by misrepresentation, slander, or talebearing, even the intentional suppression of truth by which injury may result to others is a violation of the ninth commandment.

10. "Thou shalt not covet thy neighbor's house, thou shalt not covet thy neighbor's wife, nor his manservant, nor his maidservant, nor his ox, nor his ass, nor anything that is thy neighbor's."

The tenth commandment strikes at the very root of all sins, prohibiting the selfish desire, from which springs the sinful act. He who refrains from indulging even a sinful desire for that which belongs to another will not be guilty of an act of wrong toward his fellow creatures.

God proclaimed His law with exhibitions of His power and glory, that His people might never forget the scene. He would show to all men the sacredness and permanence of His law.

God's Law Is a Law of Love

As God's great rule of right was presented before them, the people realized as never before the offensive character of sin and their own guilt in the sight of a holy God. The multitude cried out to Moses, "Speak thou with us, and we will hear: but let not God speak with us, lest we die." The leader answered, "Fear not: for God is come to prove you, and that His fear may be before your faces, that ye sin not."

Blinded and debased by slavery and heathenism, the people were not prepared to appreciate fully the far-reaching principles of God's ten precepts. Additional precepts were given, illustrating and applying the principles of the Ten Commandments. These laws were called "judgments" because the magistrates were to give judgment according to them. Unlike the Ten Commandments, they were delivered privately to Moses.

The first of these related to servants. A Hebrew could not be sold as a slave for life. His service was limited to six years; on the seventh he was to be set at liberty. The holding of slaves not of Israelitish birth was permitted, but their life and person were strictly guarded. The murderer of a slave was to be punished; an injury inflicted upon one by his master, though no more than the loss of a tooth, entitled him to his freedom.

The Israelites were to beware of indulging the spirit of cruelty from which they had suffered under their Egyptian taskmasters. The memory of their own bitter servitude should enable them to put themselves in the servant's place, to be kind and compassionate.

The rights of widows and orphans were specially guarded. "If thou afflict them in any wise," the Lord declared, "and they cry at all unto Me, I will surely hear their cry; and My wrath shall wax hot, and I will kill you with the sword; and your wives shall be widows, and your children fatherless." Aliens who united themselves with Israel were to be protected from wrong or oppression. "Thou shalt not oppress a stranger: for ye know the heart of a stranger, seeing ye were strangers in the land of Egypt."

The taking of usury from the poor was forbidden. A poor man's raiment or blanket taken as a pledge must be restored to him at nightfall. Judges were warned against perverting judgment, aiding a false cause, or receiving bribes. Slander was prohibited, and acts of kindness enjoined even toward personal enemies.

The people were reminded of the sacred obligation of the Sabbath. Yearly feasts were appointed, at which all the men of the nation were to assemble before the Lord, bringing to Him their offerings of gratitude and the firstfruits of His bounties. The object of all these regulations was stated: all were given for the good of Israel. The Lord said, "Ye shall be holy men unto Me."

These laws were to be recorded by Moses and carefully treasured as the foundation of the national law, and, with the ten precepts, the condition of the fulfillment of God's promises to Israel.

The message was now given, "Behold, I send an Angel before thee, to keep thee in the way, and to bring thee into the place which I have prepared. Beware of Him, and obey His voice, provoke Him not." Christ in the pillar of cloud and of fire was their Leader. While there were types pointing to a Saviour to come, there was also a present Saviour, who gave commands to Moses for the people and was set forth before them as the only channel of blessing.

How the "Old Covenant" Was Made

Upon descending from the mountain, "Moses came and told the people all the words of the Lord, and all the judgments: and all the people answered with one voice, and said, All the words which the Lord hath said will we do."

Then followed the ratification of the covenant. An altar was built at the foot of the mountain, and beside it twelve pillars were set up, "according to the twelve tribes of Israel," as a testimony of their acceptance of the covenant. Moses "took the book of the covenant, and read in the audience of the people." All were at liberty to choose whether they would comply with them. They had heard God's law proclaimed, and its principles had been particularized, that they might know how much this covenant involved. Again the people answered with one accord, "All that the Lord hath said will we do, and be obedient." "When Moses had spoken every precept to all the people according to the law, he took the blood, . . . and sprinkled both the book, and all the people, saying, This is the blood of the testament which God hath enjoined unto you." Hebrews 9:19, 20.

Moses had received the command, "Come up unto the Lord, thou, and Aaron, Nadab, and Abihu, and seventy of the elders of Israel." The seventy elders were to assist Moses in the government of Israel, and God put upon them His Spirit. "And they saw the God of Israel: and there was under His feet as it were a paved work of a sapphire stone, and as it were the body of heaven in his clearness." They did not behold the Deity, but they saw the glory of His presence. They had been contemplating His glory, purity, and mercy, until they could approach nearer to Him.

Moses and "his minister Joshua" were now summoned to meet with God. The leader appointed Aaron and Hur, assisted by the elders, to act in his stead. Moses waited for a summons to the presence chamber of the Most High. Though his patience and obedience were tested, he did not forsake his post. Even this favored servant of God could not at once approach into His presence and endure His glory. Six days must be employed in devoting himself to God by searching of heart, meditation, and prayer.

Upon the seventh day, which was the Sabbath, Moses was called up into the cloud. "And Moses went into the midst of the cloud, . . . and Moses was in the mount forty days and forty nights." He fasted during the entire forty days.

God Exalts a Race of Slaves

During his stay in the mount, Moses received directions for the building of a sanctuary in which the divine Presence would be specially manifested. "Let them make Me a sanctuary, that I may dwell among them" was the command of God. For the third time the observance of the Sabbath was enjoined: "It is a sign between Me and the children of Israel forever," the Lord declared, "that ye may know that I am Jehovah that doth sanctify you. Ye shall keep the Sabbath therefore; for it is holy unto you: . . . whosoever doeth any work therein, that soul shall be cut off from among his people." Exodus 31:17, 13, 14.

Henceforth the people were to be honored with the abiding presence of their King. "I will dwell among the children of Israel, and will be their God," "and the tabernacle shall be sanctified by My glory." Exodus 29:45, 43.

From a race of slaves the Israelites had been exalted above all peoples to be the peculiar treasure of the King of kings. God had separated them from the world, He had made them the depositaries of His law, and He purposed, through them, to preserve among men the knowledge of Himself.

Thus the light of heaven was to shine out to a world in darkness. A voice was to be heard appealing to all peoples to turn from idolatry to serve the living God. If the Israelites would be true to their trust, God would be their defense, and He would exalt them above all other nations.

28 / Israel Worships a Golden Calf

While Moses was absent, it was a time of waiting and suspense to Israel. The people waited eagerly for his return. Accustomed in Egypt to material representations of deity, it had been hard for them to trust in an invisible being. They had come to rely upon Moses to sustain their faith. Now he was taken from them. Week after week passed, and still he did not return. It seemed to many in the camp that their leader had deserted them or that he had been consumed by the devouring fire.

During this period of waiting, there was time to meditate upon the law of God which they had heard and to prepare their hearts to receive further revelations that He might make to them. Had they been seeking a clearer understanding of God's requirements and humbling their hearts before Him, they would have been shielded from temptation. But they soon became careless, inattentive, and lawless, especially the "mixed multitude." They were impatient to be on their way to the land flowing with milk and honey. It was only on condition of obedience that the goodly land was promised them, but they had lost sight of this. Some suggested a return to Egypt; but whether forward to Canaan or backward to Egypt, the masses were determined to wait no longer for Moses.

The "mixed multitude" had been the first to indulge murmuring and impatience and were the leaders in apostasy. Among the objects regarded by the Egyptians as symbols of deity was the ox or calf. At the sug-

This chapter is based on Exodus 32 to 34.

gestion of those who had practiced idolatry in Egypt, a calf was now made and worshiped. The people desired some image to represent God and to go before them in the place of Moses. The mighty miracles in Egypt and at the Red Sea were designed to establish faith in God as the invisible, all-powerful Helper of Israel. The desire for some visible manifestation of His presence had been granted in the pillar of cloud and of fire, and in the revealing of His glory upon Mount Sinai. But with the cloud of the Presence still before them, they turned back in their hearts to the idolatry of Egypt.

The judicial authority had been delegated to Aaron, and a vast crowd gathered about his tent. The cloud, they said, now rested permanently upon the mount; it would no longer direct their travels. They must have an image in its place; and if, as had been suggested, they should return to Egypt, they would find favor with the Egyptians by bearing this image before them as their god. (See Appendix, Note 3.)

Instead of Leading, Aaron Follows

Aaron feebly remonstrated with the people, but his wavering and timidity at the critical moment rendered them the more determined. A blind, unreasoning frenzy seemed to possess the multitude. Some remained true to their covenant with God; but the greater part joined in the apostasy. A few who ventured to denounce the proposed image making as idolatry were set upon and finally lost their lives.

Aaron feared for his own safety, and instead of nobly standing up for the honor of God, he yielded to the demands of the multitude. They willingly yielded up their ornaments, and from these he made a molten calf in imitation of the gods of Egypt.

The people proclaimed, "These be thy gods, O Israel, which brought thee up out of the land of Egypt." And Aaron basely permitted this insult to Jehovah. He did more. Seeing with what satisfaction the golden god was received, he built an altar before it and made proclamation, "Tomorrow is a feast to the Lord. And they rose up early on the morrow, and offered burnt offerings, and brought peace offerings; and the people sat down to eat . . . and rose up to play." They gave themselves up to gluttony and licentious reveling.

A religion that permits men to devote themselves to selfish or sensual gratification is as pleasing to the multitudes now as in the days of Israel. There are still pliant Aarons in the church who will yield to the desires of the unconsecrated, and thus encourage them in sin.

Israel Broke Their Solemn Promise

Only a few days had passed since the Hebrews had stood trembling before the mount, listening to the words of the Lord, "Thou shalt have no other gods before Me." The glory of God still hovered above Sinai in the sight of the congregation; but "they made a calf in Horeb, and worshiped the molten image. Thus they changed their glory into the similitude of an ox." Psalm 106:19, 20.

Moses in the mount was warned of the apostasy in the camp. "Go, get thee down," were the words of God; "thy people, which thou broughtest out of the land of Egypt, have corrupted themselves: they have turned aside quickly out of the way which I commanded them."

God's covenant with His people had been disannulled, and He declared to Moses, "Let Me alone, that My wrath may wax hot against them, and that I may consume them: and I will make of thee a great nation." The people of Israel, especially the "mixed multitude," would be constantly disposed to rebel against God, murmur against their leader, and grieve him by their unbelief and stubbornness. Their sins had already forfeited the favor of God.

If God had purposed to destroy Israel, who could plead for them? But Moses discerned ground for hope where there appeared only discouragement and wrath.

The words of God, "Let Me alone," he understood not to forbid but to encourage intercession; if entreated, God would spare His people.

God had signified that He disowned His people. He had spoken of them to Moses as "thy people, which *thou* broughtest out of Egypt." But Moses disclaimed the leadership of Israel. They were not his, but God's—"*Thy* people, which *Thou* hast brought forth . . . with great power, and with a mighty hand. Wherefore," Moses urged, "should the Egyptians speak, and say, For mischief did He bring them out, to slay them in the mountains?"

During the few months since Israel left Egypt, the report of their wonderful deliverance had spread to all surrounding nations. Terrible foreboding rested upon the heathen. All were watching to see what the God of Israel would do for His people. Should they now be destroyed, their enemies would triumph. The Egyptians would claim that their accusations were true—instead of leading His people into the wilderness to sacrifice, He had caused them to be sacrificed. The destruction of the people whom He had honored would bring reproach upon His name. How great the responsibility resting upon those whom God has highly honored, to make His name a praise in the earth!

As Moses interceded for Israel, the Lord listened to his pleadings and granted his unselfish prayer. God had proved his love for that ungrateful people, and nobly had Moses endured the trial. The prosperity of God's people was dearer to him than becoming the father of a mighty nation. God was pleased with his faithfulness and integrity, and committed to him the great charge of leading Israel to the Promised Land.

As Moses and Joshua came down from the mount and drew near the encampment, they beheld the people shouting and dancing around their idol—a scene of heathen riot, an imitation of the idolatrous feasts of Egypt. How unlike the solemn and reverent worship of God! Moses was overwhelmed. He had just come from the presence of God's glory, and he was unprepared for that dreadful exhibition of the degradation of Israel. To show his abhorrence of their crime, he threw down the tables of stone, and they were broken in the sight of all the people, signifying that as they had broken their covenant with God, so God had broken His covenant with them.

Moses Punishes the Wrongdoers

Seizing the idol, Moses cast it into the fire. He afterward ground it to powder and strewed it upon the stream that descended from the mount. Thus was shown the utter worthlessness of the god which they had been worshiping.

The great leader summoned his guilty brother. Aaron endeavored to shield himself by relating the clamors of the people, that if he had not complied with their wishes he would have been put to death. "They said unto me, Make us gods, which shall go before us: for as for this Moses, the man that brought us up out of the land of Egypt, we wot not what is become of him. And I said unto them, Whosoever hath any gold, let them break it off. So they gave it me: then I cast it into the fire, and there came out this calf." He would lead Moses to believe that a miracle had been wrought, that the gold by supernatural power changed to a calf. But his excuses were of no avail. He was justly dealt with as the chief offender.

It was Aaron, "the saint of the Lord" (Psalm 106:16), that had made the idol and announced the feast. He had failed to check the idolaters in their heaven-daring purpose. He heard unmoved the proclamation before the molten image, "These be thy gods, O Israel, which brought thee up out of the land of Egypt." He had been with Moses on the mount and there beheld the glory of the Lord. It was he who had changed that glory into the similitude of an ox. He to whom God had committed the government of the people in the absence of Moses was found sanctioning rebellion. "The Lord was very angry with Aaron to have destroyed him." Deuteronomy 9:20. But in answer to the intercession of Moses, his life was spared; and in penitence for his great sin, he was restored to the favor of God.

How Aaron Encouraged Rebellion

If Aaron had had courage to stand for the right, he could have prevented that apostasy. If he had unswervingly maintained his own allegiance to God and had reminded the people of their solemn covenant with God, the evil would have been checked. But his compliance emboldened them to go to greater lengths in sin than had before entered their minds.

To justify himself, Aaron endeavored to make the people responsible for his weakness in yielding to their demand; but notwithstanding this, they were filled with admiration of his gentleness and patience. But Aaron's yielding spirit and desire to please had blinded his eyes to the enormity of the crime he was sanctioning. His course cost the life of thousands. In contrast was the course of Moses. While faithfully executing God's judgments, he showed that the welfare of Israel was dearer to him than prosperity, honor, or life.

God would have His servants prove their loyalty by faithfully rebuking transgression, however painful that act may be. Those who are honored with a divine commission are not to aim at self-exaltation or shun disagreeable duties, but to perform God's work with unswerving fidelity.

The insubordination which Aaron had permitted, if not speedily crushed, would run riot in wickedness and involve the nation in ruin. By terrible severity the evil must be put away. Moses called to the people, "Who is on the Lord's side? let him come unto me." Those who had not joined the apostasy were to take their position at the right; those who were guilty but repentant, at the left. It was found that the tribe of Levi had taken no part in the idolatrous worship. From among other

As Moses was receiving the Ten Commandments from God on the mountaintop, Satan was at work in the camp below, inciting God's people to apostasy.

tribes there were great numbers who now signified their repentance. But a large company, mostly the "mixed multitude," persisted in their rebellion. In the name of "the Lord God of Israel," Moses now commanded those who had kept themselves clear of idolatry to gird on their swords and slay all who persisted in rebellion. "And there fell of the people that day about three thousand men." The ringleaders in wickedness were cut off, but all who repented were spared.

Men are to beware how they judge and condemn their fellowmen; but when God commands them to execute His sentence upon iniquity, He is to be obeyed. Those who performed this painful act thus manifested their abhorrence of rebellion and idolatry. The Lord honored their faithfulness by bestowing special distinction upon the tribe of Levi.

That the divine government might be maintained, justice must be visited upon the traitors. Yet even here God's mercy was displayed: He granted freedom of choice and opportunity for repentance to all. Only those were cut off who persisted in rebellion.

Why Israel's Idolatry Must Be Punished

It was necessary that this sin should be punished as a testimony to surrounding nations of God's displeasure against idolatry. As the Israelites would hereafter condemn idolatry, their enemies would throw back the charge that the people who claimed Jehovah as their God had made a calf and worshiped it in Horeb. Though compelled to acknowledge the disgraceful truth, Israel could point to the terrible fate of the transgressors as evidence that their sin had not been excused.

Love no less than justice demanded that judgment be inflicted. God cuts off those who are determined upon rebellion, that they may not lead others to ruin. In sparing the life of Cain, God had demonstrated the result of permitting sin to go unpunished. His life and teaching led to the state of corruption that demanded the destruction of the whole world by a flood. The history of the antediluvians testifies that God's great forbearance did not repress their wickedness.

So at Sinai. Unless punishment had been speedily visited upon transgression, the same results would again have been seen. The earth would have become as corrupt as in the days of Noah. Evils would have followed, greater than resulted from sparing the life of Cain. It was the mercy of God that thousands should suffer, to prevent the necessity of visiting judgments upon millions. To save the many He must punish the few.

Furthermore, as the people had forfeited divine protection, the whole nation was exposed to the power of their enemies. They would soon have fallen prey to their numerous and powerful foes. It was necessary for the good of Israel that crime should be promptly punished.

And it was no less a mercy to the sinners themselves that they should be cut short in their evil course. Had their lives been spared, the same spirit that led them to rebel against God would have been manifested in hatred and strife among themselves. They would eventually have destroyed one another.

Moses' Christlike Love for Israel

As the people were roused to see the enormity of their guilt, it was feared that every offender was to be cut off. Moses promised to plead once more with God for them.

"Ye have sinned a great sin," he said, "and now I will go up unto the Lord; peradventure I shall make an atonement for your sin." In his confession before God he said, "Oh, this people have sinned a great sin, and have made them gods of gold. Yet now if Thou wilt forgive their sin—; and if not, blot me, I pray Thee, out of Thy book which Thou hast written."

In the prayer of Moses, our minds are directed to the heavenly records in which the names of all men are inscribed, and their deeds, good or evil, are registered. The book of life contains the names of all who have entered the service of God. If any of these by stubborn persistence in sin become finally hardened against His Holy Spirit, their names will in the judgment be blotted from the book of life.

If the people of Israel were to be rejected by the Lord, Moses desired his name to be blotted out with theirs; he could not endure to see the judgments of God fall upon those who had been graciously delivered. The intercession of Moses in behalf of Israel illustrates the mediation of Christ for sinful men. But the Lord did not permit Moses to bear, as did Christ, the guilt of the transgressor. "Whosoever hath sinned against Me," He said, "him will I blot out of My book."

In deep sadness the people buried their dead. Three thousand had fallen by the sword; a plague had soon after broken out in the encampment; and now the message came to them that the divine Presence would no longer accompany them in their journeyings: "I will not go up in the midst of thee; for thou art a stiffnecked people: lest I consume thee in the way." And the command was given, "Put off thy ornaments from thee, that I may know what to do unto thee." In penitence and humiliation, "the children of Israel stripped themselves of their ornaments by the mount Horeb."

By divine direction, the tent that had served as a temporary place of worship was removed "afar off from the camp." This was further evidence that God had withdrawn His presence from them. The rebuke was keenly felt, and to the conscience-smitten multitudes it seemed a foreboding of greater calamity.

But they were not left without hope. The tent was pitched without the encampment, but Moses called it "the tabernacle of the congregation." All who were truly penitent and desired to return to the Lord were directed to repair thither to confess their sins and seek His mercy. When they returned to their tents, Moses entered the tabernacle. The people watched for some token that his intercessions in their behalf were accepted. When the cloudy pillar descended and stood at the entrance of the tabernacle, the people wept for joy, and they "rose up and worshiped, every man in his tent door."

Help From God, a Necessity

Moses had learned that in order to prevail with the people, he must have help from God. He pleaded for an assurance of God's presence: "Now therefore, I pray Thee, if I have found grace in Thy sight, show me now Thy way, that I may know Thee, that I may find grace in Thy sight: and consider that this nation is Thy people."

The answer was, "My presence shall go with thee, and I will give thee rest." But Moses was not yet satisfied. He prayed that the favor of God might be restored to His people and that the token of His presence might continue to direct their journeyings: "If Thy presence go not with me, carry us not up hence. For wherein shall it be known here that I and Thy people have found grace in Thy sight? is it not in that Thou goest with us?"

And the Lord said, "I will do this thing also that thou hast spoken: for thou hast found grace in My sight, and I know thee." Still the prophet did not cease pleading. He now made a request that no human being had ever made before: "I beseech Thee, show me Thy glory."

Moses Sees God's Glory

The gracious words were spoken, "I will make all My goodness pass before thee." Moses was summoned to the mountain summit; then the hand that made the world, that hand that "removeth the mountains, and they know not" (Job 9:5), took this creature of the dust and placed him in a cleft of the rock, while the glory of God and all His goodness passed before him.

This experience was to Moses an assurance which he counted of infinitely greater worth than all the learning of Egypt or all his attainments as a statesman or military leader. No earthly power or skill or learning can supply the place of God's abiding presence.

Moses stood alone in the presence of the Eternal One, and he was not afraid, for his soul was in harmony with his Maker. "If I regard iniquity in my heart, the Lord will not hear me." Psalm 66:18. But "the secret of the Lord is with them that fear Him; and He will show them His covenant." Psalm 25:14.

The Deity proclaimed Himself, "The Lord, The Lord God, merciful and gracious, long-suffering, and abundant in goodness and truth, keeping mercy for thousands, forgiving iniquity and transgression and sin, and that will by no means clear the guilty."

"Moses made haste, and bowed his head toward the earth, and worshiped." The Lord graciously promised to renew His favor to Israel and to do marvels such as had not been done "in all the earth, nor in any nation." During all this time, as at the first, Moses was miraculously sustained. At God's command he had prepared two tables of stone and had taken them with him to the summit; and again the Lord "wrote upon the tables the words of the covenant, the Ten Commandments." (See Appendix, Note 4.)

Moses' face shone with a dazzling light when he descended from the mountain. Aaron as well as the people "were afraid to come nigh him." Seeing their terror, he held out to them the pledge of God's reconciliation. They perceived in his voice nothing but love and entreaty, and at last one ventured to approach him. Too awed to speak, he silently pointed to the countenance of Moses and then toward heaven. The great leader understood his meaning. In their conscious guilt, they could not endure the heavenly light which, had they been obedient to God, would have filled them with joy.

Moses put a veil upon his face and continued to do so thereafter whenever he returned to the camp from communion with God.

By this brightness, God designed to impress upon Israel the exalted character of His law and the glory of the gospel revealed through Christ. While Moses was in the mount, God presented to him not only the tables of the law, but also the plan of salvation. He saw the sacrifice of Christ prefigured by all the types and symbols of the Jewish age; and it was the heavenly light streaming from Calvary, no less than the glory of the law of God, that shed such radiance upon the face of Moses.

The glory reflected in the countenance of Moses testifies that the closer our communion with God and the clearer our knowledge of His requirements, the more fully shall we be conformed to the divine image.

As Israel's intercessor veiled his countenance, so Christ, the divine Mediator, veiled His divinity with humanity when He came to earth. Had He come clothed with the brightness of heaven, men in their sinful state could not have endured the glory of His presence. Therefore He humbled Himself, and was made "in the likeness of sinful flesh" (Romans 8:3), that He might reach the fallen race and lift them up.

29 / Satan's Hatred of God's Law

The first effort of Satan to overthrow God's law—undertaken among the sinless inhabitants of heaven—seemed for a time to be crowned with success. A vast number of the angels were seduced. But Satan's apparent triumph resulted in defeat and loss, separation from God, and banishment from heaven.

When the conflict was renewed on earth, Satan again won a seeming advantage. By transgression, man became his captive. Now the way seemed open for Satan to establish an independent kingdom and to defy the authority of God and His Son. But the plan of salvation made it possible for man again to be brought into harmony with God.

Again Satan was defeated, and again he resorted to deception in the hope of converting defeat into victory. He now represented God as unjust in having permitted man to transgress His law. "Why," said the tempter, "when God knew what would be the result, did He permit man to be placed on trial and bring in misery and death?" The children of Adam gave ear to the tempter and murmured against the only Being who could save them from the destructive power of Satan.

Thousands today are echoing the same rebellious complaint against God. They do not see that to deprive man of freedom of choice would make him a mere automaton. Like the inhabitants of all other worlds, he must be subject to the test of obedience; but he is never brought into such a position that yielding to evil becomes a matter of necessity. No temptation or trial is permitted which he is unable to resist.

As men increased, almost the whole world joined the ranks of rebellion. Once more Satan seemed to have gained the victory, but the earth was cleansed by the Flood from its moral pollution.

Why God Chose Israel

Says the prophet, "Let favor be showed to the wicked, yet will he not learn righteousness: . . . and will not behold the majesty of the Lord." Isaiah 26:10. Thus it was after the Flood. The inhabitants of the earth again rebelled against the Lord. Twice God's covenant had been rejected by the world. Both the people before the Flood and the descendants of Noah cast off the divine authority. Then God entered into covenant with Abraham and took to Himself a people to become the depositaries of His law.

To seduce and destroy this people, Satan began at once to lay his snares. The children of Jacob were tempted to contract marriage with the heathen and worship their idols. But Joseph's fidelity was a testimony to the true faith. To quench this light Satan worked through Joseph's brothers to cause him to be sold as a slave. But God overruled. Both in the house of Potiphar and in the prison, Joseph received an education that, with the fear of God, prepared him for his position as prime minister of the nation. His influence was felt throughout the land, and the knowledge of God was spread far and wide. The idolatrous priests were filled with alarm. Inspired by Satan's enmity toward the God of heaven, they set themselves to quench the light.

After the flight of Moses from Egypt, idolatry seemed to conquer. Year by year the hopes of the Israelites grew fainter. Both king and people mocked the God of Israel. This spirit grew until it culminated in the Pharaoh who was confronted by Moses. When the Hebrew leader came before the king with a message from "Jehovah, God of Israel," it was not ignorance of the true God, but defiance of His power, that prompted the answer, "Who is Jehovah, that I should obey His voice? . . . I know not Jehovah." From first to last, Pharaoh's opposition was the result of hatred and defiance.

In the days of Joseph, Egypt had been an asylum for Israel. God had been honored in the kindness shown His people; and now the long-suffering One, full of compassion, gave each judgment time to do its work. The Egyptians had evidence of the power of Jehovah, and all who would might submit to God and escape His judgments. The stubbornness of the king resulted in spreading the knowledge of God and bringing many Egyptians to give themselves to His service.

The gross idolatry of the Egyptians and their cruelty during the latter part of the Hebrew sojourn should have inspired in the Israelites an abhorrence of idolatry and led them to flee for refuge to the God of their fathers. But Satan darkened their minds, leading them to imitate the practices of their heathen masters.

When the time came for Israel's deliverance, it was Satan's determination that that great people, numbering more than two million, should be held in ignorance, superstition, obscurity, and bondage that he might obliterate from their minds the remembrance of God.

When the miracles were wrought before the king, Satan wrought to counterfeit the work of God and resist His will. The only result was to prepare the way for greater exhibitions of divine power and glory.

God "brought forth His people with joy, and His chosen with gladness . . . that they might observe His statutes, and keep His laws." Psalm 105:43-45.

During the bondage in Egypt many of the Israelites had, to a great extent, lost the knowledge of God's law and had mingled its precepts with heathen customs and traditions. God brought them to Sinai, and there with His own voice declared His law.

Even while God was proclaiming His law to His people, Satan was plotting to tempt them to sin. By leading them into idolatry, he would destroy the efficacy of all worship, for how can man be elevated by adoring what may be symbolized by his own handiwork? If men could so forget their own divine relationship as to bow down to these revolting and senseless objects, then the evil passions of the heart would be unrestrained, and Satan would have full sway.

At the very foot of Sinai, Satan began to plan for overthrowing the law of God, thus carrying forward the same work he had begun in heaven. During the forty days Moses was in the mount with God, Satan was exciting doubt, apostasy, and rebellion. When Moses came from the presence of divine glory with the law they had pledged to obey, he found God's covenant people bowing in adoration before a golden image.

Satan had planned to cause their ruin. Since they had proved themselves so utterly degraded, the Lord would, he believed, divorce them from Himself. Thus would be secured the extinction of the seed of Abraham that was to preserve the knowledge of the living God, and through whom the true Seed was to come to conquer Satan. But the great rebel again was defeated. While those who stubbornly ranged themselves on the side of Satan were cut off, the people, humbled and repentant, were mercifully pardoned. The whole universe had been witness to the scenes at Sinai; all had seen the contrast between the government of God and that of Satan.

The True Sign of Loyalty to God—the Sabbath

God's claim to reverence and worship, above the gods of the heathen, is based upon the fact that He is the Creator. Says the prophet Jeremiah: "The living God. . . . hath made the earth by His power, He hath established the world by His wisdom, and hath stretched out the heavens by His discretion." "Every man is brutish in his knowledge: every founder is confounded by the graven image: for his molten image is falsehood, and there is no breath in them.' They are vanity, and the work of errors: in the time of their visitation they shall perish." Jeremiah 10:10-12, 14, 15. The Sabbath, as a memorial of God's creative power, points to Him as the maker of the heavens and the earth. It is a constant witness to His greatness, wisdom, and love. Had the Sabbath always been sacredly observed, there could never have been an atheist or an idolater.

The Sabbath, which originated in Eden, is as old as the world itself. It was observed by all the patriarchs, from creation down. When the law was proclaimed at Sinai, the first words of the fourth commandment were, "Remember the Sabbath day, to keep it holy," showing that the Sabbath was not then instituted. We are pointed back for its origin to creation. Satan aimed to tear down this great memorial. If men could be led to forget their Creator, they would make no effort to resist the power of evil, and Satan would be sure of his prey.

Satan's enmity against God's law had impelled him to war against every precept of the Decalogue. Contempt for parental authority will soon lead to contempt for the authority of God, hence Satan's efforts to lessen the obligation of the fifth commandment. In many heathen nations parents were abandoned or put to death as soon as age had rendered them incapable of providing for themselves. The mother was treated with little respect, and, upon the death of her husband, was required to submit to the authority of her eldest son. Filial obedience was enjoined by Moses; but as the Israelites departed from the Lord, the fifth commandment, with others, came to be disregarded.

Satan was "a murderer from the beginning" (John 8:44); and as soon as he obtained power over the human race, he not only prompted them to hate and slay one another, but made the violation of the sixth commandment a part of their religion.

Heathen nations were led to believe that human sacrifices were necessary to secure the favor of their deities; and the most horrible cruelties have been perpetrated under various forms of idolatry. Among these was the practice of causing their children to pass through the fire before their idols. When one came through unharmed, the people believed their offerings were accepted. The one thus delivered was regarded as specially favored by the gods, was loaded with benefits, and ever afterward held in high esteem. However aggravated his crimes, he was never punished. But should one be burned in passing through the fire, his fate was sealed; the anger of the gods could be appeased only by taking the life of the victim. In times of great apostasy these abominations prevailed, to some extent, among the Israelites.

The violation of the seventh commandment also was early practiced in the name of religion. Licentious and abominable rites were made a part of the heathen worship. The gods themselves were impure, and their worshipers gave rein to the baser passions. Religious festivals were characterized by universal, open impurity.

Polygamy was one of the sins that brought the wrath of God upon the antediluvian world. Yet after the Flood it again became widespread. It was Satan's studied effort to pervert marriage, to weaken its obligations and lessen its sacredness. In no surer way could he deface the image of God in man and open the door to misery and vice.

God Will Win the Battle

Multitudes give ear to Satan's deceptions and set themselves against God. But amid the working of evil, God's purposes move steadily forward to their accomplishment. To all created intelligences He is making manifest His justice and benevolence. The whole human race have become transgressors of God's law, but by the sacrifice of His Son they may return to God. Through the grace of Christ they may be enabled to render obedience to the Father's law. In every age God gathers out a people "in whose heart is His law." Isaiah 51:7.

God's dealings with rebellion will result in fully unmasking the work so long carried on under cover. The fruits of setting aside the divine statutes will be laid open to the view of all created intelligences. The law of God will stand fully vindicated. Satan himself, in the presence of the witnessing universe, will confess the justice of God's government and the righteousness of His law.

The terrors of Sinai were to represent to the people the scenes of the judgment. The sound of a trumpet summoned Israel to meet with God. The voice of the Archangel and the trump of God shall summon, from the whole earth, both the living and the dead to the presence of their Judge. At the great judgment day, Christ will come "in the glory of His Father with His angels." Matthew 16:27. Before Him shall be gathered all nations.

When Christ shall come in glory with His holy angels, the whole earth shall be ablaze with the terrible light of His presence. "Our God shall come, and shall not keep silence; a fire shall devour before Him, and it shall be very tempestuous round about Him. He shall call to the heavens from above, and to the earth, that He may judge His people." Psalm 50:3, 4. "The Lord Jesus shall be revealed from heaven with His mighty angels, in flaming fire taking vengeance on them that know not God, and that obey not the gospel." 2 Thessalonians 1:7, 8.

When Moses came from the divine Presence in the mount, guilty Israel could not endure the light that glorified his countenance. How much less can transgressors look upon the Son of God when He shall appear in the glory of His Father, surrounded by all the heavenly host, to execute judgment upon the transgressors of His law and the rejecters of His atonement. "The kings of the earth, and the great men, and the rich men, and the chief captains, and the mighty men" shall hide themselves "in the dens and in the rocks of the mountains," and they shall say to the mountains and rocks,

"Fall on us, and hide us from the face of Him that sitteth on the throne, . . . for the great day of His wrath is come; and who shall be able to stand?" Revelation 6:15-17.

Satan has represented that good would result from transgression, but it will be seen that "the wages of sin is death." Romans 6:23. "For, behold, the day cometh, that shall burn as an oven; and all the proud, yea, and all that do wickedly, shall be stubble; and the day that cometh shall burn them up, saith the Lord of hosts, that it shall leave them neither root nor branch." Malachi 4:1.

But amid the tempest of divine judgment, the children of God will have no cause for fear. "The Lord will be the hope of His people, and the strength of the children of Israel." Joel 3:16.

The great plan of redemption results in fully bringing back the world into God's favor. All that was lost by sin is restored. Not only man but the earth is redeemed, to be the eternal abode of the obedient. Now God's original purpose in its creation is accomplished. "The saints of the Most High shall take the kingdom, and possess the kingdom forever, even forever and ever." Daniel 7:18.

The sacred statutes which Satan has hated and sought to destroy will be honored throughout a sinless universe. "The Lord God will cause righteousness and praise to spring forth before all the nations." Isaiah 61:11.

30 / The Sanctuary: God's Dwelling Place in Israel

The command was communicated to Moses while in the mount with God, "Let them make Me a sanctuary, that I may dwell among them." Exodus 25:8. Full directions were given for the construction of the tabernacle. By their apostasy, the Israelites forfeited the divine Presence, but after they were again taken into favor with Heaven, the great leader proceeded to execute the divine command.

God Himself gave Moses the plan of that structure, its size and form, the materials to be employed, and every article of furniture it was to contain. The holy places made with hands were "figures of the true," "patterns of things in the heavens" (Hebrews 9:24, 23), a miniature representation of the heavenly temple where Christ, our great High Priest, was to minister in the sinner's behalf. God presented before Moses a view of the heavenly sanctuary and commanded him to make all things according to the pattern shown him.

For building the sanctuary, a large amount of the most costly material was required, yet the Lord accepted only freewill offerings.

All the people responded, "every one whose heart stirred him up, and every one whom his spirit made willing, and they brought the Lord's offering to the work of the tabernacle of the congregation. . . . And they came, both men and women, as many as were willinghearted, and brought bracelets, and earrings, and rings, and tablets, all jewels of gold."

While the building of the sanctuary was in progress,

This chapter is based on Exodus 25 to 40; Leviticus 4 and 16.

men, women, and children continued to bring their offerings, until those in charge of the work found that they had more than could be used. And Moses caused to be proclaimed throughout the camp, "Let neither man nor woman make any more work for the offering of the sanctuary. So the people were restrained from bringing." The Israelites' devotion, zeal, and liberality are an example worthy of imitation. All who love the worship of God will manifest the same spirit of sacrifice in preparing a house where He may meet with them. An amount sufficient to accomplish the work should be freely given, that the workmen may be able to say, as did the builders of the tabernacle, "Bring no more offerings."

The tabernacle was small, not more than fifty-five feet in length, and eighteen in breadth and height. Yet it was magnificent. The wood was that of the acacia tree, less subject to decay than any other at Sinai. The walls consisted of upright boards, set in silver sockets, and held firm by pillars and connection bars, all overlaid with gold, giving the appearance of solid gold.

Two Apartments Symbolize Two Phases of Ministry

The building was divided into two apartments by a beautiful veil, and a similar veil closed the entrance of the first apartment. These were of gorgeous colors— blue, purple, and scarlet—while inwrought with threads of gold and silver were cherubim to represent the angelic host.

The sacred tent was enclosed in an open space called the court. The entrance was at the eastern end, closed by curtains of beautiful workmanship, though inferior to those of the sanctuary. The building could be plainly seen by the people without. In the court stood the brazen altar of burnt offering. On this altar were consumed all the sacrifices made by fire unto the Lord, and its horns were sprinkled with the atoning blood. Between the altar and the door of the tabernacle was the brass laver made from the mirrors that had been the freewill offering of the women of Israel. At the laver the priests were to wash their hands and feet whenever they went into the sacred apartments or approached the altar to offer a burnt offering unto the Lord.

In the first apartment, or holy place, were the table of showbread, the candlestick, and the altar of incense. The table of showbread stood on the north; it was overlaid with pure gold. On this table the priests were each Sabbath to place twelve cakes, arranged in two piles. On the south was the seven-branched candlestick, its branches ornamented with exquisitely wrought flowers, the whole made from one solid piece of gold. The lamps were never all extinguished at one time, but shed their light by day and night.

Just before the veil separating the holy place from the most holy and the immediate presence of God stood the golden altar of incense. Upon this altar the priest was to burn incense every morning and evening; its horns were touched with the blood of the sin offering and sprinkled with blood upon the great Day of Atonement. The fire on this altar was kindled by God Himself. Day and night the holy incense diffused its fragrance throughout the sacred apartments and far around the tabernacle.

Beyond the inner veil was the holy of holies, where centered the symbolic service of atonement and intercession, the connecting link between heaven and earth. In this apartment was the ark, overlaid within and without with gold, a depository for the tables of stone, the Ten Commandments. It was called the ark of God's testament, the ark of the covenant, since the Ten Commandments were the basis of the covenant made between God and Israel.

The cover of the chest was called the mercy seat. This was wrought of one solid piece of gold, surmounted by golden cherubim on each end. The position of the cherubim, with their faces turned toward each other and looking reverently downward toward the ark, represented the reverence with which the heavenly host regard the law of God and their interest in the plan of redemption.

Above the mercy seat was the Shekinah, the manifestation of the divine Presence. Divine messages were sometimes communicated to the high priest by a voice from the cloud.

The law of God within the ark was the great rule of righteousness and judgment. That law pronounced death upon the transgressor; but above the law was the mercy seat. By virtue of the atonement, pardon was granted to the repentant sinner. "Mercy and truth are met together; righteousness and peace have kissed each other." Psalm 85:10.

A Dim Reflection of Heavenly Glory

No language can describe the glory within the sanctuary. The gold-plated walls reflecting light from the golden candlestick; the table, and altar of incense, glittering with gold; beyond the second veil the sacred ark, and above it the holy Shekinah, the manifestation of Jehovah's presence—all were but a dim reflection of the glories of the temple of God in heaven, the great center of the work for man's redemption.

About half a year was occupied in building the tabernacle. When it was completed, Moses examined all the work of the builders. "As the Lord had commanded, even so had they done it: and Moses blessed them." The multitude of Israel crowded around to look upon the sacred structure. The pillar of cloud floated over the sanctuary, and "the glory of the Lord filled the tabernacle." There was a revealing of the divine majesty, and for a time even Moses could not enter. With deep emotion the people beheld the token that the work of their hands was accepted. A solemn awe rested upon all. The gladness of their hearts welled up in tears of joy. God had condescended to abide with them.

In the days of Abraham, the priesthood was the birthright of the eldest son. Now, instead of the first-born, the Lord accepted the tribe of Levi for the work of the sanctuary. However, Aaron and his sons alone were permitted to minister before the Lord; the rest of the tribe were entrusted with the charge of the tabernacle and its furniture.

A special dress was appointed for the priests. The robe of the common priest was of white linen, woven in one piece, confined about the waist by a white linen girdle embroidered in blue, purple, and red. A linen turban or miter completed his outer costume. The priests were to leave their shoes in the court before entering the sanctuary, and also to wash both their hands and feet before ministering in the tabernacle. Thus was taught the lesson that all defilement must be put away from those who would approach the presence of God.

The garments of the high priest were of costly material and beautiful workmanship. In addition to the linen dress of the common priest, he wore a robe of blue, also woven in one piece. Around the skirt it was ornamented with golden bells and pomegranates of blue, purple, and scarlet. The ephod, a shorter garment, was confined by a girdle of the same colors. The ephod was sleeveless, and on its shoulder pieces were set two onyx stones bearing the names of the twelve tribes of Israel.

Over the ephod was the breastplate in the form of a square, suspended from the shoulders by a cord of blue. The border was formed of a variety of precious stones, the same that form the twelve foundations of the City of God. The Lord's direction was, "Aaron shall bear the names of the children of Israel in the breastplate of judgment upon his heart, when he goeth in unto the holy place, for a memorial before the Lord continually." Exodus 28:29. So, Christ, the great High Priest, pleading His blood in the sinner's behalf, bears upon His heart the name of every repentant, believing soul.

At the right and left of the breastplate were two large stones known as the Urim and Thummim. When questions were brought before the Lord, a halo of light encircling the stone at the right was a token of divine approval, while a cloud shadowing the stone at the left was evidence of denial.

Everything connected with the apparel and deportment of the priests was to impress the beholder with the holiness of God and the purity required of those who came into His presence.

The Sanctuary Ministry a Foreshadow of Heavenly Things

Not only the sanctuary but the ministry of the priests was to "serve unto the example and shadow of heavenly things." Hebrews 8:5. The ministration consisted of two divisions, a daily and a yearly service. The daily service was performed at the altar of burnt offering in the court of the tabernacle and in the holy place, while the yearly service was in the most holy.

No mortal eye but that of the high priest was to look upon the inner apartment of the sanctuary. Only once a year could he enter there. The people in reverent silence awaited his return, their hearts uplifted in prayer for the divine blessing. Before the mercy seat the high priest made the atonement for Israel, and in the cloud of glory, God met with him. His stay beyond the accustomed time filled them with fear, lest because of their sins or his own he had been slain by the glory of the Lord.

The Daily Service

Every morning and evening a lamb of a year old was burned upon the altar, symbolizing the daily consecration of the nation and their constant dependence upon the atoning blood of Christ. Only an offering "without blemish" could be a symbol of His perfect purity who was to offer Himself as "a lamb without blemish and without spot." 1 Peter 1:19. The apostle Paul says, "I beseech you therefore, brethren, by the mercies of God, that ye present your bodies a living sacrifice, holy, acceptable unto God, which is your reasonable service." Romans 12:1. Those who love Him with all the heart will desire to give Him the best service of the life, constantly seeking to bring every power of their being into harmony with His will.

In the offering of incense the priest was brought more directly into the presence of God than any other act of the daily ministration. The glory of God manifested above the mercy seat was partially visible from the first apartment. When the priest offered incense before the Lord, he looked toward the ark; and as the divine glory descended upon the mercy seat and filled the most holy place, often the priest was obliged to retire to the door of the tabernacle. As the priest looked by faith to the mercy seat which he could not see, so the people of God are now to direct their prayers to Christ, their great High Priest, who is pleading in their behalf in the sanctuary above.

The incense represents the merits and intercession of Christ, His perfect righteousness, which through faith is imputed to His people and which can alone make the worship of sinful beings acceptable to God. By blood and by incense God was to be approached— symbols pointing to the great Mediator through whom alone mercy and salvation can be granted to the repentant soul.

As the priests morning and evening entered the holy place, the daily sacrifice was ready to be offered upon the altar in the court. This was a time of intense interest; the worshipers at the tabernacle were to engage in searching of the heart and confession of sin. Their petitions ascended with the cloud of incense, while faith laid hold upon the merits of the promised Saviour prefigured by the atoning sacrifice. In later times the Jews, scattered as captives in distant lands, still at the appointed hour turned their faces toward Jerusalem and offered their petitions to the God of Israel. In this custom Christians have an example for morning and evening prayer. God looks with great pleasure upon those who bow morning and evening to seek pardon and present their requests for blessings.

The showbread was a perpetual offering, part of the daily sacrifice. It was ever before the face of the Lord (Exodus 25:30), an acknowledgment of man's dependence upon God for both temporal and spiritual food, received only through the mediation of Christ. God had fed Israel with bread from heaven, and they were still dependent upon His bounty, both for temporal food and spiritual blessings. Both the manna and the showbread pointed to Christ, the living Bread. He Himself said, "I am the living Bread which came down from heaven." John 6:48-51. The bread was removed every Sabbath, to be replaced by fresh loaves.

The most important part of the daily ministration was the service in behalf of individuals. The repentant sinner brought his offering to the door of the tabernacle, and, placing his hand upon the victim's head, confessed his sins, thus in figure transferring them from himself to the innocent sacrifice. By his own hand the animal was then slain, and the blood was carried by the priest into the holy place and sprinkled before the veil, behind which was the ark containing the law that the sinner had transgressed. By this ceremony the sin was, through the blood, transferred in figure to the sanctuary. In some cases the blood was not taken into the holy place. (See Appendix, Note 5.) But the flesh was eaten by the priest, as Moses directed, saying, "God hath given it you to bear the iniquity of the congregation." Leviticus 10:17. Both ceremonies symbolized the transfer of sin from the penitent to the sanctuary.

Such was the work that went on day by day throughout the year. The sins of Israel being thus transferred to the sanctuary, the holy places were defiled, and a special work became necessary for the removal of the sins. God commanded that an atonement be made for each of the sacred apartments, as for the altar, to "cleanse it, and hallow it from the uncleanness of the children of Israel." Leviticus 16:19.

Once a year, on the great Day of Atonement, the high priest entered the most holy place for the cleansing of the sanctuary. Two kids of the goats were brought to the door of the tabernacle and lots were cast upon them, "one lot for the Lord, and the other lot for the scapegoat." The goat upon which the first lot fell was slain as a sin offering for the people. The priest was to bring his blood within the veil and sprinkle it upon the mercy seat. "And he shall make an atonement for the holy place, because of the uncleanness of the children of Israel, and because of their transgressions in all their sins: and so shall he do for the tabernacle of the congregation."

"And Aaron shall lay both his hands upon the head of the live goat, and confess over him all the iniquities of the children of Israel, and all their transgressions in all their sins, putting them upon the head of the goat, and shall send him away by the hand of a fit man into the wilderness: and the goat shall bear upon him all their iniquities unto a land not inhabited." Not until the goat had thus been led away did the people regard themselves as freed from the burden of their sins. Every man was to afflict his soul while the work of atonement was going forward. All business was laid aside, and the whole congregation of Israel spent the day in solemn humiliation before God, with prayer, fasting, and deep searching of heart.

Truths Taught by Day of Atonement

Important truths concerning the atonement were taught by this yearly service. In the sin offerings presented during the year, a substitute had been accepted in the sinner's stead, but the blood of the victim had not made full atonement for the sin. It had only provided a means by which the sin was transferred to the sanctuary. By the offering of blood, the sinner confessed the guilt of his transgression and expressed faith in Him who was to take away the sin of the world. But he was not entirely released from the condemnation of the law. On the Day of Atonement the high priest, having taken an offering for the congregation, went into the most holy place with the blood and sprinkled it upon the mercy seat, above the tables of the law.

Thus the claims of the law, which demanded the life of the sinner, were satisfied. Then in his character of mediator the priest took the sins upon himself, and, leaving the sanctuary, bore with him the burden of Israel's guilt. He laid his hands upon the head of the scapegoat and confessed over him "all the iniquities of the children of Israel, and all their transgressions in all their sins, putting them upon the head of the goat." These sins were regarded as forever separated from the people. Such was the service performed "unto the example and shadow of heavenly things." Hebrews 8:5.

The True Heavenly Sanctuary

The earthly sanctuary was "a figure for the time then present, in which were offered both gifts and sacrifices"; its two holy places were "patterns of things in the heavens." Christ, our great High Priest, is "a minister of the sanctuary, and of the true tabernacle, which the Lord pitched and not man." Hebrews 9:9, 23; 8:2.

The apostle John was granted a view of the temple of God in heaven. He beheld there "seven lamps of fire burning before the throne." He saw an angel "having a golden censer; and there was given unto him much incense, that he should offer it with the prayers of all saints upon the golden altar which was before the throne." Revelation 4:5; 8:3. Here the prophet was permitted to behold the first apartment of the sanctuary in heaven. Again, "the temple of God was opened," and he looked within the inner veil upon the holy of holies. Here he beheld "the ark of his testament" (Revelation 11:19), represented by the sacred chest constructed by Moses to contain the law of God.

Paul declares that "the tabernacle and all the vessels of the ministry," when completed, were "the patterns of things in the heavens." Acts 7:44; Hebrews 9:21, 23. And John says that he saw the sanctuary in heaven. That sanctuary, in which Jesus ministers in our behalf, is the great original. The sanctuary built by Moses was a copy.

Important truths concerning the heavenly sanctuary and the work there carried forward for man's redemption were to be taught by the earthly sanctuary and its services.

After His ascension, our Saviour was to begin His work as our High Priest. "Christ is not entered into the holy places made with hands, which are the figures of the true; but into heaven itself, now to appear in the presence of God for us." Hebrews 9:24. Christ's ministration was to consist of two great divisions, each occupying a period of time and having a distinctive place in the heavenly sanctuary. So the typical ministration consisted of two divisions, the daily and the yearly service, and to each a department of the tabernacle was devoted.

Christ at His ascension appeared in the presence of God to plead His blood in behalf of penitent believers. So the priest in the daily ministration sprinkled the blood of the sacrifice in the holy place in the sinner's behalf.

The blood of Christ, while it was to release the repentant sinner from the condemnation of the law, was not to cancel the sin; it would stand on record in the sanctuary until the final atonement. So in the type the blood of the sin offering removed the sin from the penitent, but it rested in the sanctuary until the Day of Atonement.

In the great day of final award, the dead are to be "judged out of those things which were written in the books, according to their works." Revelation 20:12. Then the sins of all the truly penitent will be blotted from the books of heaven. Thus the sanctuary will be freed, or cleansed, from the record of sin. In the type this great work of blotting out of sins was represented by the services of the Day of Atonement, the cleansing of the earthly sanctuary accomplished by the removal of the sins by which it had been polluted.

In the final atonement the sins of the truly penitent

are to be blotted from the records of heaven, no more to be remembered or come into mind. So in the type they were borne away into the wilderness, forever separated from the congregation.

Since Satan is the direct instigator of all the sins that caused the death of the Son of God, justice demands that Satan suffer the final punishment. Christ's work for the redemption of men and the purification of the universe from sin will be closed by placing these sins upon Satan, who will bear the final penalty. So in the typical service, the yearly round of ministration closed with the purification of the sanctuary and the confessing of the sins on the head of the scapegoat.

Thus in the ministration of the tabernacle the people were taught each day the great truths relative to Christ's death and ministration, and once each year their minds were carried forward to the closing events of the great controversy between Christ and Satan, the final purification of the universe from sin and sinners.

31 / The Sin of Nadab and Abihu

After the dedication of the tabernacle, the priests were consecrated to their sacred office. These services occupied seven days; on the eighth day Aaron offered the sacrifices that God required. All had been done as God commanded, and He revealed His glory in a remarkable manner—fire came and consumed the offering upon the altar. The people raised a universal shout of praise and adoration and fell on their faces.

But soon afterward a terrible calamity fell upon the family of the high priest. Two of the sons of Aaron took each his censer and burned fragrant incense before the Lord. But they transgressed His command by the use of "strange fire." They took common instead of the sacred fire which God Himself had kindled. For this sin, fire from the Lord devoured them in the sight of the people.

Next to Moses and Aaron, Nadab and Abihu had stood highest in Israel. They had been especially honored by the Lord, having been permitted with the seventy elders to behold His glory in the mount. All this rendered their sin more grievous. Because men have received great light, because they have, like the princes of Israel, ascended to the mount and been privileged to have communion with God in the light of His glory, let them not flatter themselves that they can sin with impunity, that God will not be strict to punish their iniquity. Great privileges require virtue and holiness corresponding to the light given. Great blessings never give license to sin.

This chapter is based on Leviticus 10:1-11.

251

Nadab and Abihu had not been trained to habits of self-control. The father's yielding disposition had led him to neglect the discipline of his children. His sons had been permitted to follow inclination. Habits of self-indulgence obtained a hold on them which even the responsibility of the most sacred office had not power to break. They did not realize the necessity of exact obedience to the requirements of God. Aaron's mistaken indulgence of his sons prepared them to become the subjects of divine judgment.

Partial Obedience Not Acceptable

God cannot accept partial obedience. It was not enough that in this solemn worship nearly everything was done as He had directed. Let no one deceive himself with the belief that a part of God's commandments are nonessential, or that He will accept a substitute for that which He has required. God has placed in His Word no command which men may obey or disobey at will and not suffer the consequences.

"Moses said unto Aaron, and unto Eleazar and unto Ithamar, his sons, Uncover not your heads, neither rend your clothes; lest ye die, . . . for the anointing oil of the Lord is upon you." The great leader reminded his brother of the words of God, "Before all the people I will be glorified." Aaron was silent. The death of his sons in so terrible a sin—a sin which he now saw to be the result of his own neglect of duty—wrung the father's heart with anguish. But by no manifestation of grief must he seem to sympathize with sin. The congregation must not be led to murmur against God.

The Lord would teach His people to acknowledge the justice of His corrections, that others may fear. The divine rebuke is upon that false sympathy for the sinner which endeavors to excuse his sin. The wrongdoer does not realize the enormity of transgression, and without the convicting power of the Holy Spirit he remains in partial blindness to his sin. It is the duty of Christ's servants to show these erring ones their peril.

Many have gone down to ruin as the result of false and deceptive sympathy.

Nadab and Abihu would never have committed that fatal sin had they not first become partially intoxicated by the free use of wine. By intemperance they were disqualified for their holy office. Their minds became confused and their moral perceptions dulled so that they could not discern the difference between the sacred and the common. To Aaron and his surviving sons was given the warning, "Do not drink . . . when ye go into the tabernacle of the congregation, lest ye die." The use of spirituous liquors prevents men from realizing the sacredness of holy things or the binding force of God's requirements. All who occupied positions of responsibility were to be men of strict temperance that their minds might be clear to discriminate between right and wrong.

The same obligation rests upon every follower of Christ. "Ye are a chosen generation, a royal priesthood, a holy nation, a peculiar people." 1 Peter 2:9. When intoxicants are used, the same effects will follow as in the case of those priests of Israel. The conscience will lose its sensibility to sin till the common and the sacred will lose all difference of significance. "Whether therefore ye eat, or drink, or whatsoever ye do, do all to the glory of God." 1 Corinthians 10:31. To the church of Christ in all ages is addressed the solemn and fearful warning, "If any man defile the temple of God, him shall God destroy; for the temple of God is holy, which temple ye are." 1 Corinthians 3:17.

32 / The Grace of Christ and the New Covenant

Adam and Eve at their creation had a knowledge of the law of God; they were acquainted with its claims; its precepts were written upon their hearts. When man fell by transgression, the law was not changed, but the promise of a Saviour was given. Sacrificial offerings pointed to the death of Christ as the great sin offering.

The law of God was handed down from father to son through successive generations. But few rendered obedience. The world became so vile that it was necessary to cleanse it by the Flood from its corruption. Noah taught his descendants the Ten Commandments. As men again departed from God, the Lord chose Abraham, of whom He declared, "Abraham obeyed My voice, and kept My charge, My commandments, My statutes, and My laws." Genesis 26:5. To him was given the rite of circumcision, a pledge to remain separate from idolatry and obey the law of God. The failure of Abraham's descendants to keep their pledge was the cause of their bondage in Egypt. In their intercourse with idolaters and forced submission to the Egyptians, the divine precepts became still further corrupted with the vile teachings of heathenism. Therefore the Lord came down upon Sinai and in awful majesty spoke His law in the hearing of all the people.

He did not even then trust His precepts to the memory of a people prone to forget, but wrote them upon tables of stone. And He did not stop with giving them the Decalogue. Moses was commanded to write judgments and laws giving minute instruction as to what was required. These directions were only the principles of the Ten Commandments amplified in a specific manner, designed to guard their sacredness.

If the descendants of Abraham had kept the covenant, of which circumcision was a sign, there would have been no necessity for God's law to be proclaimed from Sinai or engraved upon tables of stone.

The sacrificial system was also perverted. Through long intercourse with idolaters, Israel had mingled many heathen customs with their worship; therefore the Lord gave them definite instructions concerning the sacrificial service. The ceremonial law was given to Moses and by him written in a book. But the law of Ten Commandments had been written by God Himself on tables of stone and preserved in the ark.

Two Laws: Moral and Ceremonial

Many try to blend these two systems, using the texts that speak of the ceremonial law to prove that the moral law has been abolished, but this is perversion of the Scriptures. The ceremonial system was made up of symbols pointing to Christ, to His sacrifice and priesthood. This ritual law with its sacrifices and ordinances was to be performed by the Hebrews until type met antitype in the death of Christ. Then all the sacrificial offerings were to cease. It is this law that Christ "took . . . out of the way, nailing it to His cross." Colossians 2:14.

But concerning the law of Ten Commandments the psalmist declares, "Forever, O Lord, Thy word is settled in heaven." Psalm 119:89. And Christ Himself says, "Think not that I am come to destroy the law. . . . Verily I say unto you, Till heaven and earth pass, one jot or one tittle shall in no wise pass from the law, till all be fulfilled." Matthew 5:17, 18. Here He teaches that the claims of God's law should hold as long as the heavens and the earth remain.

Concerning the law proclaimed from Sinai, Nehemiah says, "Thou camest down also upon Mount

Sinai, and spakest with them from heaven, and gavest them *right judgments, and true laws, good statutes and commandments.*" Nehemiah 9:13. And Paul, "the apostle to the Gentiles," declares, "the law is holy, and the commandment holy, and just, and good." Romans 7:12.

While the Saviour's death brought to an end the law of types and shadows, it did not detract from the obligation of the moral law. The very fact that it was necessary for Christ to die in order to atone for the transgression of that law, proves it to be immutable.

Christ the Mediator of the New Covenant

Those who claim that Christ came to do away with the Old Testament represent the religion of the Hebrews as consisting of mere forms and ceremonies. But this is an error. Through all the ages after the Fall, "God was in Christ, reconciling the world unto Himself." 2 Corinthians 5:19. Christ was the foundation and center of the sacrificial system. Since the sin of our first parents, the Father has given the world into the hands of Christ, that through His mediatorial work He may redeem man and vindicate the authority of the law of God. All communion between heaven and the fallen race has been through Christ. It was the Son of God that gave to our first parents the promise of redemption. Adam, Noah, Abraham, Isaac, Jacob, and Moses understood the gospel. These holy men of old held communion with the Saviour who was to come to our world in human flesh.

Christ was the leader of the Hebrews in the wilderness, the Angel who, veiled in the cloudy pillar, went before the host. It was He who gave the law to Israel. (See Appendix, Note 6.) Amid the glory of Sinai Christ declared the ten precepts of His Father's law. He gave to Moses the law engraved upon tables of stone.

Christ spoke to His people through the prophets. The apostle Peter says that the prophets "prophesied of the grace that should come unto you, searching

At the death of Christ, God made plain that the system of ordinances and sacrifices had come to an end.

what, or what manner of time the *Spirit of Christ* which was in them did signify, when it testified beforehand the sufferings of Christ and the glory that should follow." 1 Peter 1:10, 11. It is the voice of Christ that speaks through the Old Testament. "The testimony of Jesus is the spirit of prophecy." Revelation 19:10.

While personally among men, Jesus directed the minds of the people to the Old Testament. "Ye search the Scriptures, because ye think that in them ye have eternal life; and these are they which bear witness of Me." John 5:39. At this time the books of the Old Testament were the only part of the Bible in existence.

The ceremonial law was given by Christ. Even after it was no longer to be observed, the great apostle Paul pronounces this law glorious, worthy of its divine Originator. The cloud of incense ascending with the prayers of Israel represents His righteousness that alone can make the sinner's prayer acceptable to God; the bleeding victim on the altar testified of a Redeemer to come. Thus through darkness and apostasy, faith was kept alive in the hearts of men until the advent of the promised Messiah.

Jesus was the Light of the world before He came in the form of humanity. The first gleam of light that pierced the gloom came from Christ. From Him has come every ray of heaven's brightness that has fallen upon the inhabitants of the earth.

Since the Saviour shed His blood and ascended to heaven "to appear in the presence of God for us" (Hebrews 9:24), light has been streaming from the cross of Calvary and from the sanctuary above. The gospel of Christ gives significance to the ceremonial law. As truths are revealed, the character and purposes of God are made manifest. Every additional ray of light gives a clearer understanding of the plan of redemption. We see new beauty in the inspired Word and study its pages with more absorbing interest.

God did not design that Israel should build up a wall of partition between themselves and their fellowmen.

The heart of Infinite Love was reaching out toward all the inhabitants of the earth, seeking to make them partakers of His love and grace. His blessing was granted to the chosen people that they might bless others.

Abraham did not shut himself away from the people around him. He maintained friendly relations with the kings of the surrounding nations, and the God of heaven was revealed through His representative.

To the people of Egypt God manifested Himself through Joseph. Why did the Lord choose to exalt Joseph so highly among the Egyptians? He desired to place him in the palace of the king that the heavenly illumination might extend far and near. Joseph was a representative of Christ. In their benefactor the Egyptians were to behold the love of their Creator and Redeemer. In Moses also God placed a light beside the throne of earth's greatest kingdom that all might learn of the true and living God.

In the deliverance of Israel from Egypt, a knowledge of the power of God spread far and wide. Centuries after the exodus, the priests of the Philistines reminded their people of the plagues of Egypt and warned them against resisting the God of Israel.

Why God Worked With Israel

God called Israel in order to reveal Himself through them to all the inhabitants of the earth. For this purpose He commanded them to keep themselves distinct from the idolatrous nations around them.

It was just as necessary then as now that God's people be pure, "unspotted from the world." But God did not intend that His people should shut themselves away from the world so that they could have no influence upon it. It was their evil heart of unbelief that led them to hide their light instead of shedding it upon surrounding peoples, to shut themselves away in proud exclusiveness as if God's love and care were over them alone.

The covenant of grace was first made with man in

Eden. After the Fall, there was given a divine promise that the seed of the woman should bruise the serpent's head. To all men this covenant offered pardon and the assisting grace of God for future obedience through faith in Christ. It also promised eternal life on condition of fidelity to God's law. Thus the patriarchs received the hope of salvation.

This same covenant was renewed to Abraham in the promise, "In thy seed shall all the nations of the earth be blessed." Genesis 22:18. Abraham trusted in Christ for the forgiveness of sins. It was this faith that was accounted unto him for righteousness. The covenant with Abraham also maintained the authority of God's law. The testimony of God was, "Abraham obeyed My voice, and kept My charge, My commandments, My statutes, and My laws." Genesis 26:5. Though made to Adam and renewed to Abraham, this covenant could not be ratified until the death of Christ. It had existed by the promise of God; it had been accepted by faith; yet when ratified by Christ, it is called a *new* covenant. The law of God was the basis of this covenant, which was simply an arrangement for bringing men again into harmony with the divine will, placing them where they could obey God's law.

Another compact—called in Scripture the "old" covenant—was formed between God and Israel at Sinai, and was then ratified by the blood of a sacrifice. The Abrahamic covenant, ratified by the blood of Christ, is called the "second," or "new" covenant, because the blood by which it was sealed was shed after the blood of the first covenant.

But if the Abrahamic covenant contained the promise of redemption, why was another covenant formed at Sinai? In their bondage the people had to a great extent lost the knowledge of the principles of the Abrahamic covenant. In delivering them from Egypt, God sought to reveal His power and mercy, that they might be led to love and trust Him. He bound them to Himself as their deliverer from temporal bondage.

But they had no true conception of the holiness of God, of the exceeding sinfulness of their own hearts, their utter inability, in themselves, to render obedience to God's law, and their need of a Saviour.

God gave them His law with the promise of great blessings on condition of obedience: "If ye will obey My voice indeed, and keep My covenant, . . . ye shall be unto Me a kingdom of priests, and a holy nation." Exodus 19:5, 6. The people did not realize the sinfulness of their own hearts and that without Christ it was impossible for them to keep God's law. Feeling able to establish their own righteousness, they declared, "All that the Lord hath said will we do, and be obedient." Exodus 24:7. They readily entered into covenant with God. Yet only a few weeks passed before they broke their covenant and bowed down to worship a graven image. Now, seeing their sinfulness and their need of pardon, they were brought to feel their need of the Saviour revealed in the Abrahamic covenant and shadowed forth in the sacrificial offerings. Now they were prepared to appreciate the blessings of the new covenant.

The New Covenant and Justification by Faith

The terms of the "old covenant" were, Obey and live: "If a man *do*, he shall even live in them." Ezekiel 20:11. But "cursed be he that confirmeth not all the words of this law to do them." Deuteronomy 27:26. The "new covenant" was established upon "better promises," the promise of forgiveness and the grace of God to renew the heart and bring it into harmony with God's law. "This shall be the covenant that I will make with the house of Israel; After those days, saith the Lord, I *will put My law* in their inward parts, *and write it in their hearts.* . . . I will *forgive* their iniquity, and I will remember their sin no more." Jeremiah 31:33, 34.

The same law that was engraved upon tables of stone is written by the Holy Spirit upon the heart. We accept the righteousness of Christ. His blood atones for our sins. His obedience is accepted for us. Then through the grace of Christ we shall walk even as He walked. Through the prophet He declared of Himself, "I delight to do Thy will, O My God: yea, Thy law is within My heart." Psalm 40:8.

Paul clearly presents the relation between faith and the law under the new covenant: "Being *justified by faith*, we have peace with God through our Lord Jesus Christ." "Do we then make void the law through faith? God forbid: yea, we establish the law." "For what the law could not do, in that it was weak through the flesh"—it could not keep the law—"God sending His own Son in the likeness of sinful flesh, and for sin, condemned sin in the flesh: that *the righteousness of the law* might be fulfilled in us, who walk not after the flesh, but after the Spirit." Romans 5:1; 3:31; 8:3, 4.

Beginning with the first gospel promise and coming down through the patriarchal and Jewish ages to the present time, there has been a gradual unfolding of the purposes of God in the plan of redemption. The clouds have rolled back, the mists and shades have disappeared, and Jesus, the world's Redeemer, stands revealed. He who proclaimed the law from Sinai is the same that spoke the Sermon on the Mount. The great principles of love to God are only a reiteration of what He had spoken through Moses. The Teacher is the same in both dispensations.

33 / The Terrible Murmurings of God's People

The government of Israel was characterized by thorough organization, wonderful for its completeness and simplicity. God was the center of government, the sovereign of Israel. Moses stood as leader to administer the law in His name. A council of seventy was afterward chosen to assist Moses in the general affairs of the nation. Next came the priests, who consulted the Lord in the sanctuary. Chiefs, or princes, ruled over the tribes. Under these were "captains over thousands, and captains over hundreds, and captains over fifties, and captains over tens." Deuteronomy 1:15.

The Hebrew camp was separated into three great divisions. In the center was the tabernacle, the abiding place of the invisible King. Around it were stationed the priests and Levites. Beyond these were encamped all the other tribes.

The position of each tribe was specified. Each was to march and to encamp beside its own standard, as the Lord had commanded. See Numbers 2:2, 17. The mixed multitude that had accompanied Israel from Egypt were to abide upon the outskirts of the camp, and their offspring were to be excluded from the community until the third generation. See Deuteronomy 23:7, 8.

Strict order and thorough sanitary regulations were enforced, measures indispensable to the preservation of health among so vast a multitude. It was necessary also that perfect order and purity be maintained. God declared: "The Lord thy God walketh in the midst of

This chapter is based on Numbers 10 to 12.

thy camp, to deliver thee, and to give up thine enemies before thee; therefore shall thy camp be holy." Deuteronomy 23:14.

In all the journeyings of Israel, "the ark of the covenant of the Lord went before them, . . . to search out a resting place for them." Priests bearing silver trumpets were stationed near. These priests received directions from Moses, which they communicated to the people by the trumpets. It was the duty of the leaders of each company to give definite directions concerning all the movements to be made, as indicated by the trumpets.

God is a God of order. Everything connected with heaven is in perfect order; thorough discipline marks the movements of the angelic host. Success can attend order and harmonious action now no less than in the days of Israel.

God Himself directed the Israelites in their travels. The place of their encampment was indicated by the descent of the pillar of cloud; and so long as they were to remain in camp, the cloud rested over the tabernacle. When they were to continue their journey, it was lifted high above the sacred tent.

Only eleven days' journey lay between Sinai and Kadesh, on the borders of Canaan. With the prospect of speedily entering the land, the hosts of Israel resumed their march when the cloud gave the signal. What blessings might they not expect, now that they had formally been acknowledged as the chosen people of the Most High?

With reluctance many left the place where they had encamped. The scene was so closely associated with the presence of God and holy angels that it seemed too sacred to be left thoughtlessly, or even gladly. At the signal from the trumpeters, however, all eyes were turned anxiously to see in what direction the cloud would lead. As it moved toward the east, where were only mountain masses huddled together, black and desolate, a feeling of sadness and doubt arose in many hearts.

As they advanced, the way became more difficult. Their route lay through stony ravine and barren waste, "a land of deserts and of pits," "a land of drought and of the shadow of death," "a land that no man passed through, and where no man dwelt." Jeremiah 2:6. Their progress was slow and toilsome, and the multitudes were not prepared to endure the perils and discomforts of the way.

The People Demand a Meat Diet

After three days' journey open complaints were heard. These originated with the mixed multitude, many of whom were continually finding fault with the way in which Moses was leading them. Dissatisfaction is contagious, and it soon spread in the encampment.

Again they began to clamor for flesh to eat. Many of the Egyptians among them had been accustomed to a luxurious diet, and these were the first to complain.

God might as easily have provided them with flesh as with manna, but it was His purpose to supply food better suited to their wants. The perverted appetite was to be brought into a more healthy state that they might enjoy the food originally provided for man, the fruits of the earth which God gave to Adam and Eve in Eden. For this reason the Israelites had been deprived in a great measure of animal food.

Satan tempted them to regard this as unjust and cruel. He saw that unrestrained indulgence of appetite would tend to produce sensuality, and by this means the people could be more easily brought under his control. Through appetite he has, to a large extent, led men into sin from the time he induced Eve to eat of the forbidden fruit. Intemperance in eating and drinking prepares the way to disregard all moral obligations.

God brought the Israelites from Egypt that He might establish them in the land of Canaan a pure, holy, and happy people. Had they been willing to deny appetite, feebleness and disease would have been unknown among them. Their descendants would have possessed physical and mental strength, clear perceptions of truth and duty, keen discrimination, and sound judgment.

Says the psalmist: "They tempted God in their heart by asking meat for their lust. Yea, they spake against God; they said, Can God furnish a table in the wilderness? . . . can He provide flesh for His people? Therefore the Lord heard this, and was wroth." Psalm 78:18-21. They had been witnesses to the majesty, power, and mercy of God; and their unbelief and discontent incurred the greater guilt. They had covenanted to obey his authority. Their murmuring was now rebellion, and as such it must receive prompt punishment if Israel was to be preserved from anarchy and ruin. "The fire of Jehovah burnt among them, and consumed them that were in the uttermost parts of the camp." The most guilty of the complainers were slain by lightning from the cloud.

Their Demands Become Rebellious

The people in terror besought Moses to entreat the Lord for them. He did so, and the fire was quenched. But instead of leading the survivors to humiliation and repentance, this fearful judgment seemed only to increase their murmurings. In all directions the people gathered at the door of their tents, weeping and lamenting. "The mixed multitude that was among them fell a lusting: and the children of Israel also wept again, and said, Who shall give us flesh to eat? We remember the fish, which we did eat in Egypt freely; the cucumbers, and the melons, and the leeks, and the onions, and the garlic: but now our soul is dried away: there is nothing at all, besides this manna, before our eyes." Yet, notwithstanding the hardships, there was not a feeble one in all their tribes.

The heart of Moses sank. In his love for them, he had prayed that his name might be blotted from the book of life rather than that they should perish. This was their response. All their hardships, even their imaginary sufferings, they charged upon him. In his distress he was tempted even to distrust God. His prayer was almost a complaint: "Wherefore hast Thou afflicted Thy servant . . .that Thou layest the burden of all this people upon me? . . . They weep, . . . saying, Give us flesh, that we may eat. I am not able to bear all this people alone, because it is too heavy for me."

The Lord hearkened to his prayer and directed him to summon seventy men possessing sound judgment and experience to share the responsibility with him. Their influence would assist in quelling insurrection, yet serious evils would eventually result from their promotion. They would never have been chosen had Moses manifested faith corresponding to the evidences he had witnessed of God's power and goodness. Had he relied fully upon God, the Lord would have guided him continually and given him strength for every emergency.

Moses announced the appointment of the seventy elders. The great leader's charge to these chosen men might well serve as a model of judicial integrity for the judges and legislators of modern times: "Hear the causes between your brethren, and judge righteously between every man and his brother, and the stranger that is with him. Ye shall not respect persons in judgment; but ye shall hear the small as well as the great; ye shall not be afraid of the face of man; for the judgment is God's." Deuteronomy 1:16, 17.

"And the Lord came down in a cloud, and spake unto him, and took of the spirit that was upon him, and gave it unto the seventy elders: and they prophesied, and did not cease." Like the disciples on the Day of Pentecost, they were endued with "power from on high." It pleased the Lord to honor them in the presence of the congregation, that confidence might be established in them.

A strong wind blowing from the sea now brought flocks of quails, "about a day's journey on the other side, round about the camp, and about two cubits above the face of the earth."

All that day and night and the following day, the people labored in gathering the food miraculously provided. Immense quantities were secured. All that was not needed for present use was preserved by drying, so that the supply, as promised, was sufficient for a whole month.

God gave the people that which was not for their highest good because they persisted in desiring it. But they were left to suffer the result. They feasted without restraint, and their excesses were speedily punished. "The Lord smote the people with a very great plague." The most guilty among them were smitten as soon as they tasted the food for which they had lusted.

At Hazeroth, the next encampment after leaving Taberah, a still more bitter trial awaited Moses. Aaron and Miriam had occupied a position of high honor and leadership in Israel. Both had been associated with Moses in the deliverance of the Hebrews. Richly endowed with gifts of poetry and music, Miriam had led the women of Israel in song and dance on the shore of the Red Sea. In the affections of the people and the honor of Heaven she stood second only to Moses and Aaron.

But in the appointment of the seventy elders, Miriam and Aaron had not been consulted, and their jealousy was excited against Moses. They felt that their position and authority had been ignored. They regarded themselves as sharing equally with him the burden of leadership and regarded the appointment of further assistants as uncalled for.

Sin of Jealousy

Moses realized his own weakness and made God his counselor. Aaron esteemed himself more highly, and trusted less in God. He had failed in the matter of the idolatrous worship at Sinai. But Miriam and Aaron, blinded by jealousy and ambition, said, "Hath the

Lord indeed spoken only by Moses? Hath He not spoken also by us?''

Miriam found cause of complaint in events that God had especially overruled. The marriage of Moses had been displeasing to her. That he should choose a woman of another nation instead of taking a wife from among the Hebrews was an offense to her family and national pride. Zipporah was treated with ill-disguised contempt.

Though called a "Cushite woman," the wife of Moses was a Midianite and thus a descendant of Abraham. She differed from the Hebrews in being of a somewhat darker complexion. Though not an Israelite, Zipporah was a worshiper of the true God. She was of a timid, retiring disposition, and greatly distressed at the sight of suffering. For this reason Moses, on his way to Egypt, had her return to Midian.

When Zipporah rejoined her husband in the wilderness, she saw that his burdens were wearing away his strength, and she made known her fears to Jethro, who suggested measures for his relief. Here was the chief reason for Miriam's antipathy to Zipporah. Had Aaron stood firmly for the right, he might have checked the evil; but instead of showing Miriam the sinfulness of her conduct, he sympathized with her and thus came to share her jealousy.

Their accusations were borne by Moses in uncomplaining silence. Moses "was very meek, above all the men which were upon the face of the earth," and this is why he was granted divine wisdom and guidance above all others.

God had chosen Moses. Miriam and Aaron, by their murmurings, were guilty of disloyalty not only to their appointed leader, but to God Himself. "And Jehovah came down in the pillar of the cloud, and stood in the door of the tabernacle, and called Aaron and Miriam." Their claim to the prophetic gift was not denied. But to Moses a nearer communion had been granted. With *him* God spake mouth to mouth. "Wherefore then were ye not afraid to speak against My servant Moses? And the anger of the Lord was kindled against them; and He departed." In token of God's displeasure, Miriam "became leprous, white as snow." Aaron was spared but was severely rebuked in Miriam's punishment. Now, their pride humbled in the dust, Aaron confessed their sin and entreated that his sister might not be left to perish by that loathsome, deadly scourge.

In answer to the prayers of Moses, the leprosy was cleansed. Miriam was, however, shut out of the camp for seven days. The whole company abode in Hazeroth, awaiting her return.

This manifestation of the Lord's displeasure was designed to check the growing spirit of discontent and insubordination. Envy is one of the most satanic traits that can exist in the human heart. It was envy that first caused discord in heaven, and its indulgence has wrought untold evil among men.

The Bible teaches us to beware of lightly bringing accusation against those whom God has called to act as His ambassadors. "Against an elder receive not an accusation, but before two or three witnesses." 1 Timothy 5:19. He who has placed upon men the responsibility of leaders and teachers of His people will hold the people accountable for the manner in which they treat His servants. The judgment visited upon Miriam should be a rebuke to all who yield to jealousy and murmur against those upon whom God lays the burden of His work.

34 / Twelve Spies Survey Canaan

The Hebrew host encamped at Kadesh, in the wilderness of Paran, which was not far from the borders of the Promised Land. Here it was proposed by the people that spies be sent up to survey the country. The matter was presented before the Lord by Moses, and permission was granted. The men were chosen, and Moses bade them go and see the country and the people, whether they were strong or weak, few or many; also to observe the soil and its productiveness and to bring of the fruit of the land.

They went and surveyed the whole land and returned after forty days. The news of the spies' return was hailed with rejoicing. The people rushed out to meet the messengers, who had safely escaped the dangers of their perilous undertaking. The spies brought specimens of the fruit, showing the fertility of the soil. They brought a cluster of grapes so large that it was carried between two men. They also brought of the figs and pomegranates, which grew in abundance.

The people listened intently as the report was brought to Moses. "We came unto the land whither thou sentest us," the spies began, "and surely it floweth with milk and honey; and this is the fruit of it." The people were enthusiastic; they would eagerly obey the voice of the Lord and go up at once to possess the land.

But all but two of the spies enlarged upon the dangers and uttered the sentiments of their unbelieving hearts, which were filled with discouragement prompted by Satan. Their unbelief cast a gloomy

This chapter is based on Numbers 13 and 14.

shadow over the congregation. The mighty power of God, so often manifested in behalf of the chosen nation, was forgotten. The people did not call to mind how wonderfully God had delivered them from their oppressors, cutting a path through the sea and destroying the pursuing hosts of Pharaoh. They left God out of the question, as though they must depend solely on the power of arms.

In their unbelief they repeated their former error of murmuring against Moses and Aaron. "This, then, is the end of all our high hopes," they said. They accused their leaders of deceiving the people and bringing trouble upon Israel.

A wail of agony arose, mingled with the confused murmur of voices. Bold to stand in defense of the word of God, Caleb did all in his power to counteract the evil influence of his unfaithful associates. He did not contradict what had been said; the walls were high and the Canaanites strong. But God had promised the land to Israel. "Let us go up at once and possess it," urged Caleb, "for we are well able to overcome it."

But the ten, interrupting him, pictured the obstacles. "We be not able to go up against the people," they declared; "for they are stronger then we. . . . All the people that we saw in it are men of a great stature; and we were in our own sight as grasshoppers, and so we were in their sight."

Revolt and Open Mutiny

These men, having entered upon a wrong course, stubbornly set themselves against Caleb and Joshua, against Moses, and against God. They distorted the truth in order to sustain their baleful influence. "It is a land that eateth up the inhabitants thereof," they said. This was not only an evil report; it was a lying one. The spies had declared the country to be fruitful, and the people of giant stature, which would be impossible if the climate were so unhealthful that the land could be said to "eat up the inhabitants."

Revolt and open mutiny quickly followed. The people seemed bereft of reason. They cursed Moses and Aaron, forgetting that enshrouded in the cloudy pillar, the Angel of His presence was witnessing their terrible outburst of wrath. Then their feelings rose against God: "Wherefore hath the Lord brought us unto this land, to fall by the sword, that our wives and our children should be a prey? And they said one to another, Let us make a captain, and let us return into Egypt." Thus they accused not only Moses but God Himself, of deception, in promising them a land they were not able to possess.

Caleb and Joshua attempted to quiet the tumult. They rushed in among the people, and their ringing voices were heard above the tempest of rebellious grief: "If the Lord delight in us, then He will bring us into this land, and give it us; a land which floweth with milk and honey. Only rebel not ye against the Lord, neither fear ye the people of the land; for they are bread for us: their defence is departed from them and the Lord is with us: fear them not."

By the covenant of God, the land was ensured to Israel. But the false report of the unfaithful spies was accepted. The whole congregation were deluded. The traitors had done their work. If only the two men had brought the evil report and all the ten had encouraged them to possess the land in the name of the Lord, they would still have taken the advice of the two in preference to the ten, because of their wicked unbelief.

The cry was raised to stone Caleb and Joshua. The insane mob rushed forward with yells of madness, when suddenly the stones dropped from their hands, and they shook with fear. God interposed. The glory of His presence, like a flaming light, illuminated the tabernacle. None dared continue their resistance. The spies who brought the evil report crouched terror-stricken and sought their tents.

Moses now arose and entered the tabernacle. The Lord declared to him, "I will smite them with the pestilence, and disinherit them, and will make of thee a greater nation." But again Moses pleaded for his people. "I beseech Thee, let the power of my Lord be great, according as Thou has spoken, saying, The Lord is longsuffering, and of great mercy. . . . Pardon, I beseech Thee, the iniquity of this people according unto the greatness of Thy mercy, and as Thou hast forgiven this people, from Egypt even until now."

The Lord promised to spare Israel from immediate destruction; but because of their unbelief and cowardice He could not manifest His power to subdue their enemies. Therefore in His mercy He bade them turn back toward the Red Sea.

In their rebellion the people had exclaimed, "Would God we had died in this wilderness!" Now this prayer was to be granted: "As ye have spoken in Mine ears, so will I do to you: your carcasses shall fall in this wilderness; and all that were numbered of you, according to your whole number, from twenty years old and upward. . . . But your little ones, which ye said should be a prey, them will I bring in, and they shall know the land which ye have despised." And of Caleb He said, "My servant Caleb, because he had another spirit with him, and hath followed Me fully, him will I bring into the land whereinto he went; and his seed shall possess it." As the spies had spent forty days in their journey, so the hosts of Israel were to wander in the wilderness forty years.

An Example of False Repentance
When Moses made known to the people the divine decision, they knew that their punishment was just. The ten unfaithful spies, smitten by the plague, perished before the eyes of all Israel; and in their fate the people read their own doom.

Now they seemed sincerely to repent; but they sorrowed because of the result of their evil course rather than from a sense of their ingratitude and disobedience. When they found that the Lord did not relent in His decree, their self-will again arose and they declared they would not return into the wilderness. God tested their apparent submission and proved it was not real. Their hearts were unchanged, and they only needed an excuse to occasion a similar outbreak. Had they mourned for their sin when it was faithfully laid before them, this sentence would not have been pronounced; but they mourned for the judgment. Their sorrow was not repentance and could not secure a reversing of their sentence.

That night was spent in lamentation, but with the morning they resolved to redeem their cowardice. When God had bidden them go up and take the land, they had refused; and now when He directed them to retreat, they were equally rebellious.

God had made it their privilege and duty to enter the land at the time of His appointment, but through their willful neglect that permission had been withdrawn. Satan now urged them on to do the very thing in the face of divine prohibition which they had refused to do when God required it, leading them to rebel the second time. "We have sinned against the Lord," they cried. "We will go up and fight, according to all that the Lord our God commanded us." Deuteronomy 1:41. So terribly blinded had they become! The Lord had never commanded them to "go up and fight." It was not His purpose that they should gain the land by warfare, but by strict obedience to His commands.

"We have sinned," they confessed, acknowledging that the fault was in themselves and not in God, whom they had wickedly charged with failing to fulfill His promises. Though their confession did not spring from true repentance, it served to vindicate the justice of God.

The Lord still works in a similar manner to glorify His name by bringing men to acknowledge His justice. God sets counteragencies at work to make manifest the works of darkness. Though the spirit which prompted to evil is not radically changed, confessions are made that vindicate the honor of God and justify His faithful reprovers who have been opposed and misrepresented. Thus it will be when the wrath of God shall be finally poured out. Every sinner will be brought to see and acknowledge the justice of his condemnation.

How Rebellion Made Their Situation Worse

Regardless of the divine sentence, the Israelites prepared to undertake the conquest of Canaan. They were, in their own estimation, fully prepared for conflict. Contrary to the command of God and the solemn prohibition of their leaders, they went out to meet the armies of the enemy.

Moses hastened after them with the warning, "Wherefore now do ye trangress the commandment of the Lord? but it shall not prosper. Go not up, for the Lord is not among you; that ye be not smitten before your enemies."

The Canaanites had heard of the mysterious power that seemed to be guarding this people, and they now summoned a strong force to repel the invaders. The attacking army had no leader. No prayer was offered that God would give them the victory. Though untrained in war, they hoped by a fierce assault to bear down all opposition. They presumptuously challenged the foe that had not dared to attack them.

The Canaanites had stationed themselves upon a rocky tableland reached only by a steep and dangerous ascent. The immense numbers of the Hebrews could only render their defeat more terrible. Massive rocks came thundering down, marking their path with the blood of the slain. Those who reached the summit, exhausted with their ascent, were fiercely repulsed and driven back with great loss. The army of Israel was utterly defeated.

The enemies of Israel, who had awaited with trembling the approach of that mighty host, were inspired with confidence to resist them. All the reports they had heard concerning the marvelous things that God had wrought for His people, they now regarded as false; there was no cause for fear. That first defeat of Israel, by inspiring the Canaanites with courage and resolution, had greatly increased the difficulties of the conquest.

Nothing remained for Israel but to fall back from the face of their victorious foes, into the wilderness, knowing that here must be the grave of a whole generation.

35 / Korah Leads a Rebellion

The judgments visited upon the Israelites served for a time to restrain their murmuring and insubordination, but the spirit of rebellion was still in the heart. Now a deep-laid conspiracy was formed to overthrow the authority of the leaders appointed by God Himself.

Korah, the leading spirit in this movement, a cousin of Moses, was a man of ability and influence. He had become dissatisfied with his position and aspired to the dignity of the priesthood. For some time Korah had been secretly opposing the authority of Moses and Aaron, though He had not ventured upon open rebellion. He finally conceived the bold design of overthrowing both the civil and the religious authority. Dathan and Abiram, two princes, readily joined in his ambitious schemes and determined to divide with Korah the honors of the priesthood.

The feeling among the people favored Korah. In the bitterness of their disappointment, their former doubts, jealousy, and hatred returned, and again their complaints were directed against their patient leader. They forgot that they were under divine guidance, that the presence of Christ went before them, and that from Him Moses received directions.

Unwilling to die in the wilderness, they were ready to believe that it was not God but Moses who had pronounced their doom. Although the marks of God's displeasure at their perverseness were still before them, they did not take the lesson to heart.

He who reads the secrets of all hearts had given His

This chapter is based on Numbers 16 and 17.

277

people warning and instruction as might have enabled them to escape the deception of these designing men. They had seen the judgment of God on Miriam because of her jealousy and complaints against Moses. The Lord had declared: "With him will I speak mouth to mouth." "Wherefore, then," He added, "were ye not afraid to speak against My servant Moses?" Numbers 12:8. These instructions were not intended for Aaron and Miriam alone, but for all Israel.

Korah and his fellow conspirators were of the number who went up with Moses into the mount and beheld the divine glory. But a temptation, slight at first, had been harbored until their minds were controlled by Satan. They first whispered their discontent to one another and then to leading men of Israel. At last they really believed themselves actuated by zeal for God.

They were successful in alienating two hundred and fifty princes. With these influential supporters they felt confident of greatly improving upon the administration of Moses and Aaron.

Jealousy had given rise to envy, and envy to rebellion. And they deceived themselves and one another into thinking that Moses and Aaron had themselves assumed the positions they held, that these leaders had exalted themselves in taking the priesthood and government. They were no more holy than the people, and it should be enough for them to be on a level with their brethren, who were equally favored with God's presence and protection.

Korah's Method: Praise the People

Korah and his associates enlisted the support of the congregation. The charge that the murmurings of the people had brought the wrath of God was declared a mistake. They said that the congregation were not at fault, since they desired nothing more than their rights; but Moses was an overbearing ruler; he had reproved the people as sinners when they were a holy people.

Korah's hearers thought they saw clearly that their

troubles might have been prevented if Moses had pursued a different course. Their exclusion from Canaan was in consequence of the mismanagement of Moses and Aaron. If Korah would be their leader and encourage them by dwelling upon their good deeds instead of reproving their sins, they would have a very prosperous journey; instead of wandering in the wilderness they would proceed directly to the Promised Land.

Korah's success with the people increased his confidence. He claimed that God had authorized him to make a change in the government before it should be too late.

Unfair Attack on Moses

But many were not ready to accept Korah's accusations against Moses. His patient, self-sacrificing labors came up before them, and conscience was disturbed. It was therefore necessary to assign some selfish motive; the old charge was reiterated, that he had led them out to perish in the wilderness that he might seize their possessions.

As soon as the movement gained sufficient strength to warrant an open rupture, Korah publicly accused Moses and Aaron of usurping authority. "Ye take too much upon you," said the conspirators. "Seeing all the congregation are holy, every one of them, and the Lord is among them: wherefore then lift ye up yourselves above the congregation of the Lord?"

Moses had not suspected this deep-laid plot, and he fell upon his face in silent appeal to God. He arose calm and strong. Divine guidance had been granted. "Even tomorrow," he said, "the Lord will show who are His, and who is holy and . . . whom He hath chosen will He cause to come near unto Him." Those who aspired to the priesthood were to come each with a censer and offer incense at the tabernacle. Even the priests, Nadab and Abihu, had been destroyed for venturing to offer "strange fire" in disregard of a divine command. Yet Moses challenged his accusers, if they dared enter upon so perilous an appeal, to refer the matter to God.

Singling out Korah and his fellow Levites, Moses said, "Seemeth it but a small thing unto you, that the God of Israel hath separated you from the congregation of Israel, to bring you near to Himself to do the service of the tabernacle of the Lord. . . ? And He hath brought thee near to Him, and all thy brethren the sons of Levi with thee: and seek ye the priesthood also? for which cause thou and all thy company are gathered together against the Lord. And what is Aaron, that ye murmur against him?"

Dathan and Abiram had not taken so bold a stand as had Korah; and Moses summoned them to appear before him, that he might hear their charges against him. But they insolently refused to acknowledge his authority: "Is it a small thing that thou hast brought us up out of a land that floweth with milk and honey, to kill us in the wilderness, except thou make thyself altogether a prince over us? Moreover thou hast not brought us into a land that floweth with milk and honey, or given us inheritance of fields and vineyards: wilt thou put out the eyes of these men? We will not come up."

Thus they declared that they would no longer submit to be led about like blind men, now toward Canaan, and now toward the wilderness, as best suited Moses' ambitious designs. He was represented in the blackest character of a tyrant and usurper. The exclusion from Canaan was charged upon him.

Moses made no effort at self-vindication. He solemnly appealed to God in the presence of the congregation and implored Him to be his judge.

The Great Test: Whom Would God Acknowledge?

On the morrow, the two hundred and fifty princes, with Korah at their head, presented themselves with their censers, while the people gathered to await the result. It was not Moses who assembled the congregation to behold the defeat of Korah and his company, but the rebels, in their blind presumption, had called them together to witness their victory. A large part of the congregation openly sided with Korah.

Korah had withdrawn from the assembly to join Dathan and Abiram when Moses, accompanied by the seventy elders, went down with a last warning to the men who had refused to come to him. Moses, by divine direction, bade the people, "Depart, I pray you, from the tents of these wicked men, and touch nothing of theirs, lest ye be consumed in all their sins." The warning was obeyed, for an apprehension of impending judgment rested upon all. The chief rebels saw themselves abandoned by those whom they had deceived, but they stood with their families in defiance of the divine warning.

Moses now declared in the hearing of the congregation: "Hereby ye shall know that the Lord hath sent me to do all these works; for I have not done them of mine own mind. If these men die the common death of all men . . . then the Lord hath not sent me. But if the Lord make a new thing, and the earth open her mouth, and swallow them up, with all that appertain unto them, and they go down quick into the pit, then ye shall understand that these men have provoked the Lord."

As he ceased speaking, the solid earth parted and the rebels went down alive into the pit, with all that pertained to them, and "they perished from among the congregation." The people fled, self-condemned as partakers in the sin.

But the judgments were not ended. Fire flashing from the cloud consumed the two hundred and fifty princes who had offered incense. These men were not destroyed with the chief conspirators. They were permitted to see their end and to have opportunity for repentance; but their sympathies were with the rebels, and they shared their fate.

The entire congregation were sharers in their guilt, for all had, to a greater or lesser degree, sympathized with them. Yet the people who had permitted themselves to be deceived were still granted space for repentance.

The Angel who went before the Hebrews sought to save them from destruction. The judgment of God had come very near and appealed to them to repent. Now, if they would respond to God's providence, they might be saved. But their rebellion was not cured. They returned to their tents that night terrified, but not repentant.

They had been flattered by Korah until they really believed themselves to be a very good people, wronged and abused by Moses. They had fondly cherished the hope that a new order of things was about to be established in which praise would be substituted for reproof, and ease for anxiety and conflict. The men who had perished had spoken flattering words and professed great interest and love for them, and the people concluded that Moses had by some means been the cause of their destruction.

The Israelites had proposed to put both Moses and Aaron to death. Yet that night of probation was not passed in repentance and confession, but in devising some way to resist the evidence which showed them to be the greatest of sinners. They still cherished hatred of the men of God's appointment and braced themselves to resist their authority.

"On the morrow all the congregation of the children of Israel murmured against Moses and against Aaron, saying, Ye have killed the people of the Lord." And they were about to proceed to violence against their faithful, self-sacrificing leaders.

Moses' Love for Erring Israel

Divine glory was seen in the cloud above the tabernacle, and a voice spoke to Moses and Aaron, "Get you up from among this congregation, that I may consume them as in a moment."

Moses lingered, in this fearful crisis manifesting the true shepherd's interest for the flock of his care. He pleaded that God might not utterly destroy the people of His choice.

But the minister of wrath had gone forth; the plague was doing its work of death. By his brother's direction, Aaron took a censer and hastened into the midst of the congregation to "make an atonement for them." "And he stood between the dead and the living." The plague was stayed, but not until fourteen thousand of Israel lay dead.

Now the people were compelled to believe the unwelcome truth that they were to die in the wilderness. "Behold," they exclaimed, "we die, we perish, we all perish." They confessed that they had sinned in rebelling against their leaders and that Korah and his company had suffered the just judgment of God.

Do not the same evils still exist that lay at the foundation of Korah's ruin? Pride and ambition are widespread and open the door to envy and striving for supremacy. The soul is alienated from God and unconsciously drawn into the ranks of Satan. Like Korah and his companions, many are thinking, planning, and working so eagerly for self-exaltation that they are ready to pervert the truth, falsifying and misrepresenting the Lord's servants. By persistently reiterating falsehood, they at last come to believe it to be truth.

The Hebrews were not willing to submit to the directions and restrictions of the Lord. They were unwilling to receive reproof. This was the secret of their murmuring against Moses. All through the history of the church God's servants have had the same spirit to meet.

Rejection of light darkens the mind and hardens the heart, so that it is easier to take the next step in sin, to reject still clearer light, until at last habits of wrongdoing become fixed. He who faithfully preaches God's word, condemning sin, too often incurs hatred. Soothing their consciences with deception, the jealous and disaffected sow discord in the church and weaken the hands of those who would build it up.

284 / FROM ETERNITY PAST

Every advance made by those whom God has called to lead His work has been misrepresented by the jealous and faultfinding. Thus it was in the time of Luther, of the Wesleys, and other reformers. Thus it is today.

Korah and his companions rejected light until they became so blinded that striking manifestations of power were not sufficient to convince them; they attributed them all to human or satanic agency. The same thing was done by the people. Notwithstanding the most convincing evidence of God's displeasure, they dared to attribute His judgments to Satan, declaring that Moses and Aaron had caused the death of good and holy men. They committed the sin against the Holy Spirit. "Whosoever speaketh a word against the Son of man," said Christ, "it shall be forgiven him: but whosoever speaketh against the Holy Ghost, it shall not be forgiven him." Matthew 12:32. It is through the Holy Spirit that God communicates with man; and those who deliberately reject this agency as satanic have cut off the channel of communication between the soul and Heaven.

If the Spirit's work is finally rejected, there is no more that God can do for the soul. The transgressor has cut himself off from God, and sin has no remedy to cure itself. "Let him alone" (Hosea 4:17) is the divine command. Then "there remaineth no more sacrifice for sins, but a certain fearful looking for of judgment and fiery indignation, which shall devour the adversaries." Hebrews 10:26, 27.

36 / Forty Years of Wandering in the Wilderness

For nearly forty years the children of Israel were lost to view in the obscurity of the desert. In the rebellion at Kadesh they had rejected God, and God had for the time rejected them. Since they had proved unfaithful to His covenant, they were not to receive the sign of the covenant, the rite of circumcision. Their desire to return to the land of slavery had shown them to be unworthy of freedom; and the Passover, instituted to commemorate deliverance from bondage, was not to be observed.

Yet the continuance of the tabernacle service testified that God had not utterly forsaken His people. And His providence still supplied their wants. "The Lord thy God . . . knoweth thy walking through this great wilderness: these forty years the Lord thy God hath been with thee; thou hast lacked nothing." Deuteronomy 2:7. God cared for Israel even during these years of banishment: "Thou gavest also Thy good Spirit to instruct them. . . . In the wilderness . . . their clothes waxed not old, and their feet swelled not." Nehemiah 9:20, 21.

The wilderness was to serve as a discipline for the rising generation, preparatory to their entrance into the Promised Land. Moses declared, "As a man chasteneth his son, so the Lord thy God chasteneth thee," "to humble thee, and to prove thee, to know what was in thine heart, whether thou wouldest keep His commandments, or no. And He . . . suffered thee to hunger, and fed thee with manna, which thou knewest not, neither did thy fathers know; that He might make thee know that man doth not live by bread only, but by every word that proceedeth out of the mouth of the Lord doth man live." Deuteronomy 8:5, 2, 3.

"In all their affliction He was afflicted, and the Angel of His presence saved them; in His love and in His pity He redeemed them; and He bare them, and carried them all the days of old." Isaiah 63:9.

The revolt of Korah had resulted in the destruction of fourteen thousand of Israel. And isolated cases showed the same spirit of contempt for divine authority.

On one occasion one of the mixed multitude that had come up with Israel from Egypt left his own part of the camp, and entering that of the Israelites, claimed the right to pitch his tent there. A dispute arose between him and an Israelite, and the matter, being referred to the judges, was decided against the offender.

Enraged at this decision, he cursed the judge and blasphemed the name of God. He was immediately brought before Moses. The man was placed in ward until the will of God could be ascertained. God Himself pronounced sentence. By divine direction the blasphemer was conducted outside the camp and stoned to death. Those who had been witnesses to the sin placed their hands upon his head, thus solemnly testifying to the truth of the charge against him. Then they threw the first stones, and the people who stood by afterward joined in executing the sentence. [See Leviticus 24:14; Deuteronomy 17:7.]

Should Sabbath Breakers Be Stoned?

Had this man's sin been permitted to pass unpunished, others would have been demoralized; and as the result many lives must eventually have been sacrificed.

The mixed multitude that came up with the Israelites from Egypt professed to have renounced idolatry and to worship the true God; but they were more or less corrupted with idolatry and irreverence. They leavened the camp with idolatrous practices and murmurings against God.

Soon an instance of Sabbath violation occurred. The Lord's announcement that He would disinherit Israel had roused a spirit of rebellion. One of the people, angry at being excluded from Canaan and determined to show his defiance of God's law, ventured upon the open transgression of the fourth commandment by going out to gather sticks upon the Sabbath. During the sojourn in the wilderness, the kindling of fires upon the seventh day had been prohibited. The prohibition was not to extend to the land of Canaan, but, in the wilderness, fire was not needed for warmth. This was a willful and deliberate violation of the fourth commandment—a sin of presumption.

The case was brought by Moses before the Lord, and the direction was given, "The man shall be surely put to death; all the congregation shall stone him with stones without the camp." Numbers 15:35. The sins of blasphemy and willful Sabbathbreaking received the same punishment, being equally an expression of contempt for the authority of God.

Many who reject the Sabbath as Jewish urge that, if it is to be kept, the penalty of death must be inflicted for its violation. But blasphemy received the same punishment as did Sabbathbreaking. Though God may not now punish the transgression of His law with temporal penalties, yet in the final judgment death is the portion of those who violate His sacred precepts.

During the entire forty years in the wilderness, the people were every week reminded of the Sabbath by the miracle of the manna. Yet God declares through His prophet, "My Sabbaths they greatly polluted." Ezekiel 20:13-24. And this is enumerated among the reasons for the exclusion of the first generation from the Promised Land.

The period of their desert sojourn being ended, "the people abode in Kadesh." Numbers 20:1. From that scene of rejoicing on the shores of the Red Sea to the wilderness grave which ended a lifelong wandering— such had been the fate of millions who with high hopes had come forth from Egypt. Sin had dashed from their lips the cup of blessing. Would the next generation learn the lesson?

Every week for forty years, God's people in the wilderness were reminded of the Sabbath by the miracle of the manna.

37 / Moses Fails on the Border of Canaan

From the smitten rock in Horeb first flowed the living stream that refreshed Israel in the desert. During all their wanderings, wherever the need existed, by a miracle water gushed out beside their encampment.

It was Christ that caused the refreshing stream to flow for Israel. "They drank of that spiritual Rock that followed them: and that Rock was Christ." 1 Corinthians 10:4. He was the source of all temporal as well as spiritual blessings. "They thirsted not when He led them through the deserts: He caused the waters to flow out of the rock for them: He clave the rock also, and the waters gushed out." "They ran in the dry places like a river." Isaiah 48:21; Psalm 105:41.

As the life-giving waters flowed from the smitten rock, so from Christ, "smitten of God," "wounded for our transgressions," "bruised for our iniquities" (Isaiah 53:4, 5), the stream of salvation flows for a lost race. As the rock had been once smitten, so Christ was to be "once offered to bear the sins of many." Hebrews 9:28. Our Saviour was not to be sacrificed a second time. It is only necessary for those who seek the blessings of His grace to ask in the name of Jesus; then will flow forth afresh the life-giving blood, symbolized by the flowing water for Israel.

Just before the Hebrew host reached Kadesh, the living stream ceased that for many years had gushed out beside their encampment. The Lord would prove whether they would trust His providence or imitate the unbelief of their fathers.

This chapter is based on Numbers 20:1-13.

They were now in sight of the hills of Canaan, but a little distance from Edom, through which lay the appointed route to Canaan. The direction had been given to Moses, "Command thou the people, saying, Ye are to pass through the coast of your brethren the children of Esau, . . . and they shall be afraid of you. . . . Ye shall buy meat of them for money, that ye may eat; and ye shall also buy water of them for money, that ye may drink." Deuteronomy 2:4-6.

These directions should have been sufficient to explain why their supply of water had been cut off; they were about to pass through a well-watered, fertile country, in a direct course to the land of Canaan. The cessation of the miraculous flow of water should therefore have been a cause of rejoicing, a token that the wilderness wandering was ended. But the people seemed to have given up all hope that God would bring them into Canaan, and they clamored for the blessings of the wilderness.

The water ceased before they had reached Edom. There was opportunity for a little time to walk by faith instead of sight. But the first trial developed the same spirit manifested by their fathers. They forgot the hand that had for so many years supplied their wants. Instead of turning to God for help, they murmured, in desperation exclaiming, "Would God that we had died when our brethren died before the Lord!" (that is, had been destroyed in the rebellion of Korah).

Moses and Aaron, the leaders, went to the door of the tabernacle and fell upon their faces. Moses was directed, "Take the rod, and gather thou the assembly together, thou, and Aaron thy brother, and speak ye unto the rock before their eyes; and it shall give forth his water, and thou shalt bring forth to them water out of the rock."

The two brothers were now aged men. Long had they borne with the rebellion of Israel. But now, at last the patience of Moses gave way. "Hear now, ye rebels," he cried, "must we fetch you water of this rock?" Instead of speaking to the rock, as God had commanded him, he smote it twice with the rod.

The water gushed forth in abundance, but a great wrong had been done. Moses had spoken from irritated feelings. "Hear now, ye rebels," he said. This accusation was true, but even truth is not to be spoken in passion or impatience. When he took it upon himself to accuse them, he grieved the Spirit of God. His lack of self-control was evident. Thus the people were given occasion to question whether his past course had been under the direction of God. They had now found the pretext desired for rejecting the reproofs God had sent through His servant.

Moses Distrusted God

Moses manifested distrust of God. "Shall we bring water?" he questioned, as if the Lord would not do what He promised. "Ye believed Me not," the Lord declared to the two brothers, "to sanctify Me in the eyes of the children of Israel." When the water failed, their own faith in God's promise had been shaken by the rebellion of the people. The first generation had been condemned to perish in the wilderness because of their unbelief. Would these also fail?

Wearied and disheartened, Moses and Aaron had made no effort to stem the current of popular feeling. They might have set the matter before the people in such a light as would have enabled them to bear this test. They might have quelled the murmuring before asking God to do the work for them. What a train of evil might have been prevented!

The rock, being a symbol of Christ, had been once smitten, as Christ was to be once offered. It was needful only to speak to the rock, as we have only to ask for blessings in the name of Jesus. By the second smiting of the rock, the significance of this beautiful figure of Christ was destroyed.

More than this, Moses and Aaron assumed power that belongs only to God. The leaders of Israel should have improved the occasion to impress the people with reverence for God and to strengthen faith in His power and goodness. When they angrily cried, "Must *we* fetch you water out of this rock?" they put themselves in God's place, as though the power lay within themselves. Moses had lost sight of his Almighty Helper and had been left to mar his record by human weakness. The man who might have stood firm and unselfish to the close of his work had been overcome at last.

God did not on this occasion pronounce judgments upon those who had so provoked Moses and Aaron. All the reproof fell upon the leaders. Moses and Aaron had felt themselves aggrieved, losing sight of the fact that the murmuring was not against them but against God. Looking to themselves, they unconsciously fell into sin and failed to set before the people their guilt before God.

"The Lord spake unto Moses and Aaron, Because ye believed Me not, to sanctify Me in the eyes of the children of Israel, therefore ye shall not bring this congregation into the land which I have given them." They must die before crossing the Jordan. They were not chargeable with willful or deliberate sin; they had been overcome by a sudden temptation, and their contrition was immediate and heartfelt. The Lord accepted their repentance, though because of the harm their sin might do among the people, He could not remit its punishment.

Moses told the people that since he had failed to ascribe the glory to God, he could not lead them into the Promised Land. He bade them mark the severe punishment visited upon him and then consider how God must regard their murmurings in charging upon a mere man the judgments which they had brought upon themselves. He told them he had pleaded with God for a remission of the sentence and had been refused.

Throughout their journeyings as they had complained of the difficulties in the way, Moses had told them, "Your murmurings are against God. It is not I, but God, who has wrought in you deliverance." But his hasty words, "Shall *we* bring water?" were a virtual admission of their charge and would thus justify their murmurings. The Lord would remove this impression forever from their minds by forbidding Moses to enter the Promised Land. Here was unmistakable evidence that their leader was not Moses. The Lord had said, "Behold, I send an Angel before thee, to keep thee in the way, and to bring thee into the place which I have prepared. Beware of Him, and obey His voice: . . . for My name is in Him." Exodus 23:20, 21.

Why the Sin of Moses and Aaron Must Be Punished

"The Lord was wroth with me for your sakes," said Moses. The transgression was known to the whole congregation. Had it been passed by lightly, the impression would have been given that impatience under great provocation might be excused in those in responsible positions. But when because of that one sin Moses and Aaron were not to enter Canaan, the people knew that God is no respecter of persons.

Men of all future time must see the God of heaven as impartial, in no case justifying sin. God's goodness and love engage Him to deal with sin as an evil fatal to the peace and happiness of the universe.

God had forgiven the people greater transgressions, but He could not deal with sin in the leaders as in those who were led. He had honored Moses above every other man upon the earth. The fact that he had enjoyed so great light and knowledge made his sin more grievous. Past faithfulness will not atone for one wrong act. The greater the light and privileges granted to man, the more aggravated his failure and the heavier his punishment.

Moses' sin was one of common occurrence. The psalmist says that "he spake unadvisedly with his lips." Psalm 106:33. To human judgment this may seem a light thing, but if God dealt so severely with this sin in His most faithful and honored servant, He will not excuse it in others. The spirit of self-exaltation, the disposition to censure our brethren, is displeasing to God. The more important one's position, the greater the necessity that he cultivate patience and humility.

If those who stand in positions of responsibility take to themselves the glory that is due to God, Satan has gained a victory. There is not an impulse of our nature or an inclination of the heart, but needs to be, moment by moment, under the control of the Spirit of God. Therefore however great one's light, however much he may enjoy divine favor, he should ever walk humbly, pleading in faith that God will control every impulse.

The burdens placed upon Moses were very great. Few men will ever be so severely tried as he was. Yet this was not to excuse his sin. However great the pressure brought upon the soul, transgression is our own act. It is not in the power of earth or hell to compel anyone to do evil. However severe or unexpected the assault, God has provided help for us and in His strength we may conquer.

38 / Why the Long Journey Around Edom

The encampment of Israel at Kadesh was but a short distance from the borders of Edom, and both Moses and the people greatly desired to follow the route through this country to the Promised Land. Accordingly they sent a message to the Edomite king:

"Thus saith thy brother Israel, . . . behold, we are in Kadesh, a city in the uttermost of thy border. Let us pass, I pray thee, through thy country: we will not pass through the fields, or through the vineyards, neither will we drink of the water of the wells: we will go by the king's highway, we will not turn to the right hand nor to the left, until we have passed thy borders."

To this courteous request, a threatening refusal was returned: "Thou shalt not pass by me, lest I come out against thee with the sword."

The leaders of Israel sent a second appeal to the king, with the promise, "We will go by the highway; and if I and my cattle drink of thy water, then I will pay for it: I will only, without doing else, go through on my feet."

"Thou shalt not go through," was the answer. Armed bands of Edomites were already posted at the difficult passes, and the Hebrews were forbidden to resort to force. They must make the long journey around the land of Edom.

Had the people trusted in God, the Captain of the Lord's host would have led them through Edom. The inhabitants of the land, instead of manifesting hostility, would have shown them favor. But the Israelites did

This chapter is based on Numbers 20:14-29; 21:1-9.

not act promptly upon God's word, and the golden opportunity passed. When they were at last ready to present their request to the king, it was refused. Ever since they left Egypt, Satan had been at work to throw hindrances in their way that they might not inherit Canaan. And by their own unbelief they had repeatedly opened the door for him.

When God bids His children go forward, Satan tempts them to displease the Lord by hesitation and delay. He seeks to kindle strife, murmuring, or unbelief, and thus deprive them of the blessings God desires to bestow. God's servants should be minutemen. Any delay on their part gives time for Satan to work to defeat them.

The Edomites were descendants of Abraham and Isaac. For the sake of these His servants, God had given them Mount Seir for a possession. They were not to be disturbed unless by their sins they should place themselves beyond His mercy. The Hebrews were to utterly destroy the inhabitants of Canaan, who had filled up the measure of their iniquity; but the Edomites were still probationers and were to be mercifully dealt with. God manifests compassion before He inflicts judgments.

The Israelites were forbidden either then or at any future time to revenge the affront given them in the refusal of passage through the land. They must not expect to possess any part of the land of Edom. God had promised them a goodly inheritance, but they were not to feel that they alone had rights in the earth and seek to crowd out all others. They were to beware of doing the Edomites injustice. They were to trade with them, promptly paying for all they received. As an encouragement to trust in God and obey His word, they were reminded, "The Lord thy God hath blessed thee; . . . thou hast lacked nothing." They had a God rich in resources. They should exemplify the principle, "Thou shalt love thy neighbor as thyself."

Had they passed through Edom as God had purposed, the passage would have proved a blessing to the inhabitants of the land to become acquainted with God's people and His worship and to witness how the God of Jacob prospered those who loved and feared Him. But all this the unbelief of Israel had prevented. Again they must traverse the desert and quench their thirst from the miraculous spring, which, had they but trusted in Him, they would no longer have needed.

Aaron Dies in Moses' Arms

Accordingly the hosts of Israel again made their way over the sterile wastes that seemed even more dreary after a glimpse of the green spots among the hills and valleys of Edom. From the mountain range overlooking this gloomy desert rises Mount Hor, whose summit was to be the place of Aaron's death and burial. When the Israelites came to this mountain, the divine command was addressed to Moses:

"Take Aaron and Eleazar his son, and bring them up unto mount Hor: and strip Aaron of his garments, and put them upon Eleazar his son: and Aaron shall be gathered unto his people, and shall die there." Numbers 20:25, 26.

Together these two aged men and the younger one toiled up the mountain height. The heads of Moses and Aaron were white. Their long and eventful lives had been marked with the deepest trials and the greatest honors that had ever fallen to the lot of man. All their powers had been developed, exalted, and dignified by communion with the Infinite One. Their countenances gave evidence of great intellectual power, firmness and nobility of purpose, and strong affections.

Many years together they had breasted unnumbered dangers, but the time was at hand when they must be separated. They moved on very slowly, for every moment in each other's society was precious. The ascent was steep and toilsome; and as they often paused to rest, they communed together of the past and the future. Before them was spread out the scene of their desert wanderings. In the plain below were encamped the vast hosts of Israel, for whom these chosen men had spent the best portion of their lives and made great sacrifices. Somewhere beyond the mountains of Edom was the path leading to the Promised Land, that land whose blessings Moses and Aaron were not to enjoy. A solemn sadness rested upon their countenances as they remembered what had barred them from the inheritance of their fathers.

Aaron's work for Israel was done. Forty years before, at the age of eighty-three, God had called him to unite with Moses in his great mission. He had held up the great leader's hands when the Hebrew hosts gave battle to Amalek. He had been permitted to ascend Mount Sinai, to behold the divine glory. The Lord had honored him with the sacred consecration of high priest. He had sustained him in the holy office by terrible manifestations of judgment in the destruction of Korah and his company. When his two sons were slain for disregarding God's express command, he did not rebel or even murmur.

Yet the record of his noble life had been marred when he yielded to the clamors of the people and made the golden calf at Sinai, and again when he united with Miriam in murmuring against Moses. And he, with Moses, offended the Lord at Kadesh by disobeying the command to speak to the rock that it might give forth water.

Aaron bore the names of Israel upon his breast. He communicated to the people the will of God. He entered the most holy place on the Day of Atonement, "not without blood," as a mediator for all Israel. It was the exalted character of that sacred office as representative of our great High Priest that made Aaron's sin at Kadesh of so great magnitude.

With deep sorrow Moses removed from Aaron the holy vestments and placed them upon Eleazar, his successor by divine appointment. For his sin at Kadesh, Aaron was denied the privilege of officiating as God's high priest in Canaan—of offering the first sacrifice in the goodly land. Moses was to continue leading the people to the very borders of Canaan, but was not to enter it. Had these servants of God borne unmurmuringly the test at Kadesh, how different would have been their future! A wrong act can never be undone. It may be that the work of a lifetime will not recover what has been lost in a single moment of temptation or thoughtlessness.

As the people looked about upon their vast congregation, they saw that nearly all the adults who left Egypt had perished in the wilderness. They remembered the sentence pronounced against Moses and Aaron. Some were aware of the object of that mysterious journey to the summit of Mount Hor, and their solicitude was heightened by bitter memories and self-accusings.

Lessons From the Death of Aaron

Moses and Eleazar were at last discerned slowly descending the mountainside. Upon Eleazar were the sacerdotal garments, showing that he had succeeded his father in the sacred office. As the people gathered about, Moses told them that Aaron had died in his arms upon Mount Hor and that they there buried him. The congregation broke forth in mourning and lamentation. "They mourned for Aaron thirty days, even all the house of Israel."

The Scriptures give only the simple record, "There Aaron died, and there he was buried." Deuteronomy 10:6. In striking contrast, in modern times the funeral services of a man of high position are often made the occasion of extravagant display. When Aaron died, there were only two of his nearest friends to attend his burial. That lonely grave was forever hidden from the sight of Israel. God is not honored in the great display and extravagant expense incurred in returning bodies to the dust.

The death of Aaron forcibly reminded Moses that his

own end was near. He deeply felt the loss of the one who had shared his joys and sorrows for so many years. Moses must now work alone; but he knew God was his friend, and upon Him he leaned more heavily.

Soon after leaving Mount Hor the Israelites suffered defeat in an engagement with Arad, one of the Canaanite kings. But as they sought help from God, divine aid was granted and their enemies were routed. This victory, instead of inspiring gratitude, made them boastful and self-confident.

They continued their journey toward the south through a hot valley, destitute of shade or vegetation. They suffered weariness and thirst. Again they failed to endure the test of faith and patience. By dwelling on the dark side they separated themselves farther from God. They lost sight of the fact that but for their murmurings when the water ceased at Kadesh, they would have been spared the journey around Edom. They flattered themselves that if God and Moses had not interfered, they might now have been in possession of the Promised Land. After making their lot altogether harder than God designed, they cherished bitter thoughts concerning His dealings with them and finally became discontented with everything. Egypt looked more desirable than liberty and the land to which God was leading them!

What Happens in Unbelief

"And the people spake against God, and against Moses, Wherefore have ye brought us up out of Egypt to die in the wilderness? for there is no bread, neither is there any water; and our soul loatheth this light bread."

Moses faithfully set before the people their great sin. God's power alone had preserved them in "that great and terrible wilderness, wherein were fiery serpents, and scorpions, and drought, where there was no water." Deuteronomy 8:15. In all the way they had found water, bread from heaven, and peace and safety under the shadowy cloud by day and the pillar of fire by night. Angels had ministered to them as they climbed rocky heights or threaded the rugged paths of the wilderness. There was not a feeble one in all their ranks. Their feet had not swollen in their long journeys; neither had their clothes grown old. God had subdued before them the fierce beasts of prey and venomous reptiles of forest and desert.

God's Protecting Hand Removed

Shielded by divine powers, they had not realized the countless dangers by which they were surrounded. In their unbelief they anticipated death, and now the Lord permitted death to come upon them. The poisonous serpents that infested the wilderness were called fiery serpents, on account of their sting, it causing violent inflammation and speedy death. As the protecting hand of God was removed, great numbers of the people were attacked by these venomous creatures.

In almost every tent were the dying or the dead. Often the silence of night was broken by piercing cries that told of fresh victims. All were busy ministering to sufferers or endeavoring to protect those not yet stricken. When compared with the present suffering, their former difficulties and trials seemed unworthy of a thought.

The people now came to Moses with confessions and entreaties. "We have sinned," they said, "for we have spoken against the Lord, and against thee." Only a little before, they had accused him of being the cause of all their distress and afflictions. But as soon as real trouble came, they fled to him as the only one who could intercede with God for them. "Pray unto the Lord, that He take away the serpents from us."

Moses was divinely commanded to make a serpent of brass and to elevate it among the people. To this, all who had been bitten were to look and find relief. The joyful news was sounded that all who had been bitten might look upon the brazen serpent and live. Many had already died, and when Moses raised the serpent upon the pole, some would not believe that merely gazing upon that metallic image could heal them; these perished in their unbelief.

Yet many had faith in the provision God had made. Fathers, mothers, brothers, and sisters were engaged in helping suffering, dying friends to fix their languid eyes upon the serpent. If these, though faint and dying, could only once look, they were perfectly restored.

The Brazen Serpent a Type of the Saviour

The lifting up of the brazen serpent was to teach Israel an important lesson. They could not save themselves from the poison in their wounds. God alone was able to heal. Yet they were required to show their faith in the provision He had made. They must look in order to live. By looking upon the serpent their faith was shown. They knew that there was no virtue in the serpent itself, but it was a symbol of Christ.

Heretofore many had brought offerings to God and felt that so doing made ample atonement for their sins. The Lord would now teach them that their sacrifices had no more power than the serpent of brass, but were to lead their minds to Christ, the great sin offering.

"As Moses lifted up the serpent in the wilderness," even so was "the Son of man lifted up: that whosoever believeth in Him should not perish, but have eternal life." John 3:14, 15. All who have lived upon earth have felt the deadly sting of "that old serpent, called the devil, and Satan." Revelation 12:9. The fatal effects of sin can be removed only by the provision that God has made. The Israelites saved their lives because they believed God's word and trusted in the means provided for their recovery. So the sinner may look to Christ and live. He receives pardon through faith in the atoning sacrifice. Christ has power and virtue to heal the repenting sinner.

While the sinner cannot save himself, he still has something to do to secure salvation. "Him that cometh to Me," says Christ, "I will in no wise cast out." John

6:37. We must *come* to Him; and when we repent, we must believe that He accepts and pardons us. Faith is the gift of God, but the power to exercise it is ours. Faith is the hand by which the soul takes hold upon divine offers of grace and mercy.

Many have cherished the idea that they could do something to make themselves worthy. They have not looked away from self, believing that Jesus is an all-sufficient Saviour. We must not think our own merits will save us. Christ is our only hope of salvation.

When we see our sinfulness, we should not fear that we have no Saviour or that He has no thoughts of mercy toward us. At this very time He is inviting us to come to Him and be saved.

Many of the Israelites saw no help in the remedy which Heaven had appointed. They knew that without divine aid their own fate was certain; but they continued to lament their sure death until their eyes were glazed. They might have had instant healing. While we realize our helpless condition without Christ, we are not to yield to discouragement, but rely upon the merits of a crucified and risen Saviour. Look and live. Jesus will save all who come unto Him. Not one who trusts in His merits will be left to perish.

Many wander in the mazes of philosophy in search of reasons they will never find, while they reject the evidence God has been pleased to give. God gives sufficient evidence on which to base faith; and if this is not accepted, the mind is left in darkness. If those who were bitten by the serpents had stopped to doubt and question before they would look, they would have perished. It is our duty to look, and the look of faith will give life.

39 / The Conquest of Bashan

After passing south of Edom, the Israelites turned northward toward the Promised Land. Their route now lay over a vast, elevated plain, swept by cool, fresh breezes, a welcome change from the parched valley. They pressed forward, buoyant and hopeful. The command had been given, "Distress not the Moabites, neither contend with them in battle: for I will not give thee of their land for a possession; because I have given Ar unto the children of Lot." The same was repeated concerning the Ammonites, also descendants of Lot.

The hosts of Israel soon reached the country of the Amorites. This strong, warlike people had crossed the Jordan, made war upon the Moabites, and gained a portion of their territory. The route to the Jordan lay directly through this territory, and Moses sent a friendly message to Sihon, the Amorite king: "Let me pass through thy land. . . . Thou shalt sell me meat for money, that I may eat; and give me water for money, that I may drink: only I will pass through on my feet."

The answer was a decided refusal, and all the hosts of the Amorites were summoned to oppose the invaders. This formidable army struck terror to the Israelites. So far as skill in warfare was concerned, their enemies had the advantage. To all human appearance, a speedy end would be made of Israel.

But Moses kept his gaze upon the cloudy pillar. The token of God's presence was still with them. At the same time he directed them to do all that human power could do in preparing for war. Their enemies were con-

This chapter is based on Deuteronomy 2; 3:1-11.

fident that they would blot out the Israelites from the land. But from the Possessor of all lands the mandate had gone forth to Israel: "Rise ye up, take your journey, and pass over the river Arnon: behold I have given into thine hand Sihon the Amorite, king of Heshbon, and his land: begin to possess it, and contend with him in battle. This day will I begin to put the dread of thee and the fear of thee upon the nations that are under the whole heaven, who shall hear report of thee, and shall tremble, and be in anguish because of thee."

How God Revealed His Love to Wicked Nations

These nations on the borders of Canaan would have been spared had they not stood, in defiance of God's word, to oppose Israel. The Lord gave Abraham the promise, "In the fourth generation they shall come hither again: for the iniquity of the Amorites is not yet full." Genesis 15:16. God spared them four hundred years to give unmistakable evidence that He was the only true God. All His wonders in bringing Israel from Egypt were known. They might have known the truth, but they rejected the light and clung to their idols.

When the Lord brought His people a second time to the borders of Canaan, additional evidence of His power was granted those heathen nations. They saw that God was with Israel in the victory over King Arad and the Canaanites and in the miracle to save those perishing from the sting of the serpents. The Israelites in all their journeyings and encampments had done no injury to the people or their possessions. On reaching the border of the Amorites, Israel had asked permission only to travel directly through the country, promising to observe the same rules that had governed their intercourse with other nations. When the Amorite king refused and defiantly gathered his hosts for battle, their cup of iniquity was full, and God would now exercise His power for their overthrow.

The Israelites crossed the river Arnon and advanced upon the foe. An engagement took place. The armies of

Israel were victorious, and they were soon in possession of the country of the Amorites. The Captain of the Lord's host vanquished the enemies of His people. He would have done the same thirty-eight years before, had Israel trusted in Him.

The army of Israel eagerly pressed forward and soon reached a country that might well test their courage and faith in God. Before them lay the powerful kingdom of Bashan, crowded with great stone cities that to this day excite the wonder of the world—"threescore cities . . . with high walls, gates, and bars, besides unwalled towns a great many." The houses were constructed of huge black stones, of such size as to make the buildings impregnable to any force brought against them. It was a country filled with wild caverns and rocky strongholds. The inhabitants, descendants from a giant race, were of marvelous size and strength, so distinguished for violence and cruelty as to be the terror of all surrounding nations. Og, the king, was remarkable for size even in a nation of giants.

But the cloudy pillar moved forward, and the Hebrew hosts advanced to Edrei, where the giant king awaited their approach. Og had skillfully chosen the place of battle—the city of Edrei, situated on the border of a tableland rising abruptly from the plain and covered with jagged rocks. It could be approached only by narrow pathways, steep and difficult of ascent. In case of defeat, his forces could find refuge in that wilderness of rocks, where it would be impossible for strangers to follow.

Moses Trusted God

Confident of success, the king came forth with an immense army upon the open plain. When the Hebrews looked on that giant of giants towering above the soldiers of his army, when they beheld the seemingly impregnable fortress behind which unseen thousands were entrenched, the hearts of many quaked with fear. But Moses was calm and firm; the Lord had said concerning the king of Bashan, "Fear him not: for I will deliver him, and all his people, and his land, into thy hands; and thou shalt do unto him as thou didst unto Sihon king of the Amorites."

Not mighty giants nor walled cities, armed hosts nor rocky fortresses, could stand before the Captain of the Lord's host. The Lord led the army, the Lord conquered in behalf of Israel. The giant king and his army were destroyed, and the Israelites soon took possession of the whole country. Thus was blotted from the earth that strange people who had given themselves up to abominable idolatry.

Israel's Fatal Mistake

Many recalled the events which nearly forty years before had doomed Israel to long desert wandering. The report of the spies concerning the Promised Land was in many respects correct. The cities were walled and very great and inhabited by giants. But they could now see the fatal mistake of their fathers in distrusting the power of God. This had prevented them from at once entering the goodly land.

God had promised His people that if they would obey His voice, He would go before them and fight for them. He would drive out the inhabitants of the land. But now Israel must advance against alert and powerful foes and contend with well-trained armies that had been preparing to resist.

Their fathers had signally failed. But the trial was now more severe than when God had commanded Israel to go forward. The difficulties had greatly increased since they refused to advance when bidden to do so.

God still tests His people. And if they fail He brings them again to the same point, and the second time the trial will be more severe than the first.

The mighty God of Israel is our God. In Him we may trust, and if we obey His requirements, He will work for us as He did for His ancient people. The way will

sometimes be so barred by obstacles, apparently insur-
mountable, as to dishearten those who will yield to discouragement; but God is saying, Go forward. The difficulties that fill your soul with dread will vanish as you
move forward in the path of obedience, humbly trusting in God.

40 / Balaam Tries to Curse Israel

In preparation for the immediate invasion of Canaan, the Israelites encamped beside the Jordan above its entrance into the Dead Sea, just opposite the plain of Jericho, on the borders of Moab. The Moabites had not been molested by Israel, yet they had watched with troubled forebodings all that had taken place in the surrounding countries. The Amorites, before whom they had been forced to retreat, had been conquered by the Hebrews. The territory the Amorites had wrested from Moab was now in possession of Israel. The hosts of Bashan had yielded before the mysterious power enshrouded in the cloudy pillar, and the giant strongholds were occupied by the Hebrews.

The Moabites dared not risk an attack upon them, but they determined, as Pharaoh had done, to enlist sorcery to counteract the work of God. The people of Moab were closely connected with the Midianites, and Balak, the king of Moab, secured their cooperation against Israel by the message, "Now shall this company lick up all that are round about us, as the ox licketh up the grass of the field." Balaam of Mesopotamia was reported to possess supernatural powers, and his fame had reached Moab. Accordingly, messengers were sent to secure his divinations and enchantments against Israel.

The ambassadors at once set out on their long journey. Upon finding Balaam they delivered the message of their king: "Behold, there is a people come out from Egypt: behold, they cover the face of the earth, and

This chapter is based on Numbers 22 to 24.

309

they abide over against me: come now therefore, I pray thee, curse me this people; for they are too mighty for me: peradventure . . . I may drive them out of the land: for I wot that he whom thou blessest is blessed, and he whom thou cursest is cursed."

Balaam was once a prophet of God. But he had apostatized and given himself up to covetousness; yet he still professed to be a servant of the Most High. When the messengers announced their errand, he well knew that it was his duty to refuse the rewards of Balak, but he urged the messengers to tarry that night, declaring that he could give no answer till he had asked counsel of the Lord. Balaam knew that his curse could not harm Israel. But his pride was flattered by the words, "He whom thou blessest is blessed, and he whom thou cursest is cursed." The bribe of costly gifts excited his covetousness, and while professing obedience to the will of God, he tried to comply with the desires of Balak.

In the night the angel of God came to Balaam with the message, "Thou shalt not go with them; thou shalt not curse the people: for they are blessed."

How One Sin Opened the Door to Satan's Control

In the morning, Balaam dismissed the messengers but did not tell them what the Lord had said. Angry that his visions of gain had been dispelled, he exclaimed, "Get you into your land: for the Lord refuseth to give me leave to go with you."

Balaam "loved the wages of unrighteousness." 2 Peter 2:15. The sin of covetousness had made him a timeserver; through this one fault Satan gained entire control of him. The tempter is ever presenting worldly gain and honor to entice men from the service of God. Thus many are induced to venture out of the path of strict integrity. One wrong step makes the next easier, and they become more and more presumptuous. They will do and dare most terrible things once they have given themselves to the control of avarice and desire for power. Many flatter themselves that they can depart from strict integrity for a time and change their course when they please. Such are entangling themselves in the snare of Satan, and it is seldom that they escape.

When the messengers reported to Balak the prophet's refusal, they did not intimate that God had forbidden him. Supposing that Balaam's delay was to secure a richer reward, the king sent princes more in number and more honorable than the first with authority to concede to any terms Balaam might demand. Balak's urgent message was, "Let nothing, I pray thee, hinder thee from coming unto me: for I will promote thee unto very great honor, and I will do whatsoever thou sayest unto me: come, . . . curse me this people."

In response, Balaam professed great conscientiousness and integrity—no amount of gold and silver could induce him to go contrary to the will of God. But he longed to comply with the king's request. Although the will of God had already been made known to him, he urged the messengers to tarry that he might further inquire of God.

In the night, the Lord appeared to Balaam and said, "If the men come to call thee, rise up, and go with them; but yet the word which I shall say unto thee, that shalt thou do." Thus far the Lord would permit Balaam to follow his own will, because he was determined upon it. He chose his own course and then endeavored to secure the sanction of the Lord.

Thousands at the present day are pursuing a similar course. Their duty is plainly set before them in the Bible or clearly indicated by circumstances and reason. But because these evidences are contrary to their inclinations, they set them aside and presume to go to God to learn their duty. They pray long and earnestly for light. But God will not be trifled with. He often permits such persons to follow their own desires and suffer the result. "My people would not hearken to My voice. . . . So I gave them up unto their own hearts' lust: and they walked in their own counsels." Psalm 81:11, 12. When one clearly sees a duty, let him not go to God with the prayer that he may be excused from performing it.

A Donkey "Sees" More Than a Prophet

The messengers from Moab, annoyed at Balaam's delay and expecting another refusal, set out on their homeward journey without further consultation. Every excuse for complying with the request of Balak had now been removed. But Balaam was determined to secure the reward. Taking the beast upon which he was accustomed to ride, he set out and pressed eagerly forward, impatient lest he fail to gain the coveted reward.

But "the angel of the Lord stood in the way for an adversary against him." The animal saw the divine messenger unperceived by the man and turned aside from the highway into a field. With cruel blows, Balaam brought the beast back into the path. But again, in a narrow place shut in by walls, the angel appeared. The animal, trying to avoid the menacing figure, crushed her master's foot against the wall. Balaam knew not that God was obstructing his path. The man became exasperated, and beating the ass unmercifully, forced it to proceed.

Again, "in a narrow place, where there was no way to turn either to the right hand or to the left," the angel appeared, and the poor beast, trembling with terror, fell to the earth under its rider. Balaam's rage was unbounded, and with his staff he smote the animal more cruelly than before. God now opened its mouth, and by "the dumb ass speaking with man's voice" He "forbade the madness of the prophet." 2 Peter 2:16. "What have I done unto thee," it said, "that thou hast smitten me these three times?"

Furious, Balaam answered the beast as he would have addressed an intelligent being: "Because thou hast mocked me, I would there were a sword in mine hand, for now would I kill thee."

The eyes of Balaam were now opened, and he beheld

the angel of God standing with drawn sword ready to slay him. In terror "he bowed down his head, and fell flat on his face." The angel said, "Behold, I went out to withstand thee, because thy way is perverse before me: and the ass saw me, and turned from me these three times: unless she had turned from me, surely now also I had slain thee, and saved her alive."

Balaam owed his life to the poor animal he had treated so cruelly. The man who claimed to be a prophet of the Lord was so blinded by covetousness and ambition that he could not discern the angel of God visible to his beast. "The god of this world hath blinded the minds of them which believe not." 2 Corinthians 4:4. How many rush on in forbidden paths, transgressing the divine law, and cannot discern that God and His angels are against them! Like Balaam they are angry at those who would prevent their ruin.

"A righteous man regardeth the life of his beast: but the tender mercies of the wicked are cruel." Proverbs 12:10. Few realize as they should the sinfulness of abusing animals or leaving them to suffer from neglect. The animals were created to serve man, but he has no right to cause them pain by harsh treatment.

He who will abuse animals because he has them in his power is both a coward and a tyrant. Many do not realize that their cruelty will ever be known, because the poor dumb animals cannot reveal it. But could the eyes of these men be opened, they would see an angel of God standing as a witness to testify against them in the courts above. A day is coming when judgment will be pronounced against those who abuse God's creatures.

Balaam Prevented From Cursing Israel

When he beheld the messenger of God, Balaam exclaimed in terror, "I have sinned; for I knew not that thou stoodest in the way against me; now therefore, if it displease thee, I will get me back again." The Lord suffered him to proceed on his journey, but his words would be controlled by divine power. God would give evidence to Moab that the Hebrews were under the guardianship of Heaven, and this He did when He showed them how powerless Balaam was to utter a curse against them.

The king of Moab, informed of the approach of Balaam, went out to receive him. When he expressed his astonishment at Balaam's delay, in view of the rich rewards awaiting him, the prophet's answer was, "Have I now any power at all to say anything? the word that God putteth in my mouth, that shall I speak." Balaam greatly regretted this restriction; he feared that his purpose could not be carried out.

The king, with the chief dignitaries of the kingdom, escorted Balaam to "the high places of Baal," from which he could survey the Hebrew host. How little the Israelites knew of what was taking place so near them! How little they knew of the care of God, extended over them by day and by night!

Balaam had some knowledge of the sacrificial offerings of the Hebrews, and he hoped that by surpassing them in costly gifts he might ensure the accomplishment of his sinful projects. Seven altars were erected, and he offered a sacrifice upon each. He then withdrew to a "high place" to meet with God.

With the nobles and princes of Moab, the king stood beside the sacrifice, watching for the return of the prophet. He came at last, and the people waited for the words that should paralyze forever that strange power exerted in behalf of the hated Israelites. Balaam said:

> The king of Moab hath brought me from Aram,
> Out of the mountains of the east,
> Saying, Come, curse me Jacob,
> And come, defy Israel.
> How shall I curse, whom God hath not cursed? . . .
> Who can count the dust of Jacob,
> And the number of the fourth part of Israel?
> Let me die the death of the righteous,
> And let my last end be like his!

As Balaam looked upon the encampment of Israel he beheld with astonishment the evidence of their prosperity. They had been represented to him as a rude, disorganized multitude, infesting the country in roving bands, a pest and terror to surrounding nations. But their appearance was the reverse of all this. He saw the vast extent and perfect arrangement of their camp, everything bearing the marks of discipline and order. He was shown the favor with which God regarded Israel and their distinctive character as His chosen people. They were not to stand upon a level with other nations, but to be exalted above them all. "The people shall dwell alone, and shall not be reckoned among the nations." How strikingly was this prophecy fulfilled in the afterhistory of Israel! Through all the years, they have remained a distinct people.

Balaam Sees God's Favor on Israel

Balaam beheld the increase and prosperity of the true Israel of God to the close of time, the special favor of the Most High attending those who love and fear Him. He saw them supported by His arm as they entered the dark valley of the shadow of death. And he beheld them coming forth from their graves, crowned with glory, honor, and immortality. He saw the redeemed rejoicing in the unfading glories of the earth made new. As he saw the crown of glory on every brow and looked forward to that endless life of happiness, he uttered the solemn prayer, "Let me die the death of the righteous, and let my last end be like his!"

If Balaam had had a disposition to accept the light God had given, he would at once have severed all connection with Moab. He would have returned to God with deep repentance. But Balaam loved the wages of unrighteousness.

Balak had expected a curse that would fall like a withering blight upon Israel, and he passionately exclaimed, "What hast thou done unto me? I took thee to curse mine enemies, and, behold, thou hast blessed them altogether." Balaam professed to have spoken from a conscientious regard for the will of God the words that had been forced from his lips by divine power. "Must I not take heed to speak that which the Lord hath put in my mouth?"

Balak Tries Again

Balak decided that the imposing spectacle presented by the vast encampment of the Hebrews had so intimidated Balaam that he dared not practice his divinations against them. The king determined to take the prophet to some point where only a small part of the host might be seen. Again seven altars were erected, whereon were placed the same offerings as at the first. The king and his princes remained by the sacrifices, while Balaam retired to meet with God. Again the prophet was entrusted with a divine message, which he was powerless to alter or withhold.

When he appeared, the question was put to him, "What hath the Lord spoken?" The answer struck terror to the heart of king and princes:

> God is not a man, that He should lie, . . .
> Behold, I have received commandment to bless:
> And He hath blessed; and I cannot reverse it.
> He hath not beheld iniquity in Jacob,
> Neither hath He seen perverseness in Israel:
> The Lord his God is with him,
> And the shout of a king is among them.

The great magician had tried his power of enchantment, but while the Hebrews were under the divine protection no people or nation, aided by all the power of Satan, should be able to prevail against them. All the world should wonder that a man should be so controlled by divine power as to utter, instead of imprecations, rich and precious promises in sublime poetry. When Satan should inspire evil men to misrepresent and destroy God's people, this occurrence would would strengthen their courage and faith in God.

The king of Moab, disheartened and distressed, exclaimed, "Neither curse them at all, nor bless them at all." Yet he determined to make another trial. He now conducted Balaam to Mount Peor, where was a temple devoted to the licentious worship of Baal. Here the same number of sacrifices were offered. But Balaam made no pretense of sorcery. He looked abroad upon the tents of Israel, and the divine message came from his lips:

How goodly are thy tents, O Jacob,
And thy tabernacles, O Israel!
As the valleys are they spread forth,
   as gardens by the river's side. . . .
And his King shall be higher than Agag,
   and his kingdom shall be exalted. . . .
Blessed is he that blesseth thee,
   and cursed is he that curseth thee.

Balaam prophesied that Israel's king would be greater than Agag. This was the name given to the kings of the Amalekites, who were at this time a very powerful nation. But Israel, if true to God, would subdue all her enemies. The King of Israel was the Son of God; and His throne was one day to be established in the earth, and His power to be exalted above all earthly kingdoms.

Balaam Loses All He Tried to Gain

Balak was overwhelmed with disappointed hope, fear, and rage. He was indignant that Balaam could have given him the least encouragement of a favorable response. He regarded with scorn the prophet's compromising, deceptive course, and exclaimed fiercely, "Therefore now flee thou to thy place: I thought to promote thee unto great honor; but, lo, the Lord hath kept thee back from honor." The answer was that the king had been forewarned that Balaam could speak only the message given him from God.

Before returning to his people, Balaam uttered a

beautiful prophecy of the world's Redeemer and the final destruction of the enemies of God:

> I shall see Him, but not now:
>   I shall behold Him, but not nigh:
> There shall come a Star out of Jacob,
>   and a Scepter shall rise out of Israel,
> And shall smite the corners of Moab,
>   and destroy all the children of Sheth.

He closed by predicting the complete destruction of Moab and Edom, of Amalek and the Kenites, thus leaving to the Moabitish king no ray of hope.

Disappointed in his hopes of wealth and promotion, and conscious that he had incurred the displeasure of God, Balaam returned from his self-chosen mission. The controlling power of the Spirit of God left him, and his covetousness prevailed. He was ready to resort to any means to gain the reward promised by Balak. Balaam knew that the prosperity of Israel depended upon their obedience to God. There was no way to cause their overthrow but by seducing them into sin.

He immediately returned to Moab and laid his plans before the king to separate the children of Israel from God by enticing them into idolatry. If they could be led to engage in the licentious worship of Baal and Ashtaroth, their omnipotent Protector would become their enemy, and they would fall prey to the fierce, warlike nations around them. This plan was readily accepted by the king, and Balaam remained to assist in carrying it into effect.

Balaam witnessed the success of his diabolical scheme. He saw the curse of God visited upon His people, and thousands falling under His judgments. But the divine justice that punished sin in Israel did not permit the tempters to escape. In the war of Israel against the Midianites, Balaam was slain. He had felt a presentiment that his end was near when he exclaimed, "Let me die the death of the righteous, and let my last end be like his!'' But he had not chosen to live the life of the righteous; his destiny was fixed with the enemies of God.

The fate of Balaam was similar to that of Judas. Both men tried to unite the service of God and mammon, and met with signal failure. Balaam acknowledged the true God; Judas believed in Jesus. Balaam hoped to make the service of Jehovah the steppingstone to the acquirement of riches and worldly honor; Judas expected by his connection with Christ to secure wealth and promotion in that worldly kingdom which he believed the Messiah was about to set up. Both Balaam and Judas received great light, but a single cherished sin poisoned the entire character and caused their destruction.

One cherished sin will, little by little, debase the character. The indulgence of one evil habit breaks down the defenses of the soul and opens the way for Satan to lead us astray. The only safe course is to pray, as did David, "Hold up my goings in Thy paths, that my footsteps slip not." Psalm 17:5.

41 / How Balaam Led Israel Into Sin

With renewed faith in God the victorious armies of Israel had returned from Bashan and were confident of the immediate conquest of Canaan. Only the river Jordan lay between them and the Promised Land. Just across the river was a rich plain watered with streams and shaded by luxuriant palm trees. On the western border rose the towers and palaces of Jericho, "the city of palm trees."

On the eastern side of Jordan was a plain several miles in width and extending some distance along the river. This sheltered valley had the climate of the tropics. Here the Israelites encamped and in the acacia groves found an agreeable retreat.

But amid these attractive surroundings they were to encounter an evil more deadly than hosts of armed men or wild beasts of the wilderness. That country, rich in natural advantages, had been defiled by the inhabitants. In the public worship of Baal, the most degrading scenes were enacted. On every side were places noted for idolatry and licentiousness, the names suggestive of corruption.

The Israelites' minds became familiar with the vile thoughts constantly suggested. Their life of ease produced its demoralizing effect, and almost unconsciously they were departing from God into a condition where they would fall prey to temptation.

During the time of their encampment beside Jordan, Moses was preparing for the occupation of Canaan. In this work the great leader was fully employed. But to

This chapter is based on Numbers 25.

the people this time of suspense was most trying, and before many weeks had elapsed their history was marred by frightful departures from virtue and integrity.

Midianitish women began to steal into the camp. It was the object of these women to seduce the Hebrews into transgression of the law of God and lead them into idolatry. These motives were studiously concealed under the garb of friendship.

At Balaam's suggestion, a grand festival in honor of their gods was appointed by the king of Moab. It was secretly arranged that Balaam should induce the Israelites to attend. He was regarded as a prophet of God and had little difficulty in accomplishing his purpose. Great numbers of the people joined him in witnessing the festivities. Beguiled with music and dancing, and allured by the beauty of heathen vestals, they cast off their fealty to Jehovah. Wine beclouded their senses and broke down the barriers of self-control. Having defiled their consciences by lewdness, they were persuaded to bow down to idols. They offered sacrifice upon heathen altars and participated in degrading rites.

The poison spread like a deadly infection through the camp of Israel. Those who would have conquered in battle were overcome by the wiles of women. The people seemed infatuated. The rulers and leading men were among the first to transgress, and so many of the people were guilty that the apostasy became national. "Israel joined himself unto Baalpeor." When Moses was aroused to perceive the evil, not only were the Israelites participating in the licentious worship at Mount Peor, but the heathen rites were observed in the camp of Israel. The aged leader was filled with indignation, and the wrath of God was kindled.

Their iniquitous practices did that for Israel which all the enchantments of Balaam could not do—they separated them from God. A terrible pestilence broke out in the camp, to which tens of thousands fell prey.

God commanded that the leaders in apostasy be put to death, and this order was promptly obeyed. Then their bodies were hung up in sight of all Israel that the congregation, seeing the leaders so severely dealt with, might have a deep sense of God's abhorrence of their sin. All felt that the punishment was just, and the people with tears and humiliation confessed their sin.

While they were thus weeping before God at the door of the tabernacle, Zimri, one of the nobles of Israel, came boldly into the camp accompanied by a Midianitish harlot, whom he escorted to his tent. Never was vice bolder or more stubborn. Zimri "declared his sin as Sodom" and gloried in his shame.

The priests and leaders had prostrated themselves in grief and humiliation, entreating the Lord to spare His people, when this prince in Israel flaunted his sin in the sight of the congregation, as if to defy the vengeance of God and mock the judges of the nation. Phinehas, the son of Eleazar the high priest, rose up, and seizing a javelin, "went after the man of Israel into the tent" and slew them both. Thus the plague was stayed. The priest who had executed the divine judgment was honored before all Israel.

Phinehas Made an Atonement for Israel

Phinehas "hath turned My wrath away from the children of Israel," was the divine message. "He was zealous for his God, and made an atonement for the children of Israel."

The judgments visited upon Israel destroyed the survivors of that vast company who, nearly forty years before, had incurred the sentence, "They shall surely die in the wilderness." During their encampment on the plains of Jordan, "of them whom Moses and Aaron the priest numbered, when they numbered the children of Israel in the wilderness of Sinai, . . . there was not left a man of them, save Caleb the son of Jephunneh, and Joshua the son of Nun." Numbers 26:64, 65.

God had sent judgments upon Israel for yielding to

the enticements of the Midianites, but the tempters were not to escape the wrath of divine justice. "Avenge the children of Israel of the Midianites," was the command of God to Moses; "afterward shalt thou be gathered unto thy people." One thousand men were chosen from each of the tribes and sent out under the leadership of Phinehas. "And they warred against the Midianites, as the Lord commanded Moses. . . . And they slew . . . five kings of Midian: Balaam also the son of Beor they slew with the sword."

Such was the end of them that devised mischief against God's people. When men "gather themselves together against the soul of the righteous," the Lord "shall bring upon them their own iniquity, and shall cut them off in their own wickedness." Psalm 94:21, 23.

Strong Men Conquered by Women

When through yielding to temptation the Hebrews transgressed God's law, their defense departed from them. When the people of God are faithful to His commandments, "there is no enchantment against Jacob, neither is there any divination against Israel." Hence all the wily arts of Satan are exerted to seduce them into sin. If those who profess to be the depositaries of God's law become transgressors of its precepts, they will be unable to stand before their enemies.

The Israelites who could not be overcome by arms or the enchantments of Midian fell a prey to her harlots. Such is the power that woman, enlisted in the service of Satan, has exerted to destroy souls. "She hath cast down many wounded: yea, many strong men have been slain by her." Proverbs 7:26. It was thus that Joseph was tempted. Thus Samson betrayed his strength into the hands of the Philistines. Here David stumbled. And Solomon, the wisest of kings, became a slave of passion and sacrificed his integrity to the same bewitching power.

Satan has studied with fiendish intensity for thousands of years and through successive generations has wrought to overthrow princes in Israel by the same temptations so successful at Baalpeor. As we approach the close of time, on the borders of the heavenly Canaan, Satan will redouble his efforts to prevent the people of God from entering the goodly land. He will prepare his temptations for those in holy office; if he can lead them to pollute their souls, he can through them destroy many. By worldly friendships, the charms of beauty, pleasure seeking, mirth, feasting, or the winecup, he tempts to violation of the seventh commandment.

Those who will dishonor God's image and defile His temple in their own persons will not scruple at any dishonor to God that will gratify the desire of their depraved hearts. It is impossible for the slave of passion to realize the sacred obligation of the law of God, to appreciate the atonement, or to place a right value upon the soul. Goodness, purity, truth, reverence for God, and love for sacred things—all are consumed in the fires of lust. The soul becomes a blackened and desolate waste. Beings formed in the image of God are dragged down to a level with the brutes.

Dangers of Ungodly Associates

By leading the followers of Christ to associate with the ungodly and unite in their amusements, Satan is most successful in alluring them into sin. God requires of His people now as great a distinction from the world in customs, habits, and principles as He required of Israel anciently. The warnings given the Hebrews against assimilating with the heathen were not more explicit than are those forbidding Christians to conform to the spirit and customs of the ungodly. We cannot be too decided in shunning the company of those who exert an influence to draw us away from God. While we pray, "Lead us not into temptation," we are to shun temptation so far as possible.

When the Israelites were in ease and security they were led into sin. Ease and self-indulgence left the citadel of the soul unguarded, and debasing thoughts found entrance. Traitors within the walls overthrew the strongholds of principle and betrayed Israel into the power of Satan. It is thus that Satan seeks to ruin the soul. A long preparatory process, unknown to the world, goes on in the heart before the Christian commits open sin. The mind does not come down at once from purity and holiness to depravity, corruption, and crime. By the indulgence of impure thoughts, sin once loathed will become pleasant.

We cannot walk the streets of our cities without encountering flaring notices of crime to be presented in some novel or to be acted at some theater. The course pursued by the base and vile is kept before the people in periodicals, and everything that can excite passion is brought before them in exciting stories. They hear so much of debasing crime that the conscience becomes hardened, and they dwell upon these things with greedy interest.

Many amusements popular with those who claim to be Christians tend to the same end as did those of the heathen. Through the drama Satan has worked for ages to excite passion and glorify vice. The opera, the dance, the card table, Satan employs to open the door to sensual indulgence. In every gathering for pleasure where pride is fostered or appetite indulged, where one is led to forget God and lose sight of eternal interests, there Satan is binding his chains about the soul.

How to Overcome Temptation

The heart must be renewed by divine grace. He who attempts to build up a virtuous character independent of the grace of Christ is building his house upon shifting sand. In the fierce storms of temptation it will surely be overthrown. David's prayer should be the petition of every soul: "Create in me a clean heart, O God; and renew a right spirit within me." Psalm 51:10.

Yet we have a work to do to resist temptation. Those who would not fall prey to Satan's devices must guard well the avenues of the soul; avoid reading, seeing, or hearing that which will suggest impure thoughts. This will require earnest prayer and unceasing watchfulness. The abiding influence of the Holy Spirit will attract the mind upward to dwell on pure and holy things. "Wherewithal shall a young man cleanse his way? by taking heed thereto according to Thy word." "Thy word," says the psalmist, "have I hid in mine heart, that I might not sin against Thee." Psalm 119:9, 11.

Israel's sin at Bethpeor brought the judgments of God upon the nation. The same sins may not now be punished as speedily, but nature has affixed terrible penalties, penalties which, sooner or later, will be inflicted upon every transgressor. These sins more than any other have caused the fearful degeneracy of our race, and the weight of disease and misery with which the world is cursed. Men may succeed in concealing their transgression from their fellowmen, but they will reap the result in suffering, disease, or death. And beyond this life stands the judgment. "They which do such things shall not inherit the kingdom of God," but with Satan and evil angels shall have their part in that "lake of fire" which "is the second death." Galatians 5:21; Revelation 20:14.

42 / God Teaches His Law to a New Generation

The Lord announced to Moses that the appointed time for the possession of Canaan was at hand. As the aged prophet stood upon the heights overlooking the Promised Land, with deep earnestness he pleaded, "O Lord God, Thou hast begun to show Thy servant Thy greatness, and Thy mighty hand: for what god is there in heaven or in earth, that can do according to Thy works, and according to Thy might? I pray Thee, let me go over, and see the good land that is beyond Jordan, that goodly mountain, and Lebanon."

The answer was, "Speak no more unto Me of this matter. Get thee up into the top of Pisgah, and lift up thine eyes westward, and northward, and southward, and eastward, and behold it with thine eyes: for thou shalt not go over this Jordan."

Without a murmur Moses submitted to the decree of God. And now his great anxiety was for Israel. From a full heart he poured forth the prayer, "Let the Lord, the God of the spirits of all flesh, set a man over the congregation . . . which may bring them in; that the congregation of the Lord be not as sheep which have no shepherd." Numbers 27:16, 17.

The answer came, "Take thee Joshua, the son of Nun, a man in whom is the Spirit, and lay thine hand upon him; and set him before Eleazar the priest, and before all the congregation; and give him a charge in their sight. And thou shalt put some of thine honor upon him, that all the congregation of the people of Israel may be obedient." Verses 18-20.

This chapter is based on Deuteronomy 3 to 6; 28.

Joshua, a man of wisdom, ability, and faith, was chosen to succeed him. He was solemnly set apart as the leader of Israel. The words of the Lord concerning Joshua came through Moses to the congregation, "At his word shall they go out, and at his word they shall come in, both he, and all the children of Israel with him, even all the congregation." Verse 21.

Moses stood before the people to repeat his warnings and admonitions. His face was illumined with a holy light, his hair white with age. But his form was erect, and his eye was clear and undimmed. With deep feeling he portrayed the love and mercy of their Almighty Protector.

"Ask from the one side of heaven unto the other, whether there hath been any such thing as this great thing is, or hath been heard like it? Did ever people hear the voice of God speaking out of the midst of the fire, as thou hast heard, and live? or hath God assayed to go and take him a nation from the midst of another nation, by temptations, by signs, and by wonders, and by war, and by a mighty hand, and by a stretched-out arm, and by great terrors, according to all that the Lord your God did for you in Egypt before your eyes?"

"Because the Lord loved you, and because He would keep the oath which He had sworn unto your fathers, hath the Lord brought you out with a mighty hand, and redeemed you out of the house of bondmen, from the hand of Pharaoh king of Egypt. Know therefore that the Lord thy God, He is God, the faithful God, which keepeth covenant and mercy with them that love Him and keep His commandments to a thousand generations." Deuteronomy 7:8, 9.

The people of Israel had often felt impatient and rebellious because of their long wandering in the wilderness; but the Lord had not been chargeable with this delay in possessing Canaan. He was more grieved than they because He could not bring them into immediate possession of the Promised Land and display before all nations His mighty power. With their distrust of God, they had not been prepared to enter Canaan. Had their fathers yielded in faith to the direction of God, walking in His ordinances, they would long before have been settled in Canaan, a prosperous, holy, happy people. Their delay dishonored God and detracted from His glory in the sight of surrounding nations.

"Behold," Moses said, "I have taught you statutes and judgments, even as the Lord my God commanded me, that ye should do so in the land whither ye go to possess it. Keep therefore and do them; for this is your wisdom and your understanding in the sight of the nations, which shall hear all these statutes, and say, Surely this great nation is a wise and understanding people."

And he challenged the Hebrew host: "What nation is there so great, that hath statutes and judgments so righteous as all this law, which I set before you this day?" The laws which God gave His ancient people were wiser, better, and more humane than those of the most civilized nations of the earth. God's law bears the stamp of the divine.

The land which was to be theirs on condition of obedience was thus described to them—and how must these words have moved the hearts of Israel as they remembered that he who so glowingly pictured the blessings of the goodly land had been, through their sin, shut out from sharing the inheritance of his people:

"The land, whither ye go to possess it, is a land of hills and valleys, and drinketh water of the rain of heaven"; "a land of brooks of water, of fountains and depths that spring out of valleys and hills; a land of wheat, and barley, and vines, and fig trees, and pomegranates; a land of olive oil, and honey; a land wherein thou shalt eat bread without scarceness, thou shalt not lack anything in it; a land whose stones are iron, and out of whose hills thou mayest dig brass"; "a land which the Lord thy God careth for: the eyes of the Lord thy God are always upon it, from the beginning of the year even unto the end of the year."

"And it shall be, when the Lord thy God shall have brought thee into the land which He sware unto thy fathers, to Abraham, to Isaac, and to Jacob, to give thee great and goodly cities, which thou buildest not, and houses full of all good things, which thou filledst not, and wells digged, which thou diggedst not, vineyards and olive trees, which thou plantedst not; when thou shalt have eaten and be full; then beware lest thou forget the Lord." "Take heed unto yourselves, lest ye forget the covenant of the Lord our God. . . . For the Lord thy God is a consuming fire, even a jealous God." If they should do evil in the sight of the Lord, then, said Moses, "Ye shall soon utterly perish from off the land whereunto ye go over Jordan to possess it."

Moses completed the work of writing all the laws, statutes, and judgments which God had given him, and regulations concerning the sacrificial system. The book containing these was placed for safe keeping in the side of the ark.

Blessings Conditional

Still the great leader was filled with fear that the people would depart from God. In a sublime and thrilling address he set before them the blessings that would be theirs on condition of obedience, and the curses that would follow upon transgression:

"If thou shalt hearken diligently unto the voice of the Lord thy God, to observe and to do all his commandments which I command thee this day," "blessed shalt thou be in the city, and blessed shalt thou be in the field," in "the fruit of thy body, and the fruit of thy ground, and the fruit of thy cattle. . . . Blessed shall be thy basket and thy store. . . . The Lord shall cause thine enemies that rise up against thee to be smitten before thy face. . . . The Lord shall command the blessing upon thee in thy storehouses, and in all that thou settest thine hand unto."

"But it shall come to pass, if thou wilt not . . . observe to do all His commandments and His statutes which I command thee this day; that all these curses shall come upon thee," "and thou shalt become an astonishment, a proverb, and a byword, among all nations whither the Lord shall lead thee." "And the Lord shall scatter thee among all people, from one end of the earth even unto the other. . . . And among these nations shalt thou find no ease, neither shall the sole of thy foot have rest: but the Lord shall give thee there a trembling heart, and failing of eyes, and sorrow of mind: and thy life shall hang in doubt before thee; and thou shalt fear day and night, and shalt have none assurance of thy life: In the morning thou shalt say, Would God it were even! And at even thou shalt say, Would God it were morning!"

By the Spirit of Inspiration, looking far down the ages, Moses pictured the terrible scenes of Israel's final overthrow as a nation and the destruction of Jerusalem by the armies of Rome. The horrible sufferings of the people during the siege of Jerusalem under Titus centuries later were vividly portrayed: "He shall besiege thee in all thy gates, until thy high and fenced walls come down, wherein thou trustedst, throughout all thy land. . . . Thou shalt eat the fruit of thine own body, the flesh of thy sons and of thy daughters . . . in the siege, and in the straitness, wherewith thine enemies shall distress thee." "The tender and delicate women among you, which would not adventure to set the sole of her foot upon the ground for delicateness and tenderness, her eye shall be evil toward the husband of her bosom, . . . and toward her children which she shall bear: for she shall eat them for want of all things secretly in the siege and straitness, wherewith thine enemy shall distress thee in thy gates."

Moses closed with these impressive words: "I call heaven and earth to record this day against you, that I have set before you life and death, blessing and cursing: therefore choose life, that both thou and thy seed may live: that thou mayest love the Lord thy God, and that thou mayest obey His voice, and that thou mayest cleave unto Him: for He is thy life, and the length of thy days: that thou mayest dwell in the land which the Lord sware unto thy fathers, to Abraham, to Isaac, and to Jacob, to give them."

The more deeply to impress these truths upon all minds, the great leader embodied them in sacred verse. The people were to commit to memory this poetic history and teach it to their children and children's children, that it might never be forgotten.

When their children should ask in time to come, "What mean the testimonies, and the statutes, and the judgments which the Lord our God hath commanded you?" then the parents were to repeat the history of God's gracious dealings with them—how the Lord had wrought for their deliverance that they might obey His law: "The Lord commanded us to do all these statutes, to fear the Lord our God, for our good always, that He might preserve us alive, as it is at this day. And it shall be our righteousness, if we observe to do all these commandments before the Lord our God, as He hath commanded us."

43 / The Death of Moses

In all dealings of God with His people, there is, mingled with His love and mercy, the most striking evidence of His strict and impartial justice. The great Ruler of nations had declared that Moses was not to lead Israel into the goodly land, and the earnest pleading of God's servant could not secure a reversing of His sentence. Yet he had faithfully sought to prepare the congregation to enter the promised inheritance. At the divine command, Moses and Joshua repaired to the tabernacle, while the pillar of cloud came and stood over the door. Here the people were solemnly committed to the charge of Joshua. The work of Moses as leader of Israel was ended.

Still he forgot himself in his interest for his people. In the presence of the multitude Moses, in the name of God, addressed to his successor these words of holy cheer: "Be strong and of a good courage: for thou shalt bring the children of Israel into the land which I sware unto them: and I will be with thee." He then turned to the elders and officers of the people, giving them a solemn charge to obey faithfully the instructions he had communicated to them from God.

As the people gazed upon the aged man so soon to be taken from them, they recalled with new appreciation his parental tenderness, his wise counsels, and his untiring labors. They bitterly remembered that their own perversity had provoked Moses to the sin for which he must die.

God would lead them to feel that they were not to make the life of their future leader as trying as they had

This chapter is based on Deuteronomy 31 to 34.

made that of Moses. God speaks to His people in blessings bestowed, and when these are not appreciated, He speaks to them in blessings removed.

That very day there came to Moses the command, "Get thee up . . . unto Mount Nebo, . . . and behold the land of Canaan, which I give unto the children of Israel for a possession: and die in the mount whither thou goest up, and be gathered unto thy people." Moses was now to depart on a new and mysterious errand. He must go forth to resign his life into the hands of his Creator. He knew that he was to die alone; no earthly friend would be permitted to minister to him in his last hours. There was a mystery and awfulness about the scene from which his heart shrank. The severest trial was his separation from the people with whom his life had so long been united. But with unquestioning faith he committed himself and his people to God's love and mercy.

Moses' Last Blessing

For the last time Moses stood in the assembly of his people. Again the Spirit of God rested upon him, and in sublime and touching language he pronounced a blessing upon each of the tribes, closing with a benediction upon them all:

> The eternal God is thy dwelling place,
> And underneath are the everlasting arms. . . .
> And Israel dwelleth in safety,
> The fountain of Jacob alone,
> In a land of corn and wine;
> Yea, his heavens drop down dew.
> Happy art thou, O Israel:
> Who is like unto thee,
> A people saved by Jehovah,
> The shield of thy help.
>   Deuteronomy 33:27-29

Moses turned from the congregation, and in silence and alone made his way up "the mountain of Nebo, to the top of Pisgah.'' Upon that lonely height he stood and gazed with undimmed eye upon the scene spread out before him.

Far away to the west lay the blue waters of the Great Sea. In the north Mount Hermon stood out against the sky. To the east was the tableland of Moab. And beyond lay Bashan, the scene of Israel's triumph. To the south stretched the desert of their long wanderings.

In solitude Moses reviewed his life of hardships since he turned from courtly honors and from a prospective kingdom in Egypt, to cast his lot with God's chosen people. He called to mind those long years in the desert with the flocks of Jethro, the appearance of the Angel in the burning bush, and his call to deliver Israel. Again he beheld the mighty miracles of God's power displayed in behalf of the chosen people and His long-suffering mercy during the years of their wandering and rebellion. Only two of all the adults in the vast army that left Egypt had been found so faithful that they could enter the Promised Land. His life of trial and sacrifice seemed to have been almost in vain.

Yet he knew that his mission and work were of God's appointing. When first called to lead Israel from bondage, he shrank from the responsibility, but he had not cast aside the burden. Even when the Lord had proposed to release him and destroy rebellious Israel, Moses could not consent. He had enjoyed special tokens of God's favor; he had obtained a rich experience during the sojourn in the wilderness in the communion of His love. He felt he had made a wise decision in choosing to suffer affliction with the people of God rather than to enjoy the pleasures of sin for a season.

As he looked back upon his experience, one wrong act marred the record. If that transgression could be blotted out, he felt that he would not shrink from death. He was assured that repentance and faith in the promised Sacrifice were all that God required, and again Moses confessed his sin and implored pardon in the name of Jesus.

Now a panoramic view of the Land of Promise was presented to him, not faint and uncertain in the dim distance, but standing clear, distinct, and beautiful to his delighted vision. In this scene it was presented not as it then appeared, but as it would become, with God's blessing. There were mountains clothed with cedars, hills gray with olives and fragrant with the odor of the vine, wide green plains bright with flowers and rich in fruitfulness, palm trees, waving fields of wheat and barley, sunny valleys musical with the ripple of brooks and the song of birds, goodly cities and fair gardens, lakes rich in "the abundance of the seas," grazing flocks upon the hillsides, and even amid the rocks the wild bees' hoarded treasures. It was indeed such a land as Moses, inspired by the Spirit of God, had described to Israel.

Moses Has Preview of Israel's History

Moses saw the chosen people in Canaan, each of the tribes in its own possession. He had a view of their history—the long, sad story of their apostasy and its punishment. He saw them dispersed among the heathen, the glory departed from Israel, her beautiful city in ruins, and her people captives in strange lands. He saw them restored to the land of their fathers and at last brought under the dominion of Rome.

He was permitted to behold the first advent of our Saviour. He saw Jesus as a babe in Bethlehem. He heard the voices of the angelic host break forth in the glad song of praise to God and peace on earth. He beheld in the heavens the star guiding the Wise Men of the east to Jesus, and a great light flooded his mind as he recalled those prophetic words, "There shall come a Star out of Jacob, and a Scepter shall rise out of Israel." Numbers 24:17. He beheld Christ's humble life in Nazareth, His ministry of love and sympathy and healing, His rejection by a proud, unbelieving nation. Amazed, he listened to their boastful exaltation of the law of God, while they despised and rejected Him by whom the law was given. He saw Jesus upon Olivet as with weeping He bade farewell to the city of His love.

As Moses beheld the final rejection of that people for whom he had toiled, prayed, and sacrificed, for whom he had been willing that his own name should be blotted from the book of life, as he listened to those fearful words, "Behold, your house is left unto you desolate" (Matthew 23:38), his heart was wrung with anguish. Bitter tears fell from his eyes in sympathy with the sorrow of the Son of God.

Moses Sees the Crucifixion and the Earth Made New

He followed the Saviour to Gethsemane and beheld the agony in the garden, the betrayal, the mockery and scourging, the crucifixion. Moses saw that as he had lifted up the serpent in the wilderness, so the Son of God must be lifted up, that whosoever would believe on Him "should not perish, but have eternal life." John 3:15. Grief, indignation, and horror filled the heart of Moses as he viewed the hypocrisy and satanic hatred manifested by the Jewish nation against their Redeemer.

He heard Christ's agonizing cry, "My God, My God, why hast Thou forsaken Me?" Mark 15:34. He saw Him lying in Joseph's new tomb. The darkness of hopeless despair seemed to enshroud the world. But he looked again, and beheld Him a conqueror ascending to heaven escorted by adoring angels and leading a multitude of captives.

Moses beheld the disciples of Jesus as they went forth to carry His gospel to the world. Though Israel "according to the flesh" had failed to be the light of the world, though they had forfeited their blessings as His chosen people, yet God had not cast off the seed of Abraham. All who through Christ should become the children of faith were to be counted as Abraham's seed, inheritors of the covenant promises. Like Abraham they were called to make known to the world the law of God and the gospel of His Son. Moses saw the light of the gospel shining through the disciples of Jesus, and thousands from the lands of the Gentiles flocking to the brightness of its rising. He rejoiced in the increase and prosperity of Israel.

And now another scene passed before him. He had been shown the work of Satan in leading the Jews to reject Christ while they professed to honor His Father's law. He now saw the world under a similar deception in professing to accept Christ while they rejected God's law. He had heard from the priests and elders the frenzied cry, "Away with Him!" "Crucify Him, crucify Him!" And now he heard from professedly Christian teachers the cry, "Away with the law!"

He saw the Sabbath trodden under foot and a spurious institution established in its place. Moses was filled with astonishment and horror. How could those who believed in Christ set aside the law which is the foundation of His government in heaven and earth? With joy Moses saw the law of God still honored and exalted by a faithful few. He saw the last great struggle of earthly powers to destroy those who keep God's law. He heard God's covenant of peace with those who have kept His law, as He utters His voice from His holy habitation. He saw the second coming of Christ in glory, the righteous dead raised to immortal life, and the living saints translated without seeing death and together ascending with songs of gladness to the City of God.

Still another scene opens to his view—the earth freed from the curse, lovelier than the fair Land of Promise so lately spread out before him. There is no sin, and death cannot enter. With joy unutterable, Moses looks upon the scene, a more glorious deliverance than his brightest hopes have ever pictured. Their earthly wanderings forever past, the Israel of God have at last entered the goodly land.

Again the vision faded, and his eyes rested upon the land of Canaan in the distance. Then, like a tired warrior, he lay down to rest. "So Moses the servant of the Lord died there in the land of Moab, according to the word of the Lord. And he buried him in a valley in the land of Moab, over against Beth-peor: but no man knoweth of his sepulcher." Many would have been in danger of committing idolatry over his dead body, had they known the place of his burial. For this reason it was concealed from men. Angels of God buried the body of His faithful servant and watched over the lonely grave.

But he was not long to remain in the tomb. Christ Himself, with the angels who had buried Moses, came down from heaven to call forth the sleeping saint. Satan had exulted at his success in causing Moses to sin and thus come under the dominion of death. The great adversary declared that the divine sentence, "Dust thou art, and unto dust shalt thou return" (Genesis 3:19), gave him possession of the dead. The power of the grave had never been broken, and all who were in the tomb he claimed as his captives, never to be released.

As the Prince of life and the shining ones approached the grave, Satan was alarmed for his supremacy. He stood to dispute an invasion of the territory that he claimed as his own. He declared that even Moses was not able to keep the law of God. He had taken to himself the glory due to Jehovah, the very sin which had caused Satan's banishment from heaven, and by transgression had come under the dominion of Satan. The archtraitor reiterated the original charges he had made of God's injustice toward him.

Christ might have brought against him the cruel work which his deceptions had wrought in heaven, causing the ruin of a vast number of its inhabitants. He might have pointed to the falsehoods told in Eden that had led to Adam's sin and brought death upon the human race. He might have reminded Satan that it was his own work in tempting Israel to murmuring and rebellion which had wearied the longsuffering patience of their leader and in an unguarded moment surprised him into the sin for which he had fallen under death. But Christ referred all to His Father, saying, "The Lord rebuke thee." Jude 9. The Saviour entered into no dispute with His adversary, but then and there began His work of breaking the power of the fallen foe and bringing the dead to life. Here was evidence of the supremacy of the Son of God. Satan was despoiled of his prey; the righteous dead would live again. Moses came forth from the tomb glorified and ascended with his Deliverer to the City of God.

God shut Moses out of Canaan to teach a lesson which should never be forgotten—that He requires exact obedience and that men are to beware of taking to themselves the glory due their Maker. He could not grant the prayer of Moses that he share the inheritance of Israel, but He did not forget or forsake His servant. On the top of Pisgah, God called Moses to an inheritance infinitely more glorious than the earthly Canaan.

Upon the mount of transfiguration, Moses was present with Elijah, who had been translated. And thus the prayer of Moses was at last fulfilled. He stood upon "the goodly mountain," within the heritage of his people, bearing witness to Him in whom all the promises to Israel centered. Such is the last scene revealed to mortal vision in the history of that man so highly honored of Heaven.

44 / Crossing the Jordan

Never till their departed leader was taken from them had the Israelites so fully realized the value of his wise counsels, his parental tenderness, and his unswerving faith.

Moses was dead, but his influence was to live on. As the glow of the descending sun lights up mountain peaks after the sun has sunk behind the hills, so the works of the holy and the good shed light upon the world long after the actors themselves have passed away. "The righteous shall be in everlasting remembrance." Psalm 112:6.

While the people were filled with grief at their great loss, they were not left alone. The pillar of cloud rested over the tabernacle by day and the pillar of fire by night. God would still be their guide and helper if they would walk in the way of His commandments.

Joshua was now the acknowledged leader of Israel. Courageous, persevering, unmindful of self, and, above all, inspired by a living faith in God—such was the character of the man chosen to conduct the armies of Israel. He had acted as prime minister to Moses, and by his quiet, unpretending fidelity, his steadfastness when others wavered, his firmness to maintain the truth in the midst of danger, he had given evidence of his fitness to succeed Moses.

With great anxiety Joshua looked forward to the work before him; but his fears were removed by the assurance of God, "As I was with Moses, so I will be with thee: I will not fail thee, nor forsake thee. . . .

This chapter is based on Joshua 1 to 5:12.

Unto this people shalt thou divide for an inheritance the land, which I sware unto their fathers to give them." "Every place that the sole of your foot shall tread upon, that have I given unto you." "Only be thou strong and very courageous, that thou mayest observe to do according to all the law, which Moses My servant commanded. . . . This book of the law shall not depart out of thy mouth; but thou shalt meditate therein day and night." "Turn not from it to the right hand or to the left . . . for then thou shalt make thy way prosperous, and then thou shalt have good success."

"Arise," had been the first message of God to Joshua, "go over this Jordan, thou, and all this people, unto the land which I do give to them." Joshua knew that whatever God should command, He would make a way for His people to perform. In this faith the intrepid leader at once began arrangements for an advance.

Just opposite where the Israelites encamped was the strongly fortified city of Jericho, the key to the whole country. It would present a formidable obstacle to Israel. Joshua therefore sent two young men as spies to ascertain something as to its population, resources, and strength of fortifications. The inhabitants of the city, terrified and suspicious, were on the alert, and the messengers were in great danger. They were, however, preserved by Rahab, a woman of Jericho, at the peril of her own life. In return for her kindness, they gave her a promise of protection when the city should be taken.

People of Jericho Already Terrified

The spies returned with the tidings, "Truly the Lord hath delivered into our hands all the land; for even all the inhabitants of the country do faint because of us." It had been declared to them in Jericho, "We have heard how the Lord dried up the water of the Red Sea for you, when ye came out of Egypt; and what ye did unto the two kings of the Amorites, that were on the other side Jordan, Sihon and Og, whom ye utterly destroyed. And as soon as we had heard these things, our hearts did melt, neither did there remain any more courage in any man, because of you: for the Lord your God, He is God in heaven above, and in earth beneath.''

Orders were now issued to make ready for an advance. The people were to prepare a three-days' supply of food, and the army was to be put in readiness for battle. Leaving their encampment the host descended to the border of the Jordan. All knew that without divine aid they could not hope to make the passage. At this time of year the melting snows of the mountains so raised the Jordan that the river overflowed, making it impossible to cross. God willed that the passage over Jordan should be miraculous.

Joshua, by divine direction, commanded the people to put away their sins and free themselves from all outward impurity, ''for tomorrow,'' he said, ''the Lord will do wonders among you.'' The ''ark of the covenant'' was to lead the way, borne by the priests from its place in the center of the camp, toward the river. ''Hereby ye shall know that the living God is among you, and that He will without fail drive out from before you the Canaanites. . . . Behold, the ark of the covenant of the Lord of all the earth passeth over before you into Jordan.''

At the appointed time the onward movement began, the ark, borne upon the shoulders of the priests, leading. There was a vacant space of more than half a mile about the ark. All watched with deep interest as the priests advanced down the bank of the Jordan. They saw the sacred ark move steadily toward the surging stream, till the feet of the bearers were dipped into the waters. Then suddenly the tide above was swept back, while the current below flowed on, and the bed of the river was laid bare.

The priests advanced to the middle of the channel and stood there while the entire host descended and crossed to the farther side. The power that stayed the waters of Jordan was the same that had opened the Red Sea to their fathers forty years before. When the people had all passed over, the ark itself was borne to the western shore. No sooner had "the soles of the priests' feet . . . lifted up unto the dry land" than the imprisoned waters rushed down, a resistless flood, in the natural channel of the stream.

While the priests bearing the ark were still in the midst of Jordan, twelve men, one from each tribe, took up each a stone from the riverbed where the priests were standing and carried them over to the western side. These stones were to be set up as a monument in the first camping place beyond the river, as Joshua said, "That all the people of the earth might know the hand of the Lord, that it is mighty: that ye might fear the Lord your God forever."

This miracle was an assurance to Israel of God's continued presence and protection, an evidence that He would work for them through Joshua as He had wrought through Moses. The Lord had declared to Joshua before the crossing, "This day will I begin to magnify thee in the sight of all Israel, that they may know that, as I was with Moses, so I will be with thee."

When the tidings that God had stayed the waters of Jordan before the children of Israel reached the kings of the Amorites and Canaanites, their hearts melted with fear. To the Canaanites, to all Israel, and to Joshua himself, unmistakable evidence had been given that the living God, the King of heaven and earth, was among His people. He would not fail them nor forsake them.

A short distance from Jordan the Hebrews made their first encampment in Canaan. The suspension of the rite of circumcision and the discontinuance of the Passover had been an evidence of the Lord's displeasure at their desire to return to the land of bondage. Now, however, the years of rejection were ended. The sign of the covenant was restored. The rite of circumcision was performed upon all the people who had been born in the wilderness. And the Lord declared to Joshua, "This day have I rolled away the reproach of Egypt from off you."

Heathen nations had reproached the Lord and His people because the Hebrews had failed to take possession of Canaan soon after leaving Egypt. Their enemies had triumphed because Israel had wandered so long in the wilderness, and they had mockingly declared that the God of the Hebrews was not able to bring them into the Promised Land. The Lord had now signally manifested His power and favor in opening the Jordan before His people.

The Passover was celebrated, "and the manna ceased on the morrow after they had eaten of the old corn of the land; neither had the children of Israel manna any more; but they did eat of the fruit of the land of Canaan." The long years of their desert wanderings were ended. The feet of Israel were at last treading the Promised Land.

45 / The Miraculous Fall of Jericho

The Hebrews had entered Canaan, but they had not subdued it. It was inhabited by a powerful race, who stood ready to oppose the invasion of their territory. Their horses and iron battle chariots, their knowledge of the country, and their training in war would give them great advantage. Further, the country was guarded by "cities great and fenced up to heaven." Deuteronomy 9:1. Only in the assurance of a strength not their own could the Israelites hope for success in the impending conflict.

The large and wealthy city of Jericho lay just a little distance from their camp at Gilgal. This proud city, behind its massive battlements, offered defiance to the God of Israel. Jericho was especially devoted to Ashtaroth, the goddess of the moon. Here centered all that was vilest and most degrading in the religion of the Canaanites. The people of Israel, in whose minds were fresh the fearful results of their sin at Beth-peor, could look upon this heathen city only with disgust and horror.

To reduce Jericho was seen by Joshua to be the first step in the conquest of Canaan. Withdrawing from the encampment to meditate and to pray, he beheld an armed warrior of commanding presence "with his sword drawn in his hand." To Joshua's challenge, "Art thou for us, or for our adversaries?" the answer was given, "As Captain of the host of the Lord am I now come." The mysterious stranger was Christ, the Exalted One. Awe-stricken, Joshua fell upon his face

This chapter is based on Joshua 5:13-15; 6; 7.

and worshiped, and heard the assurance, "I have given into thine hand Jericho, and the king thereof, and the mighty men of valor," and he received instruction for the capture of the city.

In obedience to the divine command, Joshua marshaled the armies of Israel. No assault was to be made. They were simply to make the circuit of the city, bearing the ark of God and blowing trumpets. The ark of God, surrounded by a halo of divine glory, was borne by priests clad in the dress denoting their sacred office. The army of Israel followed. Such was the procession that compassed the doomed city.

No sound was heard but the tread of that mighty host and the solemn peal of the trumpets, echoing among the hills and resounding through the streets of Jericho.

With wonder and alarm the watchmen of the city reported to those in authority. When they beheld that mighty host marching around their city once each day, with the sacred ark and the attendent priests, the mystery of the scene struck terror to the hearts of priest and people. Again they would inspect their strong defenses, feeling certain they could successfully resist the most powerful attack. Many ridiculed the thought that any harm would come to them through these singular demonstrations. Others were awed as they beheld the procession each day. They remembered that the Red Sea had once parted before this people and that a passage had just been opened for them through the river Jordan.

God's Simple Method of Conquering Jericho

For six days Israel made the circuit of the city. The seventh day came, and with the first dawn of light, Joshua marshaled the armies of the Lord. Now they were to march seven times around Jericho, and at a mighty peal from the trumpets to shout with a loud voice, for God had given them the city.

The vast army marched solemnly around the walls. All was silent, save the measured tread of many feet.

The watchers on the walls looked on with rising fear as, the first circuit ended, there followed a second, then a third, a fourth, a fifth, a sixth. What could be the object of these mysterious movements?

They had not long to wait. As the seventh circuit was completed, the long procession paused. The trumpets, which for an interval had been silent, now broke forth in a blast that shook the very earth. The walls of solid stone, with their massive towers and battlements, tottered and heaved from their foundations, and with a crash fell to the earth. The inhabitants of Jericho were paralyzed with terror, and the hosts of Israel marched in and took possession of the city.

The Israelites had not gained the victory by their own power; and as the firstfruits of the land, the city, with all that it contained, was to be devoted as a sacrifice to God. In the conquest of Canaan the Israelites were not to fight for themselves, not to seek for riches or self-exaltation, but for the glory of Jehovah their king. The command had been given, "Keep yourselves from the accursed thing, lest ye make yourselves accursed, . . . and make the camp of Israel a curse, and trouble it."

All the inhabitants, with every living thing, were put to the sword. Only faithful Rahab with her household was spared in fulfillment of the promise of the spies. The city palaces and temples, its magnificent dwellings with all their luxurious appointments, the rich draperies and the costly garments were given to the flames. That which could not be destroyed by fire, "the silver, and the gold, and the vessels of brass and of iron," was to be devoted to the service of the tabernacle. Jericho was never to be rebuilt as a stronghold; judgments were threatened on anyone who should presume to restore the walls that divine power had cast down.

The utter destruction of the people of Jericho was a fulfillment of commands previously given concerning the inhabitants of Canaan: "Thou shalt smite them, and utterly destroy them." "Of the cities of these peo-

ple, . . . thou shalt save alive nothing that breatheth."
Deuteronomy 7:2; 20:16.

To many these commands seem contrary to the
spirit of love and mercy enjoined in other portions of
the Bible. But they were in truth the dictates of infinite
wisdom and goodness. God was about to establish Israel in Canaan. They were not only to be inheritors of
the true religion, but to disseminate its principles
throughout the world. The Canaanites had abandoned
themselves to debasing heathenism, and it was necessary that the land be cleared of what would surely prevent the fulfillment of God's gracious purposes.

The inhabitants had been granted ample opportunity
for repentance. Forty years before, the judgments on
Egypt had testified to the power of the God of Israel.
The overthrow of Midian, of Gilead and Bashan, had
further shown that He was above all gods. His abhorrence of impurity had been demonstrated in the judgments on Israel for their participation in the abominable rites of Baal-peor. All these events were known to
the inhabitants of Jericho. Many shared Rahab's conviction, though they refused to obey it, that the God of
Israel "is God in heaven above, and upon the earth beneath." Like the men before the Flood, the Canaanites
lived only to blaspheme Heaven and defile the earth.
Both love and justice demanded the execution of these
rebels against God and foes to man.

"By faith the walls of Jericho fell down." Hebrews
11:30. The Captain of the Lord's host communicated
only with Joshua. He did not reveal Himself to all the
congregation, and it rested with them to believe or
doubt the words of Joshua. *They* could not see the host
of angels who attended them under the leadership of
the Son of God. They might have reasoned: "How ri-
diculous, marching daily around the walls of the city,
blowing trumpets of rams' horns. This can have no effect upon those towering fortifications." But it was to
be impressed upon their minds that their strength was
not in the wisdom of man, nor in his might, but only in

the God of their salvation. God will do great things for those who trust in Him. He will help His believing children in every emergency, if they will place their entire confidence in Him and faithfully obey Him.

Why Israel Was Defeated at Ai

Soon after the fall of Jericho, Joshua determined to attack Ai, a small town among the ravines a few miles west of the Jordan Valley. Spies brought the report that the inhabitants were few, and only a small force would be needed to overthrow it.

The great victory that God had gained for them had made the Israelites self-confident. They failed to realize that divine help alone could give them success. Even Joshua laid his plans for the conquest of Ai without seeking counsel from God.

The Israelites had begun to look with contempt upon their foes. An easy victory was expected, and three thousand men were thought sufficient to take the place. These advanced nearly to the gate of the city, only to encounter determined resistance. Panic-stricken at the numbers and thorough preparation of their enemies, they fled in confusion down the steep descent. The Canaanites "chased them from before the gate, . . . and smote them in the going down." Though the loss was small as to numbers—thirty-six men slain—the defeat was disheartening. "The hearts of the people melted, and became as water."

Joshua looked upon their ill success as an expression of God's displeasure. In distress and apprehension he "rent his clothes, and fell to the earth upon his face before the ark of the Lord until the eventide, he and the elders of Israel, and put dust upon their heads."

"Alas, O Lord God," he cried, "wherefore hast Thou at all brought this people over Jordan, to deliver us into the hand of the Amorites, to destroy us? . . . O Lord, what shall I say, when Israel turneth their backs before their enemies! For the Canaanites and all the inhabitants of the land shall hear of it, and shall environ us round, and cut off our name from the earth: and what wilt Thou do unto Thy great name?"

The answer was, "Get thee up; wherefore liest thou thus upon thy face? Israel hath . . . transgressed My covenant which I commanded them." It was a time for prompt and decided action, not for despair and lamentation. There was secret sin in the camp, and it must be searched out and put away. "Neither will I be with you any more, except ye destroy the accursed from among you."

One Family's Sin Brings Defeat to All Israel

God's command had been disregarded by one of those appointed to execute His judgments. And the nation was held accountable for the guilt of the transgressor: "*They* have even taken of the accursed thing, and have also stolen, and dissembled also." The lot was to be employed for the detection of the guilty, the matter being left in doubt for a time that the people might feel their responsibility and thus be led to searching of heart and humiliation before God.

Early in the morning, Joshua gathered the people together, and the solemn and impressive ceremony began. Step by step the investigation went on. Closer and closer came the fearful test. First the tribe, then the family, then the household, then the man was taken, and Achan the son of Carmi, of the tribe of Judah, was pointed out by the finger of God as the troubler of Israel.

Joshua solemnly adjured Achan to acknowledge the truth. The wretched man made full confession of his crime: "Indeed I have sinned against the Lord God of Israel. . . . When I saw among the spoils a goodly Babylonish garment, and two hundred shekels of silver, and a wedge of gold of fifty shekels weight, then I coveted them, and took them; and, behold, they are hid in the earth in the midst of my tent." Messengers removed the earth at the place specified, and "it was hid in his tent, and the silver under it. And they . . .

brought them unto Joshua, . . . and laid them out before the Lord."

"Why hast thou troubled us?" said Joshua. "The Lord shall trouble thee this day." As the people had been held responsible for Achan's sin and had suffered from its consequences, they were to take part in its punishment. "All Israel stoned him with stones." In the book of Chronicles his memorial is written— "Achar, the troubler of Israel." 1 Chronicles 2:7.

Achan's sin was committed in defiance of direct, solemn warnings and mighty manifestations of God's power. The fact that divine power alone had given victory to Israel, that they had not come into possession of Jericho by their own strength, gave solemn weight to the command prohibiting them from partaking of the spoils. God had overthrown this stronghold, and to Him alone the city with all that it contained was to be devoted.

Achan Refuses to Repent

Of the millions of Israel there was but one man who had dared to transgress the command of God. Achan's covetousness was excited by that costly robe of Shinar; even when it had brought him face to face with death he called it "a *goodly* Babylonish garment." And he appropriated the gold and silver devoted to the treasury of the Lord; he robbed God of the first fruits of the land of Canaan. How rarely does the violation of the tenth commandment so much as call forth censure. The enormity of this sin, and its terrible results, are the lessons of Achan's history.

Achan had cherished greed of gain until it became a habit, binding him in fetters well-nigh impossible to break. He would have been filled with horror at the thought of bringing disaster upon Israel; but his perceptions were deadened by sin, and when temptation came, he fell an easy prey.

We are as directly forbidden to indulge covetousness as was Achan to appropriate the spoils of Jericho.

**When confronted by Joshua, Achan confessed
his sin but remained unrepentant.**

We are warned, "Ye cannot serve God and mammon." "Take heed, and beware of covetousness." "Let it not be once named among you." Matthew 6:24; Luke 12:15; Ephesians 5:3. We have before us the fearful doom of Achan, of Judas, of Ananias and Sapphira. Back of all these we have Lucifer. Yet, notwithstanding all these warnings, covetousness abounds.

Everywhere its slimy track is seen. It creates dissension in families; it excites envy and hatred in the poor against the rich; it prompts the grinding oppression of the rich toward the poor. And this evil exists not in the world alone, but in the church. How common to find selfishness, avarice, neglect of charities, and robbery of God "in tithes and offerings." Many a man comes to church and sits at the table of the Lord, while among his possessions are hidden unlawful gains, things that God has cursed. For a "goodly Babylonish garment" multitudes sacrifice their hope of heaven. The cries of the suffering and poor are unheeded; the gospel light is hindered in its course; practices give the lie to the Christian profession; yet the covetous professor continues to heap up treasures. "Will a man rob God? Yet ye have robbed Me," saith the Lord. Malachi 3:8.

The Difference Between Genuine and Forced Confessions

For one man's sin the displeasure of God will rest upon His church till the transgression is searched out and put away. The influence most to be feared by the church is not that of open opposers, infidels, and blasphemers, but of inconsistent ones that keep back the blessing of the God of Israel and bring weakness upon His people. With humiliation and searching of heart, let each seek to discover the hidden sins that shut out God's presence.

Achan had seen the armies of Israel return from Ai defeated and disheartened, yet he did not come forward and confess his sin. He had seen Joshua and the elders bowed to the earth in grief too great for words.

But he still kept silence. He had listened to the proclamation that a great crime had been committed, and had even heard its character definitely stated. But his lips were sealed. His soul thrilled with terror as he saw his tribe pointed out, then his family and his household! But still he uttered no confession, until the finger of God was placed upon him. Then, when his sin could no longer be concealed, he admitted the truth.

There is a vast difference between admitting facts after they have been proved, and confessing sins known only to ourselves and to God. Achan's confession only served to show that his punishment was just. There was no genuine repentance, no contrition, no change of purpose, no abhorrence of evil.

So confessions will be made by the guilty when they stand before the bar of God, after every case has been decided for life or death. An acknowledgment of sin will be forced from the soul by an awful sense of condemnation and a fearful looking for of judgment. But such confessions cannot save the sinner.

When the records of heaven shall be opened, the Judge will not declare to man his guilt, but will cast one penetrating, convicting glance, and every deed, every transaction of life, will be vividly impressed upon the memory of the wrongdoer. The sins hidden from men will then be proclaimed to the whole world.

46 / The Blessings and the Curses

After the execution of the sentence on Achan, Joshua was commanded to marshal all the men of war and again advance against Ai. The power of God was with His people, and they were soon in possession of the city.

The people were eager to obtain settlement in Canaan; as yet they had no homes or lands for their families, and to gain these they must drive out the Canaanites. But a higher duty demanded their first attention. They must renew their covenant of loyalty to God.

In the last instructions of Moses, directions had been given for a convocation upon Mounts Ebal and Gerizim at Shechem, for the recognition of the law of God. In obedience, the men, "the women and the little ones, and the strangers that were conversant among them" left Gilgal and marched through the country of their enemies to the vale of Shechem, near the center of the land. Though surrounded by unconquered foes, "the terror of God was upon the cities that were round about them" (Genesis 35:5), and the Hebrews were unmolested.

Here both Abraham and Jacob had pitched their tents. Here the latter bought the field in which the tribes were to bury the body of Joseph. Here also was the well that Jacob had dug.

The spot chosen was worthy to be the theater where this impressive scene was to be enacted. The lovely valley, its green fields dotted with olive groves, watered with brooks from living fountains, and

This chapter is based on Joshua 8.

hemmed with wild flowers, spread out invitingly between the barren hills. Ebal and Gerizim, upon opposite sides of the valley, nearly approach each other, their lower spurs seeming to form a natural pulpit, every word spoken on one being distinctly audible on the other. The mountainsides, receding, afford space for a vast assemblage.

A monument of great stones was erected upon Mount Ebal. Upon these stones, previously prepared by a covering of plaster, the law was inscribed—not only the ten precepts spoken from Sinai and engraved on tables of stone, but the law communicated to Moses and written in a book. Beside this monument was built an altar of unhewn stone upon which sacrifices were offered unto the Lord. Because of their transgressions of God's law, Israel had justly incurred His wrath, and it would be at once visited but for the atonement of Christ, represented by the altar of sacrifice.

Six tribes were stationed upon Mount Gerizim, the others on Ebal, the priests with the ark occupying the valley between. In the presence of this vast assembly, Joshua read the blessings that follow obedience to God's law. All the tribes on Gerizim responded, "Amen." He then read the curses, and the tribes on Ebal in like manner gave their assent, thousands upon thousands of voices uniting in the solemn response. Following this came the reading of the law of God, together with the statutes and judgments delivered by Moses.

Israel had received the law from the mouth of God at Sinai, and its sacred precepts, written by His own hand, were preserved in the ark. Now it had been written where all could read for themselves the conditions of the covenant under which they were to hold possession of Canaan. It had not been many weeks since Moses gave the whole book of Deuteronomy in discourses to the people, yet now Joshua read the law again.

Not alone the men of Israel, but "all the women and the little ones" listened to the reading of the law, for it was important that they also should know and do their duty. Moses commanded: "At the end of every seven years, . . . when all Israel is come to appear before the Lord thy God in the place which He shall choose, thou shalt read this law before all Israel in their hearing. Gather the people together, men, and women, and children, and thy stranger that is within thy gates, that they may hear, and that they may learn, and fear the Lord your God, and observe to do all the words of this law: and that their children, which have not known anything, may hear, and learn to fear the Lord your God, as long as ye live in the land whither ye go over Jordan to possess it." Deuteronomy 31:10-13.

Why We Must Diligently Study God's Word

Satan is ever at work endeavoring to pervert what God has spoken, to darken the understanding and lead men into sin. God is constantly seeking to draw men close under His protection, that Satan may not practice his deceptive power upon them. He has condescended to speak to them with His own voice, to write with His own hand the living oracles committed to men as a perfect guide. Because Satan is so ready to divert the affections from the Lord's promises and requirements, the greater diligence is needed to fix them in the mind.

The facts and lessons of Bible history should be presented in simple language, adapted to the comprehension of the young. Parents can interest their children in the varied knowledge found in the sacred pages. But they must be interested themselves. Those who desire their children to love and reverence God must talk of His goodness, His majesty, and His power, as revealed in His Word and in the works of creation.

Every chapter and every verse of the Bible is a communication from God to men. If studied and obeyed, it would lead God's people, as the Israelites were led, by the pillar of cloud by day and the pillar of fire by night.

47 / A Canaanite Tribe Deceives Israel

From Shechem the Israelites returned to their encampment at Gilgal. Here a strange deputation represented that they had come from a distant country. This seemed confirmed by their appearance. Their clothing was old and worn, their sandals patched, their provisions moldy, and the skins that served them for wine bottles were rent and bound up as if hastily repaired on the journey.

In their "far off" home—professedly beyond the limits of Palestine—they had heard of the wonders which God had wrought and had sent to make a league with Israel. The Hebrews had been specially warned against entering into any league with the idolaters of Canaan, and a doubt as to the truth of the strangers' words arose in the minds of the leaders.

"Peradventure ye dwell among us," they said. To this the ambassadors replied, "We are thy servants." But when Joshua directly demanded of them, "Who are ye? and from whence come ye?" they added, "This our bread we took hot for our provision out of our houses on the day we came forth to go unto you; but now, behold, it is dry, and it is moldy: and these bottles of wine, which we filled, were new; and, behold, they be rent: and these our garments and our shoes are become old by reason of the very long journey."

The Hebrews "asked not counsel at the mouth of the Lord. And Joshua made peace with them, and made a league with them, to let them live: and the princes of

This chapter is based on Joshua 9 and 10.

the congregation sware unto them." The treaty was entered into. Three days afterward the truth was discovered. "They heard that they were their neighbors, and that they dwelt among them." The Gibeonites had resorted to stratagem to preserve their lives.

The indignation of the Israelites heightened when, after three days' journey, they reached the cities of the Gibeonites near the center of the land. But the princes refused to break the treaty, though secured by fraud, because they had "sworn unto them by the Lord God of Israel." "And the children of Israel smote them not." The Gibeonites had pledged themselves to renounce idolatry and accept the worship of Jehovah, and the preservation of their lives was not a violation of God's command to destroy the idolatrous Canaanites. Though the oath had been secured by deception, it was not to be disregarded. No consideration of gain, of revenge, or self-interest can in any way affect the inviolability of an oath or pledge. He that "shall ascend into the hill of the Lord," and "stand in His holy place," is "he that sweareth to his own hurt, and changeth not." Psalm 24:3; 15:4.

How the Gibeonites Made Themselves to Be Slaves

The Gibeonites were permitted to live, but were attached as bondmen to the sanctuary to perform menial services. "Joshua made them that day hewers of wood and drawers of water for the congregation, and for the altar of the Lord." These conditions they gratefully accepted, glad to purchase life on any terms. "Behold, we are in thine hand," they said to Joshua; "as it seemeth good and right unto thee to do unto us, do."

Gibeon, the most important of their towns, "was a great city, as one of the royal cities, . . . and all the men thereof were mighty." It is a striking evidence of the terror with which the Israelites had inspired the inhabitants of Canaan, that the people of such a city should have resorted to so humiliating an expedient to save their lives.

But it would have fared better with the Gibeonites had they dealt honestly with Israel. Their deception brought them only disgrace and servitude. God had made provision that all who would renounce heathenism and connect with Israel should share the blessings of the covenant. With few exceptions this class were to enjoy equal favors and privileges with Israel.

Such was the footing on which the Gibeonites might have been received. It was no light humiliation to those citizens of a royal city, "all the men whereof were mighty," to be made hewers of wood and drawers of water. Thus through all their generations, their servile condition would testify to God's hatred of falsehood.

Joshua's Long Day

The submission of Gibeon filled the kings of Canaan with dismay. Steps were at once taken for revenge on those who had made peace with the invaders. Five of the Canaanite kings entered into confederacy against Gibeon. The Gibeonites were unprepared for defense and sent a message to Joshua at Gilgal: "Slack not thy hand from thy servants; come up to us quickly, and save us, and help us: for all the kings of the Amorites that dwell in the mountains are gathered together against us." The danger threatened not the people of Gibeon alone, but also Israel. This city commanded the passes to central and southern Palestine, and it must be held if the country was to be conquered.

The inhabitants of the besieged city had feared that Joshua would reject their appeal, because of the fraud which they had practiced. But since they had submitted to Israel and had accepted the worship of God, he felt under obligation to protect them. And the Lord encouraged him. "Fear them not," was the divine message; "for I have delivered them into thine hand; there shall not a man of them stand before thee." "So Joshua ascended from Gilgal, he, and all the people of war with him, and all the mighty men of valor."

Scarcely had the confederate princes mustered their

armies about the city when Joshua was upon them. The immense host fled up the mountain pass to Beth-horon, and having gained the height they rushed down the precipitous descent upon the other side. Here a fierce hailstorm burst upon them. "The Lord cast down great stones from heaven: . . . they were more which died with hailstones than they whom the children of Israel slew with the sword."

While the Amorites were continuing their headlong flight, Joshua, looking down from the ridge above, saw that the day would be too short for the accomplishment of his work. If not fully routed, their enemies would renew the struggle. "Then spake Joshua to the Lord, . . . and he said in the sight of Israel, Sun, stand thou still upon Gibeon; and thou, Moon, in the valley of Ajalon. And the sun stood still, and the moon stayed, until the people had avenged themselves upon their enemies. . . . The sun stood still in the midst of heaven, and hasted not to go down about a whole day."

Before evening fell, God's promise to Joshua had been fulfilled. The enemy had been given into his hand. Long were the events of that day to remain in the memory of Israel. "There was no day like that before it or after it, that Jehovah hearkened unto the voice of a man: for the Lord fought for Israel." "The sun and moon stood still in their habitation: at the light of Thine arrows they went, and at the shining of Thy glittering spear. Thou didst march through the land in indignation, Thou didst thresh the heathen in anger. Thou wentest forth for the salvation of Thy people." Habakkuk 3:11-13.

Joshua had received the promise that God would overthrow these enemies of Israel, yet he put forth as earnest effort as though success depended upon the armies of Israel alone. He did all that human energy could do, and then he cried in faith for divine aid. The secret of success is the union of divine power with human effort. The man who commanded, "Sun, stand thou still upon Gibeon; and thou, Moon, in the valley of Ajalon," is the man who for hours lay prostrate upon the earth in prayer at Gilgal. Men of prayer are men of power.

This mighty miracle testifies that the creation is under the control of the Creator. In this miracle, all who exalt nature above the God of nature stand rebuked.

At His own will God summons the forces of nature to overthrow the might of His enemies—"fire and hail; snow, and vapor; stormy wind fulfilling His word." Psalm 148:8. We are told of a greater battle to take place in the closing scenes of earth's history, when "the Lord hath opened His armory, and hath brought forth the weapons of His indignation." Jeremiah 50:25.

The revelator describes the destruction that is to take place when the "great voice out of the temple of heaven" announces, "It is done." He says, "There fell upon men a great hail out of heaven, every stone about the weight of a talent." Revelation 16:17, 21.

48 / Home at Last

The victory at Beth-horon was speedily followed by the conquest of southern Canaan. "Joshua smote all the country of the hills and of the south, and of the vale. . . . And all these kings and their land did Joshua take at one time, because the Lord God of Israel fought for Israel."

The tribes of northern Palestine, terrified at the success which had attended the armies of Israel, now entered into a league against them. "And they went out, they and all their hosts with them." This army was much larger than any that the Israelites had before encountered in Canaan—"much people, even as the sand that is upon the seashore in multitude, with horses and chariots very many. And when all these kings were met together, they came and pitched together at the waters of Merom, to fight against Israel."

Again a message of encouragement was given to Joshua: "Be not afraid because of them: for tomorrow about this time will I deliver them up all slain before Israel."

Near Lake Merom he fell upon the camp of the allies, and "the Lord delivered them into the hand of Israel, who smote them, and chased them . . . until they left them none remaining." At the command of God the chariots were burned, and the horses lamed, and thus rendered unfit for use in battle. The Israelites were not to put their trust in chariots or horses, but "in the name of the Lord their God."

One by one, the cities were taken, and Hazor, the

This chapter is based on Joshua 10:40-43; 11; 14 to 22.

stronghold of the confederacy, was burned. The war was continued for several years, but its close found Joshua master of Canaan. "And the land had rest from war."

But though the power of the Canaanites had been broken, they had not been fully dispossessed. Joshua was not, however, to continue the war. The whole land, both the parts already conquered and that yet unsubdued, was to be apportioned among the tribes. And it was the duty of each tribe to fully subdue its own inheritance. If the people should prove faithful to God, He would drive out their enemies from before them.

The location of each tribe was determined by lot. Moses himself had fixed the bounds of the country as it was to be divided among the tribes and had appointed a prince from each tribe to attend to the distribution. Forty-eight cities in different parts of the country were assigned the Levites as their inheritance.

Caleb Asks for the Most Difficult Place

Caleb and Joshua were the only ones among the spies who had brought a good report of the Land of Promise, encouraging the people to go up and possess it in the name of the Lord. Caleb now reminded Joshua of the promises then made, as the reward of his faithfulness: "The land whereon thy feet have trodden shall be thine inheritance, and thy children's forever, because thou hast wholly followed the Lord." He therefore presented a request that Hebron be given him for a possession. Here had been the home of Abraham, Isaac, and Jacob, and here, in the cave of Machpelah, they were buried.

Hebron was the seat of the dreaded Anakim, whose formidable appearance had terrified the spies and destroyed the courage of all Israel. This was the place which Caleb, trusting in the strength of God, chose for his inheritance.

"Behold, the Lord hath kept me alive," he said,

"these forty and five years, even since the Lord spake this word unto Moses: . . . and now, lo, I am this day fourscore and five years old. As yet I am as strong this day as I was in the day that Moses sent me: as my strength was then, even so is my strength now, for war, both to go out, and to come in. Now therefore give me this mountain, whereof the Lord spake in that day; for thou heardest in that day how the Anakim were there, and that the cities were great and fenced: if so be the Lord will be with me, then I shall be able to drive them out, as the Lord said."

His claim was immediately granted. "Joshua blessed him, and gave unto Caleb the son of Jephunneh, Hebron for an inheritance," "because that he wholly followed the Lord God of Israel." Caleb had believed God's promise that He would put His people in possession of Canaan. He had endured the long wandering in the wilderness, sharing the disappointments and burdens of the guilty. Yet he made no complaint, but exalted the mercy of God that preserved him in the wilderness when his brethren were cut off. He did not ask for himself a land already conquered, but the place which, above all others, the spies had thought impossible to subdue. The brave old warrior was desirous of giving the people an example that would honor God and encourage the tribes to subdue the land which their fathers had deemed unconquerable.

Trusting in God to be with him he "drove thence the three sons of Anak." Having thus secured a possession for himself and his house, he did not settle down to enjoy his inheritance but pushed on to further conquests for the benefit of the nation and the glory of God.

The cowards and rebels had perished in the wilderness, but the righteous spies ate of the grapes of Eshcol. The unbelieving had seen their fears fulfilled. They had declared it impossible to inherit Canaan, and they did not possess it. But those who trusted in the strength of their Almighty Helper, entered the goodly land. Through faith the ancient worthies "subdued kingdoms, . . . escaped the edge of the sword, out of weakness were made strong, waxed valiant in fight, turned to flight the armies of the aliens." "This is the victory that overcometh the world, even our faith." Hebrews 11:33, 34; 1 John 5:4.

Another claim revealed a spirit widely different from that of Caleb. The children of Joseph, the tribe of Ephraim with the half tribe of Manasseh, demanded a double portion of territory. The lot designated for them was the richest in the land, including the fertile plain of Sharon; but many of the principal towns in the valley were still in possession of the Canaanites, and the tribes shrank from the toil and danger of conquering their possessions, and desired an additional portion in territory already subdued. The tribe of Ephraim was one of the largest in Israel, as well as the one to which Joshua himself belonged. "Why hast thou given me but one lot and one portion to inherit," they said, "seeing I am a great people?"

But the inflexible leader's answer was, "If thou be a great people, then get thee up to the wood country, and cut down for thyself there in the land of the Perizzites and of the giants, if Mount Ephraim be too narrow for thee."

Their reply showed the real cause of complaint. They lacked faith and courage to drive out the Canaanites. "The hill is not enough for us," they said; "and all the Canaanites that dwell in the land of the valley have chariots of iron."

Had the Ephraimites possessed the courage and faith of Caleb, no enemy could have stood before them. Their desire to shun hardship and danger was firmly met by Joshua: "Thou art a great people, and hast great power," he said; "thou shalt drive out the Canaanites, though they have iron chariots, and though they be strong." With the help of God they need not fear the chariots of iron.

Heretofore Gilgal had been the headquarters of the

nation and the seat of the tabernacle. But now the tabernacle was to be removed to its permanent location—Shiloh, a little town in Ephraim near the center of the land, and of easy access to all the tribes. Here a portion of the country had been thoroughly subdued, so that worshipers would not be molested. "And the whole congregation of the children of Israel assembled together at Shiloh, and set up the tabernacle of the congregation there."

The ark remained at Shiloh for three hundred years, until, because of the sins of Eli's house, it fell into the hands of the Philistines.

The sanctuary service was finally transferred to the temple at Jerusalem, and Shiloh fell into ruins. Long afterward its fate was made use of as a warning to Jerusalem. "Go ye now unto My place which was in Shiloh," the Lord declared by Jeremiah, "where I set My name at the first, and see what I did to it for the wickedness of My people Israel. . . . Therefore will I do unto this house, which is called by My name, wherein ye trust, and unto the place which I gave to you and to your fathers, as I have done to Shiloh." Jeremiah 7:12, 14.

"When they had made an end of dividing the land," Joshua presented his claim. He asked for no extensive province, but only a single city, Timnath-serah, "the portion that remains"—a standing testimony to the noble character and unselfish spirit of the conqueror, who, instead of being the first to appropriate the spoils of conquest, deferred his claim until the humblest of his people had been served.

Cities of Refuge

Six cities assigned to the Levites were appointed as cities of refuge, "that the slayer may flee thither, which killeth any person . . . unawares. And they shall be unto you cities for refuge . . . ; that the manslayer die not, until he stand before the congregation in judgment." Numbers 35:11. This merciful provision was necessary because the punishment of murder devolved on the nearest relative or the next heir of the deceased. In cases where guilt was clearly evident, it was not necessary to wait for a trial by magistrates. The avenger might pursue the criminal and put him to death wherever he should be found. The Lord did not abolish this custom but made provision to ensure the safety of those who should take life unintentionally.

The cities of refuge were within a half day's journey of every part of the land, the roads leading to them always kept in good repair. Signposts were erected bearing the word *Refuge* in plain, bold characters, that the fleeing one might not be delayed for a moment. Any person—Hebrew, stranger, or sojourner—might avail himself of this provision. The case of the fugitive was to be fairly tried by proper authorities, and only when found innocent of intentional murder was he protected in the city of refuge. The guilty were given up to the avenger. At the death of the high priest, however, all who had sought shelter in the cities of refuge were at liberty to return to their possessions.

In a trial for murder, the accused was not to be condemned on the testimony of one witness, even though circumstantial evidence might be strong against him. "Whoso killeth any person, the murderer shall be put to death by the mouth of the witnesses: but one witness shall not testify against any person to cause him to die." Numbers 35:30. It was Christ who gave to Moses these directions for Israel; and when personally on earth the Great Teacher repeated the lesson that one man's testimony is not to acquit or condemn. One man's opinions are not to settle disputed questions. "In the mouth of two or three witnesses every word may be established." Matthew 18:16.

If the one tried for murder were proved guilty, no atonement or ransom could rescue him. "Ye shall take no satisfaction for the life of a murderer, which is guilty of death: but he shall be surely put to death." "The land cannot be cleansed of the blood that is shed therein, but by the blood of him that shed it.'' Numbers 35:31, 33. The safety and purity of the nation demanded that the sin of murder be severely punished.

The cities of refuge were a symbol of the refuge provided in Christ. The Saviour has by the shedding of His own blood provided for the transgressors of God's law a sure retreat, into which they may flee for safety from the second death. No power can take out of His hands the souls that go to Him for pardon.

He who fled to the city of refuge could make no delay. There was no time to say farewell to loved ones. Weariness was forgotten, difficulties were unheeded. The fugitive dared not slacken his pace until he was within the city.

As loitering and carelessness might rob the fugitive of his only chance for life, so delays and indifference may prove the ruin of the soul. Satan, the great adversary, is on the track of every transgressor of God's holy law, and he who does not earnestly seek shelter in the eternal refuge will fall prey to the destroyer.

The prisoner who at any time went outside the city of refuge was abandoned to the avenger of blood. Even so, it is not enough that the sinner *believe* in Christ for pardon of sin; he must, by faith and obedience, *abide* in Him.

Civil War Avoided

Two tribes, Gad and Reuben, with half the tribe of Manasseh, had received their inheritance before crossing the Jordan. The wide upland plains and rich forests of Gilead and Bashan had attractions not to be found in Canaan itself. The two and a half tribes, desiring to settle here, had pledged to furnish their proportion of armed men to accompany their brethren across the Jordan and share their battles till they also should enter upon their inheritance. When the ten tribes entered Canaan, forty thousand of ''the children of Reuben, and the children of Gad, and half the tribe of Manasseh, . . . prepared for war passed over before the Lord unto battle, to the plains of Jericho." Joshua 4:12, 13. For years they fought bravely by the side of their brethren. As they had united with their brethren in the conflicts, so they shared the spoils. They returned "with much riches, . . . and with very much cattle, with silver, and with gold, and with brass, and with iron, and with very much raiment," all of which they were to share with those who had remained with the families and flocks.

With an anxious heart Joshua witnessed their departure, knowing how strong would be the temptations in their isolated and wandering life to fall into the customs of the heathen tribes that dwelt upon their borders.

While Joshua and other leaders were still oppressed with anxious forebodings, strange tidings reached them. Beside the Jordan, the two and a half tribes had erected a great altar similar to the altar of burnt offering at Shiloh. The law of God prohibited on pain of death the establishment of another worship than that at the sanctuary; it would lead the people away from the true faith.

It was decided to send a delegation to obtain from the two and a half tribes an explanation of their conduct. Ten princes, one from each tribe, were chosen. At their head was Phinehas, who had distinguished himself by his zeal in the matter of Peor.

The ambassadors, taking it for granted that their brethren were guilty, met them with sharp rebuke. They bade them remember how judgments had been visited upon Israel for joining themselves to Baal-peor. Phinehas stated to the children of Gad and Reuben that if they were unwilling to abide in that land without an altar for sacrifice, they would be welcome to share in the possessions and privileges of their brethren on the other side.

In reply, the accused explained that their altar was not intended for sacrifice, but simply as a witness that, although separated by the river, they were of the same faith as their brethren in Canaan. They had feared that in future years their children might be excluded as having no part in Israel. This altar, erected after the pattern of the altar of the Lord at Shiloh, would be a witness that its builders were also worshipers of the living God.

With great joy the ambassadors accepted this explanation, and the people united in rejoicing and praise to God.

The children of Gad and Reuben now placed upon their altar an inscription pointing out the purpose for which it was erected. They said, "It shall be a witness between us that Jehovah is God." Thus they endeavored to prevent future misapprehension and remove what might be a cause of temptation.

How to Avoid Useless Strife

Often difficulties arise from a simple misunderstanding, and without courtesy and forbearance, serious results may follow. The ten tribes resolved to act promptly and earnestly; but instead of making courteous inquiry to learn the facts in the case, they met their brethren with censure and condemnation. Had the men of Gad and Reuben retorted in the same spirit, war would have been the result. It is important that laxness in dealing with sin be avoided; it is equally important to shun harsh judgment and groundless suspicion.

No one was ever reclaimed from a wrong position by censure and reproach, but many are thus driven further from the right path to harden their hearts against conviction. A courteous, forbearing deportment may save the erring.

While honestly seeking to promote the cause of true religion, the Reubenites were misjudged and severely censured; yet they listened with courtesy and patience to the charges of their brethren before attempting to make their defense, and then fully explained their motives and showed their innocence.

Even under false accusation, those in the right can afford to be calm and considerate. God is acquainted with all that is misunderstood and misinterpreted by men, and we can safely leave our case in His hands. He will vindicate the cause of those who put their trust in Him.

The prayer of Christ just before His crucifixion was that His disciples might be one as He is one with the Father, that the world might believe that God had sent Him. This touching prayer reaches down the ages, even to our day. While we are not to sacrifice one principle of truth, it should be our constant aim to reach this state of unity. Said Jesus, "By this shall all men know that ye are My disciples, if ye have love one to another." John 17:20.

49 / The Last Words of Joshua

The wars and conquest ended, Joshua had withdrawn to the peaceful retirement of his home at Timnath-serah. "And it came to pass a long time after that the Lord had given rest unto Israel from all their enemies round about, that Joshua . . . called for all Israel, and for their elders, and for their heads, and for their judges, and for their officers."

As Joshua felt the infirmities of age stealing upon him and realized that his work must soon close, he was filled with anxiety for the future of his people. "Ye have seen," he said, "all that the Lord your God hath done unto all these nations because of you; for the Lord your God is He that hath fought for you." Although the Canaanites had been subdued, they still possessed a considerable portion of the land promised to Israel, and Joshua exhorted his people not to forget the Lord's command to dispossess these idolatrous nations.

The tribes had dispersed to their possessions, the army had disbanded, and it was looked upon as a difficult and doubtful undertaking to renew the war. But Joshua declared: "The Lord your God, He shall expel them from before you, and drive them from out of your sight; and ye shall possess their land, as the Lord your God hath promised unto you. Be ye therefore very courageous to keep and to do all that is written in the book of the law of Moses, that ye turn not aside therefrom to the right hand or to the left."

God had faithfully fulfilled His promises to them.

This chapter is based on Joshua 23 and 24.

"Ye know in all your hearts and in all your souls," he said, "that not one thing hath failed of all the good things which the Lord your God spake concerning you; all are come to pass unto you, and not one thing hath failed thereof."

As the Lord had fulfilled His promises, so He would fulfill His threatenings. "It shall come to pass, that as all good things are come upon you, which the Lord your God promised you; so shall the Lord bring upon you all evil things. . . . When ye have transgressed the covenant of the Lord, . . . then shall the anger of the Lord be kindled against you, and ye shall perish quickly from off the good land which He hath given unto you."

In all His dealings with His creatures, God has maintained the principles of righteousness by revealing sin in its true character—by demonstrating that its sure result is misery and death. The unconditional pardon of sin never has been, and never will be. Such pardon would fill the unfallen universe with consternation. God has faithfully pointed out the results of sin, and if these warnings were not true, how could we be sure that His promises would be fulfilled?

Before the death of Joshua the heads and representatives of the tribes again assembled at Shechem. No spot in all the land possessed so many sacred associations. Here were the mountains Ebal and Gerizim, the silent witnesses of those vows which now, in the presence of their dying leader, they had assembled to renew. God had given them a land for which they did not labor, and cities which they built not, vineyards and oliveyards which they planted not. Joshua reviewed once more the history of Israel, recounting the wonderful works of God, that all might have a sense of His love and mercy and might serve Him "in sincerity and in truth."

By Joshua's direction the ark had been brought from Shiloh. This symbol of God's presence would deepen the impression he wished to make upon the people. After presenting the goodness of God toward Israel, he called upon them to choose whom they would serve. The worship of idols was still to some extent secretly practiced, and Joshua endeavored now to bring them to a decision that should banish this sin from Israel. "If it seem evil unto you to serve Jehovah," he said, "choose you this day whom ye will serve." Joshua desired to lead them to serve God, not by compulsion, but willingly. To engage in His service merely from hope of reward or fear of punishment would avail nothing. Open apostasy would not be more offensive to God than hypocrisy and mere formal worship.

The Importance of Right Choice

The aged leader urged the people to consider what he had set before them. If it seemed evil to serve Jehovah, the source of power, the fountain of blessing, let them that day choose whom they would serve—"the gods which your fathers served," from whom Abraham was called out, "or the gods of the Amorites, in whose land ye dwell."

These last words were a keen rebuke to Israel. The gods of the Amorites had not been able to protect their worshipers. Because of their debasing sins, that wicked nation had been destroyed, and the good land which they once possessed had been given to God's people. What folly for Israel to choose the deities for whose worship the Amorites had been destroyed!

"As for me and my house," said Joshua, "we will serve Jehovah." The same holy zeal that inspired the leader's heart was communicated to the people. His appeals called forth the unhesitating response, "God forbid that we should forsake Jehovah, to serve other gods."

Before there could be any permanent reformation, the people must feel their utter inability in themselves to render obedience to God. While they trusted their own righteousness, it was impossible for them to secure pardon; they could not meet the claims of God's perfect law, and it was in vain that they pledged themselves to serve God. Only by faith in Christ could they secure pardon of sin and receive strength to obey God's law. They must trust wholly in the merits of the promised Saviour.

With deep earnestness they once more reiterated their pledge of loyalty: "The Lord our God will we serve, and His voice will we obey.

"So Joshua made a covenant with the people that day, and set them a statute and an ordinance in Shechem. . . . So Joshua let the people depart, every man unto his inheritance."

His work was done. He had "wholly followed the Lord." The noblest testimony to his character as a leader is the history of the generation that enjoyed his labors: "Israel served the Lord all the days of Joshua, and all the days of the elders that overlived Joshua."

50 / The Blessing of Tithes and Offerings

In the Hebrew economy one tenth of the income of the people was set apart to support the public worship of God. "All the tithe . . . is the Lord's: it is holy unto the Lord." Leviticus 27:30.

But the tithing system did not originate with the Hebrews. From earliest times the Lord claimed a tithe as His. Abraham paid tithes to Melchizedek, priest of God. See Genesis 14:20. Jacob promised the Lord, "Of all that Thou shalt give me I will surely give the tenth unto Thee." Genesis 28:22. God is the source of every blessing to His creatures, and to Him man's gratitude is due.

The Lord declares, "The silver is Mine, and the gold is Mine." Haggai 2:8. It is God who gives men power to get wealth. As an acknowledgment that all things came from Him, the Lord directed that a portion of His bounty should be returned to Him.

"The tithe . . . *is* the Lord's." "The seventh day *is* the Sabbath of the Lord thy God." Exodus 20:10. God reserved a specified portion of man's time and of his means, and no man could, without guilt, appropriate either for his own interests.

The tithe was to be exclusively devoted to the Levites, who had been set apart for the service of the sanctuary. But this was by no means the limit of the contributions for religious purposes. The tabernacle, as afterward the temple, was erected wholly by freewill offerings; and to provide for necessary repairs and other expenses, Moses directed that each should contribute a half shekel for "the service of the tabernacle." From time to time, sin offerings and thank offerings were brought to God. And liberal provision was made for the poor.

The people were constantly reminded that God was the true proprietor of their fields, their flocks, and their herds. He sent them sunshine and rain for their seedtime and harvest, and He made them stewards of His goods.

As the men of Israel, laden with the firstfruits of field and orchard and vineyard, gathered at the tabernacle, there was a public acknowledgment of God's goodness. When the priest accepted the gift, the offerer said, "A Syrian ready to perish was my father"; and he described the sojourn in Egypt and the affliction from which God had delivered Israel. "He hath brought us into this place, and hath given us this land, even a land that floweth with milk and honey. And now, behold, I have brought the firstfruits of the land, which Thou, Jehovah, hast given me." Deuteronomy 26:5, 9, 10.

The Secret of Prosperity

Says the wise man, "There is that scattereth, and yet increaseth; and there is that withholdeth more than is meet, but it tendeth to poverty." Proverbs 11:24. The same lesson is taught in the New Testament by the apostle Paul: "He which soweth sparingly shall reap also sparingly; and he which soweth bountifully shall reap also bountifully. . . . God is able to make all grace abound toward you; that ye, always having all sufficiency in all things, may abound to every good work." 2 Corinthians 9:6-8.

God intended that Israel should be light bearers to all the earth. The Lord has ordained that the diffusion of light and truth in the earth shall be dependent upon the efforts and offerings of those who partake of the heavenly gift. He might have made angels the ambassadors of His truth; but in His love and wisdom He called men to become colaborers with Himself, by choosing them to do this work.

In the days of Israel the tithe and freewill offerings were needed to maintain the divine service. Should the people of God give less in this age? The principle laid down by Christ is that our offerings to God should be in proportion to the light and privileges enjoyed. "Unto whomsoever much is given, of him shall be much required." Luke 12:48. "Freely ye have received, freely give." Matthew 10:8. As we have before us the unparalleled sacrifice of the glorious Son of God, should not our gratitude find expression in more abundant gifts?

The work of the gospel, as it widens, requires greater provision to sustain it than was called for anciently. This makes the law of tithes and offerings of even more urgent necessity now. If His people were liberally to sustain His cause by voluntary gifts, God would be honored and many more souls would be won to Christ.

The plan of Moses to raise means for the building of the tabernacle was highly successful. He made no grand feast. He did not invite the people to scenes of gaiety, dancing, and amusement. Neither did he institute lotteries. The Lord directed Moses to accept gifts from everyone that gave willingly, from his heart. And the offerings came in so great abundance that Moses bade the people cease bringing, for they had supplied more than could be used.

God has made men His stewards. Saith the Lord, "Them that honor Me, I will honor." 1 Samuel 2:30. "God loveth a cheerful giver" (2 Corinthians 9:7), and when His people with grateful hearts bring their gifts and offerings to Him, "not grudgingly, or of necessity," His blessing will attend them, as He has promised.

51 / God's Care for the Economically Disadvantaged

To promote the assembling of the people for religious service, as well as to provide for the poor, a second tithe of all the increase was required. Concerning the first tithe, the Lord declared, "I have given the children of Levi *all the tenth* in Israel." Numbers 18:21. The second tithe, they were for two years to bring to the place where the sanctuary was established. After presenting a thank offering to God and a portion to the priest, the offerers were to use the remainder for a religious feast, in which the Levite, the stranger, the fatherless, and the widow should participate.

Every third year this second tithe was to be used at home, in entertaining the Levite and the poor. This tithe would provide a fund for charity and hospitality.

And further provision was made for the poor. After recognition of the claims of God, nothing more distinguishes the laws given by Moses than the liberal, tender, and hospitable spirit enjoined toward the poor. Although God had promised to bless His people, He declared that the poor should never cease out of the land. Then, as now, persons were subject to misfortune, sickness, and loss of property; yet so long as they followed the instruction given by God, there were no beggars among them, neither any who suffered for food.

The law of God gave the poor a right to a certain portion of the produce of the soil. When hungry, a man was at liberty to go to his neighbor's field, orchard, or vineyard, and eat to satisfy his hunger.

All the gleanings of harvest field, orchard, and vineyard belonged to the poor. "When thou cuttest down thine harvest in thy field," said Moses, "and hast forgot a sheaf in the field, thou shalt not go again to fetch it. . . . When thou beatest thine olive tree, thou shalt not go over the boughs again. . . . When thou gatherest the grapes of thy vineyard, thou shalt not glean it afterward: it shall be for the stranger, for the fatherless, and for the widow. And thou shalt remember that thou wast a bondman in the land of Egypt." Deuteronomy 24:19-22. Also see Leviticus 19:9, 10.

The Mercy of God to Poor People

Every seventh year special provision was made for the poor. At seedtime, which followed the ingathering, the people were not to sow; they should not dress the vineyard in the spring; and they must expect neither harvest nor vintage. The yield of this year was to be free for the stranger, the fatherless, and the widow, and even for the creatures of the field. See Exodus 23:10, 11; Leviticus 25:5.

But if the land ordinarily produced only enough to supply the wants of the people, how were they to subsist during the year when no crops were gathered? The promise of God made ample provision: "I will command My blessing upon you in the sixth year," He said, "and it shall bring forth fruit for three years. And ye shall sow the eighth year, and eat yet of the old fruit until the ninth year; until her fruits come in ye shall eat of the old store." Leviticus 25:21, 22.

The sabbatical year was to be a benefit to both land and people. The soil, lying untilled for one season, would afterward produce more plentifully. The people were released from the pressing labors of the field. All enjoyed greater leisure, opportunity for the restoration of their physical powers, more time for meditation and acquainting themselves with the teachings of the Lord, and for the instruction of their households.

In the sabbatical year the Hebrew slaves were to be

set at liberty. "When thou sendest him out free from thee, thou shalt not let him go away empty. Thou shalt furnish him liberally out of thy flock, and out of thy floor, and out of thy winepress: of that wherewith the Lord thy God hath blessed thee thou shalt give unto him." Deuteronomy 15:13, 14.

The hire of a laborer was to be promptly paid. "At his day thou shalt give him his hire, neither shall the sun go down upon it; for he is poor and setteth his heart upon it." Deuteronomy 24:15.

Special directions were also given concerning the treatment of fugitives from service: "Thou shalt not deliver unto his master the servant which is escaped from his master unto thee: he shall dwell with thee, even among you, . . . where it liketh him best: thou shalt not oppress him." Deuteronomy 23:15, 16.

To the poor, the seventh year was a year of release from debt. The Hebrews were to lend money without interest to their needy brethren. To take usury from a poor man was expressly forbidden: "If thy brother be waxen poor, and fallen in decay with thee; then thou shalt relieve him: yea, though he be a stranger, or a sojourner; that he may live with thee. Take thou no usury of him, or increase: but fear thy God; that thy brother may live with thee. Thou shalt not give him thy money upon usury, nor lend him thy victuals for increase." Leviticus 25:35-37. If the debt remained unpaid until the year of release, the principal itself could not be recovered. "If there be among you a poor man of one of thy brethren, . . . thou shalt not harden thine heart, nor shut thine hand from thy poor brother. . . . Beware that there be not a thought in thy wicked heart, saying, The seventh year, the year of release, is at hand; and thine eye be evil against thy poor brother, and thou givest him nought; and he cry unto the Lord against thee, and it be sin unto thee." "The poor shall never cease out of the land: therefore I command thee, saying, Thou shalt open thine hand wide unto thy brother, to thy poor, and to thy needy, in thy land," "and shalt surely lend him sufficient for his need, in that which he wanteth." Deuteronomy 15:7-9, 11, 8.

None need fear that their liberality would bring them to want. "Thou shalt lend unto many nations," God said, "but thou shalt not borrow; and thou shalt reign over many nations, but they shall not reign over thee." Deuteronomy 15:6.

Preventing Extremes of Wealth or Poverty

After "seven times seven years" came the great year of release—the jubilee. "Then shalt thou cause the trumpet of the jubilee to sound . . . throughout all your land. And ye shall hallow the fiftieth year, and proclaim liberty throughout all the land unto all the inhabitants thereof: . . . and ye shall return every man unto his family." Leviticus 25:9, 10.

"On the tenth day of the seventh month, in the Day of Atonement," the trumpet of jubilee was sounded, calling upon all the children of Jacob to welcome the year of release.

As in the sabbatical year, the land was not to be sown or reaped, and all that it produced was to be regarded as the rightful property of the poor. Hebrew slaves who did not receive their liberty in the sabbatical year were now set free.

But that which especially distinguished the year of jubilee was the reversion of all landed property to the family of the original possessor. No one was at liberty to trade his estate. Neither was he to sell his land unless poverty compelled him to do so. Whenever he or any of his kindred might desire to redeem it, the purchaser must not refuse to sell it. If unredeemed, it would revert to its possessor or his heirs in the year of jubilee.

The Lord declared to Israel: "The land shall not be sold forever: for the land is Mine; for ye are strangers and sojourners with Me." Leviticus 25:23. God was the rightful owner, the original proprietor. It was to be impressed upon the minds of all that the poor and unfortunate have as much right to a place in God's world as the wealthy.

Such were the provisions made by our merciful Creator to lessen suffering, to bring some ray of hope, to flash some gleam of sunshine into the life of the destitute and distressed.

Great evils result from the continued accumulation of wealth by one class, and the poverty of another. The sense of this oppression would arouse the passions of the poorer class. There would be a feeling of despair and desperation which would tend to demoralize society and open the door to crimes of every description. The regulations that God established were to promote social equality. The sabbatical year and the jubilee would in a great measure set right that which had gone wrong in the social and political economy of the nation.

These regulations, designed to bless the rich no less than the poor, would restrain avarice and cultivate a noble spirit of benevolence. By fostering goodwill between all classes, they would promote stability of government.

We are all woven together in the great web of humanity. Whatever we can do to benefit others will reflect in blessing on ourselves. The law of mutual dependence runs through all classes of society. The poor are not more dependent upon the rich than are the rich upon the poor. While the one class ask a share in the blessings God has bestowed upon their wealthier neighbors, the other need the faithful service, the strength of brain and bone and muscle, that are the capital of the poor.

God's Plan Would Solve Socio-economic Problems Today

Many urge with great enthusiasm that all men should have an equal share in temporal blessings. But this was not the purpose of the Creator. A diversity of condition is one of the means by which God designs to develop character. He intends that those who have worldly

Pilgrims from near and far made their way to Jerusalem each year for the sacred Passover festival.

possessions shall regard themselves as stewards of His goods, entrusted to be employed for the benefit of the needy.

Christ has said that we shall have the poor always with us. The heart of our Redeemer sympathizes with the lowliest of His earthly children. He tells us that they are His representatives on earth, placed among us to awaken in our hearts the love He feels toward the suffering and oppressed. An act of cruelty or neglect toward them is regarded as done to Him.

If the law given by God for the benefit of the poor had continued to be carried out, how different would be the present condition of the world, morally, spiritually, and temporally! Such widespread destitution as is now seen in many lands would not exist.

The principles which God has enjoined would prevent the terrible evils that result from the oppression of the rich toward the poor and the suspicion and hatred of the poor toward the rich. While they might hinder the amassing of great wealth, they would prevent the ignorance and degradation of tens of thousands whose ill-paid servitude is required to build up these colossal fortunes. They would bring a peaceful solution of problems that now threaten the world with anarchy and bloodshed.

52 / Annual Feasts of Rejoicing

The people of Israel were surrounded by fierce, war-like tribes, eager to seize upon their lands; yet three times every year all the people who could make the journey were directed to leave their homes and repair to the place of assembly near the center of the land. What was to hinder their enemies from sweeping down on those unprotected households to lay them waste with fire and sword? What was to prevent an invasion that would bring Israel into captivity?

God had promised to be the protector of His people. "I will cast out the nations before thee, and enlarge thy borders: neither shall any man desire thy land, when thou shalt go up to appear before the Lord thy God thrice in the year." Exodus 34:24.

The first of these festivals, the Passover, occurred in Abib, the first month of the Jewish year, corresponding to the last of March and the beginning of April. The cold of winter was past, the latter rain had ended, and all nature rejoiced in the freshness and beauty of springtime. The grass was green on the hills and valleys, and wild flowers everywhere brightened the fields. The moon, now approaching full, made the evening delightful.

Throughout the land, bands of pilgrims were making their way toward Jerusalem. The shepherds, the herdsmen, fishers from the Sea of Galilee, husbandmen from their fields, and sons of the prophets from the sacred schools—all turned their steps toward the place where God's presence was revealed. Many went on foot. The

This chapter is based on Leviticus 23.

caravans often became very large before reaching the Holy City.

Nature's gladness awakened joy in the hearts of Israel. The grand Hebrew psalms were chanted, exalting the glory and majesty of Jehovah. At the sound of the signal trumpet, with the music of cymbals, the chorus of thanksgiving arose, swelled by hundreds of voices:

> I was glad when they said unto me,
> Let us go unto the house of the Lord.
> > Psalm 122:1

As they saw around them hills where the heathen had been wont to kindle their altar fires, the children of Israel sang:

> I will lift up mine eyes unto the mountains:
> From whence shall my help come?
> My help cometh from Jehovah,
> Who made heaven and earth.
> > Psalm 121:2

Surmounting the hills in view of the Holy City, they looked with reverent awe upon the throngs of worshipers wending their way to the temple. As they heard the trumpets of the Levites heralding the sacred service, they caught the inspiration of the hour, and sang:

> Great is the Lord, and greatly to be praised
> In the city of our God, in the mountain of His
>   holiness.
> Beautiful for situation, the joy of the whole earth,
> Is mount Zion, on the sides of the north,
> The city of the great King.
> > Psalm 48:1, 2

> Open to me the gates of righteousness:
> I will go into them, and I will praise the Lord.
> > Psalm 118:19

All the houses in Jerusalem were thrown open to the pilgrims, and rooms were furnished free. But this was not sufficient, and tents were pitched in every available space in the city and upon the surrounding hills.

On the fourteenth day of the month, at even, the Passover was celebrated, its solemn, impressive ceremonies commemorating deliverance from bondage in Egypt, and pointing forward to the sacrifice that should deliver from the bondage of sin. When the Saviour yielded up His life on Calvary, the significance of the Passover ceased, and the ordinance of the Lord's Supper was instituted as a memorial of the same event of which the Passover had been a type.

Meaning of the Festivals

The Passover was followed by the seven days' Feast of Unleavened Bread. On the second day of the feast, the firstfruits of the year's harvest were presented before God. A sheaf of grain was waved by the priest before the altar of God, an acknowledgment that all was His. Not until this ceremony had been performed was the harvest to be gathered.

Fifty days from the offering of firstfruits came Pentecost, the feast of harvest. As an expression of gratitude for grain, two loaves baked with leaven were presented before God. Pentecost occupied but one day.

In the seventh month came the Feast of Tabernacles, or ingathering. This feast acknowledged God's bounty in the products of orchard, olive grove, and vineyard. It was the crowning festival gathering of the year. The harvest had been gathered into the granaries, the fruits, oil, and wine had been stored, and now the people came with their tributes of thanksgiving to God.

This feast was an occasion of rejoicing. It occurred just after the great Day of Atonement, when assurance had been given that their iniquity should be remembered no more. At peace with God, the labors of the harvest ended and the toils of the new year not yet begun, the people could give themselves up to the sacred, joyous influences of the hour. So far as possible, all the household were to attend the feasts, and to their hospitality the servants, the Levites, the stranger, and the poor were made welcome.

Like the Passover, the Feast of Tabernacles was commemorative. In memory of their pilgrim life in the wilderness, the people were to leave their homes and dwell in booths, or arbors, formed from the green branches "of goodly trees, branches of palm trees, and the boughs of thick trees, and willow of the brook." Leviticus 23:40.

At these yearly assemblies the hearts of old and young would be encouraged in the service of God. Association of the people from different quarters of the land would strengthen the ties that bound them to God and to one another. As Israel celebrated the deliverance God had wrought for their fathers and His miraculous preservation of them during their journeyings from Egypt, so should we gratefully call to mind the ways He has devised for bringing us out from darkness into the precious light of His grace and truth.

With those who lived at a distance from the tabernacle, more than a month of every year must have been occupied in attendance upon the annual feasts. This example of devotion should emphasize the importance of religious worship, the necessity of subordinating our selfish, worldly interests to those that are spiritual and eternal. We sustain a loss when we neglect associating together to encourage one another in the service of God. We are all children of one Father, dependent upon one another for happiness. It is the proper cultivation of the social elements of our nature that brings us into sympathy with our brethren and affords us happiness.

The Feast of Tabernacles not only pointed back to the wilderness sojourn, but forward to the great day of final ingathering. The Lord shall send forth His reapers to gather the tares in bundles for the fire and to gather the wheat into His garner. At that time the wicked will be destroyed. They will become "as though they had not been." Obadiah 16. And every voice in the whole universe will unite in joyful praise to God.

When the ransomed of the Lord shall have been safely gathered into the heavenly Canaan, forever delivered from the bondage of the curse, they will "rejoice with joy unspeakable and full of glory." Christ's great work of atonement will then have been completed and their sins forever blotted out.

> And the ransomed of the Lord shall return,
> And come to Zion with songs
> And everlasting joy upon their heads: . . .
> And sorrow and sighing shall flee away.
> Isaiah 35:10

53 / The Judges, Deliverers of Israel

Satisfied with the territory already gained, the tribes' zeal flagged, and the war was discontinued. "When Israel was strong, they put the Canaanites to tribute, and did not utterly drive them out." Judges 1:28.

The Lord had faithfully fulfilled, on His part, the promises made to Israel. It only remained for them to complete the work of dispossessing the inhabitants of the land. But this they failed to do. By entering into league with the Canaanites they transgressed the command of God and failed to fulfill the condition on which He had promised to place them in possession of Canaan.

At Sinai they had been warned against idolatry. "Thou shalt not bow down to their gods, nor serve them, nor do after their works: but thou shalt utterly overthrow them, and quite break down their images." So long as they remained obedient, God would subdue their enemies: "I will send My fear before thee, and will destroy all the people to whom thou shalt come. . . . And I will send hornets before thee, which shall drive out the Hivite, the Canaanite, and the Hittite, from before thee. I will not drive them out from before thee in one year; lest the land become desolate, and the beast of the field multiply against thee. By little and little I will drive them out from before thee, until thou be increased, and inherit the land. . . . Thou shalt make no covenant with them, nor with their gods. They shall not dwell in thy land, lest they make thee sin

This chapter is based on Judges 6 to 8; 10.

against Me; for if thou serve their gods, it will surely be a snare unto thee." Exodus 23:24, 27-33.

God had placed His people in Canaan to stay the tide of moral evil, that it might not flood the world. God would give into their hands nations greater and more powerful than the Canaanites. "Ye shall possess greater nations and mightier than yourselves . . . from the wilderness and Lebanon, from the river, the river Euphrates, even unto the uttermost sea shall your coast be." Deuteronomy 11:23, 24.

But they chose ease and self-indulgence. They let slip their opportunities for completing the conquest of the land. And for many generations they were afflicted by the remnant of these idolatrous peoples, that were as "pricks" in their eyes and "thorns" in their sides. Numbers 33:55.

The Israelites were "mingled among the heathen, and learned their works." They intermarried with the Canaanites, and idolatry spread like a plague throughout the land. "Yea, they sacrificed their sons and their daughters unto devils, . . . and the land was polluted with blood." "Therefore was the wrath of the Lord kindled against His people, insomuch that He abhorred His own inheritance." Psalm 106:35, 37, 38, 40.

Until the generation that had received instruction from Joshua became extinct, idolatry made little headway, but the parents prepared the way for the apostasy of their children. The simple habits of the Hebrews had secured them physical health, but association with the heathen led to indulgence of appetite and passion, which gradually enfeebled the mental and moral powers. By their sins the Israelites were separated from God, and they could no longer prevail against their enemies. Thus they were brought into subjection to the very nations that they might have subdued.

"They forsook them out of the land of Egypt." "They provoked Him to anger with their high places, and moved Him to jealousy with their graven images." Therefore the Lord "forsook the tabernacle of Shiloh, the tent which He placed among them; and delivered His strength into captivity, and His glory into the enemy's hand." Judges 2:12; Psalm 78:58, 60, 61.

Yet He did not utterly forsake His people. There was ever a remnant who were true to Jehovah, and from time to time the Lord raised up faithful and valiant men to put down idolatry and deliver the Israelites from their enemies. But when the deliverer was dead and the people were released from his authority, they would gradually return to their idols. Thus the story of backsliding and chastisement, of confession and deliverance was repeated again and again.

The Sad Story of Continual Backsliding

The king of Mesopotamia, the king of Moab, and after them the Philistines, and the Canaanites of Hazor led by Sisera, in turn became oppressors of Israel. Othniel, Shamgar, Ehud, Deborah, and Barak were raised up as deliverers of their people. But again "the children of Israel did evil in the sight of the Lord; and the Lord delivered them into the hand of Midian."

The Midianites had been nearly destroyed by the Israelites in the days of Moses, but they had since become numerous and powerful. They thirsted for revenge, and now that the protecting hand of God was withdrawn from Israel, the opportunity had come. The whole land suffered from their ravages. Like a devouring plague they spread over the country. They came as soon as the harvests began to ripen, and remained until the last fruits had been gathered. They stripped the fields of their increase, and robbed and maltreated the inhabitants. The Israelites dwelling in the open country were forced to seek refuge in fortresses or even find shelter in caves among the mountains. For seven years this oppression continued. Then, as the people in their distress confessed their sins, God again raised up a helper for them.

To Gideon came the divine call to deliver his people. He was engaged at the time in threshing wheat. Not daring to beat it out on the ordinary threshing floor, he had resorted to a spot near the winepress. The season of ripe grapes being still far off, little notice was now taken of the vineyards. As Gideon labored in secrecy, he sadly pondered the condition of Israel and how the oppressor's yoke might be broken.

How the Lord Called Gideon

Suddenly the "Angel of the Lord" appeared and addressed him with the words, "Jehovah is with thee, thou mighty man of valor."

"O my Lord," was his answer, "if the Lord be with us, why then is all this befallen us? and where be all His miracles which our fathers told us of? . . . The Lord hath forsaken us, and delivered us into the hands of the Midianites."

The Messenger of heaven replied, "Go in this thy might, and thou shalt save Israel from the hand of the Midianites: have I not sent thee?"

Gideon desired some token that the one now addressing him was the Covenant Angel, who in time past had wrought for Israel. Hastening to his tent, he prepared from his scanty store a kid and unleavened cakes, which he brought forth and set before Him. But the Angel bade him, "Take the flesh and the unleavened cakes, and lay them upon this rock, and pour out the broth." Gideon did so, and then the sign he desired was given: with the staff in His hand, the Angel touched the flesh and the unleavened cakes, and a flame bursting from the rock consumed the sacrifice. Then the Angel vanished.

Gideon's father, Joash, who shared in the apostasy of his countrymen, had erected at Ophrah a large altar to Baal. Gideon was commanded to destroy this altar and to erect an altar to Jehovah over the rock on which the offering had been consumed, and there present a sacrifice to the Lord. The offering of sacrifice had been committed to the priests and restricted to the altar at Shiloh; but He who had established the ritual service had power to change its requirements. Gideon must declare war on idolatry before going out to battle with the enemies of his people.

Gideon performed the work in secret, with the aid of his servants accomplishing the whole in one night. Great was the rage of the men of Ophrah when they came next morning to pay their devotions to Baal. Joash, who had been told of the Angel's visit, stood in defense of his son. "Will ye plead for Baal? Will ye save him? he that will plead for him, let him be put to death whilst it is yet morning." If Baal could not defend his own altar, how could he be trusted to protect his worshipers?

All thoughts of violence toward Gideon were dismissed. When he sounded the trumpet of war, the men of Ophrah were among the first to gather to his standard. Heralds were dispatched to his own tribe of Manasseh, and also to Asher, Zebulun, and Naphtali, and all answered the call.

How Could Gideon Be Sure?

Gideon prayed, "If Thou wilt save Israel by mine hand, as Thou hast said, behold, I will put a fleece of wool in the floor; and if the dew be on the fleece only, and it be dry upon all the earth besides, then shall I know that Thou wilt save Israel by mine hand, as Thou hast said." In the morning the fleece was wet, while the ground was dry. But now a doubt arose, since wool naturally absorbs moisture when there is any in the air; the test might not be decisive. Hence he asked that the sign be reversed. His request was granted.

Thus encouraged, Gideon led out his forces to give battle to the invaders. "All the Midianites and the Amalekites and the children of the east were gathered together, and went over, and pitched in the valley of Jezreel." The entire force under Gideon's command numbered only thirty-two thousand men. But with the vast host of the enemy spread out before him, the word of the Lord came: "The people that are with thee are too many for Me to give the Midianites into their hands, lest Israel vaunt themselves against Me, saying, Mine own hand hath saved me. Now therefore . . . proclaim in the ears of the people, saying, Whosoever is fearful and afraid, let him return and depart early from mount Gilead.'' Those unwilling to face danger and hardship would add no strength to the armies of Israel.

Gideon was filled with astonishment at the declaration that his army was too large. But the Lord saw the pride and unbelief in the hearts of His people. Aroused by the appeals of Gideon, they had readily enlisted; but many were filled with fear when they saw the multitudes of Midian. Yet, had Israel triumphed, those very ones would have taken glory to themselves instead of ascribing victory to God.

Only Three Hundred Left

Gideon obeyed the Lord's direction, and with a heavy heart saw more than two thirds of his force depart for their homes. Again the word of the Lord came to him: "The people are yet too many; bring them down unto the water, and I will try them for thee there: and it shall be, that of whom I say unto thee, This shall go with thee, the same shall go with thee; and of whomsoever I say unto thee, This shall not go with thee, the same shall not go.''

The people were led down to the waterside, expecting to make an immediate advance upon the enemy. A few hastily took a little water in the hand and sucked it up as they went on; but nearly all bowed upon their knees and leisurely drank from the surface of the stream. Those who took the water in their hands were but three hundred out of ten thousand. These were selected; all the rest were permitted to return to their homes.

Those who in time of peril were intent upon supplying their own wants were not to be trusted in an emergency. The three hundred chosen men not only possessed courage and self-control, they were men of faith. They had not defiled themselves with idolatry. God could direct them, and through them He could work deliverance for Israel. God is honored not so much by great numbers as by the character of those who serve Him.

The Israelites were stationed on the brow of a hill overlooking the valley where the invaders lay encamped "like locusts for multitude; and their camels were without number, as the sand which is upon the seashore for multitude." Gideon trembled as he thought of the conflict of the morrow. But the Lord bade him go down to the camp of the Midianites. He would there hear something for his encouragement.

Waiting in the darkness and silence, he heard a soldier relating a dream to his companion: "Lo, a cake of barley bread tumbled into the host of Midian, and came unto a tent, and smote it that it fell, and overturned it, that the tent lay along." The other answered in words that stirred the heart of that unseen listener: "This is nothing else save the sword of Gideon the son of Joash, a man of Israel: for into his hand hath God delivered Midian, and all the host."

Gideon recognized the voice of God speaking through those Midianitish strangers. Returning to the few men under his command, he said, "Arise; for the Lord hath delivered into your hand the host of Midian."

God's Simple Battle Plan

By divine direction a plan of attack was suggested. The three hundred men were divided into three companies. To every man was given a trumpet and a torch concealed in an earthen pitcher. The men were stationed in such a manner as to approach the Midianite camp from different directions. In the dead of night, at a signal from Gideon's war horn, the three companies sounded their trumpets. Then, breaking their pitchers and displaying the blazing torches, they rushed upon the enemy with the terrible war cry, "The sword of the Lord, and of Gideon!"

The sleeping army was suddenly aroused. Upon every side was seen the light of flaming torches. In every direction was heard the sound of trumpets with the cry of the assailants. Believing themselves at the mercy of an overwhelming force, the Midianites were panic-stricken. With wild cries of alarm they fled for life, and mistaking their own companions for enemies, they slew one another.

As news of the victory spread, thousands of the men of Israel who had been dismissed to their homes returned and joined in pursuit of their fleeing enemies. Gideon sent messengers to the tribe of Ephraim, rousing them to intercept the fugitives at the southern fords. Meanwhile, with his three hundred, "faint, yet pursuing," Gideon crossed the stream hard after those who had already gained the farther side. The two princes, Zebah and Zalmunna, who escaped with fifteen thousand men, were overtaken by Gideon, their force completely scattered, and the leaders captured and slain.

One hundred and twenty thousand of the invaders perished. The power of the Midianites was broken. They were never again able to make war upon Israel. No words can describe the terror of the surrounding nations when they learned what simple means had prevailed against the power of a bold, warlike people.

The leader whom God chose to overthrow the Midianites was not a ruler, a priest, or a Levite. He thought himself the least in his father's house. But he was distrustful of himself and willing to follow the guidance of the Lord. God selects those whom He can best use. "Before honor is humility." Proverbs 15:33. He will make them strong by uniting their weakness to His might, and wise by connecting their ignorance with His wisdom.

Few can be trusted with any large measure of responsibility or success without becoming forgetful of their dependence upon God. This is why, in choosing instruments for His work, the Lord passes by those whom the world honors as great, talented, and brilliant. They are proud and feel competent to act without counsel from God.

Trust in God and obedience to His will are as essential in spiritual warfare as to Gideon and Joshua in their battles with the Canaanites. God is just as willing to work with the efforts of His people now, and to accomplish great things through weak instrumentalities. God is "able to do exceeding abundantly above all that we ask or think." Ephesians 3:20.

When at Gideon's call the men of Israel had rallied against the Midianites, the tribe of Ephraim had remained behind. As Gideon sent them no special summons, they availed themselves of this excuse not to join their brethren. But when news of Israel's triumph reached them, the Ephraimites were envious because they had not shared it.

After the rout of the Midianites, they followed up the battle and helped complete the victory. Nevertheless, they were jealous and angry, as though Gideon had been led by His own will and judgment. They did not discern God's hand in the triumph of Israel, and this showed them unworthy to be chosen as His special instruments. Returning with the trophies of victory, they angrily reproached Gideon: "Why hast thou served us thus, that thou calledst us not, when thou wentest to fight with the Midianites?"

Gideon Demonstrates Humility

"What have I done now, in comparison of you?" said Gideon. "Is not the *gleaning* of the grapes of Ephraim better than the *vintage* of Abiezer? *God* hath delivered into your hand the princes of Midian, Oreb and Zeeb: and what was I able to do in comparison of you?" Gideon's modest answer soothed the anger of the men of Ephraim, and they returned in peace to their homes. Gideon displayed a spirit of courtesy rarely witnessed.

The people of Israel, in their gratitude at deliverance from the Midianites, proposed to Gideon that he become their king, in direct violation of the principles of the theocracy. God was the king of Israel, and for them to place a man upon the throne would be a rejection of their divine Sovereign. Gideon recognized this fact. His answer shows how true and noble were his motives: "I will not rule over you, neither shall my son rule over you: the Lord shall rule over you."

But Gideon was betrayed into another error, which brought disaster upon his house and upon all Israel. The season of inactivity that succeeds a great struggle is often fraught with greater danger than is the period of conflict. To this danger Gideon was now exposed. A spirit of unrest was upon him. Instead of waiting for divine guidance, he began to plan for himself.

Because he had been commanded to offer sacrifice upon the rock where the Angel appeared to him, Gideon concluded that he had been appointed as a priest. Without waiting for divine sanction he determined to institute a system of worship similar to that carried on at the tabernacle.

With the strong popular feeling in his favor, he found no difficulty in carrying out his plan. At his request all the earrings of gold taken from the Midianites were given him as his share of the spoil. The people also collected other costly materials, together with the richly adorned garments of the princes of Midian. From the material thus furnished, Gideon constructed an ephod and a breastplate, in imitation of those worn by the high priest. His course proved a snare to himself and his family, as well as to Israel. The unauthorized worship led many of the people finally to forsake the Lord to serve idols. After Gideon's death, great numbers, among whom were his own family, joined in apostasy. The people were led away from God by the very man who once overthrew their idolatry.

Those who stand in the highest positions may lead astray. The wisest err; the strongest may falter and stumble. Our only safety lies in trusting our way implicitly to Him who has said, "Follow Me."

After the death of Gideon, the people of Israel accepted his baseborn son Abimelech as their king, who, to sustain his power, murdered all but one of Gideon's lawful children. The cruel course of Israel toward the house of Gideon was what might be expected from a people who manifested so great ingratitude to God.

More Backsliding and More Misery!

After the death of Abimelech, the rule of judges who feared the Lord served for a time to put a check on idolatry. But erelong the people returned to the practices of the heathen around them. Apostasy speedily brought punishment. The Ammonites subdued the eastern tribes and, crossing the Jordan, invaded the territory of Judah and Ephraim. On the west the Philistines came up from their plain beside the sea, burning and pillaging far and near. Israel seemed to be abandoned to the power of relentless foes.

Again the people sought help from Him whom they had forsaken and insulted. "The children of Israel cried unto the Lord, saying, We have sinned against Thee, both because we have forsaken our God, and also served Baalim." But the people mourned because their sins had brought suffering upon themselves, not because they had dishonored God by transgression of His holy law. True repentance is a resolute turning away from evil.

The Lord answered them through one of His prophets: "Did I not deliver you from the Egyptians, and from the Amorites, from the children of Ammon, and from the Philistines? . . . Ye cried to Me, and I delivered you out of their hand. Yet ye have forsaken Me, and served other gods: wherefore I will deliver you no more. Go and cry unto the gods which ye have chosen; let them deliver you in the time of your tribulation."

The Israelites now humbled themselves before the Lord. "And they put away the strange gods from

402 / FROM ETERNITY PAST

among them, and served Jehovah." And the Lord's heart of love "*was grieved* for the misery of Israel." Oh, the long-suffering mercy of our God! When His people put away the sins that had shut out His presence, He heard their prayers and at once began to work for them. A deliverer was raised up in the person of Jephthah, who made war upon the Ammonites and effectually destroyed their power. For eighteen years at this time Israel had suffered under the oppression of her foes, yet again the lesson taught by suffering was forgotten.

As His people returned to their evil ways, the Lord permitted them to be oppressed by powerful enemies, the Philistines. For many years they were constantly harassed, and at times completely subjugated, by this cruel and warlike nation. They had mingled with these idolaters, uniting in pleasure and in worship until they seemed to be one with them in spirit and interest. Then these professed friends of Israel became their bitterest enemies and sought to accomplish their destruction.

The Bible plainly teaches that there can be no harmony between the people of God and the world. Satan works through the ungodly, under cover of pretended friendship, to allure God's people into sin. When their defense is removed, then he will lead his agents to turn against them and seek to accomplish their destruction.

54 / Samson, the Strongest Yet Weakest Man

Amid widespread apostasy, the faithful worshipers of God continued to plead with Him for the deliverance of Israel. Though there was apparently no response, in the early years of the Philistine oppression a child was born through whom God designed to humble the power of these mighty foes.

To the childless wife of Manoah, "the Angel of Jehovah" appeared with the message that she should have a son through whom God would begin to deliver Israel. The Angel gave instruction concerning her own habits, and also for the treatment of her child: "Drink not wine nor strong drink, and eat not any unclean thing." The same prohibition was to be imposed upon the child, with the addition that his hair should not be cut, for he was to be consecrated to God as a Nazarite from his birth.

Importance of Prenatal Training

Fearful that they should make some mistake, the husband prayed, "Let the Man of God which Thou didst send come again unto us, and teach us what we shall do unto the child that shall be born."

When the Angel again appeared, Manoah's inquiry was, "How shall we order the child, and how shall we do unto him?" The previous instruction was repeated—"Of all that I said unto the woman let her beware. . . . All that I commanded her let her observe."

To secure for the promised child the qualifications necessary for his important work, the habits of both

This chapter is based on Judges 13 to 16.

403

mother and child were to be carefully regulated. The child will be affected for good or evil by the habits of the mother. She must be controlled by principle and practice temperance and self-denial, if she would seek the welfare of her child. Unwise advisers will urge upon the mother the necessity of gratifying every wish and impulse; but the mother is by command of God placed under solemn obligation to exercise self-control.

And fathers as well as mothers are involved in this responsibility. As the result of parental intemperance, children often lack physical strength and mental and moral power. Liquor drinkers and tobacco users may transmit their insatiable craving, inflamed blood, and irritable nerves to their children. The licentious often bequeath unholy desires, and even loathsome diseases, to their offspring. The tendency is for each generation to fall lower and lower. To a great degree, parents are responsible for the infirmities of the thousands born deaf, blind, diseased, or idiotic.

The effect of prenatal influence has been by many lightly regarded, but the instruction sent from heaven to those Hebrew parents shows how this matter is looked upon by our Creator.

A good legacy from the parents must be followed by careful training and the formation of right habits. God directed that the future judge and deliverer of Israel should be under a perpetual prohibition against the use of wine or strong drink. Lessons of temperance, self-denial, and self-control are to be taught even from babyhood.

Why the Distinction Between Clean and Unclean Foods

The distinction between articles of food as clean and unclean was based upon sanitary principles. To the observance of this distinction may be traced, in a great degree, the marvelous vitality which for thousands of years has distinguished the Jewish people. The use of stimulating and indigestible food is often injurious to health and in many cases sows the seeds of drunkenness. True temperance teaches us to dispense entirely with everything hurtful and to use judiciously that which is healthful. Few realize how much their habits of diet have to do with their health, their character, their usefulness in this world, and their eternal destiny. The body should be servant to the mind, not the mind to the body.

Samson's Strength Depends on Faithfulness to God

The divine promise to Manoah was in due time fulfilled in the birth of Samson. As the boy grew, it became evident that he possessed extraordinary physical strength. This was not, as Samson and his parents well knew, dependent upon his well-knit sinews, but upon his condition as a Nazarite, of which his unshorn hair was a symbol. Had Samson obeyed the divine commands, his would have been a nobler and happier destiny. But association with idolaters corrupted him.

The town of Zorah being near the country of the Philistines, Samson came to mingle with them on friendly terms. A young woman dwelling in the Philistine town of Timnath engaged Samson's affections, and he determined to make her his wife. To his God-fearing parents, who endeavored to dissuade him from his purpose, his only answer was, "She pleaseth me well." At last the marriage took place.

Just as he was entering on manhood, the time above all others when he should have been true to God, Samson connected himself with the enemies of Israel. He did not ask whether he could better glorify God when united with the object of his choice. To all who seek first to honor Him, God has promised wisdom. But there is no promise to those bent on self-pleasing.

How often inclination governs in the selection of husband or wife! The parties do not ask counsel of God nor have His glory in view. Satan is constantly seeking to strengthen his power over the people of God by inducing them to enter into alliance with his subjects. In order to accomplish this he endeavors to arouse unsanctified passions.

But the Lord has instructed His people not to unite with those who have not His love abiding in them: "What concord hath Christ with Belial? or what part hath he that believeth with an infidel? and what agreement hath the temple of God with idols?" 2 Corinthians 6:15, 16.

At his marriage feast, Samson was brought into familiar association with those who hated the God of Israel. The wife proved treacherous to her husband before the close of the marriage feast. Incensed at her perfidy, Samson forsook her for the time and went alone to his home at Zorah. When, afterward relenting, he returned for his bride, he found her the wife of another. His revenge, in wasting all the fields and vineyards of the Philistines, provoked them to murder her, although their threats had driven her to the deceit with which the trouble began.

Samson had already given evidence of his marvelous strength by slaying, singlehanded, a young lion, and by killing thirty of the men of Askelon. Now, moved to anger by the barbarous murder of his wife, he attacked the Philistines and smote them "with a great slaughter." Wishing a safe retreat he withdrew to "the rock Etam," in Judah.

To this place he was pursued, and the inhabitants of Judah, in great alarm, basely agreed to deliver him to his enemies. Accordingly three thousand men of Judah went up to him. Samson permitted them to bind him with two new ropes, and he was led into the camp of his enemies amid demonstrations of great joy. But "the Spirit of Jehovah came mightily upon him." He burst asunder the strong new cords as if they had been flax burned in the fire. Then seizing the first weapon at hand, the jawbone of an ass, he smote the Philistines, leaving a thousand men dead upon the field.

Had the Israelites been ready to unite with Samson and follow up the victory, they might have freed themselves from their oppressors. But they had become dispirited and had neglected the work God commanded them to perform in dispossessing the heathen. They had united with them in their degrading practices. They tamely submitted to degradation which they might have escaped had they only obeyed God. Even when the Lord raised up a deliverer for them, they would, not infrequently, desert him and unite with their enemies.

Samson's Wrong Marriage

After his victory the Israelites made Samson judge, and he ruled Israel for twenty years. But Samson had transgressed the command of God by taking a wife from the Philistines, and again he ventured among them—now his deadly enemies—in the indulgence of unlawful passion. Trusting to his great strength, he went to Gaza to visit a harlot. The inhabitants of the city learned of his presence and were eager for revenge. Their enemy was shut safely within the walls of the most strongly fortified of their cities. They felt sure of their prey, and only waited till morning to complete their triumph.

At midnight the accusing voice of conscience filled Samson with remorse as he remembered that he had broken his vow as a Nazarite. But God's mercy had not forsaken him. His prodigious strength again served to deliver him. Going to the city gate, he wrenched it from its place and carried it to the top of a hill on the way to Hebron.

He did not again venture among the Philistines but continued to seek those sensuous pleasures that were luring him to ruin. "He loved a woman in the valley of Sorek," not far from his birthplace. Her name was Delilah, "the consumer." Sorek's vineyards also had a temptation for the wavering Nazarite, who had already indulged in the use of wine, thus breaking another tie that bound him to purity and to God. The Philistines determined, through Delilah, to accomplish his ruin.

They dared not attempt to seize him while in possession of his great strength, but it was their purpose to learn the secret of his power. They therefore bribed Delilah to discover and reveal it.

A Weak Woman Subdues a Strong Man

As the betrayer plied Samson with her questions, he deceived her by declaring that the weakness of other men would come upon him if certain processes were tried. When she put the matter to the test, the cheat was discovered. Then she accused him of falsehood: "How canst thou say, I love thee, when thine heart is not with me? Thou hast mocked me these three times, and hast not told me wherein thy great strength lieth." Three times Samson had the clearest evidence that the Philistines had leagued with his charmer to destroy him; but she treated the matter as a jest, and he blindly banished fear.

Day by day a subtle power kept him by her side. Overcome at last, Samson made known the secret: "There hath not come a razor upon mine head; for I have been a Nazarite unto God from my mother's womb: If I be shaven, then my strength will go from me, and I shall become weak, and be like any other man."

A messenger was immediately dispatched to the lords of the Philistines, urging them to come without delay. While the warrior slept, the heavy masses of his hair were severed from his head. Then she called, "The Philistines be upon thee, Samson!" Suddenly awaking, he thought to exert his strength as before, but his powerless arms refused to do his bidding. He knew that "Jehovah was departed from him." Delilah began to annoy him and cause him pain, thus making a trial of his strength; for the Philistines dared not approach him till fully convinced that his power was gone. Then they seized him and, having put out both his eyes, took him to Gaza. Here he was bound with fetters in their prison house and confined to hard labor.

What a change! Weak, blind, imprisoned, degraded to the most menial service! God had borne long with him. But when he had so yielded to sin as to betray his secret, the Lord departed from him. There was no virtue in his long hair, but it was a token of his loyalty to God. When the symbol was sacrificed in the indulgence of passion, the blessings of which it was a token were forfeited.

In suffering and humiliation, a sport for the Philistines, Samson learned more of his own weakness than he had ever known before. His afflictions led him to repentance. As his hair grew, his power gradually returned. His enemies, regarding him as a fettered and helpless prisoner, felt no apprehensions.

Samson's Final Repentance and Tragic Victory

The Philistines, exulting, defied the God of Israel. A feast was appointed in honor of Dagon, the fish god. Throngs of Philistine worshipers filled the vast temple and crowded the galleries about the roof. It was a scene of festivity and rejoicing.

Then, as the crowning trophy of Dagon's power, Samson was brought in. People and rulers mocked his misery and adored the god who had overthrown "the destroyer of their country." After a time, as if weary, Samson asked permission to rest against the two central pillars which supported the temple roof.

Then he silently uttered the prayer, "O Lord God, remember me, I pray Thee, and strengthen me, I pray Thee, only this once, O God, that I may be at once avenged of the Philistines." With these words he encircled the pillars with his mighty arms, and crying, "Let me die with the Philistines!" he bowed himself and the roof fell, destroying at one crash all that vast multitude. "So the dead which he slew at his death were more than all they which he slew in his life."

The idol and its worshipers, priest and peasant, warrior and noble, were buried together beneath the ruins of Dagon's temple. And among them was the giant form of him whom God had chosen to be the deliverer of His people.

Tidings were carried to the land of Israel, and Samson's kinsmen, unopposed, rescued the body of the fallen hero. They "buried him between Zorah and Eshtaol, in the burying place of Manoah his father."

How dark and terrible the record of that life which might have been a praise to God and a glory to the nation! Had Samson been true to his divine calling, the purpose of God could have been accomplished. But he yielded to temptation, and his mission was fulfilled in bondage and death.

Physically, Samson was the strongest man upon the earth, but in self-control, integrity, and firmness, he was one of the weakest. He who is mastered by his passions is a weak man. Real greatness is measured by the power of the feelings that a man controls, not by those that control him.

Those who in the way of duty are brought into trial may be sure that God will preserve them; but if men willfully place themselves under the power of temptation, they will fall, sooner or later. The very ones whom God purposes to use as His instruments for a special work, Satan employs his utmost power to lead astray. Satan attacks us at our weak points, working through defects in the character to gain control of the whole man. He knows that if these defects are cherished, he will succeed.

But none need be overcome. Help will be given to every soul who really desires it. Angels of God that ascend and descend the ladder which Jacob saw in vision will help every soul who will, to climb even to the highest heaven.

55 / God Calls the Child Samuel

Elkanah, a Levite of Mount Ephraim, was a man of wealth and influence who loved and feared the Lord. His wife, Hannah, was a woman of fervent piety and lofty faith.

Their home was not gladdened by the voice of childhood, so the husband contracted a second marriage. But this step, prompted by lack of faith in God, did not bring happiness. Sons and daughters were added to the household, but the joy and beauty of God's sacred institution had been marred and the peace of the family broken.

Peninnah, the new wife, was jealous and narrow-minded, and bore herself with pride and insolence. To Hannah, hope seemed crushed, and life a weary burden; yet she met the trial with uncomplaining meekness.

At Shiloh Elkanah's services as a Levite were not required. Yet he went up with his family to worship and sacrifice at the appointed gatherings. Even amid the sacred festivities connected with the service of God, the evil spirit that had cursed his home intruded. After presenting the thank offerings, all the family, according to the custom, united in a solemn yet joyous feast. Elkanah gave the mother of his children a portion for herself and for each of her sons and daughters. He gave Hannah a double portion, signifying that his affection for her was the same as if she had had a son. Then the second wife, fired with jealousy, claimed the

This chapter is based on 1 Samuel 1; 2:1-11.

precedence as one highly favored of God and taunted Hannah with her childless state.

This was repeated from year to year until Hannah could endure it no longer. She wept without restraint and withdrew from the feast. Her husband vainly sought to comfort her. "Why weepest thou? and why eatest thou not? and why is thy heart grieved? Am not I better to thee than ten sons?"

Hannah uttered no reproach. The burden which she could share with no earthly friend she cast upon God. Earnestly she pleaded that He would grant her the gift of a son to train for Him. And she made a vow that if her request were granted she would dedicate her child to God from its birth.

Hannah had drawn near to the entrance of the tabernacle and in the anguish of her spirit "prayed, . . . and wept sore." In those evil times, such scenes of worship were rarely witnessed. Eli the high priest, observing Hannah, supposed that she was overcome with wine. Thinking to administer a deserved rebuke, he said sternly, "How long wilt thou be drunken? put away thy wine from thee."

Pained and startled, Hannah answered gently, "No, my lord, I am a woman of a sorrowful spirit: I have drunk neither wine nor strong drink, but have poured out my soul before the Lord. Count not thine handmaid for a daughter of Belial: for out of the abundance of my complaint and grief have I spoken hitherto."

The high priest was deeply moved, for he was a man of God. In place of rebuke he uttered a blessing: "Go in peace: and the God of Israel grant thee thy petition that thou hast asked of Him."

Hannah Gives Samuel to God

Hannah received the gift which she had earnestly entreated. As she looked upon the child, she called him Samuel—"asked of God." As soon as the little one was old enough to be separated from his mother, she fulfilled her vow. He was her only son, the special gift of Heaven; but she had received him as a treasure consecrated to God, and she would not withhold from the Giver His own.

Hannah journeyed with her husband to Shiloh and presented to the priest her precious gift, saying, "For this child I prayed; and the Lord hath given me my petition which I asked of Him: therefore also I have lent him to the Lord; as long as he liveth he shall be lent to the Lord." Eli, himself an overindulgent father, was awed and humbled as he beheld this mother's great sacrifice in parting with her only child, that she might devote him to the service of God. He felt reproved for his own selfish love, and in humiliation and reverence bowed before the Lord and worshiped. The mother's heart was filled with joy and praise, and she poured forth her gratitude to God.

From Shiloh, Hannah returned to her home at Ramah, leaving Samuel to be trained for service in the house of God. From the earliest dawn of intellect she had taught her son to regard himself as the Lord's. Every day he was the subject of prayers. Every year she made a robe of service for him, and as she went up with her husband to worship at Shiloh, she gave the child this reminder of her love. Every fiber of the little garment had been woven with prayer that he might be pure, noble, and true. She earnestly pleaded that he might attain that greatness which Heaven values, that he might honor God and bless his fellowmen.

What a reward was Hannah's! And what an encouragement to faithfulness is her example! There are opportunities committed to every mother. The humble round of duties which women regard as a wearisome task should be looked upon as a grand and noble work. The mother may make straight paths for the feet of her children, through sunshine and shadow, to the glorious heights above. But it is only when she seeks in her own life to follow Christ that the mother can hope to form the character of her children after the divine pattern. Let every mother go often to her Saviour with the prayer, "Teach us, how shall we order the child, and what shall we do unto him?" Wisdom will be given her.

"The child Samuel grew on, and was in favor both with the Lord, and also with men." Samuel's youth was not free from evil influences or sinful example. The sons of Eli feared not God, nor honored their father; but Samuel did not seek their company nor follow their evil ways. It was his constant endeavor to become what God would have him.

The loveliness of Samuel's character drew forth the warm affection of the aged priest. He was kind, generous, obedient, and respectful. Eli, pained by the waywardness of his own sons, found comfort and blessing in the presence of his charge. No father ever loved his child more tenderly than did Eli this youth. Filled with anxiety and remorse by the profligate course of his own sons, Eli turned to Samuel for comfort.

Every year saw more important trusts committed to him. While yet a child, a linen ephod was placed upon him as a token of his consecration to the work of the sanctuary. Young as he was when brought to minister in the tabernacle, Samuel had duties to perform, according to his capacity. These were not always pleasant, but they were performed with a willing heart. He regarded himself as God's servant and his work as God's work. His efforts were accepted because they were prompted by love to God and a sincere desire to do His will. Thus Samuel became a co-worker with the Lord of heaven and earth.

Integrity in Little Things

To perform every duty as unto the Lord throws a charm around the humblest employment and links the workers on earth with the holy beings who do God's will in heaven. Integrity in little things, the performance of little acts of fidelity and little deeds of kindness, will gladden the path of life. And when our work on earth is ended, it will be found that every one of the little duties faithfully performed has exerted an influence for good that can never perish.

The youth of our time may become as precious in the sight of God as was Samuel. By faithfully maintaining their Christian integrity they may exert a strong influence in the work of reform. God has a work for every one of them. Never did men achieve greater results for God and humanity than may be achieved in our day by those who will be faithful to their God-given trust.

56 / Eli and His Wicked Sons

Eli, priest and judge in Israel, wielded a great influence over the tribes of Israel. But he did not rule his own household. He was an indulgent father. He did not correct the evil habits and passions of his children. Rather than contend with them, he would give them their own way.

The priest and judge of Israel had not been left in darkness as to the duty of governing the children God had given to his care. But Eli shrank from this duty, because it involved crossing the will of his sons and would make it necessary to punish and deny them. He indulged his children in whatever they desired and neglected the work of fitting them for the service of God and the duties of life.

The father became subject to the children. His sons had no proper appreciation of the character of God or of the sacredness of His law. From childhood they had been accustomed to the sanctuary and its service, but they had lost all sense of its holiness and significance. The father had not checked their disrespect for the solemn services, and when they reached manhood they were full of the deadly fruits of skepticism and rebellion.

Though wholly unfit, they were placed as priests in the sanctuary to minister before God. These wicked men carried their disregard of authority into the service of God. The sacrifices, pointing forward to the death of Christ, were designed to preserve in the hearts of the people faith in the Redeemer to come. Hence it

This chapter is based on 1 Samuel 2:12-36.

Hannah's careful rearing of Samuel stood in sharp contrast to Eli's lax approach to bringing up his sons.

was of the greatest importance that the Lord's directions concerning them be strictly heeded. In the peace offerings the fat alone was to be burned upon the altar. A certain specified portion was reserved for the priests, but the greater part was returned to the offerer to be eaten by him and his friends in a sacrificial feast. Thus all hearts were to be directed in gratitude and faith to the great Sacrifice that was to take away the sin of the world.

The sons of Eli, not content with the part of the peace offerings allotted them, demanded an additional portion. These sacrifices gave the priests an opportunity to enrich themselves at the expense of the people. They not only demanded more than their right, but refused to wait even until the fat had been burned as an offering to God. They persisted in claiming whatever portion pleased them, and, if denied, threatened to take it by violence.

This irreverence robbed the service of its holy significance, and the people "abhorred the offering of the Lord." The great antitypical sacrifice to which they were to look forward was no longer recognized. "Wherefore the sin of the young men was very great before the Lord."

These unfaithful priests dishonored their sacred office by their vile, degrading practices. Many of the people, filled with indignation at the corrupt course of Hophni and Phinehas, ceased to come to the place of worship. Ungodliness, profligacy, and even idolatry, prevailed to a fearful extent.

Eli had greatly erred in permitting his sons to minister in holy office. Excusing their course on one pretext and another, he became blinded to their sins. But at last he could no longer hide his eyes from the crimes of his sons. The people complained of their violent deeds, and the high priest dared remain silent no longer. His sons saw the grief of their father, but their hard hearts were not touched. They heard his mild admonitions, but they were not impressed, nor would they change their evil course. Had Eli dealt justly with his wicked sons, they would have been punished with death. Dreading thus to bring public disgrace and condemnation upon them, he sustained them in the most sacred positions of trust. He permitted them to corrupt the service of God and inflict upon the cause of truth an injury which years could not efface. But God took the matter in hand.

Eli's Unfaithfulness Leads to Ruin

"There came a man of God unto Eli, and said unto him, Thus saith the Lord, . . . Wherefore . . . honorest [thou] thy sons above Me, to make yourselves fat with the chiefest of all the offerings of Israel My people? Wherefore the Lord God of Israel saith, I said indeed that thy house, and the house of thy father, should walk before Me forever: but now the Lord saith, Be it far from Me; for them that honor Me I will honor, and they that despise Me shall be lightly esteemed. . . . And I will raise Me up a faithful priest, that shall do according to that which is in Mine heart and in My mind: and I will build him a sure house; and he shall walk before Mine anointed forever."

Those who in blind affection for their children indulge them in their selfish desires and do not rebuke sin and correct evil make it manifest that they honor their wicked children more than they honor God. Eli should first have attempted to restrain evil by mild measures; but if these did not avail he should have subdued the wrong by the severest means. We are just as responsible for evils that we might have checked in others by exercise of parental or pastoral authority, as if the acts had been our own.

Eli overlooked the faults and sins of his sons in their childhood, flattering himself that after a time they would outgrow their evil tendencies. Many are now making a similar mistake. They foster wrong tendencies in their children, urging as an excuse, "They are too young to be punished. Wait till they become older and can be reasoned with." Thus the children grow up with traits of character that are a lifelong curse to them.

There is no greater curse upon households than to allow youth to have their own way. The children soon lose all respect for their parents, all regard for authority, and are led captive at the will of Satan. The influence of an ill-regulated family is disastrous to society. It accumulates a tide of evil that affects families, communities, and governments.

Eli's family life was imitated throughout Israel in thousands of homes. Actions speak louder than the most positive profession of godliness. Great are the evils of parental unfaithfulness under any circumstances; they are tenfold greater in the families of teachers of the people.

Effective Agents of Satan

When men use their sacred calling as a cloak for selfish or sensual gratification, they make themselves effective agents of Satan. Like Hophni and Phinehas, they cause men to "abhor the offering of the Lord." They may pursue their evil course in secret for a time, but when at last their true character is exposed, the faith of the people receives a shock that often results in a distrust of all who profess to teach the Word of God. The message of the true servant of Christ is doubtfully received. The question constantly arises, "Will not this man prove to be like the one we thought so holy, and found so corrupt?"

In Eli's reproof to his sons are words of solemn and fearful import: "If one man sin against another, the judge shall judge him; but if a man sin against the Lord, who shall entreat for him?" Had their crimes injured only their fellowmen, the judge might have made reconciliation by appointing a penalty and requiring restitution; and thus the offenders might have been pardoned. But their sins were so interwoven with their ministration as priests of the Most High, the work of

God was so profaned and dishonored before the people, that no expiation could be accepted for them. Their own father, though himself a high priest, dared not make intercession in their behalf; he could not shield them from the wrath of a holy God. Of all sinners, those are most guilty who cast contempt upon the means that Heaven has provided for man's redemption, who "crucify to themselves the Son of God afresh, and put Him to an open shame." Hebrews 6:6.

57 / Punishment: The Ark Taken

God could not communicate with the high priest and his sons. Their sins had shut out the presence of His Holy Spirit. But the child Samuel remained true to Heaven, and the message of condemnation to the house of Eli was Samuel's commission as a prophet of the Most High.

"When Eli was laid down in his place, and his eyes began to wax dim, that he could not see; and ere the lamp of God went out in the temple of the Lord, where the ark of God was, and Samuel was laid down to sleep; . . . the Lord called Samuel."

Supposing the voice to be that of Eli, the child hastened to the bedside of the priest, saying, "Here am I; for thou calledst me." The answer was, "I called not, my son; lie down again."

Three times Samuel was called and thrice he responded in like manner. Then Eli was convinced that the mysterious call was the voice of God. The Lord had passed by His chosen servant, the man of hoary hairs, to commune with a child. This in itself was a bitter yet deserved rebuke to Eli and his house.

No envy or jealousy was awakened in Eli's heart. He directed Samuel to answer, "Speak, Lord; for Thy servant heareth."

Once more the voice was heard and the child answered, "Speak; for Thy servant heareth."

"And the Lord said to Samuel, Behold, I will do a thing in Israel, at which both the ears of everyone that heareth it shall tingle. In that day I will perform against

This chapter based on 1 Samuel 3 to 7.

Eli all things which I have spoken concerning his house: when I begin, I will also make an end. For I have told him that I will judge his house forever for the iniquity which he knoweth; because his sons made themselves vile, and he restrained them not. . . . The iniquity of Eli's house shall not be purged with sacrifice nor offering forever.''

Samuel was filled with amazement at the thought of having so terrible a message committed to him. In the morning he went about his duties as usual, but with a heavy burden on his young heart. The Lord had not commanded him to reveal the fearful denunciation; hence he remained silent. He trembled lest some question compel him to declare the divine judgments against one whom he loved and reverenced. Eli was confident that the message foretold some great calamity to him and his house. He called Samuel and charged him to relate faithfully what the Lord had revealed. The youth obeyed, and the aged man bowed in humble submission to the appalling sentence. "It is the Lord," he said; "let Him do what seemeth Him good."

Eli Loses His Last Chance

Yet Eli did not manifest true repentance. He failed to renounce his sin. Year after year the Lord delayed His threatened judgments. Much might have been done to redeem the failures of the past, but the aged priest took no effective measures to correct the evils that were polluting the sanctuary of the Lord and leading thousands in Israel to ruin. The forbearance of God caused Hophni and Phinehas to harden their hearts and become still bolder in transgression.

The messages of warning and reproof to his house were made known by Eli to the whole nation. By this means he hoped to counteract the evil influence of his past neglect. But the warnings were disregarded by the people, as they had been by the priests. The people of surrounding nations also became bolder in their idolatry and crime. They felt no sense of guilt for their sins, as they would have felt had the Israelites preserved their integrity. It became necessary for God to interpose, that the honor of His name might be maintained.

"Now Israel went out against the Philistines to battle, and pitched beside Ebenezer: and the Philistines pitched in Aphek." This expedition was undertaken by the Israelites without counsel from God, without the concurrence of high priest or prophet. "And the Philistines put themselves in array against Israel: and when they joined battle, Israel was smitten before the Philistines: and they slew of the army in the field about four thousand men." As the shattered and disheartened force returned to their encampment, "the elders of Israel said, Wherefore hath the Lord smitten us today before the Philistines?" They did not see that their own sins had been the cause of this terrible disaster.

And they said, "Let us fetch the ark of the covenant of the Lord out of Shiloh unto us, that, when it cometh among us, it may save us out of the hand of our enemies." The Lord had given no command or permission that the ark should come into the army; yet the Israelites felt confident that victory would be theirs, and uttered a great shout when it was borne into the camp by the sons of Eli.

The Philistines looked upon the ark as the god of Israel. They said, "What meaneth the noise of this great shout in the camp of the Hebrews? And they understood that the ark of the Lord was come into the camp. And the Philistines were afraid; for they said, God has come into the camp. And they said, Woe unto us! . . . These are the gods that smote the Egyptians with all the plagues in the wilderness. Be strong, and quit yourselves like men, O ye Philistines, that ye be not servants unto the Hebrews, as they have been to you: quit yourselves like men, and fight."

The Philistines made a fierce assault, which resulted in great strength. Thirty thousand men lay dead upon the field, and the ark of God was taken, the two sons of Eli having fallen while fighting to defend it.

The most terrifying calamity that could occur had befallen Israel. The ark of God was in the possession of the enemy. The symbol of the abiding presence and power of Jehovah was removed from the midst of them. In former days, miraculous victories had been achieved whenever it appeared. The visible symbol of the most high God had rested over it in the holy of holies. But now it had brought no victory, and there was mourning throughout Israel.

The law of God, contained in the ark, was a symbol of His presence, but they had cast contempt upon the commandments and had grieved the Spirit of the Lord from among them. When the people did not honor His revealed will by obedience to His law, the ark could avail them little more than a common box. They looked to it as the idolatrous nations looked to their gods. They transgressed the law it contained, for their worship of the ark led to hypocrisy and idolatry.

Tragic News Kills Eli

When the army went out to battle, Eli had tarried at Shiloh. With troubled forebodings he awaited the result of the conflict, "for his heart trembled for the ark of God." Outside the gate of the tabernacle he sat by the highway day after day, anxiously expecting the arrival of a messenger from the battlefield.

At length a Benjamite "with his clothes rent, and with earth upon his head," rushed to the town and repeated to eager throngs the tidings of defeat. The sound of wailing and lamentation reached the watcher beside the tabernacle. The messenger was brought to him, and the man said, "Israel is fled before the Philistines, and there hath been also a great slaughter among the people, and thy two sons also, Hophni and Phinehas, are dead." Eli could endure all this, terrible as it was, for he had expected it. But when the messenger added, "and the ark of God is taken," a look of unutterable anguish passed over his countenance. The thought that his sin had dishonored God and caused

Him to withdraw His presence from Israel was more than he could bear. He fell, "and his neck brake, and he died."

The wife of Phinehas feared the Lord. The death of her father-in-law and her husband, and above all, the terrible tidings that the ark of God was taken, caused her death. She felt that the last hope of Israel was gone; and she named the child born in this hour of adversity, Ichabod, or "inglorious," with her dying breath mournfully repeating the words, "The glory is departed from Israel: for the ark of God is taken."

But the Lord had not wholly cast aside His people, and He employed the ark to punish the Philistines. The divine invisible presence would still attend it to bring terror and destruction to the transgressors of His holy law. The wicked may triumph for a time as they see Israel suffering chastisement, but the time will come when they too must meet the sentence of a holy, sin-hating God.

Heathen Gods Cannot Stand Before the Ark of God

The Philistines removed the ark in triumph to Ashdod and placed it in the house of their god Dagon. They imagined that the power which had attended the ark would be theirs, and that this, united with the power of Dagon, would render them invincible.

But entering the temple the following day, they beheld a sight which filled them with consternation. Dagon had fallen upon his face before the ark of Jehovah. The priests reverently lifted the idol and restored it to its place.

But the next morning they found it strangely mutilated, again lying upon the earth before the ark. The upper part of this idol was like that of a man, and the lower part in the likeness of a fish. Now the human form had been cut off, and only the body of the fish remained. Priests and people were horror-struck; they looked upon this as an evil omen, foreboding destruction to themselves and their idols before the God of the

Hebrews. They removed the ark from their temple and placed it in a building by itself.

The inhabitants of Ashdod were smitten with a distressing and fatal disease. Remembering the plagues inflicted upon Egypt, the people attributed their afflictions to the presence of the ark among them. It was decided to convey it to Gath. But the plague followed, and the men of that city sent it to Ekron. Here the people received it with terror, crying, "They have brought about the ark of the God of Israel to us, to slay us and our people." The work of the destroyer went on, until "the cry of the city went up to heaven."

Fearing longer to retain the ark among the homes of men, the people next placed it in the open field. There followed a plague of mice, which infested the land, destroying the products of the soil in the storehouse and in the field. Utter destruction now threatened the nation.

For seven months the ark remained in Philistia. The Israelites made no effort for its recovery. But the Philistines were anxious to free themselves from its presence. Instead of being a source of strength to them it was a burden and heavy curse. Yet they knew not what course to pursue. The people called for the princes of the nation, with the priests and diviners, and inquired, "What shall we do to the ark of Jehovah? tell us wherewith we shall send it to his place?" They were advised to return it with a costly trespass offering. "Then," said the priests, "ye shall be healed."

The Ark Sent to Beth-shemesh

In accordance with prevailing superstition the Philistine lords directed the people to make representations of the plagues by which they had been afflicted "five golden emerods, and five golden mice, according to the number of the lords of the Philistines: for," said they, "one plague was on you all, and on your lords."

These wise men acknowledged a mysterious power accompanying the ark. Yet they did not counsel the people to turn from their idolatry to serve the Lord. They still hated the God of Israel, though compelled by judgments to submit to His authority. Such submission cannot save the sinner. The heart must be yielded to God—must be subdued by divine grace—before repentance can be accepted.

How great is the long-suffering of God toward the wicked! Ten thousand unnoticed mercies were silently falling in the pathway of ungrateful, rebellious men. But when they refused to listen to the voice of God in His created works, and in the warnings, counsels, and reproofs of His word, He was forced to speak through judgments.

The priests and the diviners admonished the people not to imitate the stubbornness of Pharaoh and the Egyptians, and thus bring upon themselves still greater afflictions. A plan which won the consent of all was now proposed. The ark, with the golden trespass offering, was placed upon a new cart, thus precluding all danger of defilement. To this cart were attached two kine upon whose necks a yoke had never been placed. Their calves were shut up at home and the cows left free to go where they pleased. If the ark should thus be returned to the Israelites by way of Beth-shemesh, the nearest city of the Levites, the Philistines would accept this as evidence that the God of Israel had done unto them this great evil; "but if not," they said, "then we shall know that it is not His hand that smote us; it was a chance that happened to us."

On being set free, the kine turned from their young and took the direct road to Beth-shemesh. Guided by no human hand, the patient animals kept on their way. The divine Presence accompanied the ark safely to the very place designated.

The men of Beth-shemesh were reaping in the valley, "and saw the ark, and rejoiced to see it. And the cart came into the field of Joshua, a Beth-shemite, and stood there, where there was a great stone: and they clave the wood of the cart, and offered the kine a burnt offering unto the Lord." The Philistines had followed the ark "unto the border of Beth-shemesh" and had witnessed its reception. The plague had ceased, and they were convinced that their calamities had been a judgment from the God of Israel.

The People of Israel Do Worse Than the Philistines

The men of Beth-shemesh quickly spread the tidings that the ark was in their possession, and the people from the surrounding country flocked to welcome its return. Sacrifices were offered. Had the worshipers repented of their sins, God's blessing would have attended them. But while they rejoiced at the return of the ark as a harbinger of good, they had no true sense of its sacredness. They permitted it to remain in the harvest field. As they continued to gaze upon the sacred chest, they began to conjecture wherein lay its peculiar power. At last, overcome by curiosity, they removed the coverings and ventured to open it.

Israel had been taught to regard the ark with awe and reverence. Only once a year was the high priest permitted to behold the ark of God. Even the heathen Philistines had not dared to remove its coverings. Angels of heaven, unseen, ever attended it in all its journeyings. The irreverent daring of the people at Beth-shemesh was speedily punished. Many were smitten with sudden death.

The survivors were not led by this judgment to repent of their sin, but only to regard the ark with superstitious fear. Eager to be free from its presence, the Beth-shemites sent a message to the inhabitants of Kirjath-jearim, inviting them to take it away. With joy the men of this place welcomed the sacred chest and placed it in the house of Abinadab, a Levite. This man appointed his son Eleazar to take charge of it, and it remained there for many years.

Samuel's call to the prophetic office had come to be acknowledged by the whole nation. By faithfully delivering the divine warning to the house of Eli, painful and trying as the duty had been, Samuel had given proof of his fidelity; "and the Lord was with him, and did let none of his words fall to the ground. And all Israel from Dan even to Beersheba knew that Samuel was established to be a prophet of the Lord."

Samuel visited the cities and villages throughout the land, seeking to turn the hearts of the people to the God of their fathers, and his efforts were not without good results. After suffering the oppression of their enemies for twenty years, the Israelites "mourned after the Lord." Samuel counseled them, "If ye do return unto the Lord with all your hearts, then put away the strange gods and Ashtaroth from among you, and prepare your hearts unto the Lord, and serve Him only." Practical religion was taught in the days of Samuel, as taught by Christ when He was on earth.

Repentance is the first step that must be taken by all who would return to God. We must individually humble our souls before God and put away our idols. When we have done all that we can do, the Lord will manifest to us His salvation.

Samuel Becomes a Judge

A large assembly was gathered at Mizpeh. Here a solemn fast was held. With deep humiliation the people confessed their sins, and they invested Samuel with the authority of judge.

The Philistines interpreted this gathering to be a council of war and set out to disperse the Israelites before their plans could be matured. Tidings of their approach caused great terror in Israel. The people entreated Samuel, "Cease not to cry unto the Lord our God for us, that He will save us out of the hand of the Philistines."

While Samuel was in the act of presenting a lamb as a burnt offering, the Philistines drew near for battle. Then the Mighty One, who had parted the Red Sea and made a way through Jordan for Israel, again manifested His power. A terrible storm burst upon the advancing host, and the earth was strewn with the bodies of mighty warriors.

The Israelites had stood trembling with hope and fear. When they beheld the slaughter of their enemies, they knew that God had accepted their repentance. Though unprepared for battle, they seized the weapons of the slaughtered Philistines and pursued the fleeing host. This victory was gained upon the very field where, twenty years before, Israel had been smitten before the Philistines, the priests slain, and the ark of God taken. The Philistines were now so completely subdued that they surrendered the strongholds which had been taken from Israel and refrained from acts of hostility for many years. Other nations followed this example, and the Israelites enjoyed peace until the close of Samuel's sole administration.

That the occasion might never be forgotten, Samuel set up a great stone as a memorial called Ebenezer, "the stone of help," saying to the people, "Hitherto hath Jehovah helped us."

58 / The Schools of the Prophets

God had commanded the Hebrews to make their children acquainted with His dealings with their fathers. The mighty works of God and the promise of the Redeemer to come were to be often recounted. Figures and symbols caused the lessons to be firmly fixed in the memory. The young mind was trained to see God alike in the scenes of nature and the words of revelation. The stars, trees and flowers, the mountains, the brooks, all spoke of the Creator. Worship at the sanctuary and the utterances of the prophets were a revelation of God.

Such was the training of Moses in Goshen; of Samuel by Hannah; of David in Bethlehem; of Daniel before captivity separated him from his fathers; of Christ at Nazareth; such the training by which the child Timothy learned from his grandmother Lois, and his mother Eunice.

Further provision was made for the instruction of the young by the schools of the prophets. If a youth desired to search deeper into truth that he might become a teacher in Israel, these schools were open to him. To serve as a barrier against widespread corruption, to provide for the moral and spiritual welfare of youth, to promote the prosperity of the nation by furnishing qualified leaders and counselors, Samuel gathered young men who were pious, intelligent, and studious. These were called the sons of the prophets. The instructors, well versed in divine truth, had themselves enjoyed communion with God and received of His Spirit. They enjoyed the confidence of the people.

In Samuel's day there were two of these schools—at Ramah and at Kirjath-jearim. Others were established later.

The pupils sustained themselves by tilling the soil or in mechanical employment. In Israel it was regarded a crime to allow children to grow up in ignorance of useful labor. Every child was taught some trade, even though he was to be educated for holy office. Many religious teachers supported themselves by manual labor. Even so late as the time of the apostles, Paul and Aquila earned a livelihood by tentmaking.

The chief subjects of study in these schools were the law of God, sacred history, sacred music, and poetry. Instruction was different from that in the theological schools of the present day, from which many students graduate with less knowledge of God and religious truth than when they entered. It was the object of all study to learn the will of God and man's duty toward Him. In sacred history were traced the footsteps of Jehovah. Great truths set forth by the types were brought to view, and faith grasped the central object of all that system—the Lamb of God that was to take away the sin of the world.

Students were taught how to pray, how to approach their Creator, how to exercise faith in Him, and how to understand and obey the teachings of His Spirit. The Spirit of God was manifested in prophecy and sacred song.

Uplifting Music Taught

Music was made to lift the thoughts to that which is pure and elevating, and to awaken in the soul devotion and gratitude to God. How many employ this gift to exalt self instead of using it to glorify God! A love for music becomes one of the most successful agencies by which Satan allures the mind from duty and from contemplation of eternal things.

Music forms a part of God's worship in the courts above, and we should endeavor in our songs of praise to approach as nearly as possible to the harmony of the heavenly choirs. Singing is as much an act of worship as is prayer. The heart must feel the spirit of the song to give it right expression.

Are there not some lessons which the educators of our day might learn with profit from the ancient schools of the Hebrews? Real success in education depends upon the fidelity with which men carry out the Creator's plan.

The true object of education is to restore the image of God in the soul. Sin has well-nigh obliterated the image of God in man. To bring him back to the perfection in which he was first created is the great object of life. It is the work of parents and teachers, in the education of the youth, to cooperate with the divine purpose. Every faculty, every attribute with which the Creator has endowed us, is to be employed for His glory and for the uplifting of our fellowmen.

Were this principle given the attention which its importance demands, there would be a radical change in some current methods of education. Instead of appealing to pride and selfish ambition, teachers would endeavor to awaken love for goodness, truth, and beauty. The student would seek not to excel others but to fulfill the purpose of the Creator and to receive His likeness. Instead of being actuated by the desire for self-exaltation, which dwarfs and belittles, the mind would be directed to the Creator.

"The fear of the Lord is the beginning of wisdom; and *the knowledge of the Holy* is understanding." Proverbs 9:10. To impart this knowledge and to mold the character in harmony with it should be the object of the teacher's work. The psalmist says, "All Thy commandments are righteousness"; and "through Thy precepts I get understanding." Psalm 119:172, 104. Through the volume of inspiration and the book of nature we are to obtain a knowledge of God.

The mind gradually adapts itself to the subjects upon which it dwells. If occupied with commonplace matters only, it will become dwarfed and enfeebled. If never required to grapple with difficult problems, it will almost lose the power of growth. As an educating power the Bible is without a rival. It came fresh from the fountain of eternal truth, and a divine hand has preserved its purity through all the ages. It lights up the far-distant past, where human research seeks vainly to penetrate. Here only can we find a history of our race unsullied by human prejudice or pride. Here are recorded the struggles, defeats, and victories of the greatest men this world has ever known. Here the curtain that separates the visible from the invisible world is lifted, and we behold the conflict of the opposing forces of good and evil, from the first entrance of sin to the final triumph of righteousness. All is but a revelation of the character of God. The student is brought into communion with the infinite mind. Such a study cannot fail to expand and invigorate the mental powers.

The Bible unfolds principles that are the cornerstone of society and which are the safeguard of the family. Studied and obeyed, the Word of God would give to the world men of strength and solidity of character, of keen perception and sound judgment—men who would be a blessing to the world.

All true science is an interpretation of the handwriting of God in the material world. Science brings from her research only fresh evidences of the wisdom and power of God. Rightly understood, both the book of nature and the Written Word make us acquainted with God by teaching us something of the wise and beneficent laws through which He works.

Teachers should copy the example of the Great Teacher, who drew illustrations that simplified His teachings and impressed them more deeply upon the minds of His hearers. The birds in the leafy branches, the flowers of the valley, the lofty trees, the fruitful lands, the springing grain, the barren soil, the setting sun gilding the heavens with golden beams—all served as means of instruction. He connected the visible works of the Creator with the words of life which He spoke.

Religion Conducive to Health and Happiness

The things of nature speak to man of his Creator's love. This world is not all sorrow and misery. "God is love" is written upon every opening bud, upon the petals of every flower, and upon every spire of grass. There are flowers upon thistles, and thorns are hidden by roses. All things in nature testify to God's desire to make His children happy. His prohibitions are not intended merely to display His authority; He has the well-being of His children in view. He does not require them to give up anything that would be for their best interest to retain.

The opinion that religion is not conducive to health or happiness is one of the most mischievous of errors. Scripture says: "The fear of the Lord tendeth to life: and he that hath it shall abide satisfied." Proverbs 19:23. The words of wisdom "are life unto those that find them, and health to all their flesh." Proverbs 4:22.

True religion brings man into harmony with the laws of God, physical, mental, and moral. It teaches self-control, serenity, temperance. Religion ennobles the mind, refines the taste, and sanctifies the judgment. Faith in God's love and overruling providence lightens the burdens of anxiety and care. It fills the heart with joy and contentment in the highest or lowliest lot. Religion tends to promote health, to lengthen life, and to heighten our enjoyment of all its blessings. It opens a never-failing fountain of happiness. No real joy can be found in the path forbidden by Him who knows what is best.

The physical as well as the religious training in the schools of the Hebrews may be profitably studied. There is an intimate relation between the mind and the body. In order to reach a high standard of moral and intellectual attainment, the laws that control our physical being must be heeded.

And now, as in the days of Israel, every youth should acquire a knowledge of some branch of manual labor. Even if it were certain that one would never need to resort to manual labor for support, still he should be taught to work. Without physical exercise, no man can have vigorous health. The discipline of well-regulated labor is essential to a strong and active mind and a noble character.

Every student should devote a portion of each day to active labor. Thus the youth would be shielded from many evil and degrading practices that are often the result of idleness. This is all in keeping with the primary object of education.

Let the youth see the tender love the Father in heaven has manifested toward them, and the dignity and honor to which they are called—even to become the sons of God—and thousands would turn with contempt from selfish aims and pleasures that have hitherto engrossed them. They would learn to hate sin, not merely from hope of reward or fear of punishment, but from a sense of its inherent baseness.

God does not bid the youth to be less aspiring. By the grace of God they are to be directed to objects as much higher than mere selfish and temporal interests as the heavens are higher than the earth.

And the education begun in this life will be continued in the life to come. "Eye hath not seen, nor ear heard, neither have entered into the heart of man, the things which God hath prepared for them that love Him." 1 Corinthians 2:9. The fullness of joy and blessing will be reached in the hereafter. Eternity alone can reveal the glorious destiny to which man, restored to God's image, may attain.

59 / Saul, the First King of Israel

The government of Israel was administered in the name of God. The work of Moses, of the seventy elders, of the rulers and judges was simply to enforce the laws that God had given; they had no authority to legislate for the nation. This was the condition of Israel's existence as a nation.

The Lord foresaw that Israel would desire a king, but He did not change the principles on which the state was founded. The king was to be the vicegerent of the Most High. God was the head of the nation. (See Appendix, Note 7.)

When the Israelites first settled in Canaan, the nation prospered under the rule of Joshua. But intercourse with other nations brought a change. The people adopted many of the customs of their heathen neighbors and ceased to prize the honor of being God's chosen people. Attracted by the pomp and display of heathen monarchs, they tired of their own simplicity. Jealousy sprang up between the tribes. Internal dissensions made them weak. They were exposed to the invasion of heathen foes, and the people were coming to believe that the tribes must be united under a strong central government. They desired to be freed from the rule of their divine Sovereign. Thus the demand for a monarchy became widespread throughout Israel.

Under Samuel's administration the nation had prospered, order had been restored, godliness promoted, and the spirit of discontent checked for the time. But with advancing years the prophet appointed his two

This chapter is based on 1 Samuel 8 to 12.

sons to act as his assistants. The young men were stationed at Beersheba to administer justice among the people near the southern border of the land.

They did not prove worthy but "turned aside after lucre, and took bribes, and perverted judgment." They had not copied the pure, unselfish life of their father. He had been to some extent too indulgent with his sons, and the result was apparent in their character.

A pretext was thus furnished for urging the change long secretly desired. "All the elders of Israel gathered themselves together, and came to Samuel unto Ramah, and said unto him, Behold, thou art old, and thy sons walk not in thy ways: now make us a king to judge us like all the nations." Had the evil course of his sons been known to him, he would have removed them without delay, but this was not what the petitioners desired. Samuel saw that their real motive was discontent and pride. No complaint had been made against Samuel. All acknowledged the integrity and wisdom of his administration. The aged prophet uttered no reproach, but carried the matter to the Lord in prayer and sought counsel from Him alone.

The Lord Warns Israel of Their Mistake

The Lord said unto Samuel: "Hearken unto the voice of the people in all that they say unto thee: for they have not rejected thee, but they have rejected Me, that I should not reign over them. According to all the works which they have done since the day that I brought them up out of Egypt even unto this day, wherewith they have forsaken Me, and served other gods, so do they also unto thee."

The days of Israel's greatest prosperity had been those in which they acknowledged Jehovah as their King, when the laws and the government which He had established were regarded as superior to those of other nations. But by departing from God's law the Hebrews had failed to become the people that God desired to make them. Then all the evils which were the result of their own sin and folly they charged upon the government of God.

The Lord permitted the people to follow their own choice, because they refused to be guided by His counsel. When men choose to have their own way, He often grants their desires that they may be led to realize their folly. That which the heart desires contrary to the will of God will in the end be a curse rather than a blessing.

Samuel was instructed to grant the request of the people, but to warn them of the Lord's disapproval and make known what would be the result of their course. He faithfully set before them the burdens that would be laid upon them and the contrast between such oppression and their present free and prosperous condition. Their king would imitate the pomp and luxury of other monarchs. Grievous exactions upon their persons and property would be necessary. The goodliest of their young men he would require for his service. They would be made charioteers and horsemen and runners before him. They must fill the ranks of his army and be required to till *his* fields, reap *his* harvests, and manufacture implements of war for *his* service. To support his kingly state he would seize the best of their lands. The most valuable of their servants and of their cattle he would take and "put them to his own work." Besides all this, the king would require a tenth of all their income, the profits of their labor or the products of the soil. "Ye shall be his servants," concluded the prophet. "And the Lord will not hear you in that day." When once a monarchy was established, they could not set it aside at pleasure.

The People Reject God as King

But the people returned the answer, "Nay; but we will have a king over us; that we also may be like all the nations; and that our king may judge us, and go out before us, and fight our battles."

"Like all the nations." To be in this respect unlike other nations was a special privilege. God had separated the Israelites from every other people, to make them His own peculiar treasure. But they desired to imitate the heathen! As the professed people of God depart from the Lord, they become ambitious for the honors of the world. Many urge that by uniting with worldlings and conforming to their customs they might exert a stronger influence over the ungodly. But all who pursue this course separate from the Source of their strength. Becoming friends of the world, they are enemies of God.

With deep sadness, Samuel listened to the people. But the Lord said unto him, "Make them a king." The prophet had faithfully presented the warning, and it had been rejected. With a heavy heart he departed to prepare for the great change in the government.

Samuel's life of purity and unselfish devotion was a rebuke both to self-serving priests and to the proud, sensual congregation of Israel. His labors bore the signet of Heaven. He was honored by the world's Redeemer, under whose guidance he ruled the Hebrew nation. But the people, weary of his piety, despised his humble authority and rejected him for a man who should rule them as a king.

In the character of Samuel we see reflected the likeness of Christ. It was the holiness of Christ that stirred up against Him the fiercest passions of falsehearted professors of godliness. The Jews looked for the Messiah to break the oppressor's yoke, yet they cherished the sins that bound it upon their necks. Had Christ applauded their piety, they would have accepted Him as their king; but they would not bear His fearless rebuke of their vices. Thus it has been in every age of the world. When rebuked by the example of those who hate sin, hypocrites become the agents of Satan to persecute the faithful.

God had reserved to Himself the right to choose their king. The choice fell upon Saul, a son of Kish, of the tribe of Benjamin.

"There was not among the children of Israel a

goodlier person than he.'' Of noble and dignified bearing, comely and tall, he appeared like one born to command. Yet Saul was destitute of those higher qualities that constitute true wisdom. He had not learned to control his impetuous passions; he had never felt the renewing power of divine grace.

Saul was the son of a wealthy chief, yet he was engaged in the humble duties of a husbandman. Some of his father's animals having strayed upon the mountains, Saul went with a servant to seek for them. As they were not far from Ramah, the home of Samuel, the servant proposed that they inquire of the prophet concerning the missing property.

As they drew near to the city they were told that a religious service was about to take place, that the prophet had already arrived. Worship of God was now maintained throughout the land. There being no ministration in the tabernacle, sacrifices were for the time offered elsewhere. The cities of the priests and Levites, where the people resorted for instruction, were chosen for this purpose. The highest points in these cities were the place of sacrifice, and hence were called the ''high places.''

King Revealed to Samuel

At the gate of the city Saul was met by the prophet himself. God had revealed to Samuel that at that time the chosen king of Israel would present himself before him. As they now stood face to face, the Lord said to Samuel, "Behold the man who I spake to thee of! this same shall reign over My people."

Assuring him that the lost animals had been found, Samuel urged him to tarry and attend the feast, at the same time giving some intimation of the great destiny before him. "On whom is all the desire of Israel? Is it not on thee, and on all thy father's house?" The demand for a king had become a matter of absorbing interest to the whole nation, yet with modest self-depreciation, Saul replied, "Am not I a Benjamite, of the smallest of the tribes of Israel? and my family the least of all the families of the tribe of Benjamin? wherefore then speakest thou so to me?''

Samuel conducted the stranger to the place of assembly. At the prophet's direction, the place of honor was given to Saul, and at the feast the choicest portion was set before him. The services over, Samuel took his guest to his own home and there communed with him, setting forth the great principles on which the government of Israel had been established, thus seeking to prepare him for his high station.

When Saul departed next morning, the prophet went with him. Having passed through the town, he directed the servant to go forward. Then he bade Saul stand still to receive a message sent him from God. "Then Samuel took a vial of oil, and poured it upon his head, and kissed him, and said, Is it not because Jehovah hath anointed thee to be captain over His inheritance?'' He assured Saul that he would be qualified by the Spirit of God for the station awaiting him. "The Spirit of Jehovah will come mightily upon thee, . . . that thou do as occasion shall serve thee; for God is with thee.''

As Saul went on his way, all came to pass as the prophet had said. At Gibeah, his own city, a band of prophets returning from "the high place'' were singing the praise of God to the music of the pipe and the harp, the psaltery and the tabret. As Saul approached them, the Spirit of the Lord came upon him also, and he joined in their song of praise and prophesied with them. He spoke with great fluency and wisdom and joined earnestly in the service. Those who had known him exclaimed in astonishment, "What is this that is come unto the son of Kish? Is Saul also among the prophets?''

A great change was wrought in him by the Holy Spirit. The light of divine holiness shone in upon the darkness of the natural heart. He saw himself as he was before God. He saw the beauty of holiness. He was called to begin the warfare against sin and was made to feel that in this conflict his strength must come wholly from God. The plan of salvation, which had before seemed dim and uncertain, was opened to his understanding. The Lord endowed him with courage and wisdom for his high station.

Saul Publicly Acclaimed King

The anointing of Saul as king had not been made known to the nation. The choice of God was to be publicly manifested by lot. For this purpose Samuel convoked the people at Mizpeh. Prayer was offered for divine guidance; then followed the solemn ceremony of casting the lot. In silence the multitude awaited the issue. The tribe, the family and the household were successively designated, and then Saul, the son of Kish, was pointed out as the individual chosen.

But Saul was not in the assembly. Burdened with a sense of the great responsibility about to fall upon him, he had secretly withdrawn. He was brought back to the congregation, who observed with pride that he was of kingly bearing and noble form, being "higher than any of the people from his shoulders and upward." Samuel exclaimed, "See ye him whom the Lord hath chosen, that there is none like him among all the people?" In response one long, loud shout of joy arose from the throng, "God save the king!"

Samuel then set before the people "the manner of the kingdom," stating the principles upon which the monarchical government was based. The king was not to be an absolute monarch, but to hold his power in subjection to the will of the Most High. This address was recorded in a book. Though the nation had despised Samuel's warning, the faithful prophet still endeavored, as far as possible, to guard their liberties.

While the people in general were ready to acknowledge Saul as their king, there was a large party in opposition. For a monarch to be chosen from Benjamin, the smallest of the tribes of Israel—and to neglect both Judah and Ephraim, the largest and most powerful—was a slight which they could not brook. Those who had been most urgent in their demand for a king were the ones that refused to accept the man of God's appointment.

Leaving Samuel to administer the government as formerly, Saul returned to Gibeah. He made no attempt to maintain by force his right to the throne. He quietly occupied himself in the duties of a husbandman, leaving the establishment of his authority entirely to God.

Soon after, the Ammonites invaded the territory east of Jordan and threatened the city of Jabesh-gilead. The inhabitants tried to secure peace by offering to become tributary to the Ammonites. The cruel king would not consent but on condition that he put out the right eye of everyone.

Messengers were at once dispatched to seek help from the tribes west of Jordan. Saul, returning at night from following the oxen in the field, heard the loud wail that told of some great calamity. When the shameful story was repeated, all his dormant powers were roused. "The Spirit of God came upon Saul, . . . and he took a yoke of oxen, and hewed them in pieces, and sent them throughout all the coasts of Israel by the hands of messengers, saying, Whosoever cometh not forth after Saul and after Samuel, so shall it be done unto his oxen."

Three hundred and thirty thousand men gathered under the command of Saul. By a rapid night march, Saul and his army crossed the Jordan and arrived before Jabesh in "the morning watch." Dividing his force into three companies, he fell upon the Ammonite camp at that early hour, when, not suspecting danger, they were least secure. In the panic that followed, they were routed with great slaughter. "They which remained were scattered, so that two of them were not left together."

The promptness and bravery of Saul, as well as his generalship, were qualities which the people of Israel desired in a monarch, that they might cope with other nations. They now greeted him as their king, attributing the honor of the victory to human agencies and forgetting that without God's special blessing all their efforts would have been in vain. Some proposed to put to death those who had at first refused to acknowledge the authority of Saul. But the king interfered, saying, "There shall not a man be put to death this day: for today the Lord hath wrought salvation in Israel." Instead of taking honor to himself, he gave the glory to God. Instead of showing revenge, he manifested forgiveness. This is unmistakable evidence that the grace of God dwells in the heart.

Samuel now proposed that a national assembly be convoked at Gilgal, that the kingdom might be publicly confirmed to Saul. It was done, "and there they sacrificed sacrifices of peace offerings before the Lord; and there Saul and all the men of Israel rejoiced greatly."

Upon this plain, linked with so many thrilling associations, stood Samuel and Saul; and when the shouts of welcome to the king had died away, the aged prophet gave his parting words as ruler of the nation.

Samuel had previously set forth the principles that should govern both the king and the people, and he desired to add to his words the weight of his own example. From childhood he had been connected with the work of God, and during his long life one object had been ever before him—the glory of God and the highest good of Israel.

In consequence of sin Israel had lost faith in God and their discernment of His power and wisdom to rule the nation—lost confidence in His ability to vindicate His cause. Before they could find true peace, they must see and confess the sin of which they had been guilty.

Samuel recounted the history of Israel from the day God brought them from Egypt. The King of kings had fought their battles. Often their sins had sold them into the power of their enemies, but no sooner did they turn from their evil ways than God's mercy raised up a deliverer. The Lord sent Gideon and Barak, and "Jephthah, and Samuel, and delivered you out of the hand of your enemies on every side, and ye dwelt safe." Yet when threatened with danger they had declared, "A king shall reign over us," when, said the prophet, "Jehovah your God was your King."

In humiliation the people now confessed their sin, the very sin of which they had been guilty. "Pray for thy servants unto the Lord thy God, that we die not: for we have added unto all our sins this evil, to ask us a king."

Samuel did not leave the people in a state of discouragement, for this would have prevented all effort for a better life. To look upon God as severe and unforgiving would expose them to manifold temptations. "Fear not," was the message of God by His servant: "ye have done all this wickedness: yet turn not aside from following the Lord, but serve the Lord with all your heart; and turn ye not aside. . . . For the Lord will not forsake His people."

Samuel uttered no reproach for the ingratitude with which Israel had repaid his lifelong devotion, but he assured them of his unceasing interest for them. "God forbid that I should sin against the Lord in ceasing to pray for you: but I will teach you the good and the right way: only fear the Lord, and serve Him in truth with all your heart; for consider how great things He hath done for you."

60 / Saul Makes a Terrible Mistake

After the assembly at Gilgal, Saul disbanded the army that had at his call arisen to overthrow the Ammonites. Here was a serious error. His army was filled with hope and courage by the recent victory; and had he proceeded at once against other enemies of Israel, a telling blow might have been struck for the liberties of the nation.

Meanwhile, the Philistines were active. They had still retained some hill fortresses in the land of Israel, and now they established themselves in the very heart of the country. During the long period of their oppressive rule, the Philistines had endeavored to strengthen their power by forbidding the Israelites to practice the trade of smiths, lest they make weapons of war. The Hebrews still resorted to the Philistine garrisons for such work as needed to be done. Controlled by the abject spirit induced by long oppression, the men of Israel had, to a great extent, neglected to provide themselves with weapons of war. Bows and slings the Israelites could obtain, but none among them except Saul and his son Jonathan possessed a spear or sword.

Not until the second year of Saul's reign was an attempt made to subdue the Philistines. The first blow was struck by Jonathan, who overcame their garrison at Geba. The Philistines, exasperated, made ready for a speedy attack upon Israel. Saul proclaimed war by the trumpet, calling all men of war, including the tribes across the Jordan, to assemble at Gilgal.

The Philistines had gathered an immense force at

This chapter is based on 1 Samuel 13; 14.

447

Michmash—"thirty thousand chariots, and six thousand horsemen, and the people as the sand which is on the seashore in multitude." Saul and his army at Gilgal were appalled at the thought of the mighty forces they would have to encounter in battle. Many were so terrified that they dared not come to the encounter. Others hid in caves and amid rocks in that region. As the time drew near, desertions rapidly increased, and those who did not withdraw were filled with error.

When Saul was anointed king, he had received from Samuel explicit directions concerning the course to be pursued at this time. "Thou shalt go down before me to Gilgal," said the prohet; "and, behold, I will come down unto thee, to offer burnt offerings, and to sacrifice sacrifices of peace offerings: seven days shalt thou tarry, till I come to thee, and show thee what thou shalt do." 1 Samuel 10:8.

Discouraged by Circumstances

Day after day Saul tarried, but without encouraging the people and inspiring confidence in God. Before the time appointed by the prophet had fully expired, he allowed himself to be discouraged by the trying circumstances that surrounded him. Instead of seeking to prepare the people for the service that Samuel was coming to perform, he indulged in unbelief. The work of seeking God by sacrifice was a most solemn work; God required that His people search their hearts and repent of their sins, that the offering be made with acceptance, and His blessing attend their efforts to conquer the enemy. But Saul had grown restless; and the people, instead of trusting in God for help, were looking to the king to lead and direct them.

Yet the Lord still cared for them and did not give them up. He brought them into close places that they might be convicted of the folly of depending on man and that they might turn to Him as their only help. The time for proving Saul had come. Would he depend on God and patiently wait according to His command as

The prophet Samuel reproved King Saul for his impatience and disregard of God's commands concerning the offering of sacrifices.

one whom God could trust in trying places as the ruler of His people? Or would he be vacillating and unworthy of the sacred responsibility that had devolved upon him? Would the king listen to the Ruler of all kings? Would he turn the attention of his fainthearted soldiers to the One in whom is everlasting strength and deliverance?

With growing impatience he awaited the arrival of Samuel and attributed the distress and desertion of his army to the absence of the prophet. The appointed time came, but the man of God did not appear. God's providence had detained His servant. Feeling that something must be done to calm the people, Saul determined to summon an assembly and by sacrifice entreat divine aid. God had directed that only those consecrated to the office should present sacrifices before Him. But Saul commanded, "Bring hither a burnt offering," and he approached the altar and offered sacrifice.

Saul's Presumption

"And it came to pass, that as soon as he had made an end of offering the burnt offering, behold, Samuel came." Samuel saw at once that Saul had gone contrary to the express directions that had been given him. If Saul had fulfilled the conditions upon which divine help was promised, the Lord would have wrought a marvelous deliverance for Israel. But Saul was so well satisfied with himself that he went out to meet the prophet as one who should be commended rather than disapproved.

To Samuel's inquiry, "What hast thou done?" Saul offered excuses for his presumptuous act. "I saw that the people were scattered from me, and that thou camest not within the days appointed, and that the Philistines gathered themselves together at Michmash; therefore said I, The Philistines will come down now upon me to Gilgal, and I have not made supplication unto the Lord: I forced myself therefore, and offered a burnt offering.

"And Samuel said to Saul, Thou hast done foolishly: thou hast not kept the commandment of the Lord thy God, which He commanded thee: for now would the Lord have established thy kingdom upon Israel forever. But now thy kingdom shall not continue: the Lord hath sought Him a man after His own heart, and the Lord hath commanded him to be captain over His people. . . . And Samuel arose, and gat him up from Gilgal unto Gibeah of Benjamin."

Either Israel must cease to be the people of God, or the monarchy and the nation must be governed by divine power. In Israel no monarchy could prosper that did not in all things acknowledge the supreme authority of God.

In this time of trial, Saul's failure proved him unfit to be the vicegerent of God to His people. He would mislead Israel. His will, rather than the will of God, would be the controlling power. Since he had failed, the purpose of God must be accomplished by another. The government of Israel must be committed to one who would rule according to the will of Heaven.

The Reason for Saul's Sad Failure

Saul was in disfavor with God and yet unwilling to humble his heart in penitence. He was not ignorant of Israel's defeat when the ark of God was brought into the camp by Hophni and Phinehas; and yet, knowing all this, he determined to send for the sacred chest and its attendant priest. By this means he hoped to reassemble his scattered army and give battle to the Philistines. He would dispense with Samuel's presence and free himself from the prophet's unwelcome criticisms and reproofs.

The Holy Spirit had been granted to Saul to enlighten his understanding and soften his heart. And yet how great was his perversity! That impetuous spirit, not early trained to submission, was ever ready to rebel against divine authority. Men cannot for years pervert the powers God has given them, and then, when they choose to change, find these powers fresh and free for an opposite course.

Saul's efforts to arouse the people proved unavailing. His force reduced to six hundred men, he retired to the fortress at Geba on the south side of a deep, rugged gorge a few miles north of Jerusalem. On the north side of the valley, at Michmash, the Philistine force lay encamped, while troops went out in different directions to ravage the country.

Jonathan, the King's Son, Is Honored

God had permitted a crisis that He might rebuke Saul and teach His people a lesson of humility and faith. Because of Saul's sin in his presumptuous offering, the Lord would not give him the honor of vanquishing the Philistines. Jonathan, the king's son, who feared the Lord, was chosen. Moved by a divine impulse, he proposed to his armor-bearer that they make a secret attack upon the enemy's camp. "It may be," he urged, "that the Lord will work for us: for there is no restraint to the Lord to save by many or by few."

The armor-bearer, also a man of faith and prayer, encouraged the design. Together they withdrew from the camp secretly, lest their purpose be opposed. With earnest prayer to the Guide of their fathers, they agreed upon a sign by which they might determine how to proceed. Passing down into the gorge separating the two armies, they silently threaded their way under the cliff, partially concealed by the ridges of the valley. Approaching the fortress they were revealed to their enemies, who said tauntingly, "Behold, the Hebrews come forth out of the holes where they had hid themselves. . . . Come up to us, and we will show you a thing," meaning that they would punish the two Israelites for their daring. This challenge was the token that Jonathan and his companion had agreed to accept as evidence that the Lord would prosper their undertaking.

Choosing a secret and difficult path, the warriors made their way to a cliff that had been deemed inacces-

sible and was not strongly guarded. Thus they penetrated the enemy's camp and slew the sentinels, who,
overcome with surprise and fear, offered no resistance.

Angels of heaven shielded Jonathan and his attendant; angels fought by their side, and the Philistines fell
before them. The earth trembled as though a great multitude with horsemen and chariots were approaching.
Jonathan recognized the tokens of divine aid, and even
the Philistines knew that God was working for the deliverance of Israel. Great fear seized the host. In the
confusion the Philistines began to slay one another.

Soon the noise of the battle was heard in the camp of
Israel. The king's sentinels reported great confusion
among the Philistines and that their numbers were de-
creasing. Seeing that the Philistines were meeting with
a repulse, Saul led his army to join the assault. The Hebrews who had deserted to the enemy now turned
against them; great numbers also came out of their hiding places. As the Philistines fled, Saul's army committed terrible havoc upon the fugitives.

Again Saul Is Foolish

Determined to make the most of his advantage, the
king rashly forbade his soldiers to partake of food for
the entire day. "Cursed be the man that eateth any
food until evening, that I may be avenged on mine enemies." The victory had already been gained without
Saul's knowledge or cooperation, but he hoped to dis-
tinguish himself by the utter destruction of the vanquished army. The command to refrain from food
showed the king to be indifferent to the needs of his
people when these conflicted with his desire for self-
exaltation. He declared his object to be, not "that the
Lord may be avenged on *His* enemies," but "that *I*
may be avenged on *mine* enemies."

The people had been engaged in warfare all day and
were faint for want of food; and as soon as the hours of
restriction were over, they fell upon the spoil, and de-

voured flesh with the blood, thus violating the law that forbade the eating of blood.

During the day's battle, Jonathan, who had not heard of the king's command, unwittingly offended by eating a little honey as he passed through a wood. Saul had declared that violation of his edict should be punished with death; and though Jonathan had not been guilty of a willful sin, and though God had wrought deliverance through him, the king declared that the sentence must be executed. "God do so, and more also," was his terrible sentence; "thou shalt surely die, Jonathan."

Jonathan's Life Is Saved

Saul could not claim the honor of the victory, but he hoped to be honored for his zeal in maintaining the sacredness of his oath. The people refused to allow the sentence to be executed. Braving the anger of the king, they declared, "Shall Jonathan die, who hath wrought this great salvation in Israel? God forbid: as the Lord liveth, there shall not one hair of his head fall to the ground; for he hath wrought with God this day."

Jonathan's deliverance was a severe reproof to the king's rashness. Saul felt a presentiment that his curses would return upon his own head. He returned to his home, moody and dissatisfied.

Those most ready to excuse themselves in sin are often most severe in condemning others. Many, like Saul, when convinced that the Lord is not with them, refuse to see in themselves the cause of their trouble. They indulge in cruel judgment of others who are better than they.

Often those who are seeking to exalt themselves are brought into positions where their true character is revealed. So it was in the case of Saul. Kingly honors were dearer to him than justice, mercy, or benevolence. Thus the people were led to see their error. They had exchanged the pious prophet, whose prayers had brought down blessings, for a king, who had prayed for a curse upon them.

Had not the men of Israel interposed, Jonathan, their deliverer, would have perished by the king's decree. With what misgivings must that people afterward have followed Saul's guidance! How bitter the thought that he had been placed upon the throne by their own act!

61 / Saul Rejected as King

Saul's errors were not yet irretrievable. The Lord would grant him another opportunity to learn the lesson of unquestioning faith in His word and obedience to His commands.

When reproved by the prophet at Gilgal, Saul felt he had been treated unjustly and offered excuses for his error. Samuel loved Saul as his own son, while Saul resented Samuel's rebuke and thenceforth avoided him so far as possible.

But the Lord sent His servant with another message to Saul: "Thus saith the Lord of hosts, I remember that which Amalek did to Israel, how he laid wait for him in the way, when he came up from Egypt. Now go and smite Amalek, and utterly destroy all that they have, and spare them not; but slay both man and woman, infant and suckling, ox and sheep, camel and ass." The Lord through Moses had pronounced sentence upon the Amalekites. The history of their cruelty toward Israel had been recorded with the command, "Thou shalt blot out the remembrance of Amalek from under heaven; thou shalt not forget it." Deuteronomy 25:19.

For four hundred years execution of this sentence had been deferred; but the Amalekites had not turned from their sins. Now the time had come for the sentence, so long delayed, to be executed.

To our merciful God the act of punishment is a strange act. "As I live, saith the Lord God, I have no pleasure in the death of the wicked; but that the wicked turn from his way and live." The Lord is "merciful and

This chapter is based on 1 Samuel 15.

455

gracious, long-suffering, and abundant in goodness and truth, . . . forgiving iniquity and transgression and sin." Yet He will "by no means clear the guilty." Ezekiel 33:11; Exodus 34:6, 7. While He does not delight in vengeance, He will execute judgment upon the transgressors of His law. He is forced to do this to preserve the inhabitants of the earth from utter depravity and ruin. In order to save some, He must cut off those who have become hardened in sin.

But while inflicting judgment, God remembered mercy. The Amalekites were to be destroyed, but the Kenites, who dwelt among them, were spared. This people, though not wholly free from idolatry, were worshipers of God and friendly to Israel.

King Saul Gets Another Chance

On receiving the commission against the Amalekites, Saul at once proclaimed war. At the call to battle the men of Israel flocked to his standard. The Israelites were not to receive either the honor of the conquest or the spoils of their enemies; they were to engage in the war solely as an act of obedience to God. God intended that all nations should behold the doom of that people that had defied His sovereignty.

"Saul smote the Amalekites . . . and took Agag the king. . . . But Saul and the people spared Agag, and the best of the sheep, and of the oxen, and of the fatlings, and the lambs, and all that was good, and would not utterly destroy them: but everything that was vile and refuse, that they destroyed utterly."

This victory served to rekindle the pride that was Saul's greatest peril. Ambitious to heighten the honor of his triumphal return, Saul ventured to imitate the customs of the nations around him, and spared Agag. The people reserved for themselves the finest of the flocks, herds, and beasts of burden, excusing their sin on the ground that the cattle were to be offered as sacrifices to the Lord. It was their purpose, however, to use these merely as a substitute, to save their own cattle.

Saul's presumptuous disregard of the will of God proved that he could not be trusted with royal power as the vicegerent of the Lord. While Saul and his army were marching home in the flush of victory, there was anguish in the home of Samuel. He had received a message from the Lord: "It repenteth Me that I have set up Saul to be king: for he is turned back from following Me, and hath not performed My commandments." The prophet wept and prayed all night for a reversal of the terrible sentence.

God's repentance is not like man's repentance. Man's repentance implies a change of mind. God's repentance implies a change of circumstances and relations. Man may change his relation to God by complying with the conditions upon which he may be brought into the divine favor, or he may, by his own action, place himself outside the favoring condition. Saul's disobedience changed his relation to God; but the conditions of acceptance with God were unaltered, for with Him there "is no variableness, neither shadow of turning." James 1:17.

With an aching heart the prophet set forth the next morning to meet the erring king. Samuel cherished a hope that Saul might, by repentance, be restored to the divine favor. But Saul, debased by his disobedience, came to meet Samuel with a lie upon his lips: "Blessed be thou of the Lord; I have performed the commandment of the Lord."

To the prophet's pointed question, "What meaneth then this bleating of the sheep in mine ears, and the lowing of the oxen which I hear?" Saul answered, "They have brought them from the Amalekites: for the people spared the best of the sheep and of the oxen, to sacrifice unto the Lord thy God; and the rest we have utterly destroyed." In order to shield himself, he was willing to charge upon the people the sin of his disobedience.

The message of Saul's rejection had to be delivered before the army of Israel when they were filled with pride over a victory accredited to the valor and generalship of their king, for Saul had not associated God with the success of Israel in this conflict. When the prophet saw the evidence of Saul's rebellion, he was stirred with indignation that he should lead Israel into sin. With mingled grief and indignation he declared, "I will tell thee what the Lord hath said to me this night. . . . When thou wast little in thine own sight, wast thou not made the head of the tribes of Israel, and the Lord anointed thee king over Israel?" He repeated the command of the Lord concerning Amalek and demanded the reason of the king's disobedience.

Saul Proves His Rebellion

Saul persisted in self-justification: "Yea, I have obeyed the voice of the Lord, and have gone the way which the Lord sent me, and have brought Agag the king of Amalek, and have utterly destroyed the Amalekites. But the people took of the spoil, sheep and oxen, the chief of the things which should have been utterly destroyed, to sacrifice unto the Lord thy God in Gilgal."

In solemn words the prophet swept away the refuge of lies and pronounced the irrevocable sentence: "Hath the Lord as great delight in burnt offerings and sacrifices, as in obeying the voice of the Lord? Behold, to obey is better than sacrifice, and to hearken than the fat of rams. For rebellion is as the sin of witchcraft, and stubbornness is as iniquity and idolatry. Because thou hast rejected the word of the Lord, He hath also rejected thee from being king."

As the king heard this fearful sentence, he cried out, "I have sinned: for I have transgressed the commandment of the Lord, and thy words: because I feared the people, and obeyed their voice." Terrified, Saul acknowledged his guilt, but he still persisted in casting blame on the people.

It was not sorrow for sin, but fear of its penalty, that actuated the king of Israel as he entreated Samuel, "I pray thee, pardon my sin, and turn again with me, that I may worship the Lord.'' If Saul had had true repentance, he would have made public confession of his sin; but it was his chief anxiety to maintain his authority and retain the allegiance of the people. He desired the honor of Samuel's presence to strengthen his own influence.

"I will not return with thee," was the answer of the prophet: "for thou hast rejected the word of the Lord, and the Lord hath rejected thee from being king over Israel." As Samuel turned to depart, the king, in an agony of fear, laid hold of his mantle to hold him back, but it rent in his hands. Upon this, the prophet declared, "The Lord hath rent the kingdom of Israel from thee this day, and hath given it to a neighbor of thine, that is better than thou."

An act of justice, stern and terrible, was yet to be performed. Samuel commanded that the king of the Amalekites be brought before him. Agag, guilty and merciless, came at the prophet's command, flattering himself that the danger of death was past. Samuel declared: "As thy sword hath made women childless, so shall thy mother be childless among women. And Samuel hewed Agag in pieces before the Lord." This done, Samuel returned to Ramah.

God Did All Possible to Help Saul

When called to the throne, Saul was deficient in knowledge and had serious defects of character. But the Lord granted him the Holy Spirit and placed him where he could develop the qualities requisite for a ruler of Israel. Had he remained humble, every good quality would have been gaining strength, while evil tendencies would have lost their power. This is the work which the Lord proposes to do for all who consecrate themselves to Him. He will reveal to them their defects of character and will give to them strength to correct their errors.

Though when first called to the throne Saul was

humble and self-distrustful, success made him self-confident. The valor and military skill displayed in the deliverance of Jabesh-gilead roused the enthusiasm of the whole nation. At first he ascribed the glory to God, but afterward took honor to himself. He lost sight of his dependence on God and in heart departed from the Lord. Thus the way was prepared for his sin of presumption at Gilgal. The same blind self-confidence led him to reject Samuel's reproof. Had he been willing to confess his error, this bitter experience would have proved a safeguard for the future. If the Lord had then separated Himself entirely from Saul, He would not have again spoken to him through His prophet, entrusting him with a definite work to perform, that he might correct the errors of the past.

When Saul persisted in his stubborn self-justification, he rejected the only means by which God could work to save him from himself. At Gilgal, a religious service performed in direct opposition to the command of God placed him beyond the help that God was willing to grant. In the expedition against Amalek, the Lord was not pleased with partial obedience. God has given men no liberty to depart from His requirements.

Obedience the Fruit of Faith

"To obey is better than sacrifice." Without patience, faith, and an obedient heart, sacrificial offerings were worthless. When Saul proposed to present a sacrifice of that which God had devoted to destruction, open contempt was shown for divine authority. The service would have been an insult to Heaven. Yet many are pursuing a similar course. While they refuse to believe and obey some requirement of the Lord, they offer up to God their formal services of religion. The Lord cannot accept them if they persist in willful violation of one of His commands.

"Rebellion is as the sin of witchcraft, and stubbornness is as iniquity and idolatry." Those who set themselves against the government of God have entered into an alliance with the archapostate. He will cause everything to appear in a false light. Like our first parents, those who are under his bewitching spell see only the great benefits to be received by transgression.

Many thus led by Satan deceive themselves with the belief that they are in the service of God. In the days of Christ the Jewish scribes and elders who professed great zeal for the honor of God crucified His Son. The same spirit still exists in the hearts of those who set themselves to follow their own will in opposition to the will of God.

Saul's fatal presumption must be attributed to satanic sorcery. In his disobedience to the divine command he had been as really inspired by Satan as are those who practice sorcery; and when reproved, he added stubbornness to rebellion. He could have offered no greater insult to the Spirit of God had he openly united with idolaters.

In Saul, God had given to Israel a king after their own heart, as Samuel said, "Behold the king *whom ye have chosen, and whom ye have desired.*" 1 Samuel 12:13. His appearance accorded with their conceptions of royal dignity. His personal valor and ability in the conduct of armies were qualities they regarded as best calculated to secure respect from other nations. They did not ask for one who had true nobility of character, who possessed the love and fear of God. They were not seeking God's way, but their own. Therefore God gave them such a king as they desired—one whose character was a reflection of their own.

Had Saul relied upon God, God would have been with him. But when Saul chose to act independently of God, the Lord was forced to set him aside. Then he called to the throne "a man after His own heart" (1 Samuel 13:14)—one who would rely upon God and be guided by His Spirit; who, when he sinned, would submit to reproof and correction.

62 / David Anointed as King

David, in the freshness of boyhood, kept watch of his flocks as they grazed on the hills surrounding Bethlehem. The simple shepherd sang songs of his own composing, and the music of his harp made a sweet accompaniment to the melody of his fresh young voice. The Lord was preparing David for the work He designed to commit to his trust in after years.

"And the Lord said unto Samuel, How long wilt thou mourn for Saul, seeing I have rejected him from reigning over Israel? fill thine horn with oil, and go, I will send thee to Jesse the Bethlehemite: for I have provided Me a king among his sons. . . . Thou shalt anoint unto Me him whom I name unto thee. And Samuel did that which the Lord spake, and came to Bethlehem. And the elders of the town trembled at his coming, and said, Comest thou peaceably? And he said, Peaceably." The elders accepted an invitation to the sacrifice, and Samuel called Jesse and his sons. All the household of Jesse were present with the exception of David, the youngest son, who had been left to guard the sheep.

Before partaking of the offering feast, Samuel began his prophetic inspection of the noble-appearing sons of Jesse. Eliab was the eldest, and more nearly resembled Saul for stature and beauty than the others. As Samuel looked upon his princely bearing, he thought, "This is indeed the man whom God has chosen as successor to Saul," and waited for the divine sanction that he might anoint him.

This chapter is based on 1 Samuel 16:1-13.

But Eliab did not fear the Lord. He would have been a proud, exacting ruler. The Lord's word to Samuel was, "Look not on his countenance, or on the height of his stature; because I have refused him: for the Lord seeth not as man seeth; for man looketh on the outward appearance, but the Lord looketh on the heart." We may learn from the mistake of Samuel how vain is the estimation that rests on beauty of face or nobility of stature. The thoughts of God in relation to His creatures are above our finite minds. But we may be assured that His children will be brought to fill the place for which they are qualified and enabled to accomplish the work committed to their hands, if they will submit their will to God.

The Shepherd Boy Is Called to the Feast

Eliab passed from the inspection of Samuel, and the six brothers who were in attendance at the service followed in succession to be observed by the prophet. But the Lord did not signify His choice of any one of them. With painful suspense, Samuel had looked upon the last of the young men. Perplexed and bewildered, he inquired, "Are here all thy children?" The father answered, "There remaineth yet the youngest, and behold, he keepeth the sheep." Samuel directed that he be summoned. "We will not sit down till he come hither."

The lonely shepherd was startled by the unexpected call of the messenger who announced that the prophet had come to Bethlehem and had sent for him. Why should the prophet and judge of Israel desire to see him? But without delay he obeyed the call.

"Now he was ruddy, and withal of a beautiful countenance, and goodly to look to." As Samuel beheld the handsome, manly, modest shepherd boy, the voice of the Lord spoke: "Arise, anoint him: for this is he." David had proved himself brave and faithful in the humble office of a shepherd, and now God had chosen him to be captain of His people. "Samuel took the horn of oil, and anointed him in the midst of [from among] his brethren: and the Spirit of the Lord came upon David from that day forward." With a relieved heart the prophet returned to Ramah.

The ceremony of anointing David had been performed in secret. It was an intimation to the youth of the high destiny awaiting him, that amid all the perils of his coming years, this knowledge might inspire him to be true to the purpose of God to be accomplished by his life.

The great honor conferred upon David did not serve to elate him. As humble and modest as before his anointing, the shepherd boy returned to the hills and watched his flocks. But with new inspiration he composed his melodies and played upon his harp.

Before him spread a landscape of rich and varied beauty. He beheld the sun flooding the heavens with light, coming forth as a bridegroom out of his chamber, and rejoicing "as a strong man to run a race." There were bold summits of the hills reaching toward the sky. And beyond was God. The light of day, gilding forest and mountain, meadow and stream, carried the mind up to behold the Author of every good and perfect gift. Daily revelations of the character of his Creator filled the young poet's heart with adoration and rejoicing. The faculties of David's mind and heart were developing and coming into a more intimate communion with God. His mind was constantly penetrating into new depths for fresh themes to inspire his song and to wake the music of his harp. The rich melody of his voice poured out upon the air as if responsive to the angels' songs in heaven.

Who can measure the results of those years of toil and wandering among the lonely hills? The psalms of Israel's sweet singer were in all coming ages to kindle love and faith in the hearts of God's people, bringing them nearer to the loving heart of Him in whom all His creatures live.

David was preparing to take a high position with the

noblest of the earth. Clearer conceptions of God opened before his soul. Obscure themes were illuminated, difficulties made plain, perplexities harmonized. Each ray of new light called forth sweeter anthems of devotion to the glory of God and the Redeemer. As he beheld the love of God in the providences of his life, his heart throbbed with more fervent adoration and gratitude. His voice rang out in richer melody, his harp was swept with more exultant joy. And the shepherd boy proceeded from strength to strength, from knowledge to knowledge, for the Spirit of the Lord was upon him.

63 / David Kills Goliath

When King Saul realized that he had been rejected by God, he was filled with bitter rebellion and despair. He had no clear perception of his sin and did not reform his life, but brooded over what he thought was the injustice of God in taking the succession away from his posterity. He was ever occupied in anticipating the ruin that had been brought upon his house. He did not accept with meekness the chastisement of God; but his haughty spirit became desperate, until he was on the verge of losing his reason.

His counselors advised him to seek a skilled musician, in the hope that the soothing notes of a sweet instrument might calm his troubled spirit. David, as a skilled performer upon the harp, was brought before the king. His heaven-inspired strains had the desired effect. The dark cloud over the mind of Saul was charmed away.

Whenever necessary, David was recalled to soothe the mind of the troubled monarch. Although Saul expressed delight in David and his music, the young shepherd went from the king's house to the fields and hills of his pasture with a sense of relief.

David was growing in favor with God and man. He had been in the court of the king and had seen the responsibilities of royalty. He had penetrated some of the mysteries in the character of Israel's first king. He knew that the household of Saul, in their private life, were far from happy. These things served to bring troubled thoughts to him. But he turned to his harp and

This chapter is based on 1 Samuel 16:14-23; 17.

called forth strains that elevated his mind to the Author of every good, and the dark clouds that seemed to shadow the future were dispelled.

David's Special Educator

As Moses was trained for his work, so the Lord was fitting the son of Jesse to become the guide of His chosen people. The lonely hills and wild ravines where David wandered with his flocks were the lurking place of beasts of prey. Not infrequently lions or bears came, fierce with hunger, to attack the flocks. David was armed only with his sling and shepherd's staff; yet he gave proof of his courage in protecting his flock. Afterward describing these encounters, he said: "When there came a lion, or a bear, and took a lamb out of the flock, I went out after him, and smote him, and delivered it out of his mouth: and when he arose against me, I caught him by his beard, and smote him, and slew him." His experience developed in him courage, fortitude, and faith.

When war was declared by Israel against the Philistines, three of the sons of Jesse joined the army under Saul, but David remained at home. After a time, however, he went to visit the camp. By his father's direction he was to carry a message and a gift to his elder brothers. But, unknown to Jesse, the armies of Israel were in peril, and David had been directed by an angel to save his people.

As David drew near to the army, Israel and the Philistines were drawn up in array, army against army. Goliath, the champion of the Philistines, came forth, and with insulting language defied Israel to provide a man from their ranks who would meet him in combat. When David learned that the Philistine's defiance was hurled at them day after day without arousing a champion to silence the boaster, he was fired with zeal to preserve the honor of God.

The armies of Israel were depressed. They said one to another, "Have ye seen this man that is come up?

surely to defy Israel is he come up." In shame and indignation, David exclaimed, "Who is this uncircumcised Philistine, that he should defy the armies of the living God?"

Even as a shepherd, David had manifested daring, courage, and strength rarely witnessed, and the mysterious visit of Samuel to their father's house had awakened in the brothers suspicions of the real object of his visit. Their jealousy had been aroused.

And now the question which David asked was regarded by Eliab as a censure upon his own cowardice in making no attempt to silence the giant. The elder brother exclaimed angrily, "Why camest thou down hither? and with whom hast thou left those few sheep in the wilderness? I know thy pride, and the naughtiness of thine heart; for thou art come down that thou mightest see the battle." David's answer was respectful but decided: "What have I now done? Is there not a cause?"

David Brought Before the King

The words of David were repeated to the king, who summoned the youth before him. The shepherd said, "Let no man's heart fail because of him; thy servant will go and fight with this Philistine." Saul strove to turn David from his purpose, but the young man was not to be moved. "The Lord that delivered me out of the paw of the lion, and out of the paw of the bear, he will deliver me out of the hand of this Philistine. And Saul said unto David, Go, and the Lord be with thee."

For forty days Israel had trembled before the Philistine giant. Upon his head was a helmet of brass; he was clothed with a coat of mail that weighed five thousand shekels, and he had greaves of brass upon his legs. The coat was made of plates of brass that overlaid one another, like the scales of a fish, and no arrow could possibly penetrate the armor. The giant bore a huge javelin, also of brass. "The staff of his spear was like a weaver's beam; and his spear's head weighed six hundred shekels of iron; and one bearing a shield went before him.''

Morning and evening, Goliath had approached the camp of Israel, saying, ''Choose you a man for you, and let him come down to me. If he be able to fight with me, and to kill me, then will we be your servants: but if I prevail against him, and kill him, then shall ye be our servants. . . . I defy the armies of Israel.''

The king had small hope that David would be successful in his courageous undertaking. Command was given to clothe the youth in the king's own armor. The heavy helmet of brass was put on his head, and the coat of mail was placed on his body; the monarch's sword was at his side. Thus equipped, he started upon his errand, but erelong began to retrace his steps. The anxious spectators thought that David had decided not to risk his life. But this was far from the thought of the brave young man. When he returned he laid off the king's armor and in its stead took only his staff and a simple sling. Choosing five smooth stones out of the brook, he put them in his bag, and with his sling in his hand, drew near to the Philistine. The giant strode boldly forward, expecting to meet the mightiest of the warriors of Israel. His armor-bearer walked before him as if nothing could withstand him. As he came near he saw but a stripling. David's well-knit form, unprotected by armor, was displayed to advantage; yet between its youthful outline and the massive proportions of the Philistine, there was a marked contrast.

Goliath Despises the Youthful David

Goliath was filled with amazement and anger. ''Am I a dog,'' he exclaimed, ''that thou comest to me with staves?'' He poured upon David terrible curses, then cried in derision, ''Come to me, and I will give thy flesh unto the fowls of the air, and to the beasts of the field.''

David did not weaken. Stepping forward, he said to his antagonist: ''Thou comest to me with a sword, and with a spear, and with a shield: but I come to thee in the name of the Lord of hosts, the God of the armies of Israel, whom thou hast defied. This day will the Lord deliver thee into mine hand; and I will smite thee, and take thine head from thee; and I will give the carcasses of the host of the Philistines this day unto the fowls of the air, and to the wild beasts of the earth; that all the earth may know that there is a God in Israel. And all this assembly shall know that the Lord saveth not with sword and spear: for the battle is the Lord's, and He will give you into our hands."

This speech, given in a clear voice, rang out on the air and was distinctly heard by the listening thousands. In his rage Goliath pushed up the helmet that protected his forehead and rushed forward. "And it came to pass, when the Philistine arose, and came and drew nigh to meet David, that David hasted, and ran toward the army to meet the Philistine. And David put his hand in his bag, and took thence a stone, and slang it, and smote the Philistine in the forehead, that the stone sunk into his forehead; and he fell upon his face to the earth."

The two armies had been confident that David would be slain. But when the stone went whizzing through the air straight to the mark, they saw the mighty warrior tremble and reach forth his hands as if struck with blindness. The giant staggered, and like a smitten oak fell to the ground.

David did not wait an instant. He sprang upon the prostrate form of the Philistine and with both hands laid hold of Goliath's sword. It was lifted in the air, and the head of the boaster rolled from his trunk. A shout of exultation went up from the camp of Israel.

The Philistines were smitten with terror. The triumphant Hebrews rushed after their fleeing enemies, "to the gates of Ekron." "And the children of Israel returned from chasing after the Philistines, and they spoiled their tents."

64 / David Flees

After the slaying of Goliath, Saul kept David with him and would not permit him to return to his father's house. And "the soul of Jonathan was knit with the soul of David, and Jonathan loved him as his own soul." Jonathan and David made a covenant to be united as brethren, and the king's son "stripped himself of the robe that was upon him, and gave it to David, and his garment, even to his sword, and to his bow, and to his girdle." Yet David preserved his modesty and won the affection of the people as well as of the royal household. It was evident that the blessing of God was with him.

Saul felt that the kingdom would be more secure if there could be connected with him one who received instruction from the Lord. David's presence might be a protection to Saul when he went out with him to war.

The providence of God had connected David with Saul. David's position at court would give him a knowledge of affairs and would enable him to gain the confidence of the nation. Hardships which befell him through the enmity of Saul would lead him to feel his dependence upon God. And the friendship of Jonathan was also of God's providence, to preserve the life of the future ruler of Israel.

When Saul and David were returning from battle with the Philistines, "the women came out of all cities of Israel, singing and dancing, to meet King Saul, with tabrets, with joy, and with instruments of music." One company sang, "Saul hath slain his thousands," while

This chapter is based on 1 Samuel 18 to 22.

another company responded, "And David his ten thousands." The king was angry because David was exalted above himself. In place of subduing envious feelings, he exclaimed, "They have ascribed unto David ten thousands, and to me they have ascribed but thousands: and what can he have more but the kingdom?"

Saul's love of approbation had a controlling influence over his actions and thoughts. His standard of right and wrong was popular applause; Saul's ambition was to be first in the estimation of men. A settled conviction entered the mind of the king that David would obtain the heart of the people and reign in his stead.

The Demon of Jealousy Enters Saul's Heart

Saul opened his heart to the spirit of jealousy by which his soul was poisoned. The king of Israel was opposing his will to the will of the Infinite One. He allowed his impulses to control his judgment until he was plunged into a fury of passion. He had paroxysms of rage, when he was ready to take the life of any who dared to oppose his will. From this frenzy he would pass into despondency and self-contempt, and remorse would take possession of his soul.

He loved to hear David play upon his harp, and the evil spirit seemed to be charmed away for the time. But one day when the youth was bringing sweet music from his instrument, accompanying his voice as he sang the praises of God, Saul suddenly threw his spear at the musician. David was preserved by God and fled from the rage of the maddened king.

As Saul's hatred of David increased, he became more and more watchful to find an opportunity to take his life, but none of his plans against the anointed of the Lord were successful. David trusted in Him who is strong to deliver. "The fear of the Lord is the beginning of wisdom" (Proverbs 9:10), and David's prayer was that he might walk before God in a perfect way.

The people were not slow to see that David was a

competent person. Affairs entrusted to his hand were managed with wisdom and skill. The counsels of the young man were safe to follow, while the judgment of Saul was at times unreliable.

Saul stood in fear of him, since it was evident the Lord was with him. The king deemed that the life of David cast reproach upon him, since by contrast it presented his own character to disadvantage. Envy made Saul miserable. What untold mischief has this evil trait worked in our world! Envy is the offspring of pride, and if it is entertained in the heart, it will lead eventually to murder.

The king kept watch, hoping to find some occasion of indiscretion that might serve as an excuse to take the young man's life and still be justified before the nation for his evil act. He laid a snare, urging David to war against the Philistines with still greater vigor, promising as a reward the eldest daughter of the royal house. To this proposal David's modest answer was, "Who am I? and what is my life, or my father's family in Israel, that I should be son-in-law to the king?" The monarch manifested his insincerity by wedding the princess to another.

Michal, Saul's youngest daughter, was offered the young man on condition that evidence be given of the slaughter of a specified number of their foes. "Saul thought to make David fall by the hand of the Philistines," but David returned a victor from the battle, to become the king's son-in-law. "Michal Saul's daughter loved David," and the monarch, enraged, was still more assured that this was the man whom the Lord had said was better than he and who should reign in his place. Throwing off all disguise, he issued a command to the officers of the court to take the life of the one he hated.

Jonathan presented before the king what David had done to preserve the honor and life of the nation, and what terrible guilt would rest upon the murderer of the one whom God had used to scatter their enemies. The conscience of the king was touched. "And Saul sware, As the Lord liveth, he shall not be slain." David was brought to Saul, and he ministered in his presence as in the past.

David Leads Victorious Army

Again war was declared and David led the army against their enemies. A great victory was gained by the Hebrews, and the people praised his wisdom and heroism. This served to stir up the former bitterness of Saul against him. While the young man was playing, filling the palace with sweet harmony, Saul's passion overcame him and he hurled a javelin at David, but the angel of the Lord turned aside the deadly weapon. David escaped and fled to his own house. Saul sent spies that they might take him in the morning and put an end to his life.

Michal informed David of the purpose of her father. She urged him to flee and let him down from the window to make his escape. He fled to Samuel at Ramah, where the prophet welcomed the fugitive. It was here, amid the hills, that the honored servant of the Lord continued his work. A company of seers with him studied closely the will of God and listened reverently to the words of instruction that fell from the lips of Samuel. David learned precious lessons from the teacher of Israel. But David's connection with Samuel aroused the jealousy of the king, lest the prophet lend his influence to the advancement of Saul's rival. The king sent officers to bring David to Gibeah, where he intended to carry out his murderous design.

God Restrains Evil

The messengers went on their way intent upon taking David's life, but One greater than Saul controlled them. Met by unseen angels, they began to utter prophetic sayings and proclaimed the glory of Jehovah. Thus God manifested His power to restrain evil.

Saul was exasperated and sent other messengers.

These also were overpowered by the Spirit of God, and united with the first in prophesying. The third embassage was sent by the king, but the divine influence fell upon them also, and they prophesied.

Saul then decided that he himself would go. As soon as he should come within reach of David he intended with his own hand to slay him, whatever the consequences.

But an angel of God met him, and the Spirit of God held him in Its power. He went forward uttering prayers to God, with predictions and sacred melodies. When he came to the prophet's home in Ramah, he laid aside the outer garments that betokened his rank and lay before Samuel and his pupils under the influence of the divine Spirit. The people were drawn together to witness this strange scene, and the experience of the king was reported far and wide.

The persecutor assured David that he was at peace with him, but David had little confidence in the king's repentance. He longed to see his friend Jonathan once more. Conscious of his innocence, he sought the king's son and made a touching appeal: "What have I done? what is mine iniquity? and what is my sin before thy father, that he seeketh my life?"

Jonathan believed that his father no longer intended to take the life of David. "God forbid; thou shalt not die: behold, my father will do nothing either great or small, but that he will show it me; and why should my father hide this thing from me? It is not so."

After the remarkable exhibition of the power of God, Jonathan could not believe that his father would harm David. This would be rebellion against God.

David Hides From Saul

But David was not convinced. He declared to Jonathan, "As the Lord liveth, and as thy soul liveth, there is but a step between me and death."

At the time of the new moon, a sacred festival was celebrated in Israel. It was expected that both David and Jonathan would appear at the king's table. But David feared to be present, and it was arranged that he visit his brothers in Bethlehem. On his return he was to hide in a field not far from the banqueting hall, for three days absenting himself from the presence of the king. Jonathan would note the effect upon Saul. If no angry demonstration were made by the king, then it would be safe for David to return to court.

When the place was vacant the second day the king questioned, "Wherefore cometh not the son of Jesse to meat, neither yesterday nor today? And Jonathan answered Saul, David earnestly asked leave of me to go to Bethlehem: and he said, Let me go, I pray thee; for our family hath a sacrifice in the city; and my brother, he hath commanded me to be there: and now, if I have found favor in thine eyes, let me get away, I pray thee, and see my brethren. Therefore he cometh not unto the king's table."

When Saul heard these words, his anger was ungovernable. He declared that as long as David lived, Jonathan could not come to the throne. David should be sent for immediately, that he might be put to death. Jonathan again pleaded, "Wherefore shall he be slain? what hath he done?" This only made the king more satanic in his fury, and the spear intended for David he now hurled at his own son.

The prince was grieved and indignant. Leaving the royal presence, he repaired at the appointed time to the spot where David was to learn the king's intentions. They wept bitterly. The dark passion of the king cast its shadow upon the young men, and their grief was too intense for expression. Jonathan's last words fell upon the ear of David as they separated: "Go in peace, forasmuch as we have sworn both of us in the name of the Lord, saying, The Lord be between me and thee, and between my seed and thy seed forever."

David hastened to reach Nob. The tabernacle had been taken to this place from Shiloh, and here Ahimelech the high priest ministered. The priest looked upon

David in astonishment, as he came in haste and apparently alone. He inquired what had brought him there. The young man in his extremity resorted to deception. David told the priest he had been sent by the king on a secret errand.

David's Faith Fails

Here he manifested a want of faith in God, and his sin resulted in the death of the high priest. Had the facts been plainly stated, Ahimelech would have known what course to pursue to preserve his life. God requires that truthfulness mark His people, even in the greatest peril.

Doeg, chief of Saul's herdsmen, was paying his vows in the place of worship. At the sight of this man, David determined to make haste to secure another place of refuge. He asked Ahimelech for a sword and was told that he had none except the sword of Goliath, kept as a relic in the tabernacle. David replied, "There is none like that; give it me."

David fled to Achish, king of Gath; for he felt that there was more safety in the midst of the enemies of his people than in the dominions of Saul. But it was reported to Achish that David was the man who had slain the Philistine champion years before. Now he who had sought refuge with the foes of Israel found himself in great peril. But, feigning madness, he deceived his enemies and thus made his escape.

The first error of David was his distrust of God at Nob; his second, his deception before Achish. As trial came upon him, his faith was shaken and human weakness appeared. He saw in every man a spy and a betrayer. As he had been hunted and persecuted, perplexity and distress had nearly hidden his heavenly Father from his sight.

Every failure on the part of the children of God is due to their lack of faith. When shadows encompass the soul, we must look up; there is light beyond the darkness. David ought not to have distrusted God. He was the Lord's anointed. If he had but removed his mind from the distressing situation in which he was placed and had thought of God's power and majesty, he would have been at peace even in the midst of the shadows of death.

Among the mountains of Judah, David sought refuge. He made good his escape to the cave of Adullam, a place that with a small force could be held against a large army. "And when his brethren and all his father's house heard it, they went down thither to him." The family of David could not feel secure, knowing that at any time the unreasonable suspicions of Saul might be directed against them on account of their relation to David. They had now learned—what was coming to be generally known in Israel—that God had chosen David as the future ruler of His people. They believed that they would be safer with him.

In the cave of Adullam, the family were united in sympathy and affection. The son of Jesse could make melody with voice and harp. He had tasted the bitterness of distrust on the part of his own brothers, and the harmony that had taken the place of discord brought joy to the exile's heart.

Many had lost confidence in the ruler of Israel, for they could see that he was no longer guided by the Spirit of the Lord. "And everyone that was in distress, and everyone that was in debt, and everyone that was discontented," resorted to David, "and he became a captain over them: and there were with him about four hundred men." Here David had a little kingdom of his own, and in it order and discipline prevailed. But he was far from secure, for he received continual evidence that the king had not relinquished his murderous purpose.

At a warning of danger from a prophet of the Lord, he fled from his hiding place to the forest of Hareth. God was giving David a course of discipline to fit him to become a wise general, as well as a just and merciful king.

Saul had been preparing to ensnare David in the cave of Adullam, and when it was discovered that David had left this place of refuge, the king was enraged. The flight of David was a mystery. Had traitors in his camp informed the son of Jesse of his design?

King Saul Orders a Terrible Massacre

Saul affirmed to his counselors that a conspiracy had been formed against him, and with the offer of rich gifts and honor he bribed them to reveal who among his people had befriended David. Doeg the Edomite turned informer. Moved by ambition and avarice and by hatred of the priest who had reproved his sins, Doeg reported David's visit to Ahimelech in such a light as to kindle Saul's anger against the man of God. Maddened with rage, he declared that the whole family of the priest should perish. Not only Ahimelech, but the members of his father's house—"four-score and five persons that did wear a linen ephod"—were slain at the king's command by the murderous hand of Doeg. This is what Saul could do under the control of Satan.

This deed filled all Israel with horror. It was the king whom they had chosen that had committed this outrage. The ark was with them, but the priests of whom they had inquired were slain with the sword.

What would come next?

65 / The Largeheartedness of David

"One of the sons of Ahimelech the son of Ahitub, named Abiathar, . . . escaped, and fled after David. And Abiathar showed David that Saul had slain the Lord's priests. And David said unto Abiathar, I knew it that day, when Doeg the Edomite was there, that he would surely tell Saul: I have occasioned the death of all the persons of thy father's house. Abide thou with me, fear not: for he that seeketh my life seeketh thy life: but with me thou shalt be in safeguard."

Still hunted by the king, David's brave band repaired to the wilderness of Ziph. At this time, when there were so few bright spots in the path of David, he received an unexpected visit from Jonathan. These two friends related their varied experiences, and Jonathan strengthened the heart of David, saying, "Fear not: for the hand of Saul my father shall not find thee; and thou shalt be king over Israel, and I shall be next unto thee; and that also Saul my father knoweth." The hunted fugitive was greatly encouraged. "And they two made a covenant before the Lord: and David abode in the wood, and Jonathan went to his house."

The Ziphites sent word to Saul in Gibeah that they knew where David was hiding and they would guide the king to his retreat. But David, warned of their intentions, changed his position, seeking refuge in the mountains between Maon and the Dead Sea.

Again word was sent to Saul, "Behold, David is in the wilderness of Engedi. Then Saul took three thousand men chosen out of all Israel, and went to seek Da-

This chapter is based on 1 Samuel 22:20-23; 23 to 27.

After her husband Nabal had rebuffed David's courteous request, Abigail quickly sought out the future king in an effort to soothe his anger.

vid and his men upon the rocks of the wild goats.'' David had only six hundred men in his company. In a secluded cave the son of Jesse waited for the guidance of God as to what should be done.

As Saul was pressing his way up the mountains, he entered alone the very cavern in which David and his band were hidden. When David's men saw this they urged their leader to kill Saul. The king was now in their power—certain evidence that God Himself had delivered the enemy into their hand, that they might destroy him. David was tempted to take this view of the matter, but the voice of conscience spoke to him. ''Touch not the anointed of the Lord.''

David's men reminded their commander of the words of God, ''Behold, I will deliver thine enemy into thine hand, that thou mayest do to him as it shall seem good unto thee. Then David arose, and cut off the skirt of Saul's robe privily.''

Saul rose up and went out of the cave to continue his search, when a voice fell upon his startled ears, ''My lord the king.'' Who was addressing him? The son of Jesse, the man he had so long desired to kill. David bowed, then addressed Saul: ''Behold, this day thine eyes have seen how that the Lord hath delivered thee today into mine hand in the cave: and some bade me kill thee; but mine eye spared thee; and I said, I will not put forth mine hand against my lord; for he is the Lord's anointed. Moreover, my father, see, yea, see the skirt of thy robe in my hand: for in that I cut off the skirt of thy robe, and killed thee not, know thou and see that there is neither evil nor transgression in mine hand, and I have not sinned against thee; yet thou huntest my soul to take it.''

Saul was deeply moved as he realized how completely he had been in the power of the man whose life he sought. With softened spirit, he exclaimed, ''Is this thy voice, my son David? And Saul lifted up his voice, and wept.'' Then he declared to David: ''Thou art more righteous than I: for thou hast rewarded me good, whereas I have rewarded thee evil. . . . For if a man find his enemy, will he let him go well away? wherefore the Lord reward thee good for that thou hast done unto me this day. And now, behold, I know well that thou shalt surely be king, and that the kingdom of Israel shall be established in thine hand." And David made a covenant with Saul that he would not cut off his name.

David could put no confidence in the assurances of the king, so when Saul returned home, he remained in the mountains.

After evil-minded men do and say wicked things against the Lord's servants, the Spirit of the Lord strives with them, and sometimes they humble their hearts before those they have sought to destroy. But as they again open the door to the evil one, the old enmity is awakened and they return to the same work they repented of. Satan can use such souls with far greater power than before, because they have sinned against greater light.

The People Are Sorry They Asked for a King

"And Samuel died; and all the Israelites were gathered together, and lamented him, and buried him in his house at Ramah." A great and good prophet and an eminent judge had fallen in death. From his youth up, Samuel had walked before Israel in the integrity of his heart. Although Saul had been king, Samuel had wielded a more powerful influence than he, because his record was one of faithfulness and devotion.

The people saw what a mistake they had made in desiring a king that they might not be different from the nations around them. Many looked with alarm at the condition of society, fast becoming leavened with godlessness. Well might Israel mourn that Samuel, the prophet of the Lord, was dead.

The nation had lost him to whom the people had been accustomed to go with their great troubles—lost one who had constantly interceded with God in behalf of the best interests of its people. "The effectual fervent prayer of a righteous man availeth much." James 5:16. The king seemed little less than a madman. Justice was perverted, and order was turned to confusion.

Bitter were the reflections of the people as they looked upon Samuel's quiet resting place and remembered their folly in rejecting him as their ruler; for he had had so close a connection with Heaven that he seemed to bind all Israel to the throne of Jehovah. Samuel had taught them to love and obey God, but now he was dead. The people felt they were left to the mercies of a king who had joined to Satan and who would divorce the people from God and heaven.

David knew that Samuel's death had broken another bond of restraint from the actions of Saul, and he felt less secure than when the prophet lived. So he fled to the wilderness of Paran. In these desolate wilds, realizing that the prophet was dead and the king was his enemy, he sang:

> He that keepeth thee will not slumber.
> Behold, He that keepeth Israel
> Shall neither slumber nor sleep. . . .
> The Lord shall preserve thy going out and thy
> coming in
> From this time forth, and even forevermore.
> Psalm 121:3-8

Nabal, the Hard-Hearted Farmer

David and his men protected the flocks and herds of a wealthy man named Nabal, who had vast possessions in Paran. Nabal's character was churlish and niggardly.

It was the time of sheepshearing, a season of hospitality. David and his men were in need of provisions, and the son of Jesse sent ten young men to Nabal, bidding them greet him: "Peace be both to thee, and peace be to thine house, and peace be unto all that thou hast. And now I have heard that thou hast shearers: now thy shepherds which were with us, we hurt them not, neither was there ought missing unto them, all the while they were in Carmel. [Not Mount Carmel, but a place in the territory of Judah.] Ask thy young men, and they will show thee. Wherefore . . . give, I pray thee, whatsoever cometh to thine hand unto thy servants, and to thy son David.''

This rich man was asked to furnish from his abundance some relief to the necessities of those who had done him such valuable service. The answer Nabal returned indicated his character: "Who is David? and who is the son of Jesse? There be many servants nowadays that break away every man from his master. Shall I then take my bread, and my water, and my flesh that I have killed for my shearers, and give it unto men, whom I know not whence they be?"

David was filled with indignation. He determined to punish the man who had denied him what was his right and had added insult to injury. This impulsive movement was more in harmony with the character of Saul than that of David. The son of Jesse had yet to learn patience.

Nabal's Wise Wife Saves the Household

Without consulting her husband, Abigail made up an ample supply of provisions, which she sent forward in the charge of servants, and herself started out to meet David. When Abigail saw David, "She hastened, and lighted off the ass, and fell before David on her face, and bowed herself to the ground, and fell at his feet, and said, Upon me, my lord, upon me let this iniquity be: and let thine handmaid, I pray thee, speak in thine audience." Abigail addressed David with as much reverence as though speaking to a crowned monarch. With kind words she sought to soothe his irritated feelings. Full of the wisdom and love of God, she made it plain that the unkind course of her husband was in no wise premeditated, but simply the outburst of an unhappy, selfish nature. She then offered her rich provision as a peace offering to the men of David.

She said, "The Lord will certainly make my lord a

sure house; because my lord fighteth the battles of the Lord, and evil hath not been found in thee all thy days." Abigail implied that David ought to fight the battles of the Lord. He was not to seek revenge for personal wrongs, even though persecuted as a traitor. "And it shall come to pass, when the Lord shall have done to my lord according to all the good that he hath spoken concerning thee, and shall have appointed thee prince over Israel; that this shall be no grief unto thee, nor offense of heart unto my lord, either that thou hast shed blood causeless, or that my lord hath avenged himself."

The piety of Abigail, like the fragrance of a flower, breathed out all unconsciously in face and word and action. The Spirit of God was abiding in her soul. Her speech, seasoned with grace, shed a heavenly influence. David trembled as he thought of his rash purpose. "Blessed are the peacemakers; for they shall be called the children of God." Matthew 5:9. Would that many more like this woman of Israel would soothe irritated feelings, prevent rash impulses, and quell great evils by words of calm wisdom.

David's passion died away under the power of Abigail's influence and reasoning. He was convinced that he had lost control of his own spirit. With humble heart, he received the rebuke, in harmony with his own words, "Let the righteous smite me; it shall be a kindness: and let him reprove me; it shall be an excellent oil." Psalm 141:5. He gave thanks and blessings because she advised him righteously. How few take reproof with gratitude and bless those who seek to save them from pursuing an evil course.

Remorse and Fear Take Nabal's Life

When Abigail returned home she found Nabal and his guests in drunken revelry. Not until the next morning did she relate to her husband what had occurred in her interview with David. When he realized how near his folly had brought him to sudden death, he seemed smitten with paralysis. He was filled with horror and sank down in helpless insensibility. After ten days he died. In the midst of his making merry, God had said to him, as to the rich man of the parable, "This night thy soul shall be required of thee." Luke 12:20.

David afterward married Abigail. He was already the husband of one wife, but the custom of the nations of his time had perverted his judgment. The bitter result of marrying many wives was sorely felt throughout all the life of David.

Again the Ziphites, hoping to secure the favor of the king, informed him of David's hiding place. Once more Saul summoned his men of arms and led them in pursuit of David. But friendly spies brought tidings to the son of Jesse; and with a few of his men, David started out to learn the location of his enemy.

It was night when they came upon the tents of the king and his attendants, and saw, unobserved, the camp quiet in slumber. In answer to David's question, "Who will go down with me to Saul to the camp?" Abishai promptly responded, "I will go down with thee."

Hidden by the shadows of the hills, David and his attendant entered the encampment. They came upon Saul sleeping, his spear stuck in the ground and a cruse of water at his head. Beside him lay Abner, his chief commander, and all around them were the soldiers, locked in slumber. Abishai raised his spear. "God hath delivered thine enemy into thine hand this day: now therefore let me smite him, I pray thee, with the spear even to the earth at once, and I will not smite him the second time." He waited for permission, but there fell upon his ear the whispered words: "Destroy him not: for who can stretch forth his hand against the Lord's anointed, and be guiltless? . . . As the Lord liveth, the Lord shall smite; . . . or he shall descend into battle, and perish. The Lord forbid that I should stretch forth mine hand against the Lord's anointed; but, I pray thee, take thou now the spear that is at his bolster, and the cruse of water, and let us go. . . . And no man saw it, nor knew it, neither awaked: . . . because a deep sleep from the Lord was fallen upon them.''

When David was at a safe distance from the camp, he cried with a loud voice to Abner, ''Art not thou a valiant man? and who is like to thee in Israel? wherefore then hast thou not kept thy lord the king? for there came one of the people in to destroy the king thy lord. This thing is not good that thou hast done. As the Lord liveth, ye are worthy to die, because ye have not kept your master, the Lord's anointed. And now see where the king's spear is, and the cruse of water that was at his bolster. And Saul knew David's voice, and said, Is this thy voice, my son David? And David said, It is my voice, my lord, O king. And he said, Wherefore doth my lord thus pursue after his servant? for what have I done? or what evil is in mine hand?''

Again King Saul Confesses He Is Wrong

Again the acknowledgment fell from the lips of the king: ''I have sinned: return, my son David; for I will no more do thee harm, because my soul was precious in thine eyes this day: behold, I have played the fool, and have erred exceedingly.''

David answered, ''Behold the king's spear! and let one of the young men come over and fetch it.'' Although Saul had made the promise, ''I will no more do thee harm,'' David did not place himself in his power.

In parting, Saul exclaimed, ''Blessed be thou, my son David: thou shalt both do great things, and also shalt still prevail.'' But the son of Jesse had no hope that the king would long continue in this frame of mind.

David despaired of reconciliation. It seemed that he should at last fall victim to the malice of the king. With the six hundred men under his command, he passed over to Achish, the king of Gath.

David's conclusion that Saul would accomplish his murderous purpose was formed without the counsel of God. Even while Saul was plotting his destruction, the

Lord was working to secure David the kingdom. Looking at appearances, men interpret the trials and tests that God permits as things that will only work their ruin. David looked on appearances and not at the promises of God. He doubted that he would ever come to the throne. Long trials had wearied his faith and exhausted his patience.

The Lord did not send David for protection to the Philistines, the most bitter foes of Israel. Yet, having lost all confidence in Saul and in those who served him, David threw himself upon the mercies of the enemies of his people. God had appointed him to set up his standard in the land of Judah, and it was want of faith that led him to forsake his post of duty.

Another of David's Mistakes

The Philistines had feared David more than Saul; and by placing himself under the protection of the Philistines, David discovered to them the weakness of his own people. Thus he encouraged these relentless foes to oppress Israel. David had been anointed to stand in defense of the people of God. The Lord would not have His servants give encouragement to the wicked by disclosing the weakness of His people.

Further, the impression was received by his brethren that he had gone to the heathen to serve their gods. By this act, many were led to hold prejudice against him. The very thing Satan desired to have him do, he was led to do. David did not renounce his worship of God nor devotion to His cause, but he sacrificed his trust in Him to his personal safety.

David was cordially received by the king of the Philistines. The king admired him and was flattered to have a Hebrew seek his protection. David brought his family, his household, and all his possessions, as did also his men. To all appearance he had come to settle permanently in the land of Philistia. This was gratifying to Achish, who promised to protect the fugitive Israelites.

At David's request, the king graciously granted Ziklag as a possession. In a town wholly separated for their use, David and his men might worship God with more freedom than in Gath, where heathen rites could prove a source of evil.

While dwelling in this isolated town David made war upon the Geshurites, the Gezrites, and the Amalekites, and left none alive to bring tidings to Gath. He gave Achish to understand that he had been warring against his own nation, the men of Judah. By this dissembling he strengthened the hand of the Philistines, for the king said, "He hath made his people Israel utterly to abhor him; therefore he shall be my servant forever." David was not walking in the counsel of God when he practiced deception.

"And it came to pass in those days, that the Philistines gathered their armies together for warfare, to fight with Israel. And Achish said unto David, Know thou assuredly, that thou shalt go out with me to battle, thou and thy men." David answered the king evasively, "Surely thou shalt know what thy servant can do." Achish pledged his word to bestow upon David a high position at the Philistine court.

But although David's faith had staggered somewhat at the promises of God, he still remembered that Samuel had anointed him king of Israel. He reviewed the mercy of God in preserving him from Saul and determined not to betray a sacred trust. Even though the king of Israel had sought his life, he would not join his forces with the enemies of his people.

66 / Saul Takes His Own Life

"The Philistines gathered themselves together, and came and pitched in Shunem," while Saul and his forces encamped but a few miles distant at the foot of Mount Gilboa. Saul felt alone and defenseless, because God had forsaken him. As he looked abroad upon the Philistine host, "he was afraid, and his heart greatly trembled."

Saul had expected that the son of Jesse would take this opportunity to revenge the wrongs he had suffered. The king was in sore distress. His own unreasoning passion to destroy the chosen of God had involved the nation in great peril. While pursuing David, he had neglected the defense of his kingdom. The Philistines, taking advantage of its unguarded condition, had penetrated into the very heart of the country. While Satan had been urging Saul to destroy David, the same malignant spirit inspired the Philistines to work Saul's ruin. How often the archenemy moves upon some unconsecrated heart to kindle strife in the church, and then, taking advantage of the divided condition of God's people, he stirs up his agents to work their ruin.

On the morrow Saul must engage the Philistines in battle. Shadows of impending doom gathered dark about him. He longed for guidance; in vain he sought counsel from God. "The Lord answered him not, neither by dreams, nor by Urim, nor by prophets."

The Lord never turned away a soul that came to Him in sincerity. Why did He turn Saul away unanswered?

This chapter is based on 1 Samuel 28; 31.

490

The king had rejected the counsel of Samuel the prophet; he had exiled David, the chosen of God; he had slain the priests of the Lord. Could he be answered when he had cut off the channels of communication that Heaven had ordained? It was not pardon for sin and reconciliation with God that Saul sought, but deliverance from his foes. By rebellion he had cut himself off from God. There could be no return but by penitence and contrition.

"Then said Saul unto his servants, Seek me a woman that hath a familiar spirit, that I may go to her, and inquire of her." Necromancy had been forbidden by the Lord, and the sentence of death was pronounced against all who practiced its unholy arts. Saul had commanded that all wizards and those that had familiar spirits should be put to death. But now, in desperation, he had recourse to that which he had condemned as an abomination.

A woman who had a familiar spirit was living in concealment at Endor. She had entered into covenant with Satan to fulfill his purposes and, in return, the prince of evil revealed secret things to her.

Disguising himself, Saul went by night with two attendants to seek the sorceress. Oh, pitiable sight! the king of Israel led captive by Satan! Trust in God and obedience to His will were the only conditions upon which Saul could be king of Israel. Had he complied with these conditions, his kingdom would have been secure; God would have been his guide, the Omnipotent his shield. Although his rebellion and obstinacy had well-nigh silenced the divine voice in the soul, there was still opportunity for repentance. But when in his peril he turned to Satan, he cut the last tie that bound him to his Maker. He placed himself fully under the control of the demoniac power which for years had brought him to the verge of destruction.

Under cover of darkness, Saul and his attendants safely passed the Philistine host. They crossed the mountain ridge to the lonely home of the sorceress of

Endor. Disguised as he was, Saul's lofty stature and kingly bearing declared that he was no common soldier. His rich gifts strengthened her suspicions. To his request the woman answered, "Saul hath . . . cut off those that have familiar spirits, and the wizards, out of the land: wherefore then layest thou a snare for my life, to cause me to die?" Then "Saul sware to her by the Lord, saying, As the Lord liveth, there shall no punishment happen to thee for this thing." And when she said, "Whom shall I bring up unto thee?" he answered, "Samuel."

After practicing her incantations, she said, "I saw gods ascending out of the earth. . . . An old man cometh up; and he is covered with a mantle. And Saul perceived that it was Samuel, and he stooped with his face to the ground, and bowed himself."

It was not God's prophet that came forth. Samuel was not present in that haunt of evil spirits. Satan could as easily assume the form of Samuel as he could assume that of an angel of light when he tempted Christ in the wilderness.

The message to Saul from the pretended prophet was, "Why hast thou disquieted me, to bring me up?" Saul answered, "I am sore distressed; for the Philistines make war against me, and God is departed from me, and answereth me no more, neither by prophets, nor dreams: therefore I have called thee, that thou mayest make known unto me what I shall do."

When Samuel was living, Saul had despised his counsel. But now, in order to communicate with Heaven's ambassador, he had recourse to the messenger of hell! Saul had placed himself fully in the power of Satan, and now he whose only delight is misery and destruction made the most of his advantage to ruin the unhappy king. In answer came the terrible message, professedly from the lips of Samuel:

"The Lord is departed from thee, and is become thine enemy. . . . The Lord hath rent the kingdom out of thine hand, and given it to thy neighbor, even to David: because thou obeyedst not the voice of the Lord, nor executedst His fierce wrath upon Amalek, therefore hath the Lord done this thing unto thee this day. Moreover the Lord will also deliver Israel with thee into the hand of the Philistines.''

Satan had led Saul to justify himself in defiance of Samuel's reproofs and warning. But now he turned on him, presenting the enormity of his sin and the hopelessness of pardon, that he might goad him to desperation. Nothing could better drive him to despair and self-destruction.

Saul was faint with fasting, terrified, and conscience-stricken. His form swayed like an oak before the tempest, and he fell prostrate to the earth.

The sorceress was filled with alarm. The king of Israel lay before her like one dead. She besought him to partake of food, urging that since she had imperiled her life in granting his desire, he should yield to her request for the preservation of his own. Saul yielded, and the woman set before him the fatted calf and bread hastily prepared.

What a scene! In the wild cave of the sorceress, in the presence of Satan's messenger, he who had been anointed of God as king over Israel sat down to eat, in preparation for the day's deadly strife.

By consulting that spirit of darkness, Saul had destroyed himself. Oppressed by the horror of despair, it would be impossible to inspire his army with courage. He could not lead the minds of Israel to look to God as their helper. Thus the prediction of evil would work its own accomplishment.

The Sad End of the "Anointed of the Lord"

The armies of Israel and the Philistines closed in mortal combat. Though the fearful scene in the cave of Endor had driven all hope from his heart, Saul fought with desperate valor. But it was in vain. "The men of Israel fled from before the Philistines, and fell down slain in Mount Gilboa." Saul had seen his soldiers falling around him and his three princely sons cut down by the sword. Himself wounded, he could neither fight nor flee. Escape was impossible and, determined not to be taken alive by the Philistines, Saul took his own life by falling upon his sword.

Thus the first king of Israel perished, with the guilt of self-murder on his soul. His life had been a failure, and he went down in dishonor and despair.

The tidings of defeat spread far and wide, carrying terror to all Israel. The people fled from the cities, and the Philistines took undisturbed possession. Saul's reign, independent of God, had well-nigh proved the ruin of his people.

On the day following, the Philistines discovered the bodies of Saul and his three sons. They cut off the head of Saul and stripped him of his armor. Then the head and the armor, reeking with blood, were sent to the country of the Philistines as a trophy of victory, "to publish it in the house of their idols, and among the people." Thus the glory of victory was ascribed to the power of false gods, and the name of Jehovah was dishonored.

In Beth-shan the bodies of Saul and his sons were hung up in chains, to be devoured by birds of prey. But the brave men of Jabesh-gilead, remembering Saul's deliverance in earlier and happier years, now manifested their gratitude by rescuing the bodies of the king and princes and giving them honorable burial. Thus the noble deed performed forty years before, secured for Saul and his sons burial by tender and pitying hands in that dark hour of defeat and dishonor.

67 / Ancient and Modern Spiritualism

The Scripture account of Saul's visit to the woman of Endor has been a perplexity to many students of the Bible. Some take the position that Samuel was actually present. But the Bible furnishes ground for a contrary conclusion.

If Samuel was in heaven, he must have been summoned from thence either by God or by Satan. None can believe for a moment that Satan had power to call the prophet from heaven to honor the incantations of an abandoned woman. Nor can we conclude that God summoned him to the witch's cave, for the Lord had already refused to communicate with Saul by dreams, by Urim, or by prophets.

The message itself is evidence of its origin. Its object was not to lead Saul to repentance, but to urge him on to ruin. This is not the work of God, but of Satan. Furthermore, the act of Saul in consulting a sorceress is cited in Scripture as one reason why he was rejected by God: "Saul died for his transgression which he committed against the Lord, even against the word of the Lord, which he kept not, and also for asking counsel of one that had a familiar spirit, *to inquire of it;* and inquired not of the Lord: therefore He slew him, and turned the kingdom unto David the son of Jesse." 1 Chronicles 10:13, 14. Saul did not communicate with Samuel, the prophet of God, but with Satan. Satan could not present the real Samuel, but a counterfeit that served his purpose of deception.

Ancient sorcery and witchcraft were founded upon a

belief in communion with the dead. Those who practiced necromancy claimed to obtain through departed spirits a knowledge of future events. "When they shall say unto you, Seek unto them that have familiar spirits, and unto wizards that peep and that mutter; should not a people seek unto their God? *for the living to the dead?*" Isaiah 8:19.

The gods of the heathen were believed to be the deified spirits of departed heroes. Thus the religion of the heathen was a worship of the dead. Speaking of the apostasy of the Israelites, the psalmist says, "They joined themselves also unto Baal-peor, and *ate the sacrifices of the dead*" (Psalm 106:28), that is, sacrifices that had been offered to the dead.

In nearly every system of heathenism, the dead were believed to communicate their will to men, and also, when consulted, to give them counsel. Even in professedly Christian lands, the practice of communicating with beings claiming to be the spirits of the departed has become widespread. Spiritual beings sometimes appear in the form of deceased friends and relate incidents connected with their lives and perform acts which they performed while living. In this way they lead men to believe that their dead friends are angels. With many their word has greater weight than the Word of God.

Many regard spiritualism as a mere imposture. Its manifestations are attributed to fraud. But while it is true that the results of trickery have often been palmed off as genuine, there have also been marked evidences of supernatural power. And many who reject spiritualism as human cunning will, when confronted with manifestations which they cannot account for, be led to acknowledge its claims.

Modern spiritualism and ancient witchcraft—all having communion with the dead as their vital principle—are founded upon that first lie by which Satan beguiled Eve in Eden: "Ye shall not surely die: for God doth know that in the day ye eat thereof, . . . ye shall be as gods.'' Genesis 3:4, 5. Alike based upon falsehood, they are alike from the father of lies.

God said: "The dead know not anything. . . . Neither have they any more a portion forever in anything that is done under the sun.'' Ecclesiastes 9:5, 6. "His breath goeth forth, he returneth to his earth; in that very day his thoughts perish.'' Psalm 146:4. The Lord declared to Israel: "The soul that turneth after such as have familiar spirits, and after wizards, to go a whoring after them, I will even set my face against that soul, and will cut him off from among his people.'' Leviticus 20:6.

The "familiar spirits'' were not the spirits of the dead, but evil angels, the messengers of Satan. The psalmist, speaking of Israel, says that "they sacrificed their sons and their daughters unto devils,'' and in the next verse he explains that they sacrificed them "unto the idols of Canaan.'' Psalm 106:37, 38. In their supposed worship of dead men, they were, in reality, worshiping demons.

Identity of Spiritualism Revealed

Modern spiritualism is a revival of the witchcraft and demon worship that God condemned of old. It is foretold in the Scriptures, which declare that "in the latter times some shall depart from the faith, giving heed to seducing spirits, and doctrines of devils.'' 1 Timothy 4:1. In the last days there will be false teachers. See 2 Peter 2:1, 2. Spiritualist teachers refuse to acknowledge Christ as the Son of God. Concerning such teachers the beloved John declares: "Who is a liar but he that denieth that Jesus is the Christ? He is antichrist, that denieth the Father and the Son. Whosoever denieth the Son, the same hath not the Father.'' 1 John 2:22, 23. Spiritualism, by denying Christ, denies both the Father and the Son, and the Bible pronounces it the manifestation of antichrist.

The lure by which spiritualism attracts the multitudes is its pretended power to draw aside the veil from the future. God has in His Word opened before us the great events of the future—all that is essential for us to know. But it is Satan's purpose to destroy men's confidence in God, lead them to seek a knowledge of what God has wisely veiled from them and despise what He has revealed in His Holy Word.

Many become restless when they cannot know the outcome of affairs. They cannot endure uncertainty and refuse to wait to see the salvation of God. They give way to rebellious feelings and run hither and thither in passionate grief, seeking intelligence concerning that which has not been revealed. If they would but trust in God and watch unto prayer, they would find divine consolation.

This haste to tear away the veil from the future reveals a lack of faith in God, and Satan inspires confidence in his power to foretell things to come. By experience gained through long ages, he can often forecast, with a degree of accuracy, some future events to deceive misguided souls and bring them under his power.

God Himself is the light of His people. He bids them fix their eyes by faith upon the glories that are veiled from human sight. They have light from the throne of heaven and have no desire to turn to the messengers of Satan.

The demon's message to Saul was not meant to reform him, but to goad him to despair and ruin. Oftener, however, it serves the tempter's purpose best to lure men to destruction by flattery. Truth is lightly regarded, and impurity permitted. Spiritualism declares that there is no death, no sin, no judgment, no retribution; desire is the highest law, and man is accountable only to himself. The barriers that God has erected to guard truth, purity, and reverence are broken down, and many are thus emboldened in sin.

God is leading His people out from the abominations of the world, that they may keep His law. Because of this, the rage of "the accuser of our brethren" knows no bounds. "The devil is come down unto you, having great wrath, because he knoweth that he hath but a short time." Revelation 12:10, 12. Satan is determined to destroy the people of God and cut them off from their inheritance. The admonition, "Watch ye and pray, lest ye enter into temptation" (Mark 14:38), was never more needed than now.

68 / David's Heavy Trial

David and his men had not taken part in the battle between Saul and the Philistines, though they had marched with the Philistines to the field of conflict. As the two armies prepared to join battle the son of Jesse found himself in great perplexity. Should he quit the post assigned him and retire from the field with ingratitude and treachery to Achish, who had protected him? Such an act would cover his name with infamy and expose him to the wrath of enemies more to be feared than Saul.

Yet he could not for a moment consent to fight against Israel and become a traitor to his country, the enemy of God and of His people. It would forever bar his way to the throne of Israel. And should Saul be slain in the engagement, his death would be charged upon David.

Far better would it have been to find refuge in God's strong fortress of the mountains than with the avowed enemies of His people. But the Lord in His great mercy did not punish His servant by leaving him in his distress and perplexity. Though David, losing his grasp on divine power, had turned aside from the path of strict integrity, it was still the purpose of his heart to be true to God. Angels of the Lord moved upon the Philistine princes to protest against the presence of David and his force with the army in the approaching conflict.

"What do these Hebrews here?" cried the Philistine lords, pressing about Achish. The latter answered, "Is not this David, the servant of Saul the king of Israel,

This chapter is based on 1 Samuel 29; 30; 2 Samuel 1.

which hath been with me these days, or these years, and I have found no fault in him since he fell unto me unto this day?''

David Sent Back to Ziklag

But the princes angrily persisted: ''Make this fellow return, that he may go again to his place which thou has appointed him, and let him go not down with us to battle, lest in the battle he be an adversary to us: for wherewith should he reconcile himself unto his master? should it not be with the heads of these men? Is not this David, of whom they sang one to another in dances, saying, Saul slew his thousands, and David his ten thousands?'' They did not believe that David would fight against his own people. In the heat of battle he could inflict greater harm on the Philistines than the whole of Saul's army.

Achish, calling David, said, ''Surely as Jehovah liveth, thou hast been upright, . . . for I have not found evil in thee since the day of thy coming unto me unto this day. Nevertheless the lords favor thee not. Wherefore now return, and go in peace, that thou displease not the lords of the Philistines.'' Thus the snare in which David had become entangled was broken.

After three days' travel David and his band of six hundred men reached Ziklag, their Philistine home. But a scene of desolation met their view. The Amalekites had avenged themselves for this incursion into their territory, had surprised the city while it was unguarded, and having sacked and burned it, had departed, taking all the women and children as captives, with much spoil.

Dumb with horror and amazement, David and his men gazed upon the smoldering ruins. Then as a sense of their terrible desolation burst upon them, those battle-scarred warriors ''lifted up their voice and wept, until they had no more power to weep.''

Here again David was chastened for the lack of faith that led him to place himself among the foes of God and

His people. David had provoked the Amalekites by his attack upon them; yet, too confident of security in the midst of his enemies, he had left the city unguarded. Maddened with grief and rage, his soldiers threatened to stone their leader.

David's Great Temptation to Discouragement

All that David held dear on earth had been swept from him. Saul had driven him from his country; the Amalekites had plundered his city; his wives and children had been made prisoners; and his friends had threatened him with death.

In this hour of utmost extremity, David looked earnestly to God for help. He "encouraged himself in the Lord," recalling many evidences of God's favor. "What time I am afraid, I will trust in thee" (Psalm 56:3), was the language of his heart. Though he could not discern a way out of the difficulty, God would teach him what to do.

Sending for Abiathar the priest, "David inquired of the Lord, saying, If I pursue after this troup, shall I overtake them?" The answer was, "Pursue: for thou shalt surely overtake them, and shalt without fail recover all."

David and his soldiers at once set out in pursuit of their fleeing foe. So rapid was their march that two hundred of the band were compelled by exhaustion to remain behind. But David with the remaining four hundred pressed forward.

Advancing, they came upon an Egyptian slave, apparently about to perish from weariness and hunger. Upon receiving food and drink he revived. He had been left to die by the invading force. Having exacted a promise that he should not be slain or delivered to his master, he consented to lead David to the camp of their enemies.

As they came in sight of the encampment a scene of revelry met their gaze. The victorious host were "spread abroad upon all the earth, eating and drinking, and dancing, because of all the great spoil that they had taken out of the land of the Philistines, and out of the land of Judah." An immediate attack was ordered. The Amalekites were surprised and thrown into confusion. The battle was continued until nearly the entire host was slain. "David recovered all that the Amalekites had carried away: and David rescued his two wives. And there was nothing lacking to them, neither small nor great, neither sons nor daughters, neither spoil, nor anything that they had taken to them: David recovered all."

But for the restraining power of God, the Amalekites would have destroyed the people of Ziklag. They decided to spare the captives, desiring to heighten the triumph by leading home a large number of prisoners to sell as slaves. Thus, unwittingly, they fulfilled God's purpose, keeping the prisoners to be restored to their husbands and fathers.

God Is Ever at Work to Counteract Evil

With great rejoicing the victors took up their homeward march. The more selfish and unruly of the four hundred urged that those who had had no part in the battle should not share the spoils. But David would permit no such arrangement. "Ye shall not do so, my brethren," he said, "with that which the Lord hath given us. . . . As his part is that goeth down to the battle, so shall his part be that tarrieth by the stuff; they shall part alike."

David and his band had captured extensive flocks and herds belonging to the Amalekites. These were called "David's spoil," and upon returning to Ziklag, he sent from this spoil presents to the elders of his own tribe of Judah. All were remembered who had befriended him and his followers in the mountain fastnesses, when he had been forced to flee for his life.

As David and his warriors labored to restore their ruined homes, they watched for tidings of the battle fought between Israel and the Philistines. Suddenly a messenger entered the town, "with his clothes rent, and earth upon his head." He was at once brought to David, before whom he bowed as a powerful prince whose favor he desired. The fugitive reported Saul's defeat and death and the death of Jonathan. But he went beyond a simple statement of facts. The stranger hoped to secure honor to himself as the slayer of the king. With an air of boasting the man related that he found the monarch of Israel wounded, and that at his own request the messenger had slain him. The crown from his head and the golden bracelets from his arms he had brought to David. He confidently expected a rich reward for the part he had acted.

David Grieved for Saul

But "David took hold on his clothes, and rent them; and likewise all the men that were with him: and they mourned, and wept, and fasted until even, for Saul, and for Jonathan his son, and for the people of the Lord, and for the house of Israel; because they were fallen by the sword."

The first shock of the fearful tidings past, David's thoughts returned to the stranger herald and the crime of which, according to his own statement, he was guilty. "Whence art thou?" And he answered, "I am the son of a stranger, an Amalekite. And David said unto him, How wast thou not afraid to stretch forth thine hand to destroy the Lord's anointed?" Twice David had refused to lift his hand against him who had been consecrated by the command of God to rule over Israel. Yet the Amalekite had accused himself of a crime worthy of death. David said, "Thy blood be upon thy head; for thy mouth hath testified against thee, saying, I have slain the Lord's anointed."

David's grief at the death of Saul was sincere and deep, evincing the generosity of a noble nature. He did not exult in the fall of his enemy. The obstacle that had barred his access to the throne of Israel was removed, but at this he did not rejoice. Now nothing in Saul's history was thought of but that which was noble and kingly. The name of Saul was linked with that of Jonathan, whose friendship had been so true and unselfish.

The song in which David gave utterance to the feelings of the heart became a treasure to his nation and to the people of God in all subsequent ages. See 2 Samuel 1:19-27.

69/ David at Last Crowned King

The death of Saul removed the dangers that had made David an exile. The way was now open for him to return to his own land. "David inquired of the Lord, saying, Shall I go up into any of the cities of Judah? And the Lord said unto him, Go up. And David said, Whither shall I go up? And he said, Unto Hebron."

David and his followers immediately prepared to obey. As the caravan entered the city, the men of Judah were waiting to welcome David as the future king of Israel. Arrangements were at once made for his coronation. "And there they anointed David king over the house of Judah." But no effort was made to establish his authority over the other tribes.

Upon learning of the brave deed of the men of Jabesh-gilead in rescuing the bodies of Saul and Jonathan and giving them honorable burial, David sent the message, "Blessed be ye of the Lord, that ye have showed this kindness unto your lord, even unto Saul, and have buried him. And now the Lord show kindness and truth unto you: and I also will requite you this kindness."

The Philistines did not oppose the action of Judah in making David a king. They hoped that because of their former kindness to David the extension of his power would work to their advantage. But David's reign was not to be free from trouble.

God had chosen David to be king of Israel, yet hardly had his authority been acknowledged by the men of Judah, when Ishbosheth, the son of Saul, was

This chapter is based on 2 Samuel 2 to 5:5.

set upon a rival throne in Israel. Ishbosheth was a weak, incompetent representative of the house of Saul, while David was preeminently qualified. Abner, the chief agent in raising Ishbosheth to kingly power, was the most distinguished man in Israel. He knew that David had been appointed by the Lord to the throne, but he was not willing that the son of Jesse should succeed to the kingdom.

Abner was ambitious and unprincipled. He had been influenced by Saul to despise the man whom God had chosen to reign over Israel. His hatred had been increased by the cutting rebuke that David had given him when the cruse of water and the spear of the king had been taken from the side of Saul as he slept.

Determined to create division in Israel whereby he himself might be exalted, he employed the representative of departed royalty to advance his own selfish ambitions. He knew that Saul's first successful campaigns had not been forgotten by the army. With determination, this rebellious leader went forward to carry out his plans.

Mahanaim, on the farther side of Jordan, was chosen as the royal residence. Here the coronation of Ishbosheth took place. His reign extended over all Israel except Judah. For two years the son of Saul enjoyed his honors in his secluded capital. But Abner, intent upon extending his power over all Israel, prepared for aggressive warfare. And "there was long war between the house of Saul and the house of David: but David waxed stronger and stronger, and the house of Saul waxed weaker and weaker."

At last Abner, becoming incensed against the incompetent Ishbosheth, deserted to David, with the offer to bring over to him all the tribes of Israel. His proposals were accepted. But the favorable reception of so famed a warrior excited the jealousy of Joab, commander-in-chief of David's army. There was a blood feud between Abner and Joab, the former having slain Asahel, Joab's brother, during the war between Israel and Judah. Now Joab basely took occasion to waylay and murder Abner.

David, upon hearing of this treacherous assault, exclaimed, "I and my kingdom are guiltless before the Lord forever from the blood of Abner the son of Ner. Let it rest on the head of Joab." In view of the unsettled state of the kingdom and the power of the murderers, David could not visit the crime with just retribution, yet he publicly manifested his abhorrence. The king followed Abner's bier as chief mourner, and at the grave he pronounced an elegy which was a cutting rebuke of the murderers.

> Died Abner as a fool dieth? . . .
> As a man falleth before wicked men,
> So fellest thou.

David's recognition of one who had been his bitter enemy won the admiration of all Israel. "For all the people and all Israel understood that day that it was not of the king to slay Abner the son of Ner." In the private circle of his trusted counselors and attendants, the king recognized his own inability to punish the murderers as he desired. He left them to the justice of God. "The Lord shall reward the doer of evil according to his wickedness."

"When Saul's son heard that Abner was dead in Hebron, his hands were feeble, and all the Israelites were troubled." Soon another act of treachery completed the downfall of the waning power. Ishbosheth was murdered by two of his captains, who, cutting off his head, hastened with it to the king of Judah, hoping thus to ingratiate themselves in his favor.

David Punishes the Murderers of His Enemy

But David did not desire the aid of treachery to establish his power. He told these murderers of the doom visited upon him who boasted of slaying Saul. "How much more," he added, "when wicked men have slain a righteous person in his own house upon his bed? Shall I not therefore now require his blood of your hand, and take you away from the earth? And David commanded his young men, and they slew them."

After the death of Ishbosheth, there was a general desire among the leading men of Israel that David become king of all the tribes. They declared, "Thou wast he that leddest out and broughtest in Israel: and the Lord said to thee, Thou shalt feed My people Israel, and thou shalt be a captain over Israel. So all the elders of Israel came to the king to Hebron; and king David made a league with them in Hebron before the Lord." Thus through the providence of God the way had been opened for him to come to the throne.

The change in the sentiments of the people was decisive. The revolution was quiet and dignified, befitting the work they were doing. Nearly half a million souls, the former subjects of Saul, thronged Hebron and its environs. The hour for the coronation was appointed. The man who had been expelled from the court of Saul, who had fled to the mountains and hills and to the caves of the earth to preserve his life, was about to receive the highest honor that can be conferred upon man by his fellowman. Priests and elders, officers and soldiers with glittering spear and helmet, and strangers from long distances, stood to witness the coronation.

David was arrayed in the royal robe. The sacred oil was put upon his brow by the high priest, for the anointing by Samuel had been prophetic of what would take place at the inauguration of the king. The time had come, and David was consecrated to his office as God's vicegerent. The scepter was placed in his hands. The covenant of his righteous sovereignty was written, and the people gave their pledges of loyalty. Israel had a king by divine appointment.

He who had waited patiently for the Lord, beheld the promise of God fulfilled. "And David went on, and grew great, and the Lord God of hosts was with him." 2 Samuel 5:10.

70 / The Prosperous Reign of David

Twenty miles from Hebron a place was selected as the future metropolis of the kingdom. It had been called Salem. Eight hundred years before, it had been the home of Melchizedek, priest of the most high God. It held a central position in the country and was protected by hills. On the border between Benjamin and Judah, it was close to Ephraim and easy of access to the other tribes.

To secure this location the Hebrews must dispossess a remnant of the Canaanites, who held a fortified position on the mountains of Zion and Moriah. This stronghold was called Jebus and its inhabitants, Jebusites. For centuries, Jebus had been looked upon as impregnable. But it was besieged and taken under the command of Joab, who, as reward, was made commander-in-chief of the armies of Israel. Jebus became the national capital, and its heathen name was changed to Jerusalem.

Hiram, king of Tyre, now lent his aid to David in erecting a palace at Jerusalem. Ambassadors were sent from Tyre, accompanied by architects and workmen and costly material.

The increasing strength of Israel in its union under David excited the hostility of the Philistines, and they again invaded the country, taking up their position but a short distance from Jerusalem. David with his men of war retired to the stronghold of Zion. "And David inquired of the Lord, saying, Shall I go up to the Philistines? wilt Thou deliver them into mine hand? And the Lord said unto David, Go up: for I will doubtless deliver the Philistines into thine hand."

This chapter is based on 2 Samuel 5:6-25; 6; 7; 9; 10.

510

David advanced at once, defeated them, and took from them the gods which they had brought to ensure victory. Exasperated by their defeat, the Philistines gathered a larger force and returned to the conflict. Again David sought the Lord, and the great I AM took the direction of the armies of Israel.

God instructed David: "Thou shalt not go up; but . . . come upon them over against the mulberry trees. And . . . when thou hearest the sound of a going in the tops of the mulberry trees, . . . then thou shalt bestir thyself: for then shalt the Lord go out before thee, to smite the host of the Philistines." If David, like Saul, had chosen his own way, success would not have attended him. But he did as the Lord commanded, and he "smote the host of the Philistines from Gibeon even to Gezer. And the fame of David went out into all lands; and the Lord brought the fear of him upon all nations." 1 Chronicles 14:16, 17.

Ark Returned to Jerusalem

Now that David was established on the throne, he turned to accomplish a cherished purpose—to bring up the ark of God to Jerusalem. It was fitting that the capital of the nation should be honored with the token of the divine Presence.

David's purpose was to make the occasion a scene of great rejoicing and imposing display. The people responded gladly. The high priest and the princes and leading men of the tribes assembled at Kirjath-jearim. David was aglow with holy zeal. The ark was brought out from the house of Abinadab and placed upon a new cart drawn by oxen, while two of the sons of Abinadab attended it.

The men of Israel followed with shouts and songs of rejoicing, a multitude of voices joining in melody with the sound of musical instruments. "David and the house of Israel played before the Lord . . . on harps, and on psalteries, and on timbrels, and on cornets, and on cymbals." With solemn gladness the vast procession wound its way along the hills and valleys toward the Holy City.

But "when they came to Nachon's threshing floor, Uzzah put forth his hand to the ark of God, and took hold of it; for the oxen shook it. And the anger of the Lord was kindled against Uzzah, and God smote him there for his rashness [marginal reading]; and there he died by the ark of God." Terror fell on the rejoicing throng. David was greatly alarmed, and in his heart questioned the justice of God. Why had that fearful judgment been sent to turn gladness into grief and mourning? Feeling that it would be unsafe to have the ark near him, David determined to let it remain where it was. A place was found for it nearby, at the house of Obed-edom.

God Requires Precise Obedience

The fate of Uzzah was a divine judgment upon the violation of a most explicit command. None but the priests, the descendants of Aaron, were to touch the ark, or even look upon it uncovered. The divine direction was, "The sons of Kohath shall come to bear it: but they shall not touch any holy thing, lest they die." Numbers 4:15. The priests were to cover the ark, and then the Kohathites must lift it by the staves, which were placed in rings on each side of the ark. They should bear the ark *"upon their shoulders."* Numbers 7:9. There had been an inexcusable disregard of the Lord's directions.

David and his people had engaged in a sacred work with glad and willing hearts, but it was not performed in accordance with the Lord's directions. The Philistines, who had no knowledge of God's law, had placed the ark upon a cart when they returned it to Israel. But the Israelites had a plain statement of the will of God in these matters, and their neglect of these instructions was dishonoring to God. Transgression of God's law had lessened Uzzah's sense of its sacredness. With unconfessed sins upon him, in face of the divine prohibition, he had presumed to touch the symbol of God's

In direct disregard of a divine command, Uzzah reached out and touched the sacred ark—and instantly fell dead beside it.

presence. God can accept no partial obedience, no lax way of treating His commandments. The death of one man, by leading the people to repentance, might prevent judgments upon thousands.

The Ark Brings Blessings to Those Who Love the Lord.

Feeling that his own heart was not wholly right with God, David feared the ark, lest some sin bring judgments upon him. But Obed-edom welcomed the sacred symbol as the pledge of God's favor to the obedient. All Israel watched to see how it would fare with his household. "And the Lord blessed Obed-edom, and all his household." David was led to realize as never before the sacredness of the law of God and the necessity of strict obedience.

At the end of three months, he resolved to make another attempt to move the ark, and he now gave earnest heed to carry out the directions of the Lord. Again a vast assemblage gathered about the dwelling place of Obed-edom. With reverent care the ark was placed upon the shoulders of men of divine appointment, and with trembling hearts the vast procession set forth. By David's direction sacrifices were offered. Rejoicing now took the place of trembling and terror. The king had laid aside his royal robes and attired himself in a plain linen ephod as worn by the priests. (The ephod was sometimes worn by others besides the priests.) In this holy service he would take his place before God on an equality with his subjects. Jehovah was to be the sole object of reverence.

Again the music of harp and cornet, trumpet and cymbal, floated heavenward, with the melody of many voices. "And David danced before the Lord," keeping time to the measure of the song.

David's dancing in reverent joy before God has been cited in justification of the modern dance, but in our day dancing is associated with folly and reveling. Morals are sacrificed to pleasure. God is not an object of thought; prayer would be out of place. Amusements that weaken love for sacred things are not to be sought by Christians. The music and dancing in joyful praise of God at the removal of the ark had not the faintest resemblance to the dissipation of modern dancing. The one exalted God's holy name. The other is a device of Satan to cause men to forget and dishonor God.

The triumphal procession approached the capital. Then a burst of song demanded of the watchers upon the walls that the gates of the Holy City be thrown open:

> Lift up your heads, O ye gates;
> And be ye lift up, ye everlasting doors;
> And the King of glory shall come in.

A band of singers and players answered:

> Who is this King of glory?

From another company came the response:

> The Lord strong and mighty,
> The Lord mighty in battle.

Then hundreds of voices, uniting, swelled the triumphal chorus:

> Lift up your heads, O ye gates;
> Even lift them up, ye everlasting doors;
> And the King of glory shall come in.

Again was heard, "Who is the King of glory?" And the voice of the great multitude, like "the sound of many waters," was heard in rapturous reply:

> The Lord of hosts,
> He is the King of glory.
>   Psalm 24:7-10

Then the gates were opened wide, and with reverent

awe the ark was deposited in the tent prepared for its reception. The service ended, the king himself pronounced a benediction upon his people.

This celebration was the most sacred event that had yet marked the reign of David. As the last beams of the setting sun bathed the tabernacle in hallowed light, the king's heart was uplifted in gratitude to God that the blessed symbol of His presence was now so near the throne of Israel.

But there was one who witnessed the scene of rejoicing with a spirit widely different. "As the ark of the Lord came into the city of David, Michal Saul's daughter, looked through a window, and saw King David leaping and dancing before the Lord; and she despised him in her heart." She went out to meet him and poured forth a torrent of bitter words, keen and cutting:

"How glorious was the king of Israel today, who uncovered himself in the eyes of the handmaids of his servants, as one of the vain fellows shamelessly uncovereth himself!"

David felt that it was the service of God which Michal had despised and he answered: "It was before the Lord, which chose me before thy father, and before all his house, to appoint me ruler over the people of the Lord, over Israel: therefore will I play before the Lord. And I will yet be more vile than thus, and will be base in mine own sight: and of the maidservants which thou hast spoken of, of them shall I be had in honor." To David's rebuke was added that of the Lord. Because of her pride and arrogance, Michal "had no child unto the day of her death."

Nation Freed From Idolatry

The removal of the ark had made a lasting impression upon the people of Israel, kindling anew their zeal for Jehovah. David endeavored to deepen these impressions. Song was made a regular part of religious worship, and David composed psalms to be sung by the people in their journeys to the annual feasts. The influence thus exerted resulted in freeing the nation from idolatry. Many of the surrounding peoples were led to think favorably of Israel's God, who had done such great things for His people.

David had erected a palace for himself, and he felt that it was not fitting for the ark of God to rest within a tent. He determined to build for it a temple of such magnificence as should express Israel's appreciation of the abiding presence of Jehovah their king. Communicating his purpose to the prophet Nathan, he received the response, "Do all that is in thine heart; for the Lord is with thee."

But that same night the word of the Lord came to Nathan, giving him a message for the king. David was to be deprived of the privilege of building a house for God, but he was granted an assurance of divine favor to him, to his posterity, and to the kingdom of Israel.

The reason David was not to build the temple was declared: "Thou hast shed blood abundantly, and hast made great wars: thou shalt not build a house unto My name. . . . Behold, a son shall be born to thee, who shall be a man of rest; and I will give him rest from all his enemies; . . . his name shall be Solomon [peaceable], and I will give peace and quietness unto Israel in his days. He shall build a house for My name." 1 Chronicles 22:8-10.

Though the cherished purpose of his heart had been denied, David received the message with gratitude. He knew that it would be an honor to his name to perform the work he had purposed to do, but he was ready to submit to the will of God. How often those who have passed the strength of manhood cling to the hope of accomplishing some great work which they are unfitted to perform! God's providence may speak, declaring that it is theirs to prepare the way for another to accomplish it. But instead of gratefully submitting to divine direction, many fall back as if slighted. If they cannot do the one thing they desire to do, they will do nothing. Many vainly endeavor to accomplish a work for which they are insufficient, while that which they might do, lies neglected. And because of this the greater work is hindered.

David, in his covenant with Jonathan, had promised that he would show kindness to the house of Saul. Mindful of this the king made inquiry, "Is there yet any that is left of the house of Saul, that I may show him kindness for Jonathan's sake?" He was told of a son of Jonathan, Mephibosheth, who had been lame from childhood. The nurse of this child had let him fall, making him a lifelong cripple. David now summoned the young man to court, and the private possessions of Saul were restored to him for the support of his household; but the son of Jonathan was himself to be the constant guest of the king. Mephibosheth had been led to cherish a strong prejudice against David as a usurper; but the monarch's continued kindness won the heart of the young man. Like his father Jonathan, he felt that his interest was one with that of the king whom God had chosen.

After David's establishment upon the throne of Israel, the nation enjoyed a long interval of peace. The surrounding peoples soon thought it prudent to desist from open hostilities, and David refrained from aggressive war. At last, however, he made war upon Israel's old enemies, the Philistines and Moabites, and made them tributary.

Hostile Nations Plot Against David

Then there was formed against David a vast coalition of surrounding nations, out of which grew the greatest wars and greatest victories of his reign and the most extensive accessions to his power. This hostile alliance had been wholly unprovoked by him. The circumstances were these:

Tidings were received at Jerusalem announcing the death of Nahash, king of the Ammonites, who had shown kindness to David when he was a fugitive from

Saul. Desiring to express his appreciation of the favor shown him in his distress, David sent a message of sympathy to Hanun, son of the Ammonite king.

The message of David was misconstrued by Hanun's counselors. They "said unto Hanun their lord, Thinkest thou that David doth honor thy father, that he hath sent comforters unto thee? hath not David rather sent his servants unto thee, to search the city, and to spy it out, and to overthrow it?" They could have no conception of the generous spirit that inspired David's message. Listening to his counselors, Hanun regarded David's messengers as spies and loaded them with scorn and insult.

The Ammonites had been permitted to carry out the evil purposes of their hearts that their real character might be revealed to David. It was not God's will that Israel enter into a league with this heathen people.

Knowing that the insult offered to Israel would surely be avenged, the Ammonites made preparation for war. The inhabitants of the region between the river Euphrates and the Mediterranean leagued with the Ammonites to crush Israel.

The Hebrews did not wait for the invasion. Under Joab they advanced toward the Ammonite capital. The united forces of the allies were overcome in the first engagement, but the next year they renewed the war. David took the field in person, and by the blessing of God inflicted a defeat so disastrous that the Syrians, from Lebanon to the Euphrates, not only gave up the war, but became tributary to Israel.

The dangers that threatened the nation with destruction proved to be the means by which it rose to greatness. Commemorating his deliverance, David sang:

> Blessed be my rock; and exalted be the God of my
> salvation:
> Even the God that executeth vengeance for me,
> and subdueth peoples under me.
> He rescueth me from mine enemies.
> Psalm 18:46-48

Throughout the songs of David, the thought was impressed on his people that Jehovah was their strength and deliverer:

> Some trust in chariots, and some in horses:
> But we will remember the name of Jehovah our
>   God.
>
> Psalm 20:7

The kingdom of Israel had now reached in extent the fulfillment of the promise given to Abraham: "Unto thy seed have I given this land, from the river of Egypt unto the great river, the river Euphrates." Genesis 15:18. Israel had become a mighty nation, respected and feared by surrounding peoples. David commanded, as few sovereigns have been able to command, the affections and allegiance of his people. He had honored God, and God was now honoring him.

But in the time of his greatest outward triumph, David met his most humiliating defeat.

71 / David's Sin of Adultery and His Repentance

The Bible has little to say in praise of men. All the good qualities men possess are the gift of God; their good deeds are performed by the grace of God through Christ. They are but instruments in His hands. All the lessons of Bible history teach that it is a perilous thing to praise men, for if one comes to lose sight of his entire dependence on God, he is sure to fall. The Bible inculcates distrust of human power and encourages trust in divine power.

The spirit of self-exaltation prepared the way for David's fall. Flattery, power, and luxury were not without effect upon him. According to the customs prevailing among Eastern rulers, crimes not to be tolerated in subjects were uncondemned in the king. All this tended to lessen David's sense of the exceeding sinfulness of sin. He began to trust to his own wisdom and might.

As soon as Satan can separate the soul from God, he will arouse the unholy desires of man's carnal nature. The work of the enemy is not, at the outset, sudden and startling. It begins in apparently small things—neglect to rely upon God wholly, the disposition to follow the practices of the world.

David returned to Jerusalem. The Syrians had already submitted, and the complete overthrow of the Ammonites appeared certain. David was surrounded by the fruits of victory and the honors of his able rule. Now the tempter seized the opportunity to occupy his mind. In ease and self-security, David yielded to Satan

This chapter is based on 2 Samuel 11; 12.

and brought upon his soul the stain of guilt. He, the Heaven-appointed leader of the nation, chosen by God to execute His law, himself trampled upon its precepts. He who should have been a terror to evildoers, by his own act strengthened their hands.

Guilty and unrepentant, David did not ask guidance from Heaven, but sought to extricate himself from the dangers in which sin had involved him. Bathsheba, whose fatal beauty had proved a snare to the king, was the wife of Uriah the Hittite, one of David's bravest and most faithful officers. The law of God pronounced the adulterer guilty of death, and the proud-spirited soldier, so shamefully wronged, might avenge himself by taking the life of the king or by exciting the nation to revolt.

Every effort which David made to conceal his guilt proved unavailing. He had betrayed himself into the power of Satan; danger surrounded him, dishonor more bitter than death was before him. There appeared but one way of escape—to add murder to adultery. David reasoned that if Uriah were slain by the hand of enemies in battle, the guilt of his death could not be traced to the king. Bathsheba would be free to become David's wife, suspicion could be averted, and the royal honor maintained.

Uriah was made the bearer of his own death warrant. The king commanded Joab, "Set ye Uriah in the forefront of the hottest battle, and retire ye from him, that he may be smitten, and die." Joab, already stained with the guilt of one murder, did not hesitate to obey the king's instructions, and Uriah fell by the sword of the children of Ammon.

David Temporarily Becomes Agent of Satan

Heretofore David's record as a ruler had won the confidence of the nation. But as he departed from God, he became for the time the agent of Satan. Yet he still held the authority that God had given him, and because of this, claimed obedience that would imperil the soul of him who should yield it. Joab, whose allegiance had been given to the king rather than to God, transgressed God's law because the king commanded it.

When David commanded that which was contrary to God's law, it became sin to obey. "The powers that be are ordained of God" (Romans 13:1), but we are not to obey them contrary to God's law. The apostle Paul sets forth the principle by which we should be governed: "Be ye followers of me, even as I also am of Christ." 1 Corinthians 11:1.

An account of the execution of his order was sent to David, but so carefully worded as not to implicate either Joab or the king. "Thy servant Uriah the Hittite is dead."

The king's answer was, "Thus shalt thou say unto Joab, Let not this thing displease thee, for the sword devoureth one as well another."

Bathsheba observed the customary days of mourning for her husband, and at their close, "David sent and fetched her to his house, and she became his wife." He who would not, even when in peril of his life, put forth his hand against the Lord's anointed, had so fallen that he could wrong and murder one of his most faithful, valiant soldiers, and hope to enjoy undisturbed the reward of his sin.

Happy they who, having ventured in this way, learn how bitter are the fruits of sin, and turn from it. God, in His mercy, did not leave David to be lured to utter ruin by the deceitful rewards of sin.

How God Intervened

There was a necessity for God to interpose. David's sin toward Bathsheba became known, and suspicion was excited that he had planned the death of Uriah. The Lord was dishonored. He had exalted David, and David's sin cast reproach upon His name. It tended to lower the standard of godliness in Israel, to lessen in many minds the abhorrence of sin.

Nathan the prophet was bidden to bear a message of

reproof to David. Terrible in its severity, Nathan delivered the divine sentence with such heaven-born wisdom as to engage the sympathies of the king, to arouse his conscience, and to call from his lips the sentence of death upon himself. The prophet repeated a story of wrong and oppression that demanded redress.

"There were two men in one city," he said, "the one rich, and the other poor. The rich man had exceeding many flocks and herds: but the poor man had nothing, save one little ewe lamb, which he had brought and nourished up: and it grew up together with him, and with his children; it did eat of his own meat, and drank of his own cup, and lay in his bosom, and was unto him as a daughter. And there came a traveler unto the rich man, and he spared to take of his own flock and of his own herd, to dress for the wayfaring man that was come unto him; but took the poor man's lamb, and dressed it for the man that was come to him."

The anger of the king was aroused. "As the Lord liveth, the man that hath done this thing is worthy to die. And he shall restore the lamb fourfold, because he did this thing, and because he had no pity."

Nathan fixed his eyes upon the king, then solemnly declared, "Thou art the man. . . . Wherefore hast thou despised the commandment of the Lord, to do evil in His sight?" The guilty may attempt, as David had done, to conceal their crime from men, to bury the evil deed forever from human sight, but "all things are naked and opened unto the eyes of Him with whom we have to do." Hebrews 4:13.

Nathan declared: "Thou hast killed Uriah the Hittite with the sword and hast taken his wife to be thy wife, and hast slain him with the sword of the children of Ammon. Now therefore the sword shall never depart from thine house. . . . Behold, I will raise up evil against thee out of thine own house, and I will take thy wives before thine eyes, and give them unto thy neighbor. . . . For thou didst it secretly; but I will do this thing before all Israel, and before the sun."

The prophet's rebuke touched the heart of David; conscience was aroused; his guilt appeared in all its enormity. With trembling lips he said, "I have sinned against the Lord." David had committed a grievous sin, toward both Uriah and Bathsheba, but infinitely greater was his sin against God.

David Punished for His Sin

David trembled, lest, guilty and unforgiven, he should be cut down by the swift judgment of God. But the message was sent him by the prophet, "The Lord also hath put away thy sin; thou shalt not die." Yet justice must be maintained. The sentence of death was transferred from David to the child of his sin. Thus the king was given opportunity for repentance, while the suffering and death of the child, as a part of his punishment, was far more bitter than his own death could have been.

When his child was stricken, David, with fasting and deep humiliation, pleaded for its life. Night after night he lay in heartbroken grief, interceding for the innocent one suffering for his guilt. Upon hearing that the child was dead, he quietly submitted to the decree of God. The first stroke had fallen of that retribution which he himself had declared just.

Many, reading the history of David's fall, have inquired, "Why did God see fit to throw open to the world this dark passage in the life of one so highly honored of Heaven?" Infidels have pointed to the character of David and have exclaimed in derision, "This is the man after God's own heart!" Thus God and his word have been blasphemed, and many, under a cloak of piety, have become bold in sin.

But the history of David furnishes no countenance to sin. It was when he was walking in the counsel of God that he was called a man after God's own heart. When he sinned, this ceased to be true of him until by repentance he had returned to the Lord. "The thing that David had done was evil in the eyes of the Lord." Though

David repented of his sin, he reaped the baleful harvest of the seed he had sown. The judgments upon him testify to God's abhorrence of sin.

David himself was broken in spirit by the consciousness of his sin and its far-reaching results. He felt humbled in the eyes of his subjects. His influence was weakened. Now his subjects, having a knowledge of his sin, would be led to sin more freely. His authority in his own household was weakened. His guilt kept him silent when he should have condemned sin. His evil example exerted its influence upon his sons, and God would not interpose to prevent the result. Thus David was severely chastised. Retribution which no repentance could avert, agony, and shame would darken his whole earthly life.

Those who, by pointing to the example of David, try to lessen the guilt of their own sins should learn from the Bible record that the way of transgression is hard. The results of sin, even in this life, will be found bitter and hard to bear.

God intended the history of David's fall to serve as a warning that even those whom He has greatly blessed are not to feel secure. And thus it has proved to those who in humility have sought to learn the lesson He designed to teach. The fall of David, one so honored by the Lord, has awakened in them distrust of self. Knowing that in God alone was their strength and safety, they have feared to take the first step on Satan's ground.

Even before the divine sentence was pronounced against David, he had begun to reap the fruit of transgression. The agony of spirit he then endured is brought to view in the thirty-second psalm:

> When I kept silence, my bones waxed old
> Through my roaring all the day long.
> For day and night thy hand was heavy upon me:
> My moisture was changed as with the drought of
> summer.
> Psalm 32:3, 4

And the fifty-first psalm is an expression of David's repentance, when the message of reproof came to him from God:

Create in me a clean heart, O God;
And renew a right spirit within me.
Cast me not away from Thy presence;
And take not Thy Holy Spirit from me. . . .
Deliver me from bloodguiltiness, O God,
      Thou God of my salvation;
And my tongue shall sing aloud of Thy
      righteousness.
                        Psalm 51:10, 11, 14

Thus the king of Israel recounted his sin, his repentance, and his hope of pardon through the mercy of God. He desired that others might be instructed by the sad history of his fall.

More Than Pardon

David's repentance was sincere. There was no effort to palliate his crime, no desire to escape the judgments threatened. He saw the defilement of his soul. He loathed his sin. It was not for pardon only that he prayed, but for purity of heart. In the promise of God to repentant sinners, he saw the evidence of his pardon and acceptance: "The sacrifices of God are a broken spirit: a broken and a contrite heart, O God, Thou wilt not despise." Psalm 51:17.

Though David had fallen, the Lord lifted him up. In the joy of his release he sang, "I acknowledged my sin unto Thee, and mine iniquity have I not hid. I said, I will confess my transgressions unto the Lord; and Thou forgavest the iniquity of my sin." Psalm 32:5. David humbled himself and confessed his sin, while Saul despised reproof and hardened his heart in impenitence.

This passage in David's history is one of the most forcible illustrations given us of the struggles and temptations of humanity, and of genuine repentance. Through all the ages, thousands of the children of God who have been betrayed into sin have remembered David's sincere repentance and confession and have taken courage to repent and try again to walk in the way of God's commandments.

Whoever will humble the soul with confession and repentance, as did David, may be sure there is hope for him. The Lord will never cast away one truly repentant soul.

72 / The Rebellion of Absalom, David's Son

"He shall restore fourfold," had been David's unwitting sentence upon himself, on listening to the prophet Nathan's parable. Four of his sons must fall, and the loss of each would be a result of the father's sin.

The shameful crime of Amnon, the firstborn, was permitted by David to pass unpunished. The law pronounced death upon the adulterer, and the unnatural crime of Amnon made him doubly guilty. But David, self-condemned for his own sin, failed to bring the offender to justice. For two years Absalom, the natural protector of the sister so foully wronged, concealed his purpose of revenge, but at a feast the drunken, incestuous Amnon was slain by his brother's command.

The king's sons, returning in alarm to Jerusalem, revealed to their father that Amnon had been slain. And they "lifted up their voice and wept: and the king also and all his servants wept very sore." But Absalom fled. David had neglected the duty of punishing Amnon, and the Lord permitted events to take their natural course. When parents or rulers neglect the duty of punishing iniquity, a train of circumstances will arise which will punish sin with sin.

It was here that Absalom's alienation from his father began. David, feeling that Absalom's crime demanded punishment, refused him permission to return. Shut out by his exile from the affairs of the kingdom, Absalom gave himself up to dangerous scheming.

At the close of two years Joab determined to effect a

This chapter is based on 2 Samuel 13 to 19.

reconciliation between father and son. He secured the services of a woman of Tekoah, reputed for wisdom. The woman represented herself to David as a widow whose two sons had been her only comfort and support. In a quarrel one had slain the other, and now the relatives demanded that the survivor be given up to the avenger of blood. And so, said the mother, "will they quench my coal which is left, and will leave to my husband neither name nor remainder upon the face of the earth." 2 Samuel 14:7. The king's feelings were touched, and he assured the woman of royal protection for her son.

She entreated the king's forbearance, declaring that he had spoken as one at fault, in that he did not fetch home again his banished. "For," she said, "we must needs die, and are as water spilt on the ground, which cannot be gathered up again; neither doth God respect any person; yet doth *He devise means, that His banished be not expelled from Him."* This tender and touching portrayal of the love of God toward the sinner is a striking evidence of the familiarity of the Israelites with the great truths of redemption. The king could not resist this appeal. The command was given, "Go therefore, bring the young man Absalom again."

The Sad Results of David's Sin

Absalom was permitted to return to Jerusalem, but not to appear at court or to meet his father. Tenderly as he loved this beautiful and gifted son, David felt it necessary that abhorrence for such a crime should be manifested. Absalom lived two years in his own house, banished from the court. His sister's presence kept alive the memory of the irreparable wrong she had suffered. In popular estimation, the prince was a hero rather than an offender, and he set himself to gain the hearts of the people.

His personal appearance was such as to win the admiration of all. "In all Israel there was none to be so much praised as Absalom for his beauty: from the sole of his foot even to the crown of his head there was no blemish in him." David's action in permitting him to return to Jerusalem, and yet refusing to admit him to his presence, enlisted in his behalf the sympathies of the people.

David was weak and irresolute, when before his sin he had been courageous and decided. This favored the designs of his son.

Through the influence of Joab, Absalom was again admitted to his father's presence. He continued his scheming, sedulously courted popular favor, and artfully turned every cause of dissatisfaction to his own advantage. Day by day this man of noble mien might be seen at the gate of the city, where a crowd of suppliants waited to present their wrongs for redress. Absalom listened, expressing sympathy with their sufferings and regret at the inefficiency of the government. "O that I were made judge in the land, that every man which hath any suit or cause might come unto me, and I would do him justice! And it was so, that when any man came nigh to do him obeisance, he put forth his hand, and took him, and kissed him."

Rebellion Grows Underground

Fomented by the prince, discontent with the government was fast spreading. Absalom was generally regarded as heir to the kingdom, and a desire was kindled that he might occupy the throne. "So Absalom stole the hearts of the men of Israel." Yet the king suspected nothing. The princely state which Absalom had assumed was regarded by David as intended to do honor to his court.

Absalom secretly sent picked men throughout the tribes to concert measures for revolt. And now the cloak of religious devotion was assumed to conceal his traitorous designs. Absalom said to the king, "I pray thee, let me go and pay my vow, which I have vowed unto the Lord, in Hebron. For thy servant vowed a vow while I abode at Geshur, in Syria, saying, If the

Lord shall bring me again indeed to Jerusalem, then I will serve the Lord.''

The fond father, comforted with this evidence of piety in his son, dismissed him with his blessing. Absalom's crowning act of hypocrisy was designed not only to blind the king but to establish the confidence of the people, and thus to lead them on to rebellion against the king whom God had chosen.

Absalom set forth for Hebron, and with him ''two hundred men out of Jerusalem, that were called, and they went in their simplicity, and they knew not anything.'' These men went, little thinking that their love for the son was leading them into rebellion against the father. At Hebron, Absalom summoned Ahithophel, a man in high repute for wisdom. Ahithophel's support made the cause of Absalom appear certain of success, attracting to his standard many influential men. As the trumpet of revolt sounded, the prince's spies throughout the country spread the tidings that Absalom was king, and many of the people gathered to him.

David Finally Aroused

Meanwhile the alarm was carried to Jerusalem. David was suddenly aroused. His own son had been plotting to seize his crown and doubtless take his life. In his great peril David shook off the depression that had long rested upon him and prepared to meet this terrible emergency. Absalom was only twenty miles away. The rebels would soon be at the gates of Jerusalem.

David shuddered at the thought of exposing his capital to carnage and devastation. Should he permit Jerusalem to be deluged with blood? His decision was taken. He would leave Jerusalem and then test his people, giving them opportunity to rally to his support. It was his duty to God and to his people to maintain the authority with which Heaven had invested him. The issue of the conflict he would trust with God.

In humility and sorrow, David passed out of the gate of Jerusalem. The people followed in long, sad procession, like a funeral train. David's bodyguard of Cherethites, Pelethites, and Gittites, under the command of Ittai, accompanied the king. But David, with characteristic unselfishness, could not consent that these strangers should be involved in his calamity. Then said the king to Ittai, "Wherefore goest thou also with us? . . . Thou art a stranger, and also an exile. Whereas thou camest but yesterday, should I this day make thee go up and down with us? seeing I go whither I may, return thou, and take back thy brethren: mercy and truth be with thee."

Ittai answered, "As the Lord liveth, and as my lord the king liveth, surely in what place my lord the king shall be, whether in death or life, even there also will thy servant be." These men had been converted from paganism, and nobly they proved their fidelity to God and their king. David accepted their devotion to his apparently sinking cause, and all passed over the brook Kidron, toward the wilderness.

Some Are Loyal to David in the Crisis

Again the procession halted. "And lo Zadok also, and all the Levites were with him, bearing the ark of the covenant of God." The presence of that sacred symbol was to the followers of David a pledge of deliverance and victory. Its absence from Jerusalem would bring terror to the adherents of Absalom.

At sight of the ark, joy and hope for a brief moment thrilled the heart of David. But soon other thoughts came. As the appointed ruler of God's heritage, the glory of God and the good of his people were to be uppermost in his mind. God had said of Jerusalem, "This is my rest" (Psalm 132:14), and neither priest nor king had a right to remove therefrom the symbol of His presence. And David's great sin was ever before him. It was not for him to remove from the capital of the nation the sacred statutes which embodied the will of their divine Sovereign, the constitution of the realm and the foundation of its prosperity.

He commanded Zadok, "Carry back the ark of God into the city: if I shall find favor in the eyes of the Lord, He will bring me again, and show me both it and His habitation: but if He thus say, I have no delight in thee; behold, here am I, let Him do to me as seemeth good unto Him."

When All Looks Dark, David Prays

As the priests turned back toward Jerusalem, a deep shadow fell upon the departing throng. Their king a fugitive, themselves outcasts, forsaken even by the ark of God—the future was dark! "And David went up by the ascent of Olivet, and wept as he went up, and had his head covered, and he went barefoot: and all the people that was with him covered every man his head, and they went up, weeping as they went up. And one told David, saying, Ahithophel is among the conspirators with Absalom." Again David was forced to recognize the results of his own sin. The defection of Ahithophel, the ablest of political leaders, was prompted by revenge for the wrong to Bethsheba, his granddaughter.

"And David said, O Lord, I pray Thee, turn the counsel of Ahithophel into foolishness." Upon reaching the top of the mount, the king bowed in prayer, casting upon God the burden of his soul and humbly supplicating divine mercy.

Hushai the Archite, a wise and able counselor, a faithful friend to David, now came to cast in his fortunes with the dethroned and fugitive king. David saw, as by a divine enlightenment, that this man was the one needed to serve the interests of the king in the councils at the capital. At David's request, Hushai returned to Jerusalem to offer his services to Absalom and defeat the crafty counsel of Ahithophel.

With this gleam of light in the darkness, the king and his followers pursued their way down the eastern slope of Olivet, through a rocky and desolate waste toward the Jordan. "And when King David came to Bahurim, behold, thence came out a man of the family of the house of Saul, whose name was Shimei, the son of Gera. . . . And he cast stones at David, and at all the servants of King David. . . . And thus said Shimei when he cursed, Come out, come out, thou bloody man, and thou man of Belial. The Lord hath returned upon thee all the blood of the house of Saul, in whose stead thou hast reigned; and the Lord hath delivered the kingdom into the hand of Absalom thy son: and, behold, thou art taken in thy mischief, because thou art a bloody man."

In David's prosperity, Shimei had not shown that he was not loyal. He had honored David upon his throne, but cursed him in his humiliation. Inspired by Satan, he wreaked his hatred upon him whom God had chastened.

David had not been guilty of wrong toward Saul or his house. Much of his life had been spent amid scenes of violence; but of all who have passed through such an ordeal, few have been so little affected by its hardening, demoralizing influence as was David.

David's nephew, Abishai, could not listen patiently to Shimei's insulting words. "Why," he exclaimed, "should this dead dog curse my lord the king? Let me go over, I pray thee, and take off his head." But the king forbade him. "Behold," he said, "my son . . . seeketh my life: how much more now may this Benjamite do it? let him alone, and let him curse; for the Lord hath bidden him. It may be that the Lord will look on mine affliction, and that the Lord will requite me good for his cursing this day."

David Knows This Trouble Is the Consequence of His Sin

While his faithful subjects wondered at his sudden reverse of fortune, it was no mystery to the king. He had often had forebodings of an hour like this. He had wondered that God had so long borne with his sins. And now in his hurried and sorrowful flight, he thought of his loved capital, the place which had been the scene of his sin. As he remembered the long-suffering of

God, he felt that the Lord would still deal with him in mercy.

David had confessed his sin and had sought to do his duty as a faithful servant of God. He had labored for the upbuilding of his kingdom. He had gathered stores of material for the building of the house of God. And now must the results of years of consecrated toil pass into the hands of his reckless, traitorous son?

He saw in his own sin the cause of his trouble. And the Lord did not forsake David. Under cruel wrong and insult he showed himself humble, unselfish, generous, and submissive. Never was the ruler of Israel more truly great in the sight of heaven than at this hour of his deepest humiliation.

In the experience through which He caused David to pass, the Lord shows that He cannot tolerate or excuse sin. David's history enables us to trace, even through darkest judgments, the working out of His purpose of mercy. He caused David to pass under the rod, but He did not destroy him. The furnace is to purify, not to consume.

God Does Not Give Absalom Wisdom

Soon after David left Jerusalem, Absalom and his army took possession of the stronghold of Israel. Hushai was among the first to greet the new-crowned monarch, and the prince was gratified at the accession of his father's old friend and counselor. Absalom was confident of success. Eager to secure the confidence of the nation, he welcomed Hushai to his court.

Absalom was surrounded by a large force, but it was mostly composed of men untrained for war. Ahithophel well knew that a large part of the nation were still true to David; he was surrounded by tried warriors commanded by able and experienced generals. Ahithophel knew that after the first burst of enthusiasm in favor of the new king, a reaction would come. Should the rebellion fail, Absalom might secure a reconciliation with his father. Then Ahithophel, as his chief counselor, would be held most guilty; upon him the heaviest punishment would fall.

To prevent Absalom from retracing his steps, Ahithophel counseled an act that would make reconciliation impossible. With hellish cunning, this unprincipled statesman urged Absalom to add the crime of incest to that of rebellion. In the sight of all Israel he was to take to himself his father's concubines, thus declaring that he succeeded to his father's throne. And Absalom carried out the vile suggestion. Thus was fulfilled the word of God to David by the prophet, "Behold, I will raise up evil against thee out of thine own house, and I will take thy wives before thine eyes, and give them unto thy neighbor. . . . For thou didst it secretly: but I will do this thing before all Israel, and before the sun." 2 Samuel 12:11, 12. Not that God prompted these acts, but He did not exercise His power to prevent them.

Ahithophel was destitute of divine enlightenment, or he could not have based the success of treason on the crime of incest. Men of corrupt hearts plot wickedness, as if there were no overruling Providence to cross their designs.

Having succeeded in securing his own safety, Ahithophel urged, "Let me now choose out twelve thousand men, and I will arise and pursue after David this night: and I will come upon him while he is weary and weakhanded, and will make him afraid: and all the people that are with him shall flee; and I will smite the king only: and will bring back all the people unto thee." Had this plan been followed, David would surely have been slain. But "the Lord had appointed to defeat the good counsel of Ahithophel, to the intent that the Lord might bring evil upon Absalom."

Hushai had not been called to the council. But after the assembly had dispersed, Absalom, who had a high regard for the judgment of his father's counselor, submitted to him the plan of Ahithophel.

Hushai saw that if the plan were followed, David

would be lost. "The counsel that Ahithophel hath given is not good at this time. For, said Hushai, thou knowest thy father and his men, that they be mighty men, and they be chafed in their minds, as a bear robbed of her whelps in the field: and thy father is a man of war, and will not lodge with the people. Behold, he is hid now in some pit, or in some other place." If Absalom's forces should pursue David, they would not capture the king; and should they suffer a reverse, it would dishearten them and work great harm to Absalom's cause. "For," he said, "all Israel knoweth that thy father is a mighty man, and they which be with him are valiant men."

Hushai Suggests an Alternate Plan
He suggested a plan attractive to a vain and selfish nature: "I counsel that all Israel be generally gathered together unto thee, from Dan even to Beersheba, as the sand that is by the sea for multitude; and that thou go to battle in thine own person. So shall we come upon him in some place where he shall be found, and we will light upon him as the dew falleth on the ground: and of him and of all the men that are with him there shall not be left so much as one. Moreover, if he be gotten into a city, then shall all Israel bring ropes to that city, and we will draw it into the river, until there be not one small stone found there.

"And Absalom and all the men of Israel said, The counsel of Hushai the Archite is better than the counsel of Ahithophel."

But there was one who clearly foresaw the result of this fatal mistake of Absalom's. Ahithophel knew that the cause of the rebels was lost. And he knew that whatever might be the fate of the prince, there was no hope for the counselor who had instigated his greatest crimes. Ahithophel had encouraged Absalom in rebellion; he had counseled him to the most abominable wickedness, to the dishonor of his father; he had advised the slaying of David; he had cut off the last possibility of his own reconciliation with the king; and now another was preferred before him by Absalom. Jealous, angry, and desperate, Ahithophel "gat him home to his house, . . . and hanged himself, and died." Such was the result of the wisdom of one who did not make God his counselor.

Hushai lost no time in warning David to escape beyond Jordan without delay: "Lodge not this night in the plains of the wilderness, but speedily pass over; lest the king be swallowed up, and all the people that are with him."

David, spent with toil and grief after that first day of flight, received the message that he must cross the Jordan that night, for his son was seeking his life. What were the feelings of the father and king in this terrible peril? In the hour of his darkest trial, David's heart was stayed upon God, and he sang:

> Lord, how are they increased that trouble me!
> Many are they that rise up against me.
> Many there be which say of my soul,
> There is no help for him in God.
> But Thou, O Lord, art a shield for me;
> My glory, and the lifter up of mine head.
> I cried unto the Lord with my voice,
> And He heard me out of His holy hill.
> I laid me down and slept;
> I awaked; for the Lord sustained me.
> I will not be afraid of ten thousands of people,
> That have set themselves against me round about.
>   Psalm 3:1-7

David and all his company, in the darkness of night, crossed the deep, swift-flowing river. "By the morning light there lacked not one of them that was not gone over Jordan."

David and his forces fell back to Mahanaim, the royal seat of Ishbosheth, a strongly fortified city surrounded by a mountainous district favorable for retreat in case of war. The country was well-provisioned, and the people were friendly to David.

Absalom, the rash and impetuous prince, soon set out in pursuit of his father. His army was large, but it was undisciplined and poorly prepared to cope with the tried soldiers of his father.

David divided his forces into three battalions under the command of Joab, Abishai, and Ittai.

The Battle That Defeated the Rebellion

From the walls of Mahanaim, the long lines of the rebel army were in full view. The usurper was accompanied by a vast host, in comparison with which David's force seemed but a handful. As the army filed out from the city gates, David encouraged his faithful soldiers, bidding them go forth trusting that the God of Israel would give them victory. But as Joab, leading the column, passed his king, the conqueror of a hundred battlefields stooped his proud head to hear the monarch's last message, "Deal gently *for my sake* with the young man, even with Absalom." And Abishai and Ittai received the same charge. But the king's solicitude, seeming to declare Absalom dearer to him than the subjects faithful to his throne, only increased the indignation of the soldiers against the unnatural son.

The place of battle was a wood near the Jordan. Among the thickets and marshes of the forest, the great numbers of undisciplined troops of Absalom's army became confused and unmanageable. And "the people of Israel were slain before the servants of David, and there was a great slaughter that day of twenty thousand men."

Absalom, seeing that the day was lost, had turned to flee when his head was caught between the branches of a widespreading tree, and, his mule going out from under him, was left hopelessly suspended, a prey to his enemies. He was found by a soldier, who spared Absalom but reported to Joab what he had seen.

Joab was restrained by no scruples. He had befriended Absalom, having twice secured his reconciliation with David, and the trust had been shamelessly betrayed. But for the advantages gained by Absalom through Joab, this rebellion could never have occurred. "And he took three darts in his hand, and thrust them through the heart of Absalom. . . . And they took Absalom, and cast him into a great pit in the wood, and laid a very great heap of stones upon him."

God's Judgment on the Rebellion

Thus perished the instigators of rebellion in Israel. Ahithophel had died by his own hand. The princely Absalom, whose beauty had been the pride of Israel, had been cut down in his youth, his dead body thrust into a pit and covered with a heap of stones, in token of everlasting reproach.

The leader of the rebellion being slain, two messengers were at once dispatched to bear the tidings to the king.

The second messenger came, crying, "Tidings, my lord the king: for the Lord hath avenged thee this day of all them that rose up against thee." From the father's lips came the question, "Is the young man Absalom safe?" Unable to conceal the heavy tidings, the herald answered, "The enemies of my lord the king, and all that rise against thee to do thee hurt, be as that young man is." David questioned no further, but with bowed head "went up to the chamber over the gate, and wept: and as he went, thus he said, O my son Absalom! my son, my son Absalom! would God I had died for thee, O Absalom, my son, my son!"

The victorious army approached the city, their shouts of triumph awaking the echoes of the hills. But as they entered the city gate the shout died away, their banners drooped in their hands, for the king was not waiting to bid them welcome. From the chamber above the gate his wailing cry was heard, "O my son Absalom! my son, my son Absalom! would God I had died for thee, O Absalom, my son, my son!"

Joab was filled with indignation. God had given them reason for triumph and gladness; the greatest rebellion ever known in Israel had been crushed. Yet this great victory was turned to mourning for him whose crime had cost the blood of thousands of brave men. The rude, blunt captain pushed his way into the presence of the king and boldly said, "Thou hast shamed this day the faces of all thy servants, which this day have saved thy life, and the lives of thy sons and of thy daughters; . . . that thou lovest thine enemies, and hatest thy friends. For thou hast declared this day, that thou regarded neither princes nor servants: for this day I perceive, that if Absalom had lived, and all we had died this day, then it had pleased thee well. Now therefore arise, go forth, and speak comfortably unto thy servants: for I swear by the Lord, if thou go not forth, there will not tarry one with thee this night: and that will be worse unto thee than all the evil that befell thee from thy youth until now."

Harsh and cruel as was the reproof, David did not resent it. Seeing that his general was right, he went down to the gate, and with words of commendation greeted his brave soldiers as they marched past him.

73 / A Man After God's Own Heart

The overthrow of Absalom did not at once bring peace. So large a part of the nation had joined in revolt that David would not return to his capital and resume his authority without an invitation from the tribes. There was no prompt and decided action to recall the king, and when at last Judah undertook to bring back David, the jealousy of the other tribes was roused. A counterrevolution followed. This, however, was speedily quelled, and peace returned to Israel.

Dangers threaten the soul from power, riches, and worldly honor. David's early life as a shepherd, with its lessons of humility, patient toil, and tender care for his flocks; communion with nature in the solitude of the hills, directing his thoughts to the Creator; the long discipline of his wilderness life, had been appointed by the Lord as preparation for the throne of Israel. And yet worldly success and honor so weakened the character of David that he was overcome by the tempter.

David Falls Again to the Sin of Pride

Intercourse with heathen peoples led to a desire to follow their national customs and kindled ambition for worldly greatness. With a view to extending his conquests, David determined to increase his army by requiring military service from all who were of proper age. To effect this, it became necessary to take a census of the population. Pride and ambition prompted this action. The numbering of the people would show the contrast between the weakness of the kingdom

This chapter is based on 2 Samuel 24; 1 Kings 1;
1 Chronicles 21; 28; 29.

when David ascended the throne and its strength and prosperity under his rule. The Scripture says, "Satan stood up against Israel, and provoked David to number Israel." The prosperity of Israel under David had been due to the blessing of God. But increasing the military resources of the kingdom would give the impression to surrounding nations that Israel's trust was in her armies, not in Jehovah.

The people of Israel did not look with favor upon David's plan for greatly extending military service. The proposed enrollment caused much dissatisfaction; consequently it was thought necessary to employ military officers in place of the priests and magistrates, who had formerly taken the census. The object was directly contrary to the principles of a theocracy. Even Joab remonstrated: "Why . . . doth my lord require this thing? Why will he be a cause of trespass to Israel? Nevertheless the king's word prevailed against Joab. Wherefore Joab departed, and went throughout all Israel, and came to Jerusalem."

David was convicted of his sin. Self-condemned, he "said unto God, I have sinned greatly, because I have done this thing: but now, I beseech thee, do away the iniquity of thy servant; for I have done very foolishly."

Next morning a message was brought by the prophet Gad: "Thus saith the Lord, Choose thee either three years' famine; or three months to be destroyed before thy foes, while that the sword of thine enemies overtaketh thee; or else three days the sword of the Lord, even the pestilence, in the land, and the angel of the Lord destroying throughout all the coasts of Israel."

David Chooses Punishment From the Lord

The king's answer was, "I am in a great strait: let us fall now into the hand of the Lord; for His mercies are great: and let me not fall into the hand of man."

The land was smitten with pestilence, which destroyed seventy thousand in Israel. "David lifted up his eyes, and saw the angel of the Lord stand between the earth and the heaven, having a drawn sword in his hand stretched out over Jerusalem.'' The king pleaded with God in behalf of Israel: ''Is it not I that commanded the people to be numbered? even I it is that have sinned, and done evil indeed; but as for these sheep, what have they done? let Thine hand, I pray Thee, O Lord my God, be on me, and on my father's house; but not on Thy people, that they should be plagued.''

The people had cherished the same sins that prompted David's action. As the Lord through Absalom's sin visited judgment upon David, so through David's error He punished the sins of Israel.

The destroying angel had stood upon Mount Moriah, ''in the threshing floor of Ornan the Jebusite.'' Directed by the prophet, David went to the mountain, ''and offered burnt offerings and peace offerings, and called upon the Lord; and He answered him from heaven by fire upon the altar of burnt offering.'' ''So the Lord was entreated for the land, and the plague was stayed from Israel.''

The spot upon which the altar was erected, henceforth ever to be regarded as holy ground, was the place where Abraham had built the altar to offer up his son, and was afterward chosen as the site of the temple.

David had reached the age of threescore and ten. The hardships and exposures of his early wanderings, his many wars, the afflictions of later years had sapped the fountain of life. Feebleness and age, with desire for seclusion, prevented a quick apprehension of what was passing in the kingdom, and again rebellion sprang up in the very shadow of the throne.

The one who now aspired to the throne was Adonijah, ''a very goodly man'' in person and bearing, but unprincipled and reckless. In his youth ''his father had not displeased him at any time in saying, Why hast thou done so?'' In youth subjected to little restraint, he now rebelled against the authority of God, who had appointed Solomon to the throne.

Shortly before his death, David gave his son and successor Solomon detailed directions for building the temple.

Solomon was better qualified than his elder brother; yet although the choice of God had been clearly indicated, Adonijah did not fail to find sympathizers. Joab, heretofore loyal to the throne, now joined the conspiracy against Solomon, as did Abiathar the priest.

The rebellion was ripe. The conspirators had assembled at a great feast to proclaim Adonijah king, when their plans were thwarted by the prompt action of Zadok the priest, Nathan the prophet, and Bathsheba the mother of Solomon. They represented the state of affairs to the king, reminding him of the divine direction that Solomon should succeed to the throne. David at once abdicated in favor of Solomon, who was immediately anointed and proclaimed king. The conspiracy was crushed.

Abiathar's life was spared, out of respect to his office and former fidelity to David; but he was degraded from the office of high priest, which passed to the line of Zadok. Joab and Adonijah were spared for the time, but after the death of David they suffered the penalty of their crime. The execution of the sentence upon the son of David completed the fourfold judgment that testified to God's abhorrence of the father's sin.

David Unselfishly Gathers Money and Material for the Temple

From the opening of David's reign, one of his most cherished plans had been that of erecting a temple to the Lord. He had provided an abundance of the costly material—gold, silver, onyx stones, and stones of divers colors, marble, and precious woods. And now other hands must build the house for the ark, the symbol of God's presence.

Seeing that his end was near, the king summoned representative men from all parts of the kingdom to receive this legacy in trust. Because of his physical weakness, it had not been expected that he would attend to this transfer in person; but the inspiration of God came upon him, and with fervor and power he was able, for the last time, to address his people. He told them of his own desire to build the temple, and of the Lord's command that the work should be committed to Solomon his son. "Now therefore," David said, "in the sight of all Israel the congregation of the Lord, and in the audience of our God, keep and seek for all the commandments of the Lord your God: that ye may possess this good land, and leave it for an inheritance for your children after you forever."

David's whole soul was moved with solicitude that the leaders of Israel should be true to God and that Solomon should obey God's law, shunning the sins that had weakened his father's authority, embittered his life, and dishonored God. Turning to his son, already acknowledged as his successor, David said: "Solomon my son, know thou the God of thy father, and serve Him with a perfect heart and with a willing mind: for the Lord searcheth all hearts, and understandeth all the imaginations of the thoughts. . . . Take heed now; for the Lord hath chosen thee to build a house for the sanctuary."

David gave Solomon minute directions for building the temple. Solomon was still young and shrank from the weighty responsibilities in the erection of the temple and the government of God's people. David said, "Be strong and of good courage, and do it: fear not, nor be dismayed, for the Lord God, even my God, will be with thee; He will not fail thee, nor forsake thee."

Again David appealed to the congregation: "Solomon my son, whom alone God hath chosen, is yet young and tender, and the work is great: for the palace is not for man, but for the Lord God." He said, "I have prepared with all my might for the house of my God," and he went on to enumerate the materials he had gathered. "Who then," he asked of the assembled multitude that had brought their liberal gifts, "who then is willing to consecrate his *service* this day unto the Lord?"

There was a ready response from the assembly. "Then the people rejoiced, for that they offered willingly, because with perfect heart they offered willingly to the Lord: and David the king also rejoiced with great joy.

"Wherefore David blessed the Lord before all the congregation: and David said, Blessed be Thou, Lord God of Israel our father, forever and ever. . . . Now therefore, our God, we thank Thee, and praise Thy glorious name. But who am I, and what is my people, that we should be able to offer so willingly after this sort? for all things come of Thee, and of Thine own have we given Thee. . . . Give unto Solomon my son a perfect heart, to keep Thy commandments, Thy testimonies, and Thy statutes, and to do all these things, and to build the palace, for the which I have made provision."

David's Example Is No Excuse for Sin Today

With deepest interest the king had gathered the rich material for building and beautifying the temple. He had composed the glorious anthems that in afteryears should echo through its courts. Now his heart was made glad in God. The chief of the fathers and the princes of Israel swelled the offerings, giving of their own possessions into the treasury. It was God alone who had imparted this disposition to His people. He, not man, must be glorified. His Spirit had made them willing. If His love had not moved upon the hearts of the people, the temple would never have been erected.

When he felt that death was approaching, the burden of David's heart was still for Solomon and for Israel, whose prosperity must so largely depend upon the fidelity of her king. "And he charged Solomon his son, saying, I go the way of all the earth; be thou strong therefore, and show thyself a man; and keep the charge of the Lord thy God, to walk in His ways, to keep His statutes, and His commandments, and His judgments, and His testimonies, . . . that thou mayest prosper in all that thou doest, and whithersoever thou turnest thyself: that the Lord may continue His own word which He spake concerning me, saying, If thy children take heed to their way, so walk before Me in truth with all their heart and with all their soul, there shall not fail thee (said He) a man on the throne of Israel.'' 1 Kings 2:1-4.

Great had been David's fall, but deep was his repentance, ardent his love, and strong his faith. The psalms of David pass from the depths of guilt and self-condemnation to the most exalted communing with God. His life record declares that sin can bring only shame and woe, but that God's love and mercy can reach to the deepest depths.

Faith will lift up the repenting soul to share the adoption of the sons of God!

Appendix

Note 1, page 177: One of the important reasons why the Lord delivered Israel from slavery to Egypt was that they might keep His holy Sabbath. The Egyptians did not give them religious liberty, so the Lord "brought forth His people . . . that they might observe His statutes, and keep His laws." Psalm 105:43-45. Evidently Moses and Aaron renewed the teaching about the holiness of the Sabbath, because Pharaoh complained to them, "Ye make [the people] rest from their burdens." Exodus 5:5. This would indicate that Moses and Aaron began a Sabbath reform in Egypt.

The Lord told the Israelites that in keeping His Sabbath day, they should "remember that you were slaves in Egypt and the Lord your God brought you out with a strong hand and an outstretched arm, and for that reason the Lord your God commanded you to keep the Sabbath day." Deuteronomy 5:15, NEB.

The observance of the Sabbath was not to be a *commemoration* of their slavery in Egypt, however. Its observance in remembrance of creation was to *include* a joyful remembrance of deliverance from religious oppression in Egypt that made Sabbath observance difficult. In the same way, their deliverance from slavery was forever to kindle in their hearts a tender regard for the poor and oppressed, the fatherless and widows: "Remember that you were slaves in Egypt. . . ; that is why I command you to do this." Deuteronomy 24:17, 18.

Note 2, page 187: The plagues the Lord sent on

Egypt humiliated their gods and cast contempt on their idol-worship. The Nile River was regarded with religious reverence, and sacrifices were offered to it as a god. The first plague was directed against it. See Exodus 7:19.

The second plague brought frogs. See Exodus 8:6. One of the Egyptian deities, Heqa was a frog-headed goddess, and frogs were considered sacred. The Apis bull was dedicated to Ptah, the cow was sacred to Hathor, and the ram represented Khemu and Amen. The disease brought upon their cattle and animals was directed against their sacred animals. See Exodus 9:3.

The ninth plague was directed against one of their greatest gods, the sun god Ra. See Exodus 10:21. The tenth plague (see Exodus 12:29) was directed against Pharaoh as a god, who was considered to be Horus, the son of Osiris.

Note 3, page 220: When the Israelites worshiped the golden calf, they professed to be worshiping God. But it was like the Egyptians' worship of Osiris, by means of an image. The Egyptians' worship of Apis was immoral, and the Israelites' worship of the golden calf apparently was the same. Moses says the Israelites "sat down to eat and to drink, and rose up to play." Exodus 32:6. The Hebrew word for "play" denotes singing and dancing, which among the Egyptians was sensual and indecent. The Hebrew word for "corrupted" in verse 7 is the same as that in Genesis 6:11, 12, which refers to the people before the Flood corrupting themselves. This explains the terrible nature of this apostasy.

Note 4, page 229: The Ten Commandments were the *basis* of the covenant the Lord made with His people. But the covenant itself was the Lord's promise to write the law in their hearts (see Jeremiah 31:31-34), so that it would be their joy to obey.

Note 5, page 246: There were two ways in which the

sin (or the record of its forgiveness) was transferred to the sanctuary from the sinner: by some of the blood of the sin offering being sprinkled before the veil behind which was the ark; or by the flesh being eaten by the priest. See Leviticus 4:1-21; 6:24-26; 10:17, 18.

Note 6, page 256: The Ten Commandments were given by Christ. See 1 Corinthians 8:6; Acts 7:38; Isaiah 63:9; Exodus 23:20-23; John 1:1-3, 14; 1 Peter 1:10, 11.

Note 7, page 437: The government of Israel was a theocracy, that is, government by God directly. When Israel and Judah repeatedly violated God's law and rejected His rulership, the Lord finally withdrew from them His direct government and left them to what they desired—subjection to man. Thus they came under the successive dominion of Babylon, Medo-Persia, the Greek Empire, and finally Rome.

Since then, there has been no government anywhere to which God has delegated the authority that He gave to the king of Israel in the days of the theocracy. The Bible teaches a separation of church and state (see Matthew 22:17-22), and therefore religious liberty for all. Earthly governments may not force the conscience or usurp the place reserved to God alone in the theocracy of Israel. Not until the second coming of Christ will God again establish His theocracy. Until then, men must not arrogate to themselves authority over the human conscience that God has not entrusted to them.